ADVANCE PRAISE FOR *So L.A.*

"Electric, funny, lively, edged prose illuminates the pages of *So L.A.*—Hoida knows how to write sentences and characters that bite right into you."

—AIMEE BENDER, AUTHOR OF
THE PARTICULAR SADNESS OF LEMON CAKE

"Bridget is a rare thing—an original writer with a unique voice. Her writing is ironic, satirical, smart, sexy and deeply tender. This is a book Joan Didion will wish she'd written!"

—CHRIS ABANI, AUTHOR OF
THE VIRGIN OF FLAMES AND *SONG FOR NIGHT*

"Bridget Hoida has crafted a remarkably fine novel. The language of this work is fresh, surprising and relentless. The novel captures California, it captures the culture, it captures this one woman's life and it captured me. This is strong stuff from a strong talent. Hoida's voice is here to stay."

—PERCIVAL EVERETT,
AUTHOR OF *ASSUMPTION* AND ERASURE

"In *So L.A.*, Bridget Hoida has crafted that rarest of books: intelligent, gorgeously written—and, best of all, fun. The charming, witty and slightly off-kilter voice of narrator Magdalena de la Cruz brings to mind the writing of Nabokov—but in a distinctly California style: Magdalena is a six-foot blonde rhinestone artist with acrylic nails and silicone breasts living in the heart of Los Angeles. She is, by turns, endearing, frustrating and heartbreaking as she tries to salvage her dissolving marriage in the wake of her brother's death. Hoida's sharp, exquisite prose awed me, and brought me to both laughter and tears."

—SHAWNA YANG RYAN,
AUTHOR OF *WATER GHOSTS*

"Both heartbreaking and hilarious, Bridget Hoida's novel is a stunning debut. Inventive and deeply poetic, charming and wickedly witty, this is a work of lasting and profound satisfactions."

—DAVID ST. JOHN, AUTHOR OF
THE RED LEAVES OF NIGHT

ABOUT THIS BOOK

MAGDALENA DE LA CRUZ breezed through Berkeley and built an empire selling designer water. She'd never felt awkward or unattractive... until she moved to Los Angeles. In L.A., where "everything smells like acetone and Errol Flynn," Magdalena attempts to reinvent herself as a geographically appropriate bombshell—with rhinestones, silicone and gin—as she seeks an escape from her unraveling marriage and the traumatic death of her younger brother, Junah.

Magdalena's Los Angeles is glitzy and glamorous but also a landscape of the absurd. Her languidly lyrical voice provides a travel guide for a city of make-believe, where even Hollywood insiders feel left out.

So

L.A.

BRIDGET HOIDA

LETTERED PRESS
LOS ANGELES . BERKELEY

Published by Lettered Press
www.LetteredPress.org

So L.A.

Library of Congress Control Number: 2012902135

ISBN 978-0-9851294-3-9

Designed and composed by Sarah Ciston

Printed in the United States of America

9 8 7 6 5 4 3 2 1

First Limited Edition

Cover photograph © CURAphotography Shutterstock.com

SOURCE ACKNOWLEDGMENTS
Some of the chapter titles are taken from headings in Robert McKee's
quintessential screenwriting book, *STORY!*
Pages 116–117 reference the *Los Angeles Times* article "3 Men,
2 Nations, 1 Dream" (Jennifer Mena, June 30, 2001, A-1).
The Bombshell Manual of Style by Laren Stover was also referenced.

FOR MY PARENTS, LYNN & JACK
(WHO RAISED ME IN THE SAN JOAQUIN VALLEY)

&

FOR JESSE, WEST & STELLA
(THE BEST PARTS ABOUT L.A.)

THE BEAUTY [of Los Angeles] is the beauty of letting things go; letting go of where you came from; letting go of old lessons; letting go of what you want for what you are, or what you are for what you want; letting go of so much—and that is a hard beauty to love.

—MICHAEL VENTURA, "GRAND ILLUSION"
LETTERS AT 3 AM: REPORTS ON ENDARKENMENT

So L.A.

THE STORY PROBLEM

THE NINE people I know in Los Angeles—and by know, I don't mean people I lunch with, I mean the nine people who have seen me naked—those nine people would never believe it, but sometimes in the San Joaquin Valley it gets so hot the fields spontaneously catch fire. Just lick and burn and an entire crop of asparagus, Tokay seedless, rutabaga, hothouse or what have you are quite literally up in smoke. They didn't believe it the first time and they won't believe it the second, when I tell them about the ash that folds like walnuts into the swimming pool and the radio warnings to keep the dog off the asphalt. People from Los Angeles aren't good at willing suspension of disbelief, unless of course it involves Hollywood-celebrity cellulite secrets and million-dollar mascara wars, so I don't much expect them to empathize with the Lodi fireman, dressed in yellow gear and aiming a single hose, not at the blaze, but at the sky. Firing water upwards into the clouds and watching it waterfall against the air and onto the charred umber.

But, before I go too far, I suppose you could say the reverse is also true. That, with help, I could find nine people from the San Joaquin who would never believe that in Los Angeles you can take a class called Striptease Aerobics, get a boob job through your belly-button or when pregnant actually schedule the premature delivery of your infant so as not to interfere with your bridge game or your husband's billion-dollar business deals.

Wait.

Who am I kidding?

No one plays bridge in Beverly Hills. Not anymore. But that's beside the point. The point is: you can schedule the birth of your babe three weeks in advance of its actual due date, because the last three weeks is the point of no return as far as your abs are concerned. So you can schedule a cesarean and in optimal situations—read: all situations except the occasional indie actress turned earth mother who, in a fit of Sundance/Cannes/Taos nostalgia decides to have her son in the saline-filtered spa of her beach house—the OB/GYN, who is also a certified plastic surgeon, makes the incision and throws in a tummy tuck for a nominal fee.

I suppose, if forced, I could find nine nice folk from the San Joaquin who wouldn't believe a bit of it. Not the scheduling, not the cesarean and certainly not the part about fishing out the placenta before finishing off the lift and tuck, but—and this is something I feel confident about having lived in both L.A. and the San Joaquin—it would be much, much harder to find them. Not only because spontaneous weather-related fire is inherently easier to believe in than neonatal manipulation, but also because, when pressed, people will believe almost anything about Los Angeles.

Take me.

What if I told you that right now I'm bobbing about in the Pacific Ocean without a life vest while *Kelley*, the yacht I fell from, continues on her course? You'd believe me, right? You'd believe that sometimes in Los Angeles it's easier to float between the legs of a man you hardly know than it is to reach an arm towards your husband—on deck—as he casts a buoy overboard?

ACTION

OPENING VALUE

W E WERE on set for the commercial shoot of our newest product, Luxe, a mineral water herbal energy supplement priced at a dollar an ounce. My husband, Ricky, and some of our middle-west investors thought it might be a little high-end, even for the high-enders, but as I was learning in L.A.—contrary to popular opinion—people like to pay more for things. They especially like to spend if the thing's got style and a certain designer charm, so we decided to charge obscene, package in glass and set sail for a professional photo shoot.

The concept was basic, but smart, and featured tanned flesh on a yacht off Malibu. I was on *Kelley*, a 51-foot Bluebay, with a grip of marine mannered extras—compliments of Pico's People: Talent and Casting Agency—while Ricky was on *Green Tambourine* with the directors, the camera crew and a rather touchy-feely Big Hollywood Somebody. Usually Ricky and I sailed together on *Chelsea Girl*, but she was getting shellacked and so we split.

The extras were supposed to delight merrily, mingling, sunning and generally having the time of their lives while I, dressed in a yellow and navy nautical bikini, stretched myself out centerfold-style near the mast, left leg bent in a point towards the sun, blond hair breezing about my back and a bottle of Luxe lingering just above the cool blue sea.

Or at least that's how it was supposed to be. But although I'm naturally blond and, or so it's been said, quite unnaturally tall, I just couldn't cast myself as a seafaring supermodel. Maybe it's that loving your body in Northern California is a mantra of the *Our Bodies, Ourselves*, Germaine Greer, *Love the Skin You're In* variety; whereas loving your body in Southern California is a devotion of the *US Weekly*, Pamela Anderson, *TMZ* type. Regardless, I just couldn't wrap my mind, or my legs for that matter, around a miniskirt, much less a yellow bikini, no matter how much we'd save in modeling royalties—which ultimately resulted in Ricky, through a megaphone no less, berating me for hiding behind a toned extra, clad in tight white trunks and a blue captain's hat, and a burgeoning starlet with manufactured boobs, respectively. This went on for a while, Ricky shouting from the camera boat, me pretending not to hear him. Ricky insisting that I was gorgeous despite my invisible breasts, me forcing the wardrobe girl to allow me into a one-piece and then (because the waist was too short for my long torso) a yellow York Parka complete with hood that I pulled snug beneath my chin.

Absolutely not, Ricky shouted across the surf, swiping his hand across his neck in a tight "cut" line, as though he were Scorsese.

So we fought.

In public.

In front of a half-dozen cameras, Pico's People and some Diamond Myst Water bigwigs. And then, when we finally compromised with a sarong and a well-placed palm, the sky turned gray and the wind, which had previously been tossing my blond hair filmically, picked up to a gust. The camera boat had to have a brief pow-wow to decide if, at $17,000 an hour, we should call it a day or sit it out.

It was cold, I'll admit that, but I'll be damned if I was going to get off the boat. Although we planned to charge more for water than most pay for gas, we couldn't afford to spend big, at least not yet, hence my begrudging debut as the face of Diamond Myst. So I shouted to Ricky, Stick it out. We can always have the guys paste in some sun at the studio.

As the extras shivered in their suits and I reached for the parka I had previously been forced to discard, Ricky and some Big Hollywood Somebody whispered and nodded. Miss Hollywood Big Somebody pointed to a break in the clouds, and it seemed that if we headed a bit north, nothing far, just a mile or two towards Zuma, we'd have at least a semblance of sunshine. And so the go-ahead was given, the anchors hoisted and the boats began to move.

SCENE ANALYSIS

FALLING OFF *Kelley* was a rookie move, even for me. The first mate shouted, Tacking starboard, and I forgot to duck. With one quick swoop of the sail I got knocked in the noggin, pushed past the coach roof, slid by the guardrails and went plop, straight into the sea.

Magdalena overboard! someone shouted on deck.

Off deck, three buoys—the horseshoe buoy, the Dan buoy, the horseshoe life-buoy fitted with a drogue—came in plop, plop, plop, right after me. Someone in red was instructed to point, and even though it was daylight they started up the search lamp and shone it in a single yellow beam at my yellow-hooded head.

In the water, my head throbbed. I tried to stay calm by chanting, When in doubt straighten out, like some kooky Hare Krishna. I reclined so my feet were close together and near the surface like they teach you at Harbor School, and I kicked the saturated sarong from my legs. I suppose I should have looked for a life vest, but instead I looked to Ricky, who had his back to me and his arm around the shoulder of Miss Big Hollywood Somebody. Both his personal transcriber and my personal assistant, along with the directors, the best boy, the grip, the lighting tech and a few dozen extras, were trying desperately to get his attention; but he was leaning into his conversation, most likely indulging Diamond Myst secrets in hushed watery whispers. And when the grip shouted, Excuse me, Mr. de la Cruz, through a bullhorn no less, he merely held up his index finger—a gesture synonymous with "This is Business, and unless the building's on fire don't bother me."

But the building is on fire! And I hit my head. Hard.

Tell him, I shouted to the grip, who clearly couldn't hear a word I was saying but to his credit was still trying to get Ricky's attention on *Green Tambourine* while everyone else on *Kelley* ran about in a panic, making small gestures of rescue. The director, bless his heart, was removing his watch and attempting to fasten it to the brass rail of the boat, the assistant to the executive assistant producer was slipping out of his topsiders while pointing to the buoys floating well beyond my reach, and the wardrobe consultant shrugged out of his intentionally wrinkled Dolce sports coat while the extras were unilaterally instructed to keep a peeled eye and point.

Life jacket, the grip shouted, still using the bullhorn, though this time apparently directing his comments towards me.

Life jacket, I thought, but continued to look only at Ricky. His back was still turned and his index finger was now outstretched and pointing at the horizon, admiring the outline of the Channel Islands as they jutted out against the shark-infested sea.

Tell him! I shouted again while rubbing my head.

But the grip merely shrugged and pantomimed the sign for "I can't hear you," before pointing again to a makeshift flotation device.

Right. I made an effort to angle myself towards an empty Styrofoam case of Diamond Myst bottles, but it drifted just out of reach.

I shut my eyes and continued to float. Trying to levitate. Trying to stay almost entirely on the surface, or at least as close as humanly possible. Trying to ignore the incessant and increasing throbbing inside my skull. Trying to believe that, any minute now, Ricky would turn around, leap over the rails and save me.

However, when I opened my eyes and looked again in his direction, I saw him reach for a bottle of Luxe and pour, first himself and then Miss Hollywood Big Somebody, a glass.

It was right then that I realized three things: one, it didn't appear as if he were coming in after me any time soon; two, the cameras were rolling; and three, the cameras were still rolling.

Even though my head throbbed and my toes stung with the chill of the salty Pacific, I knew we could never afford a do-over. We needed this shoot to come through on the first take, so I smoothed out my hair, wet my lips and tried to angle myself upright. The extras continued to point, the light shone and someone shouted, Another man overboard.

I looked, but it wasn't Ricky. Although he had turned around. Instead of leaping over the rails in my rescue, he was confidently balancing himself against the mast, near Miss Hollywood, dangling a buoy overboard and sporting a big thumbs up.

Really? I thought as a flotation device drifted within reach. Really? I gave a few graceful scissor kicks—the cameras were still rolling—and an open-armed reach, but it drifted steadily past my grasp and, instead, floating near me now were several half-empty bottles of Luxe that had also slipped off deck. I grabbed one in each hand, like flares, and raised my arms above my head, swaying them back and forth as I shouted to no one in particular, Help.

Later, I remembered something about traumatic instances and the distortion of time, so I'm not sure if it was seconds or hours before help arrived, but I know the color of the water was green, like the shell of an avocado, and just below the surface what looked like little pieces of Styrofoam bobbed past.

EXAGGERATED HEROICS

|T WOULD be nice to say that Puck did a swan dive, clearing the copper rails and bounding in after me, but he did a fireman's pole, feet first, hands out so he didn't get his white-blond hair wet. Coming in after me was just about the stupidest thing Puck could have done, but he did it anyway and I loved him ever after.

I watched him swim over to me doing a crazy crawl-like stroke and I'd be lying if I didn't admit that, from a distance, especially with a knot on my noggin and my eyes slightly crossed, he looked an awful lot like Junah. So much in fact that I thought, for maybe half a second, I was dead. Maybe heaven was an ocean and as I bobbed about it was Junah who was coming for me. But another half a second later, as the cold continued to creep through my skin, I knew I was alive, and when Puck reached me we bobbed about together.

I wanted to make sure you tightened your waist fastenings, he said, reaching over with a life vest and tugging at the Velcro fasteners for me. Don't want you to catch your death.

I smiled, my teeth already starting to chatter out of fear or cold, it was too early to tell. I can't catch, I said. Not even a Frisbee.

Good. Then we won't teach you. How about we just sit tight instead?

Sure, I said, but first smile for the camera.

What? he asked.

The camera. I pointed along the horizon to *Green Tambourine*, zipping along the water with Ricky and Big Somebody—thumbs up—on deck. It's rolling.

Really?

Would I make it up? I asked, positioning the Luxe between Puck and myself. Now smile.

He smiled and I went faint. Not for real, mind you, for the show.

Hold me damsel-style, I instructed through closed lips.

He did.

Now take the bottle and pour it on my face. Like it's a magic potion or something.

Right, he said, starting to get the picture.

And, as the mineral water mixed with sea salt fell on my face, I faked my own resuscitation and passionately kissed Puck on the lips.

Saved, I proclaimed and pronounced it a wrap.

INDUSTRY CLICHÉ

ALTHOUGH THE cameras stopped rolling, Puck and I were still out to sea, bobbing and sifting with the ebb of the current.

You do this often? Jumping in after fallen women? I asked.

Nah, you're my first. The motor's down so they'll have to circle eight. Just turn your back to the break and try not to move.

I did as he said, and as I turned Puck turned with me so I ended up reclined in what would have been his lap, his legs tucked under each of my arms and my head against his puffy orange vest.

My toes were numb and the chill—it was January—was working its way up my legs and past my knees. I squeezed and released my thighs. Squeeze, release. Squeeze, release. Puck must have felt what I was doing because after a while he was squeezing along with me.

At least if we die, we'll have toned glutes.

Hey, he ran his hand across my cheek, stopping to outline my lips with his near blue finger, we're not going to die.

I twisted so that we were holding each other and looking into his eyes I said, Promise?

Trust me, he said.

It was quiet as we bobbed about together and looked toward the sea.

Think they called Mayday? I asked.

Still holding me, he looked over my shoulder at his watch. Three minutes give or take, he said, his mouth rubbing against my cheek, Probably so.

The water lapped slowly around us as we floated quietly, the light still shining bright in our eyes.

Mayday. Mayday. This is L.A. Woman, I said, a mock radio up against my shivering lips.

Vessel L.A. Woman, this is Coast Guard Station Point Dume, Puck responded, his face so close I could taste his chai latte breath. Please state your position and the nature of your emergency.

Coast Guard, I'm in between the legs of man who is not my husband somewhere in the middle of the Pacific. Junah, the boy I loved most in the world, is dead. I'm freezing to death and I think my marriage may be over. Over.

L.A. Woman, we read you but could use a little more directional information. Can you be more precise as to your bearings?

Bearing windward, just shy of scared and positively freezing, I said and this time I meant it. I was suddenly so ice cold that even holding onto Puck was effort and I started to slip.

Copy, L.A. Woman. Hold tight. Help is on the way. We'll have you out of that water in no time.

SO HERE I am, just as promised: afloat in the Pacific Ocean, wrapped up with a man I hardly know and, chances are, you believe me right? Because it seems like something that could happen, especially in Los Angeles. Especially with my husband still on deck discussing business with Miss Hollywood Big Somebody and the best boy maneuvering the grips so the artificial sun keeps shining. *Kelley* is on her forward scoop and, as the lifeline snakes its way through the frothy blue wake, Puck snaps me to a buoy and says, blowing me a kiss, You're safe now. It's over.

As they tow me in, *Kelley* getting larger and larger while Puck shrinks into a tiny blue and yellow speck, I can't stop thinking about water and drowning, drowning and death, death and falling, falling and Junah, Junah and.

And although it is nice to be pulled to safety, and although

I'm supposed to just go with it, refrain from moving or resisting, I'm so cold that I can't help kicking my legs and swimming along. So it figures that by the time I reach the vessel I'm too exhausted to climb to the bathing platform by myself. Because there are already two more people than planned in the water, someone above fashions a short strap, with a block and tackle rigged to the end of a halyard, and they sort of scoop me up and roll me out of the water and onboard.

Of course, this isn't what's actually happening. Technically, when my body reaches the boat I'm unconscious, and so that whole bit about the block and tackle and halyard is what they'll tell me after my water fall, when I come to.

EMOTIONAL TRANSITIONS

I CAME to soaked to the bone, on a gurney in an ambulance with Ricky's face staring intently above me.

I fell, I said. Like Junah but not... My words chattered around in my teeth before I spit them out. Puck, he—

Shussh— Ricky said, stroking my forehead with his thumb. There was a paramedic at my feet rubbing something I couldn't feel all over my toes, and I was covered in some strange sort of tin foil. I tried to sit up.

Ma'am, the paramedic said, simultaneous with Ricky's softer, but sharper, Mags. Lie still.

I leaned back and the tin foil made a crinkly noise as my back slid against the firm foam mattress. I tried to move one of my arms, but Ricky gave me a look and so, keeping all limbs beneath the foil, I rubbed my elbow against my waist. I couldn't be sure, having lost the certain sensation of feeling, but it felt as though I were naked.

Am I naked? I asked Ricky.

Almost.

But the cameras. The staff. They—

The paramedic blushed and looked down at my toes.

You were frozen, Ricky said. We had to get you out of those wet clothes.

We? Did this happen before or after *Kelley* caught up with you?

Does it really matter? You're safe. Are you really going to worry about who saw what?

I tried to look away but, because I was told not to move and because Ricky's face was directly above mine, I could only close my eyes.

Where were you? I asked, eyes shut, as the ambulance wailed on towards the hospital and the tears came.

Right here, baby. I'm right here, he said.

More tears were coming now. Though I tried to hold back, they spilled over easily, like a girl slipping off the side of a boat. The first slid down my cheek and the second back along my hairline and into my ear. When I raised my arm to try to brush them back, I realized an IV restrained my wrist and then I lost it. Ricky reached up to touch my face, occasionally smoothing away a wet strand of hair while chasing tears.

It's okay, baby, he said, I'm here now. I'm sorry. I'm here.

And I tried through my tears to hear if there was another siren, Puck's siren, screaming alongside my own, but I couldn't quite hear, even with my eyes wide open.

You're going to be fine, Ricky kept on. Just a little blue is all, but it's pretty. Your lips match your eyes.

I tried to protest, but as I did, a snot bubble escaped my nose.

It was disgusting. It was funny. We kinda laughed and as Ricky reached over to wipe my upper lip, he whispered, You're safe now. It's over.

And there it was like a charm: it's over.

It's over. It's over. It's over, spilling over its toxic salt-water voodoo, out of my eyes and into the medical van, a virtual sea of endings. And right there the end began.

INCONSISTENT REALITIES

NO, THAT'S not entirely true. One thing you should know about me straight off is that I'm prone to exaggeration and fits of sparkling melodrama. But all that aside, the truth is, the end has been beginning for a long, long time. Don't get me wrong, I'm trying. Hard. To fight it. It's just that lately—well, lately it's been a lot like I said before: easier to bob about in uncertain waters than to swim towards shore.

TAKE ONE

THE BIRTH OF CHARACTER

JUNAH AND I were Polish twins, which means basically that our mother was born a Jablonowski and we were born thirteen months apart. Of course no one on my mother's side called us that. And whenever she heard it said at picnics and grape stomps she'd cover Junah's ears and hum. To her credit my mother, up until she married my father, believed you could get pregnant by sitting on a boy's lap while kissing. So it shouldn't be too surprising that she also believed you couldn't get pregnant while breastfeeding. Even still, she didn't cover my ears and I was old enough to know that being a twin of something made you more special; it meant you were never alone. So I took to telling everyone that Junah and I were legitimate twins—identical in fact—and not soon after I made my first attempt on his life.

Junah was always almost just about to die. He was born blue and it started there. Something about the umbilical chord being wrapped around his neck. But the gist of it is, he was born without breath. There was some smacking, I'm sure. Some country doctor in lavender scrubs held him upside down by his ankles and shook him and thumped with thumbs and fore-fingers on his chest. Breathe, said the doctor, but Junah went from blue to purple and then to gray. He closed up his throat and he flat out refused.

The doctors pronounced him dead after birth, the one making the delivery and the one called in to consult when things started going badly. Stillborn, they said. But they didn't know Junah and they didn't know breath: Junah held his.

Through the attempts at resuscitation he neither sucked nor pushed through the mucus that glued his gums shut, and when the doctor put his old hairy lips to the cerulean child and puffed—three short baby breaths, one soft baby thump, three short baby breaths, two soft baby thumps—Junah refused to respire. The nurse shook her head sadly. The doctor handed Junah, now upright, to his colleague. The other doctor clicked in an obvious way and passed little Junie on down to the smooth nurse who wrapped him in blankets and then, because my mother insisted, gave him to her for one final hold. My mother took Junah and held him up to her swollen sweaty face.

Breathe, she whispered.

She said it to him sweetly and rocked him in her arms with a hum.

She continued with the chorus, Breathe baby. And then, Baby breathe. She invented the mantra that would become Junah's life, and with the last line, no longer whispering, baby snatched away and doctors charting "hysterical," Junah lost his Prussian pigment, yellowed out and took his first breath.

Auh, Junah said and then he wailed.

IT WAS a miracle, Mom says, but I say it was fixed. Junah held their attention from the start. Attention on top of attention on top of a show and always wanting more. Although he didn't go about it in the normal way: he didn't hit or color on the walls or wet his bed. He was cool. Cool down to the blue of his blood and Mom loved him more because of this. She loved me, the child that had come easily, but not as much as Junah. Junah she loved like licorice. Loved his anise taste and stringy limbs. Loved him because he was born not to breathe.

When she brought him home, he was not simply Baby like I had been. No, Junah was "Baby, my baby, who almost forgot how to breathe." Junah was "Precious baby sunshine who nearly, dearly, died." Junah was "Careful around Junah." Junah was

"Don't touch" and "In a minute" and "After Junah." I mean, this isn't to say I didn't love him just as much, in fact I loved him more.

But I wasn't the type to say anything. Instead, I decided to take his life.

WRITING FROM THE INSIDE OUT

T WAS a Tuesday, two weeks before my fifth birthday, and even though absolutely nothing special was going on I had convinced my mom to let me dress Junah and myself in our Easter overalls. They were matching—mine skirted, his panted—mint linen with white blouses and buttons in the shape of birds. I loved dress-up, particularly when it involved posing as twins, and Junah never protested. He made a stunning princess and a perfectly dapper mop-headed Andy to my Raggedy Ann. On the Tuesday in question I had declared us woodland sprites and dragged him out into the vineyards to braid crowns of dandelions and grape leaves. But Junah's wouldn't stay on. First it slipped over his head into a necklace and then, when I readjusted its width, it slipped to the left and looped across his ear like an eye patch. And he wasn't helping. Not in the least.

I could lie and say I thought that maybe if I gave the crown a good hard tap it would stay in place, but I don't exactly remember it that way. What I remember was every time I tried to slide the braided greens back to the top of his head he would look up through the top of his eyelids and raise his chin, trying to see that I got it right but causing it, again, to slide hopelessly to the left. He looked so precious, so perfectly adorable with his clumsy crown that I remember wanting to kill him. Not out of frustration, or anger, or jealousy or spite. But so that I could keep him with me, so that I wouldn't have to share him with anyone else.

And that's when it happened.

Just to see what it would be like, I slipped off one of my shiny patent leather shoes and hit him, hard, on the top of his head with its heel. The sound was terrible: a muffled womp, and then he just tipped over onto the dirt and was out. I remember standing there, my hand stuffed into the mouth of my shoe, the shoe raised above my head, looking at Junah and wondering if I really had killed him what it might have meant.

There was a thin trickle of red blood weaving its way across the top of Junah's forehead, tracing in his platinum hair and pooling left towards his ear. I knelt down next to him, bits of newly pruned grape vines blurring with the green sweethearts on my white tights, and put a finger in his bloody ear. I wiggled it around like a Q-tip, trying to fit it into his ear hole like a plug. I mean it was one thing to try to kill your brother. It was another thing entirely to cause him to go deaf.

Jun? I said. Then I waited. For Junah to laugh, throw a fistful of leaves in my eyes and shout, Gotcha, before getting up and racing towards the lawn. But he didn't shout and he didn't laugh and his chest stopped moving and he started to blue.

Momma, I shrieked, my finger pressing harder into Junah's ear, Momma! Junah's making himself blue. Blue! I said loud and with breath, He's going blue again. Unfazed by the other cries, the tears and the tattles and the screams, Momma leaped when she heard the word "blue" and came running, her skirt held high above her pale knees, out to the vines beyond our yard. Breathe baby, she shouted to Junah, who lay still in the dirt. Breathe, she said again, as she lifted him by the feet and shook him upside down. Junah bobbed like a cork in a bottle of wine and then swung, syncopated to the chanting, like the tire attached to our porch.

Laney what did you do? Mom asked in between mantras.

Nothing I said, holding my hands behind my back, bloody finger and shiny shoe.

Baby, breathe, she chanted, swinging Junah's body upwards and slipping her arm under his neck to cradle his weight. She saw the blood then, dripping now into his eye, and for a moment she stopped breathing too. I could hear it, a quick sucking in of air and then a silence, not a gasp.

Junah Francis, would you please breathe? His body stilled like a dead stump of tree. Magdalena, get my keys, call 911, she said, scurrying with Junah over to the side yard where we parked the car. And then, for reasons that escaped us both, Junah's cheeks began to inflate, his lips cracked and ever so slowly he sucked at the sky like a mute whippoorwill. He inhaled and exhaled and breathed.

His head needed six stitches and my birthday was sort of cancelled. Well, at least the party part. I still got a cake with peanut butter frosting and a pile of presents wrapped in newspaper. From Junah I got a pair of pink, soft-soled ballet slippers, bundled in tissue paper inside a box that said "Freed's of London." When I opened the box he grabbed one and hit himself over the head.

See, he said, in his baby-me voice, won't hurt.

I see, I said and wore those shoes until I wore them out.

THE DEATH ROLE

WHEN JUNAH died dead, he fell off a rock.
It was a big rock.

Huge.

Junah had attached himself to the rock with brightly colored ropes and super-strong clips and clasps.

LEAN BACK, Junah had told me the first time he tied me to a rock. We were camping in Yosemite, and he had me all strung up like a marionette. We were on a small rock—small by Junah's standards—that seemed a little too tall for me. Junah scurried up first. He was like a goddamned ring-tailed lemur, my brother. Limbs and legs against a staggering granite wall. Much more impressive than the worn-out monkeys we used to peer at from behind chain link when we were kids at Mickey's Grove.

LIKE THIS, Magda-laney, he said, dipping his hand into the polka-dot chalk bag he had clipped to his waist and fitting his fingers into cracks I couldn't see from the ground. Make yourself long. Reach with your arms and push up with your legs; be as long as possible.

Like Pilates? I asked, squinting up at him, shielding the sun from my face with my hand.

Sure, Junah said and gave me a thumbs up.

He was aglow, he was awesome, he fully and wholly took away my breath.

Never climb higher than your anchor, he called down, stopping just before the peak and twisting around to look at me.

This is your anchor, he pointed to a hunk of metal stuck into a crack in the rock.

How do I know it will hold? I hollered back.

It will, Junah said. It can hold you and me and about five other people. He tugged on the rope for emphasis.

How do I know it won't slip out? I said.

It won't, Junah said, kicking the rock.

Oh, I said.

I promise.

Right.

Okay, I'm going to rappel down. I need you to hold the rope.

Rappelling is the part that looks fun about climbing rocks. Floating down in huge hops, suspended by string.

I'm going to say "rope" and then I'm going to swing out the rope. Watch it and make sure it falls straight. Don't let it hit you. Keep away from the trees.

Okay, I said, taking six giant steps back and standing wide, feet apart, just in case.

Rope, called Junah, and he swung the purple and gold rope in my direction.

I had my hands out, ready to catch it, ready to catch anything, but the rope stuck, snagged on a sharp rock that jutted out on the right. Junah repositioned his bearing and leaned to the left.

Rope, he yelled again.

This time the rope came swinging out in my direction and I caught the tail end with both hands.

Got it.

Ace, Junah said. I'm coming down now. Your job is to hold the rope out so it doesn't get tangled or caught. As I get lower it might have some play so be careful.

Play?

Slack.

Right.

Ready?

No.

Junah waited patiently at the top of the rock. Why not? he smiled.

What if I mess up?

You can't mess up. Just hold the rope.

Then he leaned back, so that it seemed as though he was parallel with the ground, or from his perspective the sky. He let go. He fell back. I shut my eyes and held the rope.

See, he shouted, it's easy.

Carefully, I peeked up at him. He was about four feet below the anchor. He jumped back again, and again, and within seconds he was next to me on the ground.

Now you go, he said.

No way.

Way, I'll go with you, he said, putting his hand on my back. Piece of cake.

I looked up again at the rock. It was bulbous at the bottom. I could easily scamper up the first few boulders no problem. Then came a bit of straight rock that appeared to be about as tall as I was and above that a ledge-like thing that Junah called a shelf. After the shelf, however, it was straight as a sheet and twenty feet at least.

How far up? I asked, willing to go to the ledge.

All the way, Junah said, nodding to a brightly colored pair of smelly, too-small shoes, Those will help.

I squeezed my feet into the rubber-soled shoes and tippy-toed about while Junah fashioned a harness out of cord and carabineers for himself. The real harness, the one with a belt, two leg holes and buckle designed specifically for alpine climbing by the boys at North Face, he gave to me along with his helmet.

You sure that's safe? I asked, eyeing his meticulous knots and reaching a hand out to test the clip-things.

Yep. And besides, I'm not going high, just to the shelf. You're going all the way up. Ready?

45

I looked first to Junah and then to the rock.

Safety check, Junah said, pulling tightly on my harness and double-checking the belt to be sure it was strung through the buckle twice with a double back. Let's clip you in, he said.

But don't I get any gloves?

How in the heck are you going to feel the rock with gloves on? he asked, giving me the silly girl look he used to throw at me when we were kids.

I shrugged.

Chalk up, Junah said, smiling and turning his hip in my direction.

I put my hand into the pouch, cringing as the gritty dust worked its way beneath my nails. Then I rubbed my palms together like I had seen him do previously and, because I couldn't help it, I smacked my left hand against his shoulder, leaving a filmy white handprint on his back.

Funny girl, he said, not bothering to wipe the mark away and walking towards the base of the rock.

Okay, start by putting your left hand there, he motioned towards a lip on the rock just above my head, your left foot here, he nodded towards a spot about three feet off the ground and then stretch your way up towards that dark gray crack up top.

Up top seemed impossibly out of reach, but Junah said, I'm serious. It's all about perception. Think yourself longer.

So I put my left hand there and my left leg here, and I stretched and tugged and felt myself rising.

Neat, I said to Junah who was still on the ground shouting out my next move like a game of Twister: Right foot green. Left hand blue. I was climbing the rock.

Look at you, Laney, Junah called up after me. You'll be a pro in no time.

No way, I said, I'm not letting people see my ass in this thing.

It sure is juicy, Junah laughed, reading the letters off my mango-colored sweats, but I won't tell anyone.

When I made it to the shelf I stopped and took a look around.

Not a bad view, is it? Junah said, beginning his ascent.

Brilliant, I said. Even though I didn't make it to the top. The rock, another one of those things they don't tell you on TV, was ridiculously cold and after a while it was hard to hold on. But I got a hell of a lot further than you would've expected if, say, you were placing a bet.

Now, said Junah, who was about fifteen feet below me on the ledge, comes the fun part.

I can't wait, I said. What do I do?

Let go, Junah said.

You're kidding, right?

Not at all. Push back with your feet and keep your legs perpendicular to the rock. Let go and fall back. You're safe, the anchor will hold you.

I bent my knees a little and bounced a bit to show I was seriously considering it, when in fact there wasn't a way in hell I was letting go.

Nope. Can't do it, I said.

But it's the fun part. Just let go and hop down. I'll only let a little slack so you won't go far. If you fall, I got the rope. It'll catch you.

I looked down at Junah and then past him to the rocky ground. You're not fooling anyone, I said to him. I know full well that you still have the scar from when I hit you with the shoe.

I forgive you, Junah said, and I promise you'll be fine. Trust me.

Trust him. I took a deep breath. Bounced some more, released with my left hand and then reached back towards the crack.

Trust me, Junah said again.

I let go and fell. But not far. Just a little bit, like maybe four feet. Because I forgot to keep my feet out in front like Junah instructed I scraped my knees against the rock and ripped off a nail, but Junah caught me and on the next rappel I jumped further, landed softer and loved him.

AND I try not to think about it, but sometimes, I can't help it.

I wonder if someone said "trust me" to Junah just before he fell.

All the way.

To the ground.

THE SUSPENSE SENTENCE

BECAUSE I was supposed to be there.

CATALYST

HERE'S THE thing I just can't get over. And not—fuck—the death part. That part, you should know, I'll never get over. But also, I'm not trying. What I can't get over. What I can't seem to wrap my mind around. Why I couldn't stop crying. Why I took up under the bed to begin with. And, perhaps, maybe even why I fell off the boat. Why I took a hiatus. Why I go under the knife. Why I glue goddamned rhinestones to canvases and drink. Is because I was supposed to be there.

We both were, Ricky and I.

But then an investor called from Vermont. And the aquaponic team just wasn't getting it. And my dad was having trouble with the osmosis project. So Ricky drove to my parents' ranch to handle it, and because he couldn't—manage it by himself that is—I rolled up my sleeping bag and went back. Early.

Two days later Junah was dead.

And just you tell me how I'm supposed to get over that? How I'm supposed to just deal with knowing that had I been there—had I said yes to Junah and no to the business—well then maybe my brother could have trusted me, not some stranger who watched as he fell.

AUDITORY CUES

A FTER JUNAH died my mom kept his voice on the answering machine, so when I called home he'd answer. According to AT&T, the month after Junah died I called home 719 times. When Ricky, armed with the phone bill, finally asked what was going on, I just dialed and pushed the receiver to his ear. He listened quietly, his face pale, before he hung up and pulled me close to his chest.

Magdalena, he whispered into my neck, Junah's gone.

I ignored him and hugged tighter, my nails pressing into his back, willing myself not to hear.

Later, in the middle of the night, when Ricky caught me, in bed with the phone pressed tight to my cheek, not talking, just listening, he said, I'm trying to understand, but—

No, I said. No you don't.

Mags, Ricky said, reaching across the bed and trying to take the phone away from me.

No! I said and held the phone to my chest as though it were a defibrillator. You didn't even listen to the whole thing.

Ricky looked confused, I heard it this morning, he said. In the kitchen—

No. You listened to half of it. The message is twenty-two seconds long. You only listened to thirteen.

Mags, Ricky said again, placing his hand on top of mine, which was still holding tight to the phone, I think—

But I counted, I said shaking. I counted.

Three days later, when I picked up the phone and dialed, a mechanical voice answered. I sat on the floor and cried until I couldn't breathe.

When Ricky came home from work and found me there, phone off the hook and beeping on the cold floor, he took me in his arms.

It's in a box, he whispered, in a closet at your parent's place. Your dad and I...we thought it was the best thing.

Best for whom? I screamed and promptly began my residency beneath the bed.

BLOCKING

WHAT YOU need, the Shrink said—after Ricky dragged me out from beneath the bed and drove me to her office—is a transitional project. Something to push you away from your perpetual grief and into a life after death.

Bullshit, my mother said, when I reported to her about my session. What we need is your brother back and a fucking shrink who fucking understands what it's like to lose a child.

Before Junah died my mother never swore and, although we grew grapes, was impartial towards wine. But after, she took to talking like an unsupervised seventh-grader and she took up the bottle too.

My father, when I told him, had a different response. He rented a Caterpillar D9 and bulldozed the barn. What the fuck is he doing? my mother asked, staring through the kitchen picture windows, a glass of cabernet in her hand.

Transitioning, I guess.

Well, does he have to be so goddamn literal about it?

EXEUNT

TURNS OUT bulldozing the barn was the best thing my dad ever did. Because when it was down, when he had it leveled and then cleared, he began again, sleeping in a worn down sack in his portable shed. He was building, he told me, a cellar with temperature-controlled barrel storage and a proper tasting room. We're going to have our own label, Magdalena. I'm through selling grapes to the big guys. We're going to do it ourselves.

For a week or two, when I wasn't crying softly under the bed, I tried to help. I tried to pretend I was interested in constructing something, in making something new, but truth be told it was all too painful. Apparently, I wasn't the only one who felt cold and bare. Ricky stopped feeling too, but unlike me he didn't take up residency under the bed, crying his eyes shut for the next three weeks; no, Ricky took up and left. Later he said that his knees hurt. That he just couldn't do it anymore, crawling on the ground and peeking under the dust ruffle, begging me to come out. He explained that he thought if he left I might come out on my own. And besides there was the business to look after. And when I think of it—Wow!—that may have been when the business began to take hold. When it became his new pet project, his Number One Girl. Not that he wasn't always obsessed, we both were. But after I went under the bed, he went a little overboard trying to keep something of our old life intact.

But try as he might, up north Junah was everywhere. And when Ricky mentioned, It might be easier if we moved to L.A.—not forever, he promised, but just for a little while. Breathe some new air. See some new sights—I crawled out from beneath the bed and moved to Los Angeles.

What the fuck was I thinking?

ARCHIVES

A FTER I came out from beneath the bed, my mother filled the gap with shoeboxes. Fifty-eight of them to be exact. Filled with articles and clippings, they're filed chronologically by date and organized front to back, 1949 to Now—except for an Asics box from October 2005 that lives instead in the top drawer of her dresser, beneath her going-out panties, that has exactly six articles inside, each and every one about what she calls "the accident."

When—nearly fifteen years earlier—my grandmother died, my mother and her sisters spent days going through her things. What they didn't leave for my grandfather or divide amongst themselves, they gave to Goodwill. The only thing they fought over was an embroidered ladybug wall hanging and the contents of a Ziploc baggie, found by Junah between some lettuce and a kohlrabi in the crisper drawer of the refrigerator. When Junah found the baggie while on the prowl for some orange cheese and handed it to my mother, she let out a strange sort of whimper and went white. My Aunts came running and that's when the fight began.

For generations extending back to the Battle of Olszynka Grochowska, the Jablonowski women have been intuitionists. That is, they pride themselves on their intuition and abilities not to *see*, but to *sense*, the future. My grandfather called it Bohunk-gypsy nonsense; but the Ziploc baggie, or rather its contents, was further proof that, although my grandmother may not have been able to foresee her own death, she clearly sensed it. Why else would she have clipped and neatly folded three *Dear Abby* articles around an aged picture of her daughters as children and then hid it in the fridge, which everyone knows is the only safe place in a fire, flood, hurricane or other unnatural disaster?

Although we never talked about it I know, after Junah died, my mom checked in the drawer by the cheese. I checked too. Just like I checked under the insoles of his hiking boots and in the liner of his sleeping bag. But unless she's keeping something from me, we both found nothing. Nothing to allude to the fact that Junah sensed anything ominous at all. Which I suppose can be explained away by the fact that he was male. Maybe only Jablonowski women have the gift, but if that's true then why didn't we sense it? Why didn't my mother or I intuit that Junah was just about to die?

THE SHRINK, when I asked her exactly that, had an easy answer. She claimed that intuitionists were nothing more than doomsayers and glorified seekers of negative energy. Magdalena, she said, fanning her legal pad in front of her face, You can find anything if you look hard enough. And if you try hard enough you can actualize it too. The human mind has an extraordinary capacity to direct energy—positive or negative—into being.

That was right about the same time I got my first formal warning about harassment and verbal threats. Because I did not—you bitch—wish for Junah to die, and I did not—I'll kill you for even thinking as much—direct it into being.

THE TALL WALL

IN ADDITION to their supposed intuition, the Jablonowski women were also tall. At six feet I'm their crown jewel. Although I never saw it that way. What I saw was a girl hunched over at her seventh-grade dance, ignoring her grandmother's pleas not to slouch, hoping—just for one song—that she would shrink short enough to be swirled in an awkward shuffle around the floor.

And because I towered over most of the boys in my sixth-through eleventh-grade classes, it was impossible for me to be pretty. To be pretty was to have Guess? Jeans that zipped just below your ankle, not two inches above. To be pretty was to have a spiral perm and jelly shoes and stretch pants with stirrups that actually stretched under your foot (and did not, for example, have to be cut off and pinned inside two pair of scrunch socks). To be pretty was to have your boyfriend's name puff-painted on your pink jean jacket and an arm full of Swatches and friendship bracelets that linked you to Heathers or Valeries or Kimberlys or Kristens.

To be pretty was to be short. Shorter, at least, than the boys. Which, at fourteen, stretched out on my extra-long day bed and flipping through *Vogue*, didn't make a whole lot of sense to me. Because when I looked at the glossy pages I didn't see short girls. I saw stringy, awkward gazelles with spaghetti limbs draped in lace and slumped artfully across the pulpits of abandoned southern churches. I saw muted beach pictorials of barely-there bikinis and legs as long as the surfboards they perched upon. But apparently, as my mother explained while she stroked my straight hair, Real people don't live in *Vogue*, Laney. They live in suburbs and neigh-borhoods and apartment complexes and farms. Real people have to work for a living and can't spend all day in their underwear flipping through magazines and imagining themselves shorter.

I'm not in my underwear, I said as I slid on a pair of super-short cut-offs. And I don't imagine myself shorter, I said as I slid the magazine under my pillow. I imagine myself tall, in a world with tall people who think that I'm pretty.

Well sounds like you're home, my mom said as she motioned out the large bay window toward Junah and my three tall cousins bent over grapes in the field. Ready to join Tall World, because it's crush time.

You so don't get it, I said as I tugged an old Esprit t-shirt and ran out into the hall. You just don't get it at all.

OUTSIDE OF the land of giants that were largely male and entirely related to me by blood, the rest of the world had pegged me as Too Tall. At least for a girl. Worse yet, in their opinion, I refused to put my long legs up to any real use. I mean sure, I helped people reach top things on shelves and such, but I refused to bump, set, spike, lay-up, free throw or triple jump. Because I was neither athletic nor pretty I was left with smart, which I embraced fully and added to it—more from necessity than from desire—some flair. Let the pretty girls have their acid-washed jeans, cinch belts and China flats. I was going to be an artist. And because real paint supplies were too expensive, I took to installation and made-do with myself. I wore argyle sweaters and color-changing lipstick. I studied the fashion magazines I hid beneath my pillow and pieced together a new vision for myself. My mom was more than happy to let me take over the Singer, and with it I learned to sew sections of Junah's old jeans into patchwork miniskirts that I adorned with safety pins and grosgrain ribbon. I was the first girl in Lodi to wear ankle socks with patent-leather pumps and, when it was cold, I pulled up mismatched leg warmers. If I couldn't be pretty then at least I'd be striking. I'd be memorable. I'd be something more than a tall girl, tugging on the hemline of her store-bought skirt and slouching in the corner.

THE SPINE OF THE STORY

AFTER JUNAH died dead—eighteen months and nine days ago—I drove home and took over his closet. I hacked off my hair with pinking shears and wore his jeans, his t-shirts and even his boxers. In the days after I sat on the porch swaddled in his things and breathed. When I couldn't smell him anymore. When the static of his sweat had stopped clinging to the soft cotton armpits and was instead replaced by my own unshowered skin, I stripped, let out a long howl and decided to become a bombshell.

If I couldn't become Junah, then I would unbecome him. Unbecome the both of us. I would re-examine the canvas and cut him out with sleek scalpels. Refashion myself in Southland skin temporarily scarred with puffy red staples. I would douse my face in designer tonics to erase the light brown spots of San Joaquin sun. I would surrender to filthy, exorbitant whims beginning with an order placed by phone to Freed's of London.

Unlike other brands (that shall remain nameless but come in that horrible pink of hair barrettes and cheap nail polish), the London slippers are peachy, like the color of my grandmother's dress-slips, and you have to sew in your own elastic ribbons with teeny tiny stitches and baby-fine thread.

Six pairs, I told the British voice across the wire: one leather, one canvas, four satin.

And which colors would you prefer, Miss?

Pink. They all have to be pink, I said. But then my voice broke and I hung up.

Later, I had Ricky call back with my credit card. He pretended to be me and said something about a cold. The woman on the end of the line pretended to understand.

Right then. Been going around. Glad you rang back up.

I know this because I was listening on the other line with my hand over the mouthpiece and a Kleenex in my mouth.

EXPOSITION

WHEN I first met Ricky I was a Central Valley bombshell, which, as anyone who's traveled far enough north to know, is quite different from the L.A. bombshell variety. In NorCal you only need to shave more than twice a week to be considered feminine, so you can imagine how little it takes to be glamorous: wear a charmeuse gown to bed instead of a t-shirt, trade your boots in for a pair of kitten heels—no matter if you kick them off at every opportunity—and always insist on gin.

When Junah died I stopped wanting to be me, and so when Ricky and I moved to L.A. I suppose you could say I wasn't really myself. Maybe, if Ricky and I had stayed up north I would have tired of gin-induced tantrums and dangling diamond earrings, maybe I would have joined forces with my father and poured my creative talents into the renovation of our vineyard, but after Junah's death Ricky felt it might be a good idea to get away for a while—"breathe some new air" were his exact words—and so we moved south where everything smelled like acetone and Errol Flynn.

IMAGE SYSTEMS

A T FIRST it almost seemed like Ricky was right: it was pretty hard, if not impossible, to imagine Junah in his dusty Teva sandals and Patagonia vest ordering burrata at Ago, queuing up behind a velvet rope outside Area or cozying up to the barista for a frothy four-dollar cup of organic, trade-free joe at Urth Caffe. No way would Junah take Gideon (our half-breed ranch dog) for a constitutional around the Laurel Canyon Dog Park, and he wouldn't be caught dead holding chopsticks at Nobu.

No.

Maybe he would be caught.

Dead there.

Since he was, in fact, dead now.

And that, I soon found, was the problem.

Junah may not have been ingrained and organic to the glittery Hollywood set, like he was in the bucolic valley, but he was ingrained and organic to me, and in myself I saw him. Which again wouldn't have been so terrible had it been in the privacy of my own home. Safely locked in the bathroom, steam from the faucet pouring hot water into the tub, it wouldn't have been the end of the world to see Junah there. But contrary to the advice of seismologists, L.A. is virtually made of glass, its reflective surfaces sweeping and expansive, and so Junah was with me everywhere I went. At the Lobby Bar of the Four Seasons Hotel he stared at me from the concave curve of a highball glass; when I did sun salutations he stretched from floor to ceiling. He walked tall with me past mirrored shop windows tinted blue and green; he hovered above the ATM in the dome-shaped double-sided glass; and even when I drove he tagged along, inching his way down Sunset or Beverly bouncing off the rearview, the odometer, the shiny chrome of twenty-inch rims. He was in my nose, in the crooked angle of my premolar bicuspids, in the natural flax of my hair.

And that's when I realized it would take a lot more than a pedicure and the moves to Chico O'Farrill's "Chico's Cha Cha Cha" to become a bombshell in the Southland. And so, if I was going to try to forget about Junah entirely, if I was serious about learning how *not* to be me, I needed to augment more than just my surroundings, I needed to augment myself. It was time to step up the bombshellization and enlist some local help.

Because I didn't know anyone else I called Ricky's sister, Cheri.

She said, Precious, it's about damn time, and then proceeded to set up emergency consultations at Neimans, Escada, Badgley Mischka, The B2V Salon and Dr. Hoefflin's.

Oh and Magdalena, don't try to dress yourself for our little outing. Just tell me your size and I'll bring something by.

Six, I said quietly into the phone.

Right. Even my fat clothes aren't that big. Plan B?

SOCIAL PROGRESSION

'M NOT going to lie and pretend that I expected our little trip to Rodeo Drive to be anything but a scene out of *Pretty Woman*.

Did I expect Cheri to transform me from a NorCal bombshell wannabe into a SoCal starlet?

Yes.

Did I expect to be met with sighs of admiration and astonishment because I was tossing down obscene amounts of money for semi-functional swatches of fabric and uncomfortable shoes with too-high heels?

Absolutely.

Did I expect designer clothes to actually fit?

You bet your sweet bippy I did.

But here's the thing. Even in Los Angeles, land of supermodels, starlets and bulimic demigods, they didn't. I mean I suppose they fit well enough if you were five-foot-eight or even five-two, but try being a staggering six feet where, on the rack or off, the hemlines always fall short.

Wow, this could really be a problem, Cheri said, holding up a pair of Rich & Skinny wide-legged jeans.

I wear a lot of dresses, I said, staring down the length of denim to where the pant leg ended and my own leg continued on.

But honey, Cheri cooed, you absolutely must have designer denim. She shuffled through the rack once more, this time as I did: with her eye towards the ground, seeking out length as opposed to color or style. I mean, as long as you have a good purse, a big enough ring and a tight pair of jeans you can get away with anything in Los Angeles.

Shorts? I suggested, thinking back to my days with the pinking shears.

Shorts? Cheri coughed, Shorts are better left for Palm Springs and strippers. But maybe, she continued, bending over and rolling the denim hem of a pair of Sevens higher by about three inches, you could have them taken in for a kind-of capri look?

You're kidding, right?

Well do you have a better idea?

Yeah, I said, taking the jeans away from Cheri and placing them back on the rack. Let's try a nice shift dress. Or a pencil skirt. I have a whole closet full of skirts.

Cheri shook her head, What you have in your closet is precisely the problem. A rack full of peasant-inspired patchouli drapes that totally mask any shape you may be working on. I think we need to keep looking. Maybe go a bit bigger and then have the waist taken in?

Which was another thing I just didn't get. Why did longer always equate to bigger? As if height were somehow proportionate to weight.

I mean where the fuck, Cheri asked, flipping frantic now through rows and racks of designer denim, does Uma Thurman shop? And Elle Macpherson and Geena friggin' Davis?

On the runway, I said, or maybe in Paris.

Cheri laughed and, with her arms loaded down with a stack of jeans, nudged me towards a dressing room without doors or dividers where the women seemed to find a strange joy in walking about half-naked in front of one another.

I cringed and made my way towards a corner where I could, with luck, fashion a cubby of sorts. However, the longer I stayed there, secluded in a corner, my chest facing the wall, the more I began to realize that part of the Loehmann's experience was prancing, or flashing yourself rather, in front of your neighbors who were doing the same. But as with everything in L.A. there was a strategy to it: you didn't just bare all, only your best. Women with big tits seemed to feel the need to remove their bras before trying on tight-fitting tanks two sizes too small. Women with buns the size of thirteen-year-old boys tugged at their Valentino jeans slowly, removing them an inch at a time while bent over beneath the greenish fluorescent lights. Then, as if that weren't enough, they would offer up unsolicited advice and beg the woman nearest to them for a second or third opinion.

And you're sure it's not too tight? a girl with a Playboy bunny tattooed to her left ankle asked Cheri, referring to the Band-Aid–sized skirt she had managed to wrap around her body.

Oh God no, Cheri said, taking in the curve of the woman's non-existent hips. It's Sue Wong, right?

Right, the girl said.

Well isn't it obvious then?

The girl spun around in front of the communal mirror and looked at her ass over her shoulder. She yanked up the on the waistband a little and, standing on her tiptoes, said to me, What do you think?

In addition to the Band-Aid she was wearing around her waist she had on a frayed tube top with the words I'M NOT AN ACTRESS spray-painted on the front. From my position in the corner—and I don't think it was just because she was on tippy-toes—I could see that the butt of her panties, visible from beneath the skirt, was also spray-painted and said, concluding the phrase on her breasts, BUT YOU CAN PUT THIS ON FILM.

I think maybe it's a little short, I said.

Cheri coughed.

The girl pulled down on the hem of her skirt and said, Really. (Not: Really? But: Really.) before she turned her back on me and studied herself in the mirror.

On me, I mean, I tried to amend. Because I'm so tall. It'd be short on me because I'm so…

Cheri coughed a second, louder time.

And then, maybe it was my imagination, but the dressing room seemed to silently shift to the corner opposite me. There was some whispering, which I tried to ignore, and a look from Cheri that said, It doesn't have to be perfect, it just has to do for now. Find something with the best name that fits and let's get the hell out of here.

I chose a silk dip-dyed halter dress, not because I liked it particularly, but because Cheri insisted it was recognizably Armani, even at a distance. The preppy bohemian tiered skirt and tank top I had met her at the door in were unfit for Macy's, let alone Neiman Marcus, and so we had come to Loehmann's to buy something I could wear to Neimans, and maybe I was getting the hang of it.

Once we were back in her Jag (we had to, in Cheri's words, fucking fetch it ourselves because fucking Loehmann's did not have a fucking valet), she dug out scissors from her purse and instructed me to clip the tags off my items, roll up the tinted window and change immediately.

Right here in the parking lot? I asked, looking around the concrete structure filled with expensive automobiles.

You know of a better place?

A dressing room? I said. A bathroom? The trunk?

Magdalena, she looked at her watch, we've already spent nearly three hours picking out your going-out outfit. If you want to actually go out, like today, you need to stop complaining and strip. I mean really, she looked through her purse for her lipgloss and cell phone, you're the one who called me. We still need to find you a decent pair of jeans, which could take God knows how long. I'm just trying to help.

While she dialed with one hand and glossed with the other, I pulled my arms out of my tank and slid the skimpy piece of bluish silk over my head. Then lifting my hips I undid my sash and shimmied out of my skirt while I simultaneously pulled the dress down over my lap.

God, you're such a prude, Cheri said, leaning over to help me tie the silky straps into a knot behind my neck. I mean nobody's looking, hello.

Sorry, I said.

Don't worry about it or about those, she said pointing to my tits. We can fix them in three to five business days. After pulling up on the e-brake she pushed a button and the convertible top slid down and into the trunk.

I busied myself transferring the items in my suede messenger bag into my new purse, but after I found I couldn't even squeeze in my wallet I gave up and stuffed a credit card, my picture ID, house key (sans chain), gloss, phone and a fist full of hundreds into the purse, which lost its slim appeal, but what else could I do?

Okay, Cheri said, making a left on red and easing her way down Third Street, let's make a list. You write I'll talk.

Her phone rang. It was Donna or maybe Barbara Ann, I couldn't tell. I was too busy making sure we didn't die in traffic. We cut off an Escalade, we agreed to meet someone for lunch, we made another left turn on red, we decided or rather Cheri decided to fuck the list and somehow—not without some major horn honking and a flip of Cheri's middle finger—we made it to Fred Segal on Melrose and Crescent Heights.

There were paparazzi in the parking lot, which both excited and pissed Cheri off, and as we made our way out of the car she whispered to me not to embarrass her. If you see a star, she said, anyone famous, don't stare and certainly don't try to talk to them. Just mind your own business and move on.

I nodded, squared off my shoulders, stuck out my chest and followed Cheri's lead as she sashayed into the store.

AT FRED Segal we actually did find a pair of jeans—though they were vintage and most likely belonged to Cleopatra Jones—and t-shirts that looked like they had less than one wash left in them before they'd evaporate into small, indistinguishable fibers. It's like that a lot with $350 t-shirts. $485 shoes give you blisters. $12,000 peels leave your cheeks burnt and pimply for three weeks. $550,000 rings from Tiffany sit unloved and unnoticed on perfectly manicured hands. It's so L.A.

AFTER OUR brief stint on Melrose we were off to Rodeo where we bought lingerie from La Perla, makeup from Chanel, shoes from Jimmy Choo and the most fantastic Python wrist bag and belt from Fendi. The salespeople were all young or at least they pretended to be, and they all knew without a doubt that they were beautiful. The worse you treated them the better they treated you. Everyone knew Cheri by first name.

Ah, Mon Cheri, my petite flower, crooned a black Adonis dressed entirely in linen, his nautical tattoo and the bulge of his muscles visible through the thin fabric. You've returned and oh! how I've missed you.

Armundo, my love, Cheri cooed, shuffling up to him and kissing him on both cheeks, how are you?

Comme ci, comme ça, he said, shrugging his shoulders and picking an imaginary piece of lint off his chest. The question is how are you and what, or shall I say *who*, is that exotic bird you've brought with you?

That, Cheri said with grand emphasis, is my sister-in-law Magdalena. Magdalena, *this* is Armundo.

Magdalena, my love, he held out his hands expectantly, how brilliant that you decided to stop by our little boutique. Come hither my sweets; let's take a look at you.

I walked over to where Armundo and Cheri were having their little tête-à-tête thankful for my new hydrophobic Gucci sunglasses that were firmly pushed against my face.

Magdalena's going through a bit of a reinvention, Cheri explained.

Understandable, Armundo sighed as he slowly rotated around me, staring hard from head to toe. She does have a bit of an ass.

She's working on it, Cheri said.

Well I should hope, came the response, but considering her height and her fabulous coloring I think we can work with it.

Fabulous, Cheri squealed.

You've got to be kidding me, I thought. But then I thought of Junah and how, if I just went with it, although he was dead, I could rebirth myself.

TAKE TWO

THE NEXT BIG THING

AFTER MY fall overboard the only thing that was *really* over was my career in water. The ad itself was a big-time boom—so successful, in fact, that there was more water than we knew what to do with. And so, citing a rise in the economy, we bought a sixteen-story executive office building on Wilshire, Ricky stepped in as acting manager and CEO of Diamond Myst, I took some time off to recover and Puck was promoted from personal transcriber to personal assistant. Which unofficially meant it was his job to keep me company at company parties and—whether or not this was in contract, I don't know—bring in B-list celebrities and industry types to spice up the water vibe. You see, after my water career washed up, Puck's took off. The commercial won some sort of Emmy or Oscar or whatever it is they give out for commercials (I'm not keeping track), and the Luxe print ads were blown up and plastered down buildings and across billboards all over Sunset.

Puck blew up too and, despite his being a bit too flamboyant for everyday life, was offered the male lead in the best Bigfoot screenplay ever written. He had like forty-five speaking lines, but it didn't really matter much because he had tons of face time as he dashingly managed to save damsel after damsel in distress.

CHANGE V. STASIS

WHEN, ALMOST four months later, I finally got around to telling the Shrink about my little sailing accident, she gasped, held her yellow legal pad to her chest and said, I really wish you would have told me about this sooner!

According to her, my fall from the boat was consistent with "behavior that bordered on reckless," as she claimed I was consciously acting out to gain Ricky's attention while simultaneously subconsciously reacting to—thus effectively recreating—my recent family trauma.

Duh, I thought to myself as I sat across from her on a plush faux-suede settee wearing a string bikini and trying not to make eye contact. Tell me something I don't know.

She announced, quite simply, that I was beginning Stage Three of the grieving process, though she was quick to caution that, Most people don't take the bargaining motif quite so literally, Magdalena. And, she added, if you continue to engage in such reckless and, might I add, life-threatening behavior, you're going to force me to break our understood patient–therapist privilege.

You're my shrink, I said in a soft voice, still not looking directly at her, pretending instead to tighten the screw that hinged the sidepiece to the frame of my oversized sunglasses with my fingernail. You can't break any confidentially agreements and you can't break up with me either.

Magdalena, she said, I'm not here to break anything. I'm here to help you. Pretending to busy yourself with your glasses is not going to change anything; neither is toying with your marital relationship, your bikini ties or your life. You're exhibiting avoidance, pure and simple.

Oh, I said, sliding my dark sunglasses onto my face so she couldn't see my wet eyes, I thought you said grief came in five stages. How can I possibly be acting out the bargaining stage if I'm so clearly still in avoidance? Isn't that Stage One?

Grief, she said, smoothing the lap lines of her skirt as she stood up and moved towards her appointment book, is a complex phenomenon. It is not uncommon for a person to find herself stuck in a stage or, as in your situation, to act out two or more stages at once. Next Friday, 4:30?

Fine, I said, reaching for my shoes, which I had slipped off next to the Zen water feature on the way in.

And Magdalena, she said as I made my way out the door, remember, grief is a process; acceptance is the goal.

ARCHIVES FROM THE MUSEUM

IN ADDITION to moving us to Los Angeles, in his efforts to help me accept my grief, Ricky gave me a Corvette.

But not just any Corvette.

No, Ricky gave me The Corvette.

A 1953 Polo White Roadster, fresh out of the National Corvette Museum. It was beautiful. Even with grief processing my vision, I could still see how pretty it was. What with its white oversized steering wheel and hand-painted racing flags on the chromed-out center. The tires were white-walled and lined—like my lips—in red, and the motor roared with Blue Flame.

It's a survivor, Ricky said as he handed me the keys. Not to be confused with some overdone restoration.

I don't know why that was so important to him but it was. He needed it to be authentic—the paint, the mileage, the Plexiglas side curtains, hell, even the tire jack was an unaugmented original, straight as it was when it came off the line.

I took the key on its little red leather Chevrolet stamped keychain and held it in my hand as Ricky walked me around the car, pointing out things like matching head and engine components and the stamped trunk mat (#4636966).

Wow, I said, feigning interest. And then, because it just felt like I should do something big to show my enthusiasm, I bit down on the silver GM YOUR KEY TO GREATER VALUE that was stamped on the key.

I thought Ricky would appreciate the gesture. I thought he would understand that, like the miner who bites into a gold nugget, I was just trying to confirm its authenticity and rule out any pyrite imposters.

But he didn't. Appreciate the gesture or understand its reference. Instead he lost his shit.

Magdalena! he shouted, snatching the key from between my teeth, What in the hell are you doing?

Appreciating, I said, after rubbing my tongue against my teeth in an attempt to get rid of the old metallic taste.

Maybe you don't understand, Ricky said as he gently, carefully examined the key, wiping my saliva off on a soft shammy he pulled from the glove compartment. This, he gestured to the car, is Number 254. You know what that means, right?

I did, but he didn't leave me room to answer. He just kept right on talking, repeating, pushing his words closer and closer together.

It means that it was number two hundred fifty-four off the line. Flint, Michigan. Out of three hundred. Three hundred hand-made total. Flint, Michigan, did I say that already? In 1953. And this, he gestured again, is only one of a handful still operational. It's a survivor, he said again, but louder this time.

Got it, I said, holding out my hand to take back the key.

But instead of handing it to me, instead of holding the door open to invite me for a spin around the block, he put the keys in his pocket, mumbling, and set to work shamming shine on an already sparkly bumper.

APPARENTLY THE wind knotting my long blond hair was supposed to help me keep my mind off things like death by falling and death by boulder. But here's the funny part: although I was allowed to sit next to Ricky twice as he drove it, I never so much as got to feel the cracked leather under my thighs on the driver's side. Which I suppose is fine, because, truth-be-told, I much prefer shitty little convertibles like Miatas, Cabrios and Capris. But Ricky insisted first on the vintage Corvette and then, when he realized the stress of driving it—we drove maybe two miles when, drenched with sweat and throwing out cuss words, he decided to turn around—he bought me a brand new tank disguised as a Mercedes SUV. Said it was impenetrable. Like me.

When Ricky pulled up to the curb outside the Shrink's office, I wasn't surprised to see he was driving the Tank. Sure, I was secretly hoping that maybe just this once he'd brave the Corvette, but really what did I expect?

SLICE OF LIFE

WELL? RICKY said as I opened the passenger's door and slid into the front seat of the Mercedes. He had expertly slid into the valet-loading zone, windows down, radio tuned to some XM talk station.

It was awful, I said, reaching across and hitting the power button, leaving us with street sounds.

It was rush hour, and everything was too loud and too bright. Not helping the matter at all was the fact that the Shrink—who repeatedly requests that I not call her that and who came highly recommended as the best in the business by none other than Eric Clapton's personal assistant, Paige—was located on Melrose and Crescent Heights, which isn't half bad if you want to hit Fred Segal, but if you live in Beverly Hills and have to be at Lynda Carter's *Hillary for President Beach Bonfire and Benefit* in Malibu in less than an hour, it's totally impossible.

Already dressed in pressed linen and a pair of John Varvatos woven slides, Ricky jutted out into traffic without so much as a signal or a wave, forcing a giant yellow Hummer with a personalized plate that read QUEENBE to lay on her horn.

I sucked in my breath, hanging tight to the passenger's door.

We drove ten blocks—from Crescent Heights to La Cienega—in silence. Which doesn't seem like much, but in L.A. on a Friday afternoon it took well over thirty minutes. Thirty minutes of intermittent silence and unnaturally loud breathing, tempered only by the opening and shutting of the sunroof (Ricky) and the click-click of the automatic door locks (me). If I'd had more breath in me, I would have told him some of the quiet dark things running past my lids in slow motion every time I shut my eyes; but I already felt dull from my avoidance, or maybe it was my bargaining, and instead I said, I want to go home.

Ricky looked first to his watch and then to the road. You look fine, he said, glancing at my printed Pucci two-piece and pareo, though I can't believe you wore that to see your therapist.

Shrink, I corrected him, yanking at my bikini ties. And it doesn't really matter, she already thinks I'm crazy.

Is that what she said? Ricky asked, suddenly interested.

No, that's not what she said. She told me her usual fat pack of lies. I clicked the door locks a few more times—lock, unlock, lock, unlock—to let Ricky know I was offended by the suggestion.

Well maybe if you tell me what she did say we could work through it.

Lock, unlock, lock, unlock—I pulled a long strand of my blond hair off my shoulder and stretched it as far as my arm would reach before saying, She told me a really long story about her brother the manic-depressive English professor. She said something about genius and madness and chemical dependency and how most of us (artists, CEOs, rock stars, grape farmers), in order to get to such great heights, also have to have the ability to fall very, very low.

That's what she said? Ricky said, switching lanes from left to right, again without so much as a glance in his rearview.

Pretty much, I said, locking and unlocking the door once more, for good measure. And that in addition to the Junah grief I'm most likely also suffering from prepartum depression.

Prepartum? Ricky asked as we stopped at a light.

Because we're having such a hard time getting pregnant.

Magdalena, Ricky said, pulling off his sunglasses so I could see his eyes, We're not trying to get pregnant.

I know, I whispered as I turned my back to Ricky and stared out the window at the Pacific Design Center, but a dog might be nice. The light turned green and Ricky cut off a bus in an effort to make a left.

She also said I should stick with the Zoloft, I clicked the locks once more. And gin.

She didn't say gin. Ricky shut the sunroof, maybe because he was concerned about sun exposure (I wasn't wearing SPF), but most likely because he didn't want anyone—in traffic, on Sunset—to overhear that his wife, Magdalena de la Cruz, the founding partner of Diamond Myst Water Corp. and Luxe mastermind, was on antidepressants.

Abandoning the door locks, I moved my finger to the automatic window button. As it rolled down I said in a loud voice, Zoloft. I'm on Zoloft.

I don't care about the Zoloft, Ricky said, rolling down his window as well. It's the gin that has me worried.

TRAFFIC WAS easing up a little and Ricky had decided to take the side streets through West Hollywood.

We were quiet for a while until, nearing Rexford, Ricky asked, Do you still want to go home?

Yes, I thought, but No is what I said aloud.

I wanted to go home, but not to the house in Beverly Hills. I wanted to go back to Berkeley, where once upon a time two idealistic grad students named Ricky de la Cruz and Magdalena Bamberger met and fell in love. I wanted to go home to the ranch in Lodi where I studied viticulture alongside the tall tanned body of a boy named Junah. But here I was stuck under a shut sunroof in the beautiful L.A. sun.

PREMISE

IN NORTHERN California I loved Ricky in a kooky, mad, crazy way. I loved the way he walked through the hills, the string of his gray hooded sweatshirt pulled tight beneath his chin, his lips moving with unspoken ideas. I loved the balmy feel of my hand in his as we passed the seminary on Euclid, atop Holy Hill. I loved that, even when he was asleep, he listened. He heard me. It was years ago, on a futon on the floor of a converted Victorian in North Berkeley, when the air smelled like wet red leaves and tasted like September, that I breathed easily from beneath our shared sheets and whispered: Baby, I have an idea.

Ricky was half asleep, his arm resting across my shoulder, the bare skin of his chest pressed tight against the naked skin of my back.

Umm? He whispered to the back of my head, smoothing out my long hair so he could kiss my ear.

What if we made water taste better?

Umm, he said again before falling asleep.

NECESSARY DIGRESSION

M AGDALENA, RICKY said as we woke to the sound of
the Campanile chimes echoing through the hills, this water
idea, I really think it can work. I mean why settle for tap when
you can have pure mountain spring? Everyone knows that water
just tastes better after a long hike up Wildcat Canyon to Inspira-
tion Point. Imagine if we could bottle that? Not just water, but the
entire experience: the mist as it sets in over the East Bay skyline
at dusk, the color of the ocean as it sparkles like a diamond in the
last ray of sunset. That's it, Magdalena! We can design water for
the rich and pour the profits—Get it? *Pour* the profits—back into
environmental causes. You and I, we can Robin Hood water.

And it didn't matter what came next. Whether I thought so
or not. All that mattered was the look of him, looking at me and
talking as though it made a difference. As though we could make
a difference, to each other, to the world. As though we could be
a better business.

But then, for the better of the business, we moved to L.A., and
it's not exactly an exaggeration to suggest that things changed.
Although, if you must know the truth, sometimes when Ricky's
driving I can almost believe it didn't happen. If I shut the sunroof and close my eyes, if I breathe through my mouth so as not
to inhale any of the new car smell, if I sit still, very still, on my
sit bones, with my toes pointed and my hands in my lap, I can
almost believe I'm in an '83 Chevy, with a chug in the tank and a
star on the dash, doing forty-three miles per hour past Stagi and
Scriven's San Joaquin sunflower farm. Junah's beside me and the
billboards for Delta bluegrass have nothing to do with a record-

ing deal and everything to do with sod.

Almost, that is, until Ricky tugs open my door and says, Earth to Magdalena, this is your party. You coming?

And when I open my eyes it's not crawdads I see, sliding off the sides of Pixie Slough, but sunshine over the Pacific Ocean, still shining impossibly bright at 6:22 in the evening, and two lit Tiki torches, and a banner reading *Hillary '08* strung out between them.

IMAGE SYSTEMS

A T LYNDA Carter's parties the bar is out back on her private beach between the artfully aged driftwood deck and the surf. Tonight's was a butterflied Brazilian theme (Isn't it always?), which meant Puck was sporting someone who looked vaguely familiar. A child star now grown? Soleil Moon Frye, perhaps? Or maybe Mallory Keaton from *Family Ties*? It was hard to tell for sure because, like every other Hollywood has-been, she had fixed herself up with all the right parts: fake tits, fake tan, a purple ranunculus in her extended hair and an off-the-shoulder frilly something-or-other, fiercely hoping that she'd be re-discovered or, at the very least, asked to appear on the newest reality show. And I, for one, didn't blame her.

Maybe even, I wished it for her.

In fact, prior to my L.A.-ification, I would have gushed. Well maybe not so much gushed as revealed that, when I was seven, I painted a crescent multi-colored moon on the down side of my blinds too. So that each night, just like Punky, I could go to sleep with the stars beside me. But if Cheri's little tutorial had any kind of effect—and it indeed did—I now knew enough to know that the third faux pas in celebrity sighting was to conflate an on-screen persona with the actual celebrity herself. So I ignored Punky completely and, as Ricky excused himself to chat up an investor's wife, looked to Puck.

Sporting tight white trunks and a Gaultier hat with bold braided passementerie trim, Puck was a vision. But when he shot me a wink near the synthetic samba ensemble I held up a finger—*un momento*—and headed in the opposite direction towards the drinks.

POINT OF VIEW

PUCK AND a drink or two is how I get through parties. Before him it was Xanax and a flask, but thank God for metrosexual men—and not just because they were last year's *de rigueur* accessory, but because I love them. Puck most especially. He likes to proclaim loudly, and in public, that he's lived in West Hollywood his whole life, but once when we were alone, spread out on my bed and drinking too much, he admitted he was raised by chicken farmers in the buckle of the Bible belt. I'm probably the only one of the bottled water set who knows this, but I'm not about to out him to find out if it's true. Not only because he said he'd father my child if Ricky didn't come around, but because back on the boat he may have just saved my life.

TEXT AND SUBTEXT

THE BAR was conveniently located at the end of the Silent Amazon Auction Forest. A path of succulents and other California-indigenous plants were set on the sand in giant clay pots and done-over to look like a rain forest, complete with—oh my God, are they really real?—live blue morpho butterflies. And I'm not sure I even agree with the politics involved, but I'll admit it was stunning. Live butterflies flying in glass columns around encased white lilies and plumeria. And the truly remarkable part was no one talked about it.

None of it.

Not the house, of course. That we could Zillow later.

Not the view. It was priceless, so nothing needed to be said.

And certainly not the butterflies. No one dared to say the unsay-able: The butterflies are so lovely in their teal and indigo, but how did they get there, and where will they go after? And is it right? And how much did *that* cost? I mean we've all seen the fish bowls at that one wedding. The drunk guest who pours in some champagne or, better yet, swallows a Japanese fighting fish whole on a dare. But butterflies! Real live butterflies?

Instead, we all just walked through the faux forest looking at the "experiences" up for silent auction. Things like swimming lessons with the Lance Armstrong of the swimming world. I forget his name, but he's young and cute and won a few Olympic golds a few years back. Things like trips to Crete and cars and a yacht complete with diving instructor and underwater photographer who will charter you and ten of your loved ones to Catalina where the diver will suit you all up and when you jump in and go under the photographer will take a family shot amid the deep blue sea. Way better than that totally overdone beach shot—everyone dressed in white shirts and jeans—don't you think? Or so says a woman on my left, a beautiful Japanese woman dressed entirely in Chanel. Silk Chanel. Off-white silk Chanel in the heat. And not a speck of sweat anywhere on her.

Oh yes, I certainly think so, I said, as I hastily scribbled my name on bid for a helicopter tour of Haiti. Not caring how much it cost, trying instead to just get the letters right: Magdalena de la Cruz and not Magdalena Bamberger, the girl perpetually posed in front of a grape vine, with her parents and now dead brother, in a worn family portrait of the Northern Californian variety.

KEY SCENIC

AT THE bar, a makeshift lean-to with a thatched roof and butterfly-flanked hula skirt wrapped around the counter, a surfer with a night job was juggling limes. It might have been cliché except of course it was the only thing about the party that actually worked.

You know, if you really want to score, you'd try bottles, I said as I put both elbows down on the bar and rested my chin on my hands. Sand's soft; they won't break if you miss.

Tried it, he said reaching below the counter to hold up a bottle of Smirnoff Vanilla Twist, but the jigger gets all full of sand.

Right. I smiled and picked up a cocktail umbrella, twirling it around in my fingers.

What are you having? he asked.

Jameson up, I said, looking at his salty hair and wondering if my instinct to push it out of his eyes meant I was ready to be a mom. And a tall glass of gin with a straw and some ice so it looks like a Sprite.

I detected a hint of admiration when he set the whiskey down and I took it up and finished it in one gulp. I wanted to tip him big. But, looking down at my silk sarong tied and knotted at my hip, I realized I didn't have any cash.

So I said, Thanks, and made off with my gin.

CONSISTENT REALITY

I T WASN'T quite dark yet, only mid-evening hazy, and Puck was predictably floating on a purple pool raft sipping a blended pink umbrella drink. His skin was the perfect blend of Caribbean caramel and Bora Bora bronze, and beneath his hat his platinum hair complemented his trunks with what can only be called panache. As he drifted down the length of the sapphire swimming pool, various starlets splashed about pretending to play volleyball, desperate for his attention. I wet my lips with my tongue, smoothed out my sarong, took a long pull on my gin straw and stepped over to the side of the pool.

Puck gave me one of those out-of-the-corner-of-his-left-eye winks and dipped his hand into the water. Palming the pool softly, he glided over to where I stood.

Need a lift? Puck asked, motioning towards his inflatable raft.

I smiled and pointed my toes towards him, as though I were seriously considering walking onboard, but when the raft floated close enough I gave it a playful push with my foot.

Come on, Puck paddled back towards the deck, it's heated. Warmer than the air actually.

I dunked a big toe in. He was right, it was warm, but I shook my head, No. I mean I would, I said, but I'm not exactly dressed for it.

What are you talking about? Puck looked up at my beaded bikini, That's not what you'd call jeans and a sweater.

True, but this isn't a swimming kind of suit. I think it may have even come with a warning: "Dry clean only. Do not submerge in water of any kind."

You're making that up.

Check the tag, I said, bending down and fishing inside the top for the label. Right here, I thrust my chest at Puck, eyeing the pool girls with a back-off look.

It says, he struggled to read the faded vintage label, Emilio Pucci, he said, palming the cup of my breast, his cheek nearly in my cleavage.

Right. Italian for don't submerge in chlorine.

Puck laughed and tipped his drink appreciatively in my direction.

I lifted my glass back at him before sucking out the last of my gin and sat down on the expertly distressed driftwood deck. Besides, I said, water and I aren't exactly mixing these days.

Oh Sugar, Puck said, just be glad you have options.

What? I asked as I rested my feet on the first step and rearranged my sarong so that it wouldn't get wet.

Don't play dumb with me, Puck said, lowering his voice to a confidential whisper. You may have the rest of the Southland fooled with your designer water and celluloid veneer, he shot me a sexy little wink, but every once in a while your Valley surfaces.

My valley? Is that the new euphemism now?

No, it is not the new euphemism, Puck said as he deflected an intentionally spiked volleyball off his back. I'm talking about your roots.

Oh, you mean my *San Joaquin* Valley? I said in a mock whisper as I fished an ice cube out of my glass.

That's the one, Puck said. He effortlessly set the ball back in the direction of a big-boobied blonde before turning back to me and leaning in so his mouth was almost touching my ear. You and I both know you only had one summer suit growing up. One swimsuit to last the whole season, and when it wore out you just went in the buff.

Right you are, I said, thinking about the neon stripped bikini that my mother had to literally steal in the middle of the night from the shower neck—where I had hung it wet and dripping—because, even though the bottom was worn indecently thin and little bits of elastic were poking through the cheap fabric ties around the neck, I refused to give it up.

Puck was from Oklahoma, but he may as well have grown up in Lodi. He knew about Slip 'n Slides and how to turn a multiperforated irrigation hose like a jump rope to maximize the spray. Granted, he had never tanned topless on top of the Stroud barn; but he was a guy, after all, and he probably knew someone who had. Someone other than the manufactured starlets he hung out with today.

Unlike Puck I didn't mind being from a dusty place that sold Hydraulic Harvesters instead of Maseratis. In fact, I missed it in a way that made my teeth ache. But like him I slid on pair after pair of designer sunglasses and hid my origins well. Not because I was afraid someone would call me out, but rather because I was afraid they'd ask me in. Ask me in for a drink, chased with some questions: The weather? The people? My family? My brother? And then how would I begin?

SOCIAL DRAMA

WHY DO you lead them on? I asked, squinting my eyes to better make out the faces of the twins who were now vying for Puck's attention in a series of what appeared to be synchronized and choreographed dives off the deck.

Why do you lead me on? Puck asked, grabbing my left foot and gently beginning to massage.

Me? I asked, imitating coy as I held my right foot above the water and wiggled my toes.

Pu-uck, one of his groupies interrupted, Taffy just quit and the sides are all lopsided. Play a match? As she spoke she successively untied and then retied the bow between the breasts of her bikini.

I'm going to float this one out, Puck said, giving me another one of his famous long-lashed, left-eyed winks, but maybe next time.

Bummer! She pouted. I guess I'll have to join you then so the teams will be fair. She ducked under the net and bounced her way over to the deck near Puck and me.

I smiled a thin-lipped pout and pushed the ice around my glass with my finger. So much for the Slip 'n Slide.

Hi-iyee, Bikini Bow splashed her way into our conversation, I'm Nikole, but my friends call me Nikki.

Puck started humming the Prince song and I started to grin, despite my firm resolve to be fierce and moody in mixed company.

Nikki extended a dripping hand in my direction and I took it.

I'm Mag—, I started to say, but then Nikki burst into an ohmigosh.

Ohmigosh! she giggled, I know you. You're the girl from that shipwreck ad. The one that Puck saves. I almost didn't recognize you. In the ad, well, you're not so pretty. I mean. As you are now. She giggled, I mean you know what I mean.

Puck laughed loudly and steered his raft in between Nikki and me.

Nikki, this is Magdalena, and I think you may be confused.

No, I interrupted Puck. That's me. The girl in the ad. Totally me.

And I wanted to explain. Wanted to say something witty about cameras, artistic expression and extraordinary accidents, but I didn't know how to make the words come out right, which was just as well because before I could say anything more Lynda Carter herself, with a wonderful running start, jumped Justice League–style into the deep end. The volley girls let out wild squeals of mock-horror as water splashed in all directions and Puck accidentally slipped off his raft and under the surface. I watched him swim silently, illuminated by recessed pool lights, beneath the blue-green glow of the glistening water, and for a moment I remembered Junah. I remembered a doughboy in the Central Valley. I remembered that I needed another drink.

DIALOGUE

JAMESON UP, Surferboy said as he saw my approach and started to pour me a glass.

Make it two, I said. He raised his eyebrows and started to pour me a double, but I cut him off with my hand.

Not double, two. One for you.

Against the rules, he said as he poured himself a shot.

Well then here's to rules, I said as I raised my glass.

Rules, he said, and our glasses touched with a clink.

I swallowed all mine in one slug and giggled when it took him nearly three sips to polish off his.

Not much experience with the whiskey, he apologized.

You'll learn, I said. How old are you anyhow? Seventeen? *How old are you?* Christ. What was I thinking? First the lame *Cocktail* reference and now this. Next thing you know the theme song from *The Graduate* will cue up. Never mind, I said, before he could answer. I don't really want to know.

I'm nineteen, he said. But my ID says I'm twenty-nine.

Of course, I said.

How old are you? Or aren't I supposed to ask?

I'm twenty-nine, I said. Can you get me a Tanqueray Ten and tonic? And while you're at it, can you tell me how I can get an ID that says I'm nineteen?

Now I can understand why a guy like me'd want a fake ID, but why would you need one? Twenty-nine's cool. I mean it's not like it's thirty, right?

He winked.

I shrugged.

95

If you're hot, he said, who cares?

Thanks, I said, but the hot part is new for me. So sometimes I forget.

No way, he said as he slid my gin across the counter. Tall glass with a straw, like a Sprite.

Way, I said, raising my expertly waxed brows and looking over my augmented breasts to my tan and tucked tummy. A year and a half ago, when I didn't yet live in L.A.—I paused to take a sip from my straw and lowered my voice to what I imagined was a throaty, sexy, whisper—I was a size six.

Surferboy chuckled and slapped a hand on the bar in mock-horror.

Oh, but it gets better, I said, leaning in confidentially so the knot of my sarong rubbed against the faux hula grass of the bar. I had bangs. Perfect blond bangs that hung across my forehead like a platinum shelf.

And they let you out of the house? Surferboy grabbed a wet rag and swiped it across the counter top, stopping just short of the place where my belly brushed the bar.

In northern California they did, but down here, I backed away from the bar and looked around at the assembled party, well let's just say, who would have guessed that I'd turn in my wranglers and upgrade my cowboys for some stiletto, snakeskin, zip-up knee-highs that couldn't ever function on any real ranch but are still, by some strange familial association, called boots?

Not me, Surferboy said, shaking his head as he worked the rag over a sticky maraschino cherry stain.

Exactly, I said, sucking on my straw. No one, most especially not me, would have thought that, after the awkward butterfly barrette stage, my bangs pinned out of my face in that silly "grow-out" style, some Pilates and an exclusive diet of gin and peanut M&Ms, I'd be hot. Or better said, I paused and took another sip for dramatic emphasis, who knew Junah would exit my life and I'd ever want to leave the ranch?

I don't know much about ranches, and I don't know any Junahs, Surferboy said as he threw the rag on a lime crate in the corner and smiled at me. But good thing for L.A., right?

I poked my straw at the ice in my glass and then, holding the straw out like a baton, said, What?

L.A., he smiled another of his heartbreak grins, it looks good on you.

Right, I said. I held out my now empty glass and nodded in the direction of the gin.

He poured dutifully, smiling all the while.

Thanks, I said. Wishing again that I had some cash so I could give the kid a tip.

Don't mention it, he said, and he leaned in close across the teak counter. If you really want I can get you the name of this guy who can get you an ID. I mean it'll cost you, but he does good work. The best I've seen. Hologram and everything. The only trouble is you've got to find a place that will snap your photo DMV–style with a blue background. See, that's where most people mess up. They go to some photo booth or passport place, but all those places got white backgrounds. It's a red flag to the cops and stuff. See, he said, pulling out his wallet from the back pocket of his jeans and flipping it open so I could see his license from behind the plastic pane.

Henderson Augustine Jones, I read off the top line. That something the ID people made up?

Nope, it's real. But people call me Gus.

Thanks for the drink, Gus.

No worries, he said, and if you need the hook up. He winked.

If only it were that easy. Find a blue background, snap a photo and flash, back to nineteen, before L.A., and Junah is still around.

I took my drink and walked towards the giving garden.

CAST DESIGN

S TANDING IN the giving garden—where for $500, $5000 or $15,000 you could purchase a pipe-cleaner butterfly with paper wings and attach it to your Louis Vuitton or to the stem of your champagne glass so that everyone knew, color-coded of course, how much you gave—the long-term girlfriend clique pretended to eat shrimp from pointed plastic skewers. They were dangerous, but fun, so I picked up a skewer and said hello.

Mag-da-lane-ah! exclaimed Adair Adams, a hand model and an aspiring actress, standing on her tippy-toes (while I slouched) so she could giving me a kiss-kiss on both cheeks. Hilarious party, no?

I smiled and nodded as I picked carefully at a jumbo shrimp, Hysterical.

Adair and the girlfriends were talking about other women's husbands, their third favorite topic after reality TV and sunless tanners.

I mean really, there should be a name for them, Cheri said as I skirted the circle, sticking close to Adair and picking on a jumbo shrimp. Cheri had been married (officially) twice and unofficially (whatever that means) three more times. Currently she was on-again-off-again with Jae Flemming, our CFO, and rumor had it she'd dated both Dennis Rodman and JFK Jr., but not at the same time.

A name for who? Treena asked, momentarily shifting her iPhone away from her ear. Treena was a Breck girl, or at least she had been in 1978. It was her biggest thing ever and, although she still had terrific hair and looked thirty-two when she was probably pushing fifty, you could tell she hadn't gotten over it.

Hot old guys, interjected Mia, a board certified pet therapist and Treena's best friend. Aren't you paying attention?

Oh, right, Treena said as her phone began singing the first three bars of "California Girls," the David Lee Roth version. Hey, she said looking at the screen, it's Gigi!

Hi Gigi! All the girls shouted into the receiver as Treena held it up and wiggled it their general direction. We're trying to come up with a name for hot old guys, she said into the phone.

How about Sean Connery hot? Geneva asked. Geneva was hard to figure out. She claimed to own her own boutique, though no one had ever been there and she never actually seemed to do anything for or about it. Like the other girlfriends she was pretty, but not in an L.A. way. No, Geneva was exotic in a couture kind of way that only works in France or on men who speak French.

Overused, Treena cut her off, before Geneva could even start.

True, Adair agreed, sucking air through the "signature" Lauren Hutton gap between her two front teeth, but that's the kind of old hot I'm talking about. I'm talking, she put her hand up to her forehead to shield her eyes as she scanned the shore, *that* hot. For a second I thought she was pointing to Ricky, and I could feel a blush beginning to red beneath my cheeks, but I soon realized that she was talking about Dean, the hot old guy to Ricky's left.

Dean had been a Diamond Myst investor, turned advisor, from the start. He even relocated his family from Marin to Bel Air to be closer to "the splash" as he called it. But unlike me, his wife Lorin took to the Southcoast like, well, a garibaldi to the Pacific. Ricky insisted that, with a little effort on my part, Lorin and I could be fast friends. So I tried a few times to join her for lunch, just as I had tried on occasion to breach the Malibu mom clique, but due to the fact that I was so painfully childless the meetings were always awkward and strained and usually ended with Lorin having to run home to break up a dispute between the nanny and the assistant nanny.

Although I had never considered him in that way before, her husband Dean no doubt *was* hot.

Specifically, as Mia pointed out, he was bald hot.

Not going bald or naturally bald, Cheri agreed, but bald because he can be.

Bald because he's tan and cut and at least fifty-three, Geneva added.

Bald because it's less effort and when he jogs on the beach his hair won't matte in sweaty clumps to his forehead, Adair said and the girls all giggled and lifted their glasses. Cheers to that.

Bald because he knows it looks good on him, I said, breaking my silence and stepping into the circle, lifting my glass too. But instead of another round of cheers I got some awkward throat clearing from the other girls and a tight-lipped smirk from Adair in response.

Dean was bald and dressed in Hugo Boss (I'm guessing, but really, could it be anything else?) and wearing one of those really wide, really expensive British ties, in tangerine. Hugo Boss, at a beach party, when all the other men were dressed in polos and board shorts, that was how hot Dean was.

And as I checked him out—now silent—with the rest of the girls, I realized he was the kind of hot I always imagined Ricky would grow into one day: brave, strong and well-groomed hot.

Unfortunately, I also learned, he was the unfaithful kind of hot.

THE PRINCIPLE OF ANTAGONISM

W HAT? I nearly swallowed an ice cube whole when Adair
inferred as much.

You mean you didn't know? she said, clearly enjoying my
surprise while simultaneously giving me a look, not quite full-
scale sass but definitely a warning about the confidential nature
of the dirt she was about to dish, letting me know I was in only
as long as I could keep my mouth shut. Which, without a doubt,
I could—at least closed tight enough for it not to get back to her.
And so she continued.

Oh my God! Cheri exclaimed, winking at Adair before she
continued. I thought everybody knew. It was classic!

Gigi, Treena said into the phone, you have to text me the
link so I can show Magdalena. There was a pause while Treena
turned away slightly and then whispered into the phone, You
know Magdalena, the blonde who's married to Ricky. Then Treena laughed.

The link? I asked, trying to ignore the laugh. Trying to ignore the fact that Gigi clearly knew who Ricky was even though
she apparently hadn't heard of me. You mean it's on the web?

Well not the act itself, Cheri clarified, I mean he may be hot,
but he's no Rick Salomon.

Ditto that, Geneva said as she raised her glass, clink-clink.

He was on *The Hills*, Mia said. Season three.

Or rather he was in the wrong place, with the wrong woman,
drunk off his ass while they were filming *The Hills*, Adair said,
regaining control of the conversation.

Here look, Treena said, shoving her iPhone into my face and

taping twice on the YouTube icon.

And with the light of a nearby Tiki torch, with fireworks shooting off a barge and booming above, I watched Heidi and Spencer accost Lauren. I suppose I could pretend I was above watching reality shows on MTV. Hell, in Northern California I may well have been, but in Los Angeles I was outwardly appalled while secretly obsessed like everyone else. So while Spencer puffed himself up in the foreground, in the background two tables to the left of his shoulder, according to Treena's pointing finger, a hot old bald guy, who could have been anyone really, held hands and then kissed his much younger date across the table.

Are you sure it's him, I asked, doubtful.

Are you kidding me, Mia said, taking the phone and maneuvering a reverse-pinch finger zoom-in before hitting pause. It's totally him. Just look at the shape of his head.

I looked but still wasn't sure.

It's way clearer on a plasma, Geneva said. Cheri has it TiVoed if you don't believe me. I must have seen it a hundred times.

Yeah, me too, Mia said. You'd think it'd get old, but somehow it never does.

No, I believe you, I said, even if I didn't. Or maybe I sincerely hoped I didn't. True, I didn't care much for Lorin, but I didn't wish home-wreckage on her either. And besides, Dean was, since we're awash in original clichés anyhow, like a father to Ricky. He was definitely more than a mentor, hell, he gave us our first million when no one else would return our calls. Dean was a family man. One of the good guys. What the hell was he doing giving drunken tongue to a woman other than his wife on reality television? And more to the point, why hadn't anyone, Ricky especially, told me?

I hear his wife TiVoed it too, Adair said. And then played it for him when he came back from Fiji.

Fiji? I knew about that trip. It happened not long after I slipped off the boat. I wasn't feeling up to the flight so Dean went with Ricky in my place.

Yeah, she was totally cool about it, Cheri said. Just sat down on the couch and pressed play. She didn't call him out on it or anything. Just let him watch and then, when it was done, demanded a Bentley.

Convertible, Geneva confirmed.

And an offshore account in her maiden name, Mia added.

But why would she stay with him? I wondered aloud.

Oh, Magdalena, Adair said, putting her hand on my arm, why would she not?

I wanted to pull away. To go someplace where life made more sense. But I was secretly wondering just what exactly went on in Fiji, wondering if the reason Ricky didn't tell me about Dean's indiscretion was because, not wanting to raise suspicions on his part, he intentionally kept me out of the loop. So I stayed put, fiddling with cold shrimp on a plastic stick.

Fuck him. I say good for her, Treena said.

Sounds like she got lucky if you ask me, Mia said.

I only wish I was so lucky, Geneva said, brushing what appeared to be invisible sand off her forearm.

Still, agreed Cheri, giving me a knowing look, you've got to do it.

Got to do what? I asked, wondering if in fact I wasn't standing next to Ricky's other woman right now.

There was another awkward moment as the girls all exchanged glances. But then Adair clicked her silk nails against the rim of her now-empty glass and looked me dead in the eye and said, Your homework, sweetie. And I'm not just talking about opening his mail, tracking the AmEx or popping in unexpectedly for lunch.

If only it were that easy, Cheri sighed.

What do you mean? I said, biting onto my straw and sipping hard on my drink.

Oh honey, Adair said, wrapping her arm around my shoulder so close I could smell her Shiseido sunscreen, you have to look at the outtakes.

No really, said Geneva, Hulu, YouTube, MTV.com, there's bonus behind the scene footage everywhere. That's like the secret to everything.

I mean thank God for Google, Mia said, raising her glass.

Yeah, and fake Match.com logons, Treena added.

Speaking of a perfect match, Adair said. Where is the waterman tonight?

Chatting up a potential investor. I'm not sure, I said.

I'd check up on that too, Adair said, giving a look to the other girls. He's kind of a catch.

I wouldn't know. We met before all this.

All what? Geneva asked.

All this, I said opening my arms to the party, the beach, the fireworks, the really awful looking impressionist ice sculpture of Brazilian titi monkey riding the hump of a baleen whale.

INCONSISTENT REALITIES

I WAS shifting back and forth on my toes, trying to squeeze my calves into tight lines of muscle and concentrating on the cut line, trying to figure out how to tell Treena, and all the girls for that matter, that Ricky and I had been real. That before all—squeeze—this we were smart and silly and awkward and better. But because I was a little off balance, and because I was annoyed all to hell and secretly hoping I would give myself a charley horse so that I could go sit in the Mercedes and contemplate Ricky's fidelity, I just said, We were different then. You know, like the kind of couple who meets under the couch?

I don't think Treena heard me at first because she nodded and ah-hummed in that way people do when they're not really listening but waiting to speak. Hum, she said and was about to begin on something else when Adair cleared her throat and said, Did you say under the couch?

Yes, a tan rattan, I said.

Adair and Cheri exchanged glances and Geneva, signaling to the waiter that we could all use another round, said, How exactly do you meet under the couch anyway?

I thought about brushing it off, changing the subject to sunspot removal or Restylane, but it appeared that they were genuinely interested. And so, wanting to be funny, wanting to raise my glass—clink-clink—I fashioned myself a single girl and, as the waiter poured, I began.

You see, I was at a friend's house and Ricky was there with his girlfriend, I said, feeling out the girls' collective reaction. A former pageant princess, I continued, with a crooked nose. I forget her name.

Treena giggled, giving me the guts to go on.

Well anyhow, I raised my voice ever so slightly, Ricky was kind of hanging by the wall with Miss Teen USA, but I could tell he had no interest in her. That he really had eyes for me. So I pretended to lose my contact lens and I was feeling around under the couch when Ricky bent down to help me. There, under the rattan, we held hands, and the rest is us. I swooped my arms out in an exaggerated shrug for emphasis, but even without the gesture I could tell that the story was working. What I could not tell and what nobody had told me was that, at about this same time, Ricky and a few of the guys had come up behind me and were listening with interest to the story I was spinning.

Oh that's just precious, Cheri said. Ricky never told me that story. But tell us, did you find the contact?

Before I could answer Ricky put his hand on my shoulder and said, No.

No, I agreed, hoping Ricky would, for once in his life, go along with it. Indulge my need to have something to say. But he kept going. He said, Magdalena doesn't even wear contact lenses. She has 20/20 vision.

I could have tried a giggle. Grabbed him by the arm and said with sugar, Isn't it hilarious! There we both were searching for a contact that didn't exist and finding true love! But instead I said, He's right. I don't. And took a gulp of my gin.

As I stood, trying to decide what I could say hurt so I could escape, Treena picked up her iPhone (no doubt to tell Gigi) while Adair, Geneva and even Cheri all turned towards the shrimp stand, giggling in whispers, to grab another skewer. There was always the headache or, if I was really going to go there, menstrual cramps, but saying cramps out loud and in public was so junior high. I needed a way out of Lynda Carter's party, not a way out of P.E.

There were giant Tiki torches made of citronella, and one of Surferboy's friends was holding up small children bearing long stick matches so the kids could light them. With a bit of strategic placement I could probably manage to catch my hair on fire, but even for me it was kind of drastic. So instead I said, My ear hurts.

Ricky laughed and looked back towards what was now his audience, but I could tell that he was pissed. Gross exaggeration was something I was supposedly "working out" with the Shrink. Instead of working on it, I had worked him up. Well honey, he said, reaching his hand towards my derrière and patting me on the ass, I'm sure if you put another diamond on it, it'll feel better.

Everyone laughed, Adair the loudest, and Ricky smirked at me.

I forced my lips into a smile. A fake smile that I gave to Ricky alone and said, You know, you're right. I think I have a rock in the car. I'll go check. And, one hand on my ear and the other tightly holding my gin, I left.

THE PROBLEM OF MELODRAMA

WITH THE exception of a half-dozen cases of Diamond Myst labels, the Mercedes had no gems. Even still, I pressed my remote keychain and opened the passenger-side door as though I might find a carat or twelve. Then I took out the pear-cut studs from my ears and threw them inside, secretly hoping that one of them would land in the driver's seat and end up sticking Ricky in the ass, fully knowing that, if I didn't fish them out eventually, they would be stolen by the carwash attendants or a valet, whoever found them first.

Fuck, I said and slammed the door, hoping that the noise would calm me, but it only kind of sucked shut, the rubber insulation vacuuming tight against itself.

Fuck, I said again, this time tossing my keys—Prada coin purse and all—as far as I could towards the beach. They hit something, probably the Spanish mosaic that separated the plumeria from the palm trees; and their jingled crash was quickly replaced by the honking siren of the car alarm, masking the sound of surf hitting sand and blocking out the ska tones of the one-man steel-drum band entirely. It was perfect. Soothing even. And if I'd had my keys I would have unlocked the door and sat inside with the windows down, lulled by the shrieking wail surrounding me on all sides. But the keys were stranded somewhere on the lean shoulder of Pacific Coast Highway, and to go after them would be tantamount to disabling the alarm. So I did the next best thing. I boosted myself up onto the hood (by way of the front bumper) and shimmied across the glistening metallic paint until my back was smack against the windshield and I was sitting on my car as though it were an oversized deck chair.

Although you'd never know it from the ground, with the car as a boost the view was stunning—I dare anyone to tell me otherwise—the sky, the moonlit beach, the twenty or so business-types who didn't trust the valet and so were fishing in their pockets and designer purses for car keys, cursing politely at their spouses and kids and angling black and green plastic remotes at various vehicles in the lot. Click-click and the honk of a Porsche joined in for the chorus; click-click, the lights of a Lexus LX470 began blinking in syncopation. Click-click. The neighborhood dogs bayed. Click-click. Someone from a beachfront villa opened a high window and peered out. Click-click. They went on and off. Off and on. Each owner checking his car against the disturbance, no one able to shut up the noise.

Magdalena, Puck shouted, breaking up my revelry, will you do the honors or should I?

On his outstretched finger hung the loop of my keys. As he walked towards me from the pedestrian path, he jangled them back and forth as a taunt.

I sighed and leaned back against the glass.

May I? Puck asked angling the remote at the side of my car. Please.

He pressed down twice on the red panic button with his thumb and the screeching stopped. He pressed down once on the green button and the dome lamp lit and the doors unlocked.

He opened the passenger's door and held it ajar in mock chivalry.

Drive you home? he asked in the general direction of the hood.

I didn't respond. Instead, I stayed as still as possible, trying to blend in with the windshield wipers.

I seeee you, he said, standing on tiptoe on the running board, looking down at me reclining against the silvery roof.

I turned my head to the left, away from him, and continued not to talk.

You know you're probably skinny enough to blend in with the fixtures, but that cotton-candy sarong is a dead giveaway, honey.

He almost had me. My cheeks were pushing into a grin and I was itching to speak. But I didn't. I held firm, hands wrapped around the side mirrors.

Okay then, he said, jiggling a bit of ice in the bottom of the glass I had left on the ground, I guess I'll just go back to the beach. If you want your drink back, you know where to find me. He stepped off the running board and turned in the direction of the party, my keys tucked into the linen waistband of his pants, his hand choking my gin.

Puck? I said, turning ever so slightly to the right and adjusting my Chanel sunglasses in the dark.

Yep?

Did Ricky send you?

He stopped and fiddled his shoe in the sand, Not exactly?

Big. Fat. Liar. I said, making my hand into a fist and tossing air in his direction.

Puck ducked, spilling what was left of my drink and clutching my keys to his chest.

You, he pointed a thin finger, have lousy aim. And besides, Ricky didn't send me to fetch you. He sent me for the keys.

Of course he did. I pushed my bare heels into the hood: the quickest way to turn off the noise.

Mags, don't get me tied up in the ponytail of your drama. If you wouldn't throw fits, hell if you wouldn't throw things, he held up the keys and jangled them again, then he wouldn't have to send anyone.

I know, I whispered, my arms shrugged.

I'm sorry, Puck said. It's none of my business.

I'm trying, okay? I am trying.

I know you are. Here, hold this, Puck said, passing up my glass and a little green flask he pulled out of his pocket.

I reached across and took both, setting them with me in the center of the hood.

Puck slid off his suede espadrilles and made the barefoot climb up the front of the Benz. But then, as though to prove how irrational my fear of heights was, he pressed his body first against me and then against the windshield where he shimmed up the glass until he was standing squarely in between the ski racks on the roof of my SUV. I bit my lip and chanted a small mantra, willing him not to fall, willing the roof not to cave in.

Calm down, he said as he squatted first to his knees and then lowered himself onto his stomach so his face hung over the top of the roof and the spiky gelled tips of his blond hair touched the top of my head.

IT WAS a big car by any means—hell, according to the Green Party it was a terrorist tank suitable for the wilds of Africa—but it was still a bit small for a picnic, especially the top where Puck lay while we passed his flask back and forth.

You know, he said, reaching his hand down to hold mine, my mother claims that the rules of every relationship are established within the first five days of knowing a person.

Didn't Dr. Phil say that?

If he did he stole it from my mother.

I brought the flask to my lips and took a sip. I shook my head and said, I suppose you're right, before passing the booze back to Puck.

Puck pulled on the flask and let it unstick from his upper lip with a pop. But the point is, he paused, looking up at the stars half-disguised by the glare of a nearby street lamp, people don't change so put up or get out.

But see, that's just the thing, I said. I never tried to change Ricky. He changed without me and now I hardly recognize him.

Poor you, said Puck, his lashes flittering like a debutante.

Excuse me?

I'm just saying, and don't go throwing things again, he said, eyeing the glass that was now filled with melted ice and a half-eaten lime impaled by a straw, that if everyone's changing maybe you should change too?

I didn't say everyone. I said Ricky.

Fine. Ricky. Ricky's changing. You change too.

I looked down at my overflowing breasts, Don't you think I've changed enough? What? Should I cut my hair too? I pulled it out in front of me and wrapped it around my neck like a rope. Maybe a dye job? Or maybe, I said, I should think about collagen? That way when I pout Ricky'll be sure to notice. I puckered my lips and made smacking noises at Puck.

Stop, Puck said as he grabbed my cheeks between his thumb and finger like a potty-mouthed child. Just stop. Stop screaming. Stop it. Leave if you have to, but knock it all off.

I tried to interject, but Puck held firm to my face and shook his head, No.

Magdalena, I'm only going to say this once and then you're on your own, so listen up: I'm done making swan dives.

He let go and I rubbed at my cheeks with fingers before saying, You didn't swan.

I didn't?

No. You jumped. Feet first with your arms out so you wouldn't get your hair wet, not that I didn't appreciate it.

That's not how I remember it, but you get the point.

Learn to float.

Float, swim, dry off, fish, I don't care so long as you keep the water in the bottles and off my back.

Puck was right. And even with him I was fighting because I was used to it, not because it made any difference. So I changed the subject.

I think Ricky's having an affair, I said, taking a long drink of my gin. Again.

Puck thinned his lips and looked up towards the sky. Technically Ricky never had an affair. He took some time off when you were in hysterics over Junah and wouldn't come out from beneath the bed, but to my knowledge you're the only girl he's slept with in the last, I don't know, decade, he said. And besides, I thought you two were over all that suspicious blamey behavior.

La, la, la, I said, while Puck was still speaking. If we're so effing over it, then why's he doing it, again? And why, answer me this, did he not tell me about Dean's reality outing?

Sweetheart, Puck said, directing a wisp of hair out of my eyes and pushing it back behind my ear, there is no again. You were camped out crying under the bed for three weeks and Ricky needed a break so he stopped trying to coax you out five times a day. But he wasn't in bed with someone else. In fact, if I remember correctly he was in the office.

If you remember? You weren't even there!

No, but you told me all about it, six maybe sixty times.

Whatever. So maybe he didn't screw around then, but he is now. I can feel her.

Puck continued to play with my hair and, as he traced a finger across my temple where the soft baby hairs grew, he asked, So what does *she* feel like?

She feels like Adair Adams. What do you know about her?

Puck sighed, I know she has a condo in the same building as Tara Reid, she doesn't work days, she takes her coffee with three Equal and one Splenda, and oh! she gives a mean blow job. Is that what you want to hear?

I took a big sip, swished the alcohol around in my mouth and swallowed. Is she screwing my husband?

Not that I know of, but so what? So what if she is. If he is. Ignore him. Confront him. Take up with the goddamned cabana boy. But do something. Something besides throwing keys and fits.

Like what?

I don't know. Have dinner. Think about it. Move in with me. And speaking of which, I'm famished. Spectacular view, he nodded to the sky, but lousy spread. You coming?

He slid off the side of the Tank and held out his hands.

THREE LEVELS OF CONFLICT

WHEN PUCK and I returned to the party Ricky was seated at a table set with sea glass, surrounded by lobster and the newbies. The lobster was flown in, live, from Maine; the newbies, a group of investors who had an excess of fun money to blow on bottled water and female presidential hopefuls, were flown in from the East Coast, France and Fiji. Skirting them, trying to stand and manage a plate and a cocktail while still having a free hand to shake, were a dozen or so overdressed interns—Cal, Stanford, MIT. Ricky was seated dead center and was in the middle of what I like to call his *A&E Biography*. You know, his well-rehearsed life story in case anyone wants to film, record, document or otherwise preserve it for some future generation. The one that starts with, *On a day that was more hazy than it was hot, my father left Juarez with six little girls, a pregnant wife and a pocket full of cauliflower seeds.* Middles out around: *After working the fields from Washington state to San Diego, learning English from schoolchildren and earning the handle "Cauliflower King," my father saved enough to buy 600 acres near Riverside, his and her Cadillacs, a house with Spanish tile and two swimming pools, even though he couldn't swim.* And climaxes somewhere near, *And that's when I said, Papa, I only have two goals: to run a Fortune 500 company and to see my face on the left side of the Wall Street Journal, next to a line drawing of Janet Reno stating her intentions to split my company for anti-trust.* If you're lucky enough to be in his office when the story spills out, he'll lean back in his leather chair, kick his boots onto his desk, stretch his arms towards the panoramic view behind his head and nod towards the wall, where the front page of the *Journal* hangs framed behind anti-glare glass.

I've heard the story maybe a gazillion times. So often, in fact, that I've stopped trying to correct his exaggerations, stopped trying to remind him that his mother came from money, stopped trying to include my name in the water-industry plot. Hell, on good days I can almost remember the first time I heard it. And then I believe him myself.

IMAGINATION

TRUTH BE told, Ricky's father learned English off the portable radio and his children suffered the consequences: Rhonda, Donna, Sherry, Cheri, Venus, Barbara Ann and Ricky. Six Spanish-speaking baby girls and one American-born prince. The Mora de la Cruz girls, with the exception of Venus (who staged political protests and came out at sixteen), grew up in the shadows of Los Angeles and came into the city as one might expect: they married well, divorced, took half and then married again to second and third husbands always a little bit older and a little bit richer than their first. Other than Barbara Ann (who had three daughters with three different daddies), they remained childless, thin, beautiful and determined above everything to choose and maintain a certain lifestyle. To erase a certain past.

In the past the Mora de la Cruzes picked grapes, asparagus, peaches and—worst of all—strawberries from the time they set foot on California soil until the youngest among them turned twelve. They moved with the harvest, living in the dust and hay of the farm labor camps from Salem to Stockton, Bellingham to Riverside. Between the nine of them they were deported—individually and collectively—thirteen times under various suspicions and circumstances. Yet somehow, with assorted auspices and finagling, they always managed to make their way back to the states.

Juan Duran de la Cruz, a.k.a. The Cauliflower King, put on a bathing suit and—unable to swim—kicked a rubber tire a treacherous fifteen miles to shore. Rhonda waded through raw sewage in the Tijuana River. Sherry and Cheri jammed themselves into boxcars with hundreds of other norteños, unable to move, hardly able to breathe. Donna rode across the border spread-eagle on the top of a freight train, her blistered hands white with holding on. And Venus, a particularly bold and quick girl of fourteen, sprinted through the backed-up traffic at the port of entry, defying Border Patrol to chase her. Barbara Ann had to pay $550 American dollars to a coyote smuggler to take her to Fresno. She rode sewn inside the bench-seat upholstery of a Volkswagen Vanagon for 149 miles; and once she crossed *la frontera* she was held hostage for another $250 in ransom, which required her to work a full five months indentured and hungry, sleeping in the dirt with rotten lettuce for a pillow. But Ricky—the only true-to-flesh American born citizen of the de la Cruz clan—holds the best yarn by far.

Caught as an infant sucking on warm milk and stuffed inside the folds of his mother's dress, Ricky was deported with his mother, Angelina, without question of the papers that secured his legitimacy. On the wrong side of the Rio Bravo, Ricky was stuffed into a Styrofoam cooler and floated across the border like Moses while his mother trailed behind. Kicking against the current and steering little Ricky away from eddies, Angelina fished crawdads from Ricky's makeshift cradle and tucked him into the tulle at the first sign of danger.

MEMORY

T'S PRETTY, that story. Pretty enough to make you fall in love. And it'd be pretty too, to think the story ended there. To think that Mom, a little muddy but no worse for the wear, follows the river upstream until she's spit out with her child on some San Diego shore. Towing the Styrofoam box behind her, she trudges through the silt to safety, her fingers prunish and her knees purple and sore. She puts her baby in the grass, where he coos and giggles from a tickle of dandelion brushing across his tummy, while she wrings out her skirts in the sun. That's the way Ricky remembers it, so damn pretty. He remembers too that shortly thereafter Dad, an uncle of no relation and all six sisters came tumbling out of the hedges and trees; and before long they were in the big house in Riverside, splashing it up in the swimming pool, the river sludge long forgotten.

Of course, it didn't happen like that. Never does. But whose gonna tell Moses that his momma pushed the cradle upstream while she swam up a sewer, filling her mouth full of piss and shit and raw scum? Who's going to tell the baby that momma held her breath, the filth and refuse still inside and trickling down her lips, and faced the immigration police face-front? That she spat the festering contents of her mouth, in one solid stream, straight into the blue-green eyes of the border patrol, and then she ran, her baby still bobbing about unawares?

Nobody. That's who. Nobody's gonna tell the baby a god-damned thing. They're not going to linger on the lack of hedges in the desert. They're not going to mention the indescribable taste shit leaves in between your teeth and on the inside of your cheeks. They're going to let him float straight onto the chosen land, and they're only going to cringe a little when the baby grows up and announces his intent to marry a yellow-headed wife.

But Ricky only ever fell for tow-, hemp- and flaxen-colored locks. His Camelot depended on it. Or at least he told me as much, back when we were grad students, happy and snuggled on top of a warped futon atop a graying hardwood floor in Berkeley.

Do you think, he would ask, fluffing a wine-stained down pillow beneath his chin and cheek and rolling on his side to face me, that the world is ready for us?

Us, maybe, but Mayor de la Cruz, no, I'd say, looking into his large brown eyes and answering the question he'd really been asking. Ricky was getting his masters in history with an emphasis in political science, and he was prone to the utopian thinking of most kids at Cal.

We'll dominate. We'll get all the votes, he continued. It'll be a landslide.

Right, I replied, tugging on the tie-dyed curtain we had stapled above the window to keep out the glare of the neighbor's kitchen light. I was a double major in viticulture and business with a minor in art. In grad school I focused on natural resources and privatization. I knew enough to know there was no Rainbow Coalition. That the children of the world would not one day join hands in a barn-raising exclamation of peace and understanding. But I also wanted it. I blame Berkeley, but somewhere deep inside it secretly thrilled me that Ricky believed in positive, evolutionary social change. That he believed in God.

Of course, I couldn't tell him that, so instead I said, If you wanna run, tell me now and we can work on finding you a cute little poster wife. I can be your behind the scenes girl; everyone has one.

Ricky pulled the pillow from beneath his head and hit me in the face with it. I'm not running anywhere, he said. And you'll never be behind the scenes.

I meant for office. My voice was muffled beneath the pillow. Maybe Ricky didn't hear, or maybe he didn't want to hear, but he didn't say anything. He only threw his body on top of mine and hit me again and again with the pillow.

I countered by locking my left leg around his waist and jabbing three tickling fingers into his armpit. But even as we rolled around, off the thick mat and onto the floor, giggling, I knew he was partially serious and I was partially right: Ricky, with his Birkenstocks and grammatically correct University Spanish, wouldn't last long in politics. He was too sensitive for that. Too smart, too. There could be no election, no office, no public. It had to be a private affair, a simple transaction. Something obvious, but with wit. Something that came to me on the road to Zacatecas.

Now don't get me wrong, like most girls I'll take Cabo or Cancun over the pit that is Juarez any day. I mean, who wouldn't want to be stretched out on some oceanside resort towel, sipping a piña colada while some village girl combs your hair into a gazillion beaded braids? Hell, I'd even take Ensenada, with its photo-op burros, dusty oversized sombreros and roaming mariachi before I willingly signed up for a trip to Zacatecas, made by car no less. But it was an invitation. An initiation into the family sort of thing extended by the Cauliflower King himself. Juan Duran de la Cruz may have reached the American Dream, but he still maintained notions of Mexican longing, and so two times a year he packed his wife, his fleet of daughters, their respective ex, current and prospective spouses and his only son and drove south. When I was invited to join the entourage, I packed a few bags, stuffed all my hair into a floppy straw hat and sat next to Ricky in the back seat of the fifth of five silver Cadillacs.

Our small, metallic parade was conducted by Juan Duran in a just-off-the-sales-floor El Dorado and caboosed by a late-model Ford pick-up filled with supplies—namely, jugs of recycled milk cartons filled with Los Angeles tap water and crates of Thousand Island dressing—tightly secured with a tarp and driven by Venus.

We left on a Thursday, late in the afternoon, and I somehow managed to sleep through the border crossing; but before long the interstate ran out and I was jolted awake by pot holes and the cursing of Juan Duran, transmitted by CB, about the fucking rocky roads ruining the fucking suspension in his fucking fleet of cars. Each time his voice, heavy with driving and accents, swore across the static of the transmitter radio, Ricky would reach across the back seat and squeeze my hand.

I'm sorry, he mouthed, in the dark of night.

It's okay, I mouthed back, waiting for a northbound truck to illuminate the car so Ricky could read my lips.

I squeezed his knee.

He whispered, I love you.

Even still, it was a long fucking night.

FACT

SOMEWHERE NEAR breakfast Juan Duran signaled, and one by one the train of now-dusty cars pulled to the left and parked near a field. The field was full of crops, something low-cut and greenish, like parsley; and speckled throughout the harvest were farmers in old Dodger caps and white t-shirts, digging up produce and depositing dirty bunches into large wooden crates beneath umbrellas of bright orange and yellow and pink.

You mean the umbrellas aren't for the workers? I asked Ricky in a hushed voice.

What? Donna, who was riding shotgun, asked.

The umbrellas, I said, pointing, you mean they aren't…

Unbelievable, Donna said, before opening her door and directing a sharp glare at Ricky. I thought she grew up on a farm. I should have guessed this from you, she said, though it was unclear to whom she was speaking. Then she slammed the door and walked off barefoot towards the lead Caddy, mumbling under her breath.

I sat in the backseat with my hat in my lap, stunned and looking at Ricky. It was a vineyard, I said quietly, a small one. When we hired people it was just a few and they used the house.

Hey, don't worry about it, Donna's second husband, Christopher, said as he pushed the tip of his foot against the e-brake and took the keys out of the ignition. She's still bitter about the scars and the smell of cilantro brings it back. Then he opened his door and slipped out after Donna, carrying her heels in his left hand and her sunglasses in the other.

Ricky slipped an arm around my shoulder and rubbed the

back of my head with his palm. Don't worry. How could you have known?

You could have told me, I thought. Should I apologize?

Nah, she'll forget about it before lunch. Just next time, maybe save your questions for when we're alone. He opened his car door and let in a burst of golden light that had been previously muted by tinted windows.

Right, I said, pulling on my hat and pushing my sunglasses against my face.

Oh, come on, Magsie, Ricky said, ducking back into the car and planting a kiss on the top of my head. Don't let it get you down. He tugged on my arm and I let him slide me across the leather seat and out of the car.

Outside, doors and trunks began to click open and slam shut as the Mora de la Cruz family poured out of their air-conditioned cars and into the heat of the Mexican morning sun. Their polo shirts and pressed Levis contrasted loudly with the tattered, muted colors of the farm around them.

We walked en masse along a cracked dirt driveway and into a stucco barn-like structure that functioned as sort of multipurpose dining room/mess hall. The girls and their men spread out and took up occupancy around the various tables, fanning each other with poorly folded maps and sun hats while Ricky, who held tightly to my hand, was corralled by his father into the kitchen.

Three old ladies tied up in faded paisley aprons—their arms covered in cornmeal to the elbows—were pounding tortillas, while a small, gold, portable radio hummed Mexican folk songs from the windowsill. When they saw Ricky they exploded into Spanish pandemonium, exclaiming and folding Ricky and Juan Duran into a sweaty embrace and littering their faces and starched black shirts with kisses and corn-covered pats. Overwhelmed, I managed to wrestle my hand from Ricky's grasp and took a seat on a wooden crate in the corner. The old lady shrieks seemed to set off some sort of chain reaction and, before long, what appeared to be the entire town had gathered around, some of the children and a few older boys singing in broken English and particled Spanish, He's here. He's here. Yup the guy from California and his son. Happy.

Of course, the Spanish part I didn't understand. My mother had been trying to teach me a working vocabulary since before I could walk, and Ricky had managed to teach me a word or two, but for the most part I nodded a lot, held up my fingers and used gestures. It worked well, but there were a few flaws. For example, my hand held like a cup to my lips seemed to be the universal sign for water (agua, duh), but even with the word there was no gesture for water from the bottles in the back of the truck and not Mexican water from a rusty pipe. So rather than ask I'd just brave the heat, follow the dirt drive back to the car, fish around under the tarp of the truck, wrestle with a gallon sized jug and pour myself a hot glass of L.A. tap. And that's how it happened. How it hit me. How I knew that it would be water, in small plastic bottles, sold to America by a Mexican son. The irony was enough to make me choke, but I didn't. Instead I spit the water from my mouth in a single stream onto the cracked brown dirt below and twisted the cap back on the recycled gallon-carton.

OF COURSE, I could have said all this to the adoring crowd assembled around Ricky, but I didn't.

Unlike Ricky I didn't say a word. Didn't correct a single fact. Didn't rearrange anything at all. Instead, I stood with my back to the sea and looked around at Ricky's assembled beach-front audience. I eyed each of the interns in turn. I scanned tanned and tucked faces illuminated by the subtle orange glow of Tiki torches and tried to figure out which one. Which slut. Which common whore was screwing my husband right under my $22,000 nose?

CLASSICAL DESIGN

IN THE car on the way home, Ricky drove and I sat in the passenger's seat, fully reclined, and took deep, big sniffs of air through my nose. I tried to be as loud as possible, pushing air in and out of my nostrils, and it worked because before long Ricky broke the silence and said, Will you please stop that?

Stop what? I asked.

That, he said.

I'm just breathing, I told him. What, should I hold my breath?

That is not breathing, he said. This is breathing. He paused and made no noise as he took in several breaths of air. What you were doing, he snorted and snowed like a flat-faced dog, is not breathing. It's gross.

Gross? I asked, sitting up while my chair back remained in the recline position. Gross is being all buddy-buddy with a man who cheats on his wife, on national television, no less.

You heard, Ricky said, his eyes on the road.

No, I did better then hear. I saw.

Well I was hoping you wouldn't.

Why? So you could keep your little secret to yourself? Too late, I said, slipping my right arm out of the seatbelt so I could turn and face him, I already know.

Know what? Christ, Mags, what the hell are you talking about?

Her, I can smell her on you. Just tell me her name and we can have it out once and for all.

Whose name? You're not making sense.

Her! I said. The girl you're screwing. Don't worry, I don't even care anymore. Just admit it so I can get over it. And then we can do whatever it is people do once they've found out. I'm sure Lorin and Dean have a really great marriage counselor they can recommend.

He was quiet for a minute. Taking everything in and then, after clenching the wheel, he said, You really want to know?

Yes, I said, my hands tight around his armrest, I really want to know.

Okay, then I'll tell you, Ricky said.

Tell me then, I said, ready to throw myself at him and or rip the wheel out of his grasp.

Magdalena, he said.

What? I asked. Just tell me.

I did, he said. Her name's Magdalena. That's who I'm screwing. Or at least that's who I used to be screwing, but I haven't really gotten any in a while.

Liar, I said as I lunged for the wheel, but Ricky was too quick for me. He slammed on the brakes while simultaneously throwing his arm in front of my body. So paternal. The car screeched to a stop in the dead middle of Sunset, and cars honked and flashed their lights as they swerved around us.

Ricky, always the thinker, pulled up the e-brake and flipped on the hazards. This enough drama for you? he asked, as a driver lay on his horn and gave us the finger as he sped by, or should I make a U-turn and drive into oncoming traffic?

I didn't answer, instead I grabbed Ricky by the shoulders, pulled him towards me and slammed my face into his. I kissed him, hard, on the mouth and when he didn't respond I bit his lip and his cheek and his tongue. When I drew blood he bit me back and threw me down onto my reclined seat and pressed himself on top of me.

Fuck me, I said. If I'm the only one you're supposedly screwing, then prove it.

Ricky pulled at his belt and unzipped his pants. He pushed

my sarong aside and tried to push himself into me without removing my bikini bottoms. When that didn't work he pulled the crotch to one side and fucked me. And fucked me.

I kept biting while he fucked. I scratched my nails across his back and pushed my breasts into his face, desperate to feel something. Anything other than empty, hollow anger and tears. But the deeper I scratched, the more vacant I felt.

Outside, cars continued to lay on their horns and occasionally someone would shout an obscenity before screaming around us.

Fuck you too, Ricky said. I didn't know if he was talking to me or to the offending driver but I didn't much care. When he was through he pushed himself off me and drove the rest of the way home.

I MUST have fallen asleep on the way back, because when I woke I was still inside the car, which was now perfectly parked inside the garage. The dome light was on, sending a weak yellow shadow across my lap, and the keys were placed strategically on the driver's seat, the circular chrome ring centered around a blinking pear-cut diamond earring.

DURATION OF MOOD

HAD a kink in my neck, a swollen lip and no idea where Ricky was. I unbuckled myself from my seat and checked my reflection in the passenger's mirror. In addition to the lip, I had mascara rings beneath both eyes, a red scratch that ran from my just-like-Cindy-Crawford mole to what was left of my last-all-night panacea pink lip-gloss and tangled blond hair that fell in sad whispers across my shoulders and back. I wet my index fingers in my mouth and then rubbed them slowly under both lids, forcing the black smudges into subtler lines that almost looked intentional.

I took a quick sweep at my hair with my hand, snagged my diamond engagement ring—not the original pave promise ring Ricky gave me years ago in grad school, but my Tiffany four-carat upgrade—in my hair and managed to rip out a few strands of blond before deciding to hell with it.

Swollen lip and runny mascara, I could say that not since Junah had I been so low, but—and here's the funny thing—I felt all right. Not exactly spectacular or anything, but as close to good as all right gets. I slept well, for one thing, which had become more rare than I cared to admit these days, and for another thing I woke up without remembering.

I mean that's not to say that later, with cotton wrapped in between my toes and the subtle vibration of the spa chair working its way up and down my spine, things didn't start coming back to me. They did. And like usual I spent the remaining half hour of filing and buffing and base coats and polish trying to pretend it all away, but for the first time in over a year my waking thought wasn't Junah. It wasn't why Junah and how Junah and Junah in vivid Technicolor tragedy. Instead it was a seatbelt digging its slick edge into my clavicle, a dry mouth, the dull glare of the dome light still lit in the garage.

CRISIS MODE

STARTED the engine and put the car in reverse. I needed to talk to the Shrink. Not that I was scheduled, and not that she worked on Saturdays, but I knew she lived near a creek—a real body, well trickle rather, of flowing water in Los Angeles—at the top of Laurel Canyon. And as I pulled up her steep drive I watched her through the kitchen window as she made pancakes for her husband and a little blond boy dressed in orange robot pajamas. I was going to knock, or at the very least honk (it's not like I intended to hover in her driveway, peeping), but there was something so precious about the perfectly domestic breakfast scene that I couldn't bear to interrupt it. And try as I might, I also couldn't seem to stop staring, to reverse and cruise the canyon at least until she was dressed, so I sat entranced until the dog—a shaggy red Irish Setter—spotted me through the blinds and began to bark.

Jesuschrist, Magdalena, she said, walking out onto her front step clutching a coffee mug, her husband, still in boxers and a t-shirt, hovering protectively behind her. I live here. This is my house.

I know, I said, rolling down my car window, that's why I came. I needed to see you, and I thought you said you were Buddhist.

It's just an expression, she said, dismissing her husband with a pat on the arm and walking over to my car. But this, she motioned towards me with her mug, this is totally inappropriate. You've crossed the line here. You know that, right? After hours and you're supposed to call my answering service.

This can't wait till Friday, I said, biting on the arm of my sunglasses. And if I had wanted to talk to a machine I would have called my fucking husband. He never answers his cell, not if he sees it's me on the ID anyway. Besides, this is an emergency, I said, running a hand through my snarled hair, hoping I looked appropriately pathetic.

The service is more than equipped to handle emergencies, she said.

THE SHRINK'S answering service was a joke. It was a number that rang up a machine attached to a pager somewhere and whenever I had the urge to "go there" with Ricky I was supposed to dial it up and vent into the phone. Supposedly this was a good way to get things off my chest without actually inciting matrimonial riot, but even though I paid extra for the service I never actually used it. Don't get me wrong, I called it plenty and then hung up. Once I was almost tempted to speak, but I kept imagining her and her Wonderland Park friends sipping iced tea and laughing their asses off as they listened to one manic caller after the next.

But I didn't say any of this out loud. Instead I lied. I lost the number, I said.

Interesting, the Shrink said, still standing opposite my car in the drive. I find it very interesting that you're resourceful enough to figure out where I live—which need I remind you is commonly referred to as stalking and is probably directly in line with a restraining order—but I digress… and then she looked at me blankly. What was I saying again?

You were saying, I said, that you find it interesting that I can figure out where you live but I can't—

Right she said, taking a sip of her coffee, that you're resourceful enough to invade my privacy, but you're apparently unable to locate the emergency number, which by the way is on the voice mail of my office phone.

Zabasearch-dot-com, I said and smiled.

But I'm unlisted, she said, shifting her weight from one foot to the other.

Totally doesn't matter. They have almost everyone, I opened the car door. Do you want to sit down?

She eyed me suspiciously and took a step back.

Oh come on, I said, sliding across the center console to the passenger's seat, you can have the driver's seat. Here, I said as I turned off the engine and threw her my key ring, you can even hold the keys.

Only if you promise this will never happen again, she said, pocketing my keys and getting into the car.

Promise, I said, my fingers crossed. But even if they weren't it wouldn't matter. We both knew I paid her too much for her supposed services. Besides, I suspected she liked me.

Alright, she said, reclining her chair a little and turning to face me, What's this all about?

Ricky's cheating on me.

She tried to hide her exasperation, but it was pretty early in the morning and so I forgave her for letting out a small sigh. Are you sure?

No. Yes. I put my feet up on the dash and tried to explain. I tried to tell her about the party, about how lonely I felt, about how everyone seemed to be looking at me funny. About Adair and Geneva, *The Hills* and the signs.

What are you talking about, signs?

Oh you know, caller ID, unexpected changes in his behavior or dress, working too much, TiVo.

And does Ricky exhibit any of these so-called signs?

Well he did work 320 hours last month, but aside from the working, the truth is I don't know just yet. I mean I'm still looking for the rest. It takes a while to watch all the bonus and behind-the-scenes footage, but I'm sure they're somewhere.

And have you expressed your infidelity concerns to Ricky?

Why do you think I spent the night in the car? I asked her.

Why do you think I showed up here, at 7 AM, wearing the same bikini as yesterday, no less?

Well—, she looked at my wrinkled pareo.

He denied it, of course.

And is this consistent with his past extra—his past behavior, she corrected herself.

You were going to say extramarital.

Was I? she asked, looking up from her coffee mug. Is it?

You know, I don't exactly remember. The last time I thought Ricky had cheated on me I was a little preoccupied, what with Junah being dead and all.

The Shrink took a deep breath and looked out the car window to where her son and her husband were watching us in the kitchen. She waved. They waved back. Magdalena, she said, do you honestly, in your heart of hearts, believe that Ricky is really cheating on you? That he ever has?

What do you think? I asked.

I think you need to go home now. I think you need to take a hot shower and get some sleep. I think we'll talk about this in more detail on Friday.

But, I said, pointing to the dash, it's only been half a session, we still have 25 more minutes.

The Shrink raised her eyebrows as she opened the car door and stepped out, We'll talk more on Friday, she said, as she handed me the keys. And if you need to talk before then, call the service.

I didn't say anything. I just slid into the driver's seat, put the car in reverse and left.

INTERNAL CONFLICT

B ACK HOME I headed straight to the kitchen where I opened the fridge and pulled out a bottle of Evian. I'd been stocking our competition regularly for about two weeks now. To piss Ricky off. But of course he hadn't noticed.

I don't know how long I was standing in the kitchen, fridge door open no less, but it must have been a while because Immelda, our housekeeper, opened her bedroom door and whispered, Magses, you all right?

Yes, I whispered, I'm great. And then, Evian still in hand, I took the stairs two at a time to the master suite. Ricky was in bed, his Hanro cotton shirt perfectly matched to his Swiss Euro-style briefs. Before, that is to say yesterday, I probably would have dumped the bottle of Evian on his head, grabbed the down comforter and made my way into the library to sleep; but I kind of told Puck that I'd refrain from throwing anything anymore and, besides, things were changing. I could feel them. So I got into bed with my dirty bikini. Without washing my face I lay on top of the covers next to Ricky where, of course, I couldn't fall asleep.

So I flipped back and forth like a sixteen-year-old in a cheap tanning bed, hoping to wake Ricky without actually touching him, but no matter how much I wiggled and flopped Ricky's side of the bed stayed perfectly still—mattress technology—and Ricky himself slept soundly.

Fuck! I said into the soft goose down batting of my pillow, Do what? I mean really, what am I supposed to do? In this situation? With myself? In this life? Just shower it all away like a Calgon commercial?

As if.

I twisted and then untwisted myself in the sheets, tugging the top sheet away from Ricky's tucked arms, but even this failed to interrupt his regulated snore. So I gave up, got up and headed to my studio.

SET CONSTRUCTION

F OR THE first month after we bought the house my art studio was in one of the eight guest bedrooms that flanked the master suite; but after I fell off the boat, which caused me, quite literally, to drop out of the water set, I decided to take up full time with art.

The creative process of an artist-in-residence, I told Ricky, really necessitates an actual residence.

Mags, Ricky said, taking my hand and marching me upstairs, you have seven rooms of your own. I don't quite understand what you mean.

What I meant was, if I worked at home, if I set up shop in one, three, seven of the bedrooms inside the house, I would actually have to work because there might actually be the possibility of Ricky or Immelda or the guy who does the bills suddenly walking in on me and expecting to see art, work, product, something other than a bedraggled girl, still in her pajamas, drinking gin with a straw and playing with rhinestones. But I couldn't say as much to Ricky and so I blamed the light; it was completely inadequate.

A glass house, I said, would be adequate for my artistic endeavors. Or at the least some very large windows on the north and west sides, which—after some contracting, construction and a short step up a disappearing staircase—put me in a studio directly above the garage.

The floors were teak and the ceilings vaulted and wood-beamed. In the afternoons and early evenings the sun would streak in and warm the oversized chaise where I would usually lie, sipping gin and holding rhinestones up to the light, refracting their beams in a rainbow of prisms about the room.

I climbed the stairs and pushed open the fort-like door in the floor, which I will not pretend didn't remind me, every single time I touched it, of Junah and a certain tree house my daddy built in the big arms of an oak tree in the Central Valley. But I tried not to think of Junah or Ricky or anything associated with how things used to be, and instead I decided to focus on art.

METHOD ACTING

RIGHT NOW I'm working in rhinestones. Some people, serious artists and my husband for instance, might say that what I do is not art. And I might agree. What I know to be art does not involve twisting stringy strands of dried glue off the corners of rhinestones. But real art, the kind that I used to do in a sort of makeshift studio near the grain shaft of our barn and again on the tarred rooftop of our co-op in Berkeley, takes a certain level of introspection, self-actualization and reveal. Although the Shrink thinks that's exactly the kind of behavior I should be engaging in right now, I strongly disagree. The very last thing I need to do is go further into myself, and so, to keep my hands busy and to keep appearances up, I paste and stick artificial gems to simulated masterpieces.

Once a month I go to the library in Beverly Hills and check out books: Monet, Mondrian and Gauguin. Expensive, museum-quality books by Taschen. Then I take the books to Kinkos. I don't have to take the books to Kinkos. Ricky bought me a library full of museum-quality books, but going to the library and then to Kinkos gives me something to do (aside from imagining Junah's still alive). So I go to Kinkos on Wilshire and I color Xerox a dozen or so prints (which is, according to copyright, blatantly illegal, but I always smile and tell the Kinko's guy that I teach kindergarten). Then I take them to my house on Bedford, shut the blinds to the staggering view and glue rhinestones all over the fucking place. I sold one for twenty-five (thousand) to this movie guy in Bel Air. Don't tell Ricky I said it, but only in Los Angeles, am I right?

And the best part? It wasn't even my best piece. I mean it was so college-radio-station-I-just-fell-in-love-with-the-Velvet-Underground-and-must-play-them-all-the-time. It was Nico for christssake. You know an imitation of the blue-green, red-purple-orangeish blocks that Warhol did? Like Marilyn and Chairman Mao. Only different. I sold him the red goddess square. I had junkie, icon and rock star too, but he only wanted the yellow-haired girl. Said it looked most like me.

What, are you high? I asked him. I don't have bangs.

Makes no difference, he said holding up the sparkle-incrusted print alongside my face. It's you all the same.

Whatever, I said and showed him the door, a personal check for twenty-five grand sticking out of the pocket of my Paper skirt.

THEATRICAL TRUTH

I WAS working, or at least pretending to work, on a Gauguin when Ricky walked in and kissed me on the cheek.

Hey babydoll, he said, gettin' up and getting' right to it. That's what I like to see.

Umm, I said, feigning an intense interest in a Xeroxed copy of a man with an axe standing next to a native woman in a rose-colored stream. This is how it was with us: At night we would fight, throwing out every mean word we knew until our throats were hoarse, our adrenaline worn and our hearts totally and completely knotted. And in the morning we woke up and Ricky pretended and I pretended that everything was okay. That nothing in the world was wrong. That is, until, I noticed Ricky was not dressed in his semi-usual Saturday shorts and Cal tee, but was instead sporting slacks and a Hermes tie.

I thought, I said, turning towards Ricky, suddenly disengaged with art, that we were lying low today. Renting a movie. Ordering take-out.

Yeah, so did I, Ricky said, checking his reflection in one of the floor-to-ceiling widows that flanked my studio, but when I woke up I noticed you were working and so I thought, Hey, she's on a roll. Why not catch up on a few things in the office?

But I was just finishing up, I said, hastily scooping rhinestones into Ziploc baggies and pulling the plug on my glue gun.

Looks to me, Ricky said, pointing to the Gauguin, that you have a long way to go.

No really, I said, I was just thinking about throwing in the towel. Taking a shower and then heading to Kings Road for a latte and some eggs Benedict. Want to join me?

Since when do you eat eggs Benedict? Ricky asked, straightening his tie.

Well not eggs Benedict, exactly, more like Florentine but with egg whites, steamed spinach and tomatoes. You know what I usually get.

I'm sure Immelda could whip that up. Besides, he said, I could really stand to get a few things cleared off my desk. And I think, he pointed again towards the barely begun Gauguin, so could you.

Just a quick coffee then? I asked, rolling the Xeroxed print up and stuffing it into a cardboard tube.

No time, babe, Ricky said as he kissed me on the head, but I'll tell you what: let's both work hard today and then tomorrow we'll do whatever you want, my treat.

And before I could get another word out. Even a small word like, No. Or Stop. Or What? Ricky ducked out the door in the floor and was gone.

Fuckity fuck, I said as I sat down on the sofa. Although I often refused to admit it, Ricky was like art. No matter how much I pretended otherwise, I still wanted to be near him. I still, regardless of our fallings out, longed for his company. His attention. His—cheesy, sappy and utterly chestnutty—touch.

AS-IF'S

AFTER I heard Ricky's car—not the 'Vette (which just in case you forgot he was still afraid to drive and which, in case you forgot again, was technically mine) but his CL 63—pull out of the garage. After I heard the garage open and then electronically shut behind him, I lit a forbidden cigarette and walked around the house.

Magses, what are you doing? Immelda, asked as she walked behind me from room to room spraying a billowy mist of organic air freshener in my wake.

Taking a drag, I said, as I puffed on a Lucky Strike from the white pack.

But you know, Immelda said, spraying in staccato spurts, that Mr. Ricky hates the cigarette smoke, she said. And that it will kill you early.

Uh huh, I said while taking a particularly deep inhale and then blowing the smoke directly into a throw pillow.

Oh Mages, no! she said, as she scooped up the pillow and began beating it with her free hand against her thigh. You remember last time you did this? she asked. You remember the drycleaners and the drapes and how mad Mr. Ricky got?

Yes, I remember, I said, ashing on the plush Quaker-style rug and rubbing it in with my bare heel. But this is my house too, remember?

Magses, she said, as he shook her head at the carpet, maybe I should call the doctor? Maybe this is another of your emergencies?

Go ahead, I said, flopping down on the chaise and pointing

with my cigarette hand toward the phone, but she's not accepting emergencies this weekend. I already tried this morning.

Jesus, Maria y Joseph, she said signing herself and making her way towards her room, a continuous spray still spouting from the non-aerosol can, I pray for you.

Thanks, I said, stomach down on the lounge, cigarette dangling between my lips.

But she only shut her door in response and, bored after a short while of just lying about with no one to talk to, I tossed my cigarette in the sink and made my way back to the studio.

INDICATED ACTING

IN THE studio I spent a good hour staring out the window wondering if Ricky was really at work or if, in fact, he wasn't out fucking. When I was good and convinced he was out fucking I picked up the phone and called my mom, who was making herself lunch.

Peanut butter and jelly for one? I joked.

You know, Magdalena, she said, I'll have you know that your father doesn't eat every meal in the barn. We do go out occasionally, when I can convince him to take a break from his barn-raising. And besides, it's not exactly like you're home to find out for yourself.

What's that supposed to mean?

Nothing, she said, as I heard a wine cork come unstuck with a pop from across the line.

But it would be nice if someone slept in this house besides me.

AFTER JUNAH died and my father took up permanent residency in the broke-down barn, I read an article that said more than 80 percent of parents who lose children separate within the first year. And although I had an urge to clip it out and mail it to Mom, just like I had the urge to tell her about it now, I resisted. Instead I said, Tell me about it. It's Saturday and Ricky is where?

Tell you about what? Mom asked as I heard her raise the bottle up to her mouth and take a swig. Tell you that if you moved back up north you wouldn't be alone? And I wouldn't be alone?

We could be together? Or that maybe if you came home once in a while, gave a damn about someone other than yourself, you could convince your father to stop working himself to death. It's not like a vineyard is going to bring… Her words were lost as she took another swig, and the lip of the bottle clicked against her front teeth.

It was getting harder. I took a breath, but then couldn't stop myself, Well maybe if you could acknowledge a simple thing like my marriage might be coming apart too, I would.

Well, maybe, she was talking around the glass rim of the bottle and her words were liquored, if you came home I'd remember you were married. Ever think of that?

Could you at least use a glass, mom? I mean seriously, would it be so hard to use a glass at least?

Why? I mean why bother anymore?

Because I can't go back there. You know that. I can't look at the house, his room. And the neighbors and their whispering. It's bad enough being a girl on the street, but I can't be the girl with the dead brother on the street. That I can't do.

Stop! Just stop. You could if you wanted. You don't.

Okay, Mom, I gotta go.

No, Magdalena, you already left and last time I checked, son trumped brother so take that to your shrink and smoke it.

WHEN SHE hung up, I wanted to cry. I wanted to scream. I wanted to know if the 80 percent of all marriages applied to siblings of deceased children too. But instead I flipped through the Neiman catalogue, dog-eared a few pages and went online to shop for vintage rhinoceros belt buckles. I bought three, had them rush delivered and then, because I had nothing at all better to do, decided to plug in the glue gun and adhere to my faux-art.

The Gauguin pastoral, once I got good and into it, was actually quite complicated considering I had to seal off a few dozen pink stones in imported cheesecloth and then beat them down with my tack hammer to achieve that slightly rippled stream effect. I also had a little run-in with the glue gun. Somehow I always managed to get hot glue stuck in between my acrylic nails and finger-skin. Only this time, when it happened, the burn was so hot that I put my finger in my mouth and also burnt my tongue. It hurt.

Fishing some ice from the minibar, I filled my mouth and suddenly realized: just because my mom was eating alone didn't mean that I had to lunch that way too. So, ice in hand, I made my way out of the studio for the second time, got dressed, slapped some product on my face and hightailed it to Bristol Farms, where I planned to make a homemade lunch for Ricky and everyone at the office. Not, mind you, because I was prone to sudden fits of generosity and good will towards my employees, but because dropping off boxed lunches would make my spying on Ricky a little less obvious.

DOING LUNCH

ONLY IN L.A. is driving a Bentley to the market run of the mill. Okay, maybe they do it in the O.C. too. But with the way everything urban is sprawling, houses skyrocketing, green-belts depleting and people pushing into every available gap between Malibu and San Onofre, we'll all be one big happy county soon enough anyhow. Not that I drove a Bentley (I drove my Tank) but I parked between two, silver on the right and black on the left, and I was very careful to stay within the painted lines. Why anyone would drive a $350,000 car to pick up some Cheerios and Charmin is beyond me. I mean, the 'Vette only cost half that and never sees yellow-lined asphalt, much less a parking lot with shopping carts! But in L.A. (that is unless you're married to Ricky) it happens all the time. Especially near the end of the week when everyone uncovers their Friday cars and the already expensive Porsches and Jaguars are replaced with their vintage counterparts, you know the 1940's and '50s throwbacks with half the horse power but twice as much class (not to mention resale value), filling up on premium gas and lingering a little longer in the left-turn lanes.

Now in case you have the wrong idea, I didn't grow up watching NASCAR, paging through *Motor Trend* or obsessing over the seconds in a quarter mile. In fact, where I'm from, vehicles come in two types: cars and trucks, with an occasional minivan thrown in for variety. In the car family you have your two and four doors, your automatic and manual transmissions, and trucks are either full-bed or pantied, four-by or limp-dicked. And that's it. But in L.A., well maybe it's because we spend so much time in them going nowhere, staring out windshields at other cars with drivers also just barely creeping along, that we take notice. And what I've noticed is that L.A. is a fucking car show. A preposterous parade of rims and tints, chrome and conversion kits. Now, don't get me wrong, I'm certainly not the type of girl to turn down a parade, but since Ricky has the only set of keys for the '53, I'm usually just hoping to catch a strand of beads on the sidelines.

Because Mr. Silver and Mr. Black Bentley were undoubtedly hiding behind the gorgeous display of organic star fruit just outside the automatic doors—that's what you do when you bring a $350,000 car to the market, you let your wife shop while you stand outside to police the parking lot for vagrant carts and Kia-driving kids—I opened my door slowly, and even though there was plenty of room to open it wider I shimmed out of the small opening in an obvious way that smacked of respect. Not that I gave a damn about the paint job of Mr. Silver or the resale value of Mr. Black, but on the off chance that I did open the door too wide and God forbid it did ding with a clunk against the passenger's side, I wanted to be sure Mrs. Silver didn't catch hell for needing the free-range eggs or emu pâté or edible rose petals that required a trip to the goddamned market in the first place. It was a small sign of female solidarity, and I figured it was the least I could do.

MISE EN SCÈNE

HIGH-END MARKETS might possibly be the best part about L.A. It's not only the lighting, muted bulbs rather than harsh fluorescents, and the hardwood as opposed to that awful sticky white linoleum, but also it's the feeling you get as you walk through the rich mahogany-shelved aisles, gazing at gourmet imports and listening to Bach, that you're not really doing an errand. Rather you feel like you're being treated. Treated to a fabulous pantry of saffron-soaked lentils and shaved daikon. Where no one shakes their head or scrunches their eyebrows when you inquire about cactus stock or cremona fruit. Where they actually sell quinoa thyme buerre blanc, you can sample anything and if you don't like it you can take it back. No really, just look—but not in an obvious way—to your left.

See her?

That blond (so blond it looks silver)-haired woman with the fierce ass and aquamarine glasses standing at aisle two? The one who just handed the checker three dozen wilted long-stemmed roses and demanded a full refund because, as is perfectly obvious, they died. And the clerk, bless her heart, just smiled and punched in the keys. Exchanging $272.18 in cash for the drooping bouquet, without batting an eye, because even if she doesn't understand it personally she's been trained to understand that in Los Angeles bitter housewives are the bread and butter of Bristol Farms, because not many people are willing, or rather able, to consistently shell out $8 an ounce for Norwegian cheese imported from albino goats. Try that in a Stater Bros., or even at a Ralphs, and you'll get your ass laughed out of the store. You'll also only pay $2.99 for a family-sized block of orange cheese, but that's not what this is about. And although it may seem like it, it's not about the roses either. It's about gestures and principles and the very real truth that what the woman with the blond bob really wants to take back is her husband, but because she can't do that she bundled up the roses that he gave her nine days ago in an apologetic action and brought them back instead. And as she stands at the counter wearing diamonds and terrycloth and not much more, you can see the loneliness radiate from her flat tummy and tiny thighs. You know that her husband still doesn't give her the time she deserves, and taking the roses back to the market in his Bentley gives her something to do. She wouldn't dare take back a rotten cantaloupe or a stale baguette, because undoubtedly those things would smell, but the roses, they make perfect sense. And Christ knows she's not the only woman to think so.

I want to tell her as much, and I suppose I could if I didn't have a schedule to keep and a gazillion box lunches to make.

HANDHELD SHOT

OMEMADE IS a relative term, especially among the Malibu Mom set. Ranging from "I transferred this adorable quiche from the chi-chi pink box I bought it in to this smashing Mottahedeh china platter" to "I had my housekeeper whip something up" to "the shortbread is store bought, but the strawberries I chopped myself" to "I actually made this in a real oven Martha Stewart-style with a recipe and lemon zester and everything." Homemade has many meanings in L.A. which is why I didn't feel the least bit bad about buying three dozen prosciutto, pesto and sun-dried tomato brie panini and passing them off as my own. I mean it's not like any idiot couldn't buy ciabatta, some pine nuts and some basil, but why bother with all that Mix Mastering when you can just go to Bristol Farms order To Go and then take it home and re-make it some. You know: crack the crusts on the pear and boysenberry tartlets so they don't looks so perfect, exchange the signature grocery wrap for some Saran brand waxed paper, put in a wicker basket, and you might as well have made it yourself, because you could have if you really wanted to.

And it's not that I didn't want to, but we were working against the clock here. Even in L.A. lunch is only so long, so if I wanted to re-wrap and be at the office to check up on Ricky before, say, 3 PM, Martha Stewart be damned. I simply could not be bothered with aioli today.

INGÉNUE

WHILE I touched up my face and scouted for shoes Immelda peeled the price tags off the tartlets and stuffed the panini into waxed-paper bags. Usually I took great pride in rewrapping them myself, but my recipe for pesto cibatta was no secret, at least not to Immelda, and like I said I was crunched for time. Hair tied up like Hepburn in *Sabrina* and lip-gloss tucked into the sash of my pintucked skirt, I motored to the office for lunch.

The valet didn't work on weekends, and so rather than hassle with parking and the underground and the elevator I saddled up to the curb and flipped on my hazards. With a basket over each arm I shut the car door with my heel and made my way inside. Although we owned the entire building, we only used the top six floors; the other ten we leased to architects, attorneys and agents. I walked past the diamond-shaped fountain misting water in the lobby and hopped on the elevator where I used a special key card to get to the penthouse and realized quite quickly that this was not at all like the movies. A-of-all, because it was *our* office, not his—although sometimes Ricky forgets that when he's, say, talking to people or breathing. B-of-all, because I didn't check in at the concierge or press the elevator button reverently to ride quietly, nervously up sixteen floors to the suite of penthouse offices where I had to bully my way past two security guards before bursting into his office with a flourish.

Why honey, he'd say hastening to tuck in his shirt, a staggering view behind him and his secretary hiding beneath his desk, why didn't you call?

In the movies, I'd scream, Because, you bastard!—before

sweeping the contents of his desk to the floor with my arm and then bursting into tears.

If it were the movies I'd be in Grace Kelly heels with a full A-line skirt, mohair sweater set and red trench coat with matching hat. Perhaps I'd carry an umbrella and throw it to the floor for emphasis, but in real life it doesn't rain in Southern California, all the Myst secretaries are gay men or fat girls and I had a key to everything—not to mention an office of my own right next to Ricky's with a view of the Getty—not that I ever used it.

RED-HANDED

THE ELEVATOR quietly hummed its ascent and when it reached the penthouse it settled with the slightest bump. The polished nickel doors slid back and, for the first time in months, I stepped inside our office. With the exception of the receptionist, who—mental note—was about twenty years younger and a hell of a lot prettier than the girl I had previously hired, not much had changed. Ricky's office was on the left with a view of the city, and mine was the mountainous Getty view on the right. We both had our respective corners, flanked by conference rooms, a computer technician, secretaries, an in-house legal team, an image consultant and, of course, Puck. Floors eleven through fifteen housed marketing, sales, accounting, design and PR, respectively. But Ricky preferred his speaker phone to personal conversations and, with the exception of round table meetings and ad campaigns, rarely set foot below the sixteenth floor. Holding a picnic basket in each arm and wearing a flouncy regatta dress, I imagined myself a sexy, blonde Dorothy, sans the ruby slippers. I stepped off the elevator and made my way across the reception area in long steps.

Ricky's door was closed. This was a good sign; it meant something private was stirring. It meant when I pressed through without knocking there would be hell to pay. It meant before I could place my hand on the knob the door opened and a leggy brunette stepped out. A leggy brunette, in the leggiest sense of the word, opened Ricky's door and ruined my moment. Worse yet, she wasn't buttoning anything, her skirt was straight, her lipliner was perfectly applied and she smelled fresh and young, like cinnamon toast. Maybe she was a professional. Maybe she knew enough to tidy up before stepping out. Maybe...

Ohmigosh! You're Magdalena Bamberger, right? She adjusted the stack of papers she was holding so that she could extend her right hand for me to shake.

What was this? The enemy offering a treaty before the terms had been discussed? I took her outstretched hand and shook it tentatively. Yes, I said, I was, but I'm de la Cruz now. Magdalena de la Cruz.

Wow! she said. You're taller than I thought you'd be.

And you thought of me because? Was she really going to give herself up this easily?

In your pictures, I mean. I've studied you, she blushed and rearranged the pile of paperwork she was holding in case it should slip.

Studied me? What the fuck? Is that like stalking me? I asked out loud.

Oh no, she said, nervously stroking her hairline for errant strands, which of course there were none of. I mean my friends sometimes accused me of it, but there's so few women in the industry doing what it is that you're doing and I'm just a tiny bit, she made a precious little squint accompanied by a teeny tiny hand gesture, okay a lot bit, obsessed with you.

I stared, incredulous. This was so not what I had rehearsed.

Not you, she was starting to get nervous, your work, rather. I'm sooo in love, enamored really, with your work.

My work? What *was* this? A decoy? A distraction? Was Ricky making his way out onto the fire escape while Cinnamon Toast held me up in the hall with her transparent compliments. It would be so like him to have a preplanned strategy just in case. Hell, he probably made her practice. Okay, he'd look at his watch, let's pretend my wife entered unannounced right, he put his finger on the chronogram button, Now! It'll take me exactly one minute and thirty-six no, make that -seven seconds to slip out the back. You, he rubbed his hand on Cinnamon Toast's knee, need to come up with something to distract her for at least that long. I know, he clapped his hands together impressed with himself, tell her you love her art. She's a sucker for that.

I pushed past Cinnamon Toast and stuck my head in Ricky's office. But there was no sign of him, and as I looked around I noticed that his office didn't have an escape. That was my office. My office sixteen floors above ground was the one that had been custom fitted with an emergency window, you know, just in case.

Oh, Cinnamon Toast said upbeat, noticing my searching look, he's not here. They're having the Fiji merger meeting in the conference room. Should be done, she looked at her watch— a pastel Philippe Charriol, the lady's jet set—by three, maybe. Didn't he tell you?

No, I said, walking into his office and looking around. Under his desk were a pair of Ugg slippers and a blue foam stress ball. His top drawer held a pack of Trident, contact lenses and about a gazillion Post-Its. No, I said again, glancing in his empty inbox, I'm so busy with my work—I tried to imitate her exact inflection—that I don't really have time for the water scene.

Cinnamon Toast looked confused, But if your work isn't water, what do you do? I mean…I thought…I'm Dior, she laughed.

I didn't.

I went to Cal too, she said.

I walked carefully over to the coat closet and peeped inside. Well, Go Bears, I said.

There's a case model of your business plan in our entrepreneurial unit. I read about you, and about Ricky too, but I was most impressed by you. How you used your background in viniculture to implement the water filtration system. It was brilliant. And besides, she gave a small shrug, I believe in the solidarity of women, I really do. And I'm not just saying that because I'm talking to you, you know? I really believe that if women don't help other women come up…. Anyhow I just graduated with a double in business and biology. I'm interning here on the purification project. They sent me upstairs to get these, she nodded to the stack of papers. I guess I'm a glorified copy girl, really, but whatever it takes to get in your door, you know what I mean?

I looked her over and remained quiet.

Wow. Am I talking too much? Because I tend to do that. All I really wanted to say is "I love your work and it was a pleasure meeting you." She held out her hand.

I shook it, noticing how soft her skin was, and said, Ditto.

And then, straightening my shoulders I handed her the baskets and said, I made lunch. Would you mind handing them out to my husband and the rest of the staff?

Not at all, she said, reaching a bangle-filled arm into the basket and looping it over her elbow. Thanks.

Don't mention it, I said and took a left towards the elevator.

I pushed the backlit chrome button that pointed down and hoped it would come fast. Like right this second. But it was on the third floor and going down, or so said the numbers above the lacquered doors, and so I shifted my weight from foot to foot and waited.

Mags, Dior said, now standing right behind me.

Yes? I said, as the doors opened and she stepped in with me. I pressed Lobby, she pressed eleven.

Um, she said as the elevator sped down, if you don't mind I do have a quick question.

I examined her professionally styled Los Angeles ponytail. It was high, but not too high, and so smooth it sheened. I was impressed and so I said, Shoot.

Well, now that you're not in on the water scene what do you do? Wine? Filtration? A mixture, you know, like Luxe?

The doors opened and she hesitated to step out.

Art. I said, as she made her way into the conference hall flanked with a stack of papers and my homemade lunch, the doors slowly shutting. I do art.

NOTES FROM THE STUDIO

I WENT home and couldn't even fathom the idea of pretending to work, again, so I spent the rest of the afternoon googling people I used to know and planning my Sunday date with Ricky. When he wasn't home at 9 PM, I poured myself a drink. And when he wasn't home at 10 PM I poured myself another. By 3 AM I stumbled to bed, drunk and alone, and when I woke up at noon the next morning there was a cold latte and a scone on my bedside table with a note that said:

> *Babydoll—*
> *Long night. Early morning. Sorry but I had to get back to the office to finish something. Vital. Will call just as soon as I can. Didn't want to wake you sleeping. So pretty. Will make it up to you. Promise.*
>
> *XOXO, Ricky*

Fuck Puck and his non-violent anti-tantrum-tossing rhetoric. I threw the latte as hard as I could against Ricky's side of the room and then went in search of the toenail clippers. I was going after Ricky's Armani suits and it wasn't going to be pretty.

WARDROBE MALFUNCTION

WHEN RICKY called three hours later I had successfully undone the seams of most of his pocket linings and was halfway through releasing the little buttons that kept the collar down around the neck of his designer shirts.

Hey Babe, he said. Want to meet me at the MoCA?

Surprised, and maybe feeling the tiniest bit guilty about the buttons, but not about the seams, I said sure, hung up and crossed the walk-in closet to my side where I set to work finding something to wear.

SITE-SPECIFIC

WHEN RICKY said on the phone to meet him at the MoCA, I thought it was a date. I thought that maybe he was making up for standing me up, again, by expressing interest in art. But when I arrived at the Basquiat exhibit I quickly realized it was a carefully disguised private school fund-raiser for one of our "fingers crossed" potential investor's kids.

When I finally managed to get Ricky out from under the protective arm of the investor's wife—she was sharing a charming little story about the catastrophe her breakfast nook was in thanks to the remodel—I angled Ricky towards the installation and tried in hushed whispers to get him to fall in love.

Though he was slightly impressed by the Charlie Parker/Joe Louis tributes, he guffawed at the painted poetry and full out snorted in front of the framed graffiti. So I quietly gave up. While he traded tech tips with the assistant vice chancellor, I stood on one foot and stared at a boarded up window, painted black and hung aslant, with the word "torepelghosts" enjambed across the center. It was on loan from a private collector in Picardy, and I needed it. Badly.

But when I suggested it to Ricky his response was usual.

Magdalena, there is no way I'm spending five dollars much less five hundred thirty-five *thousand* dollars for something I could so clearly make myself or, better yet, commission from some homeless person in Echo Park. And besides, wouldn't it break up the exhibit?

Yeah, yeah, yeah, I said within earshot of a seventh-grade teacher who was sipping Veuve Clicquot Grand Dame from a

clear plastic cup and offering her personal opinion on everything. Obviously I wouldn't break up the collection. It's not like
I'm going to strip it from the wall, I'd just like to own it is all.

Interesting, Ms. Seventh Grade said, fully inserting herself
into our conversation before taking a sip and swirling champagne from cheek to cheek before swallowing. She gestured towards me. Do you live in L.A?

Yes, I said, sipping straight from a bottle of Luxe, which I
had secretly filled with Tanqueray and tonic in the handicapped
restroom on the ground floor. We live on the west side in a cute
little place off Sunset.

I expected Ricky to interject. Although it was true, he hated
it when I inferred we lived anywhere other than Beverly Hills,
and he really hated it when I referred to our house in the dimin-
utive. Usually he'd try to be witty about it and reply with an, It's
a charming estate in Beverly Hills, Lana Turner's old house, I'm
sure you've heard of it? And although most people undoubtedly
had heard of it, what with Cheryl Crane and the murder and all,
even if they hadn't they lied and pretended they had all the same.

In fact (and you'll probably find this to be quite useful
should you ever find yourself stuck at some L.A. premiere or
promotion), most people in L.A. pretend to be in the know
about almost anything. And not just who got what augmented,
lifted and tucked, or how much it cost and who they saw on the
way out, but also about serious things, global things, things that
have absolutely nothing to do with the industry, things like long
division and Armenian genocide and the highest recorded sale
of a Basquiat original at Christies. No really, next time you're at
the Playboy mansion or riding the mechanical bull at the Saddle
Ranch, approach the first blonde you see and bring up plate tec-
tonics or the pastoral influence of Pope Innocent the Fifth and
don't be surprised if she pretends to know exactly what you are
talking about.

But back to Ricky, who never lets an opportunity to an-
nounce he lives in Beverly Hills pass him by, except of course

for right now when he didn't say anything. Not one single word, allowing Ms. Seventh Grade to Umm again as she swished and then swallowed.

And your objection, she asked, cup still in hand and pinky extended as though it were high tea, to just visiting the piece in question or perhaps buying a print—you know, so the rest of the world can still enjoy it—would be…?

Trying to gage how far I could go, I looked to Ricky, who seemed to be in deep meditation studying the number of cubes in his glass, and so I decided to go all the way.

My objection, I said, screwing the silver lid tightly onto the neck of the bottle, is traffic. Hell of a lot of it, in case you haven't noticed.

Mags, Ricky said, finding his way back into the conversation as he put his hand lightly on my arm.

But Ms. Seventh Grade just laughed and cleared her throat simultaneously. Of course, she said.

Of course, what?

Mags, Ricky said again, jingling the ice in his cup just a little.

No really? I mean who is she. Who are you, I asked, turning to look her in the eye, to suggest I'd keep it locked up at my place? I could hear my voice rising, I could feel Ricky's fingers tightening. Who's to say I wouldn't donate it? To a high school? Maybe even a private one? Hang it in the gym so that all the little rich kids can enjoy it while sweating off their sashimi take-out?

Because you wouldn't, Ricky said, aligning himself with the champagne-swishing schoolmarm. Because we—

I slammed my bottle down on a bench and said to Ricky before he could finish, Just once? Would it be so hard to take my side, just once?

Ricky opened his mouth to drink what was left of his cocktail or maybe to form some words, but I continued:

Or if not, maybe you could just keep your mouth shut? Maybe, just once, you could play along?

What are you talking about? Ricky asked my back as I stormed away. I am on your side.

I pushed through a crowd of PTA parents bidding, not-so-silently, on Botox and Brite Smiles. Right, I shouted. Sure you are.

But I am, he shouted back as he hurried to catch up with me. And when he did he grabbed my arm again and lowered his voice so I could barely hear. Through clenched teeth he said, I was disagreeing on the private part. You didn't let me finish. We went to public schools. If you donated art to anything, it sure as hell wouldn't be private.

Well you're right about that, I said. But were you going to say as much? Out loud? Or was I just supposed to intuit it?

Well if you had given me the chance before exploding, maybe I would have.

No, I shook my head.

How do you know?

Because we're here, I opened my arms wide and gestured to the banquet tables adorned with Diamond Myst and Luxe bottles, and we just unloaded a hundred thirty cases of free product to a private school that is what? Trying to raise enough money to send the senior class to Paraguay for the summer?

This, Ricky said, mocking me as he opened his arms and gestured, is business. You're the one who said "People like to pay more for things." Remember that? Well, these, he gestured wide again, are the people who can afford to pay more, and that, he nearly knocked over a pyramid of perfectly placed Luxe bottles, is your product in case you haven't noticed. I mean really, now his voice was rising, what's it going to take to get you to understand that? Where do you think the money comes from? I know you're not working right now, but that doesn't mean the world has stopped. Who do you think pays for your cars and your scarves and your thousand-dollar shoes? Who do you think keeps you in Gucci and gin while you glue sparkly little beads on canvas all day?

I do art. The beads and canvas are just temporary.

Well look around Magdalena, this is a museum. Do you see anything that looks like your art?

The room was kind of quiet now, not quite rubber-neck car crash quiet but that awkward semi-silence of people pretending to have meaningful conversations about art and how they're going to get little Aiden into Harvard, or at the very least USC, all the while waiting for it to get good and nasty between Ricky and me. Waiting for fireworks or something truly explosive so they can stop pretending to be engaged in their own discussions and openly stare without shame. They were waiting for broken glass and spilt water, but for once I refused to give it to them. Instead I scanned the instillation quizzically. You know Ricky, you're right, I said in a quiet voice. This art looks nothing like mine. Of course, that's what makes it art and not, say, a knock off or a postcard the likes of which you can buy in the gift shop.

Whatever, Ricky said. Fool yourself if you have to. All I'm saying is that someone has to pay the bills.

Yeah, and someone has to perpetually step out on his wife. I guess we both know your role in this relationship. Besides, it's not like we're starving or anything.

Well at the rate you're going we very soon might be.

I won't buy the painting, okay?

I'm not talking about the art. I'm talking about that woman you offended.

You mean Ms. Seventh Grade?

No, I mean the teacher who just happens to be married to Vincent Chell, Executive Vice President and Chief Financial Officer of Fox Sports Net.

And I give a damn because?

Because athletes drink water, Magdalena. Because Vice Presidents and CFOs and errand boys drink water too. Don't you get it?

I get it all right. And I don't think I care anymore.

Well if you want to keep making art, you damn well better.

I turned on my imported cork heel and was about to breeze out the glass doors and up the stairs when I stopped, put a hand through my hair and said, so quiet I almost couldn't hear myself speak, I thought this was going to be about us tonight.

What? Ricky asked, already saddling up to Mrs. Seventh Grade in an attempt to smooth things over.

I thought, I said, pointing first at him and then at myself, tonight was for us.

It is, why do you think it was so important for you to come?

No, not Myst. Not the business. Us. You and me. I thought it was going to be us tonight.

But Myst is us, Ricky said, refilling Mrs. Seventh Grade's plastic cup with some ice cold Luxe. It is and has always been you and me. Us.

THE BACKLOT

OUTSIDE I nodded at the valet and my colossal silver Tank
that sat idling on the curb—what do they have, some sort
of closed-circuit camera installed above the exits?—and walked
in the opposite direction, past the Disney Concert Hall, towards
First Street. There were trees on Hill Street and on Broadway and
Spring. Not enough to be considered a grove or anything, but
enough so that deciduous leaves outnumbered palm fronds almost a gazillion to one. On Hill Street, even with the dirty side-
walks and people Ricky usually referred to as "unsavory" before
unrolling his window just a crack and tossing out a dollar so they
wouldn't spit on his windshield, I could breathe deep diaphrag-
matic breaths. On the corner of Spring and Temple I looked both
ways and went in the direction that boasted the most foliage.

There are a lot of things wrong with L.A., I'll be the first to
admit that, but I found that walking her downtown streets in
a ruffle-front wrap dress wasn't one of them. Maybe it was because Ricky forbid me to unlock the car doors anywhere south
of La Brea or east of Pico, or maybe it was because downtown
L.A. with its old Times building and federal courts reminded
me of downtown Stockton, another place I was forbidden to go
to while growing up in Lodi, but a place that Junah and I frequented none the less. It always felt so reckless to get in the truck
and drive the country miles to Highway 99 when we were supposed to be peddling a paddleboat around Lodi Lake or jumping
from the rope swing at the trestle. From the 99 we would drive the
paved roads in the slow lane, never quite sure if the truck could go
more than fifty-three miles per hour without igniting in a burst

of smoke and fire, the tachometer quivering at speeds over fifty. We'd exit on Charter or Waterloo or Freemont and expecting to see brutality and mayhem, or at the very least prostitution, and were slightly disappointed to find only poverty and boarded up windows. Old Vietnamese women walking with limps, pushing jimmied shopping carts full of discount produce and cheese. Gangs of small boys wearing ratty ball caps fishing aluminum cans out of the trash or crawdads out of homemade traps set up in the polluted runoff of the delta inlets. We drove past a pencil factory and the soup kitchen, the courthouse and a blood bank advertising free pie in exchange for a pint. When, after a few trips, we got brave enough to park the truck and walk around, we found an antiquarian bookstore, an acupuncturist, a turn-of-the-century theatre and a Mexican bakery that sold bread with *milagros* baked inside. We toured the classified section of the valley newspaper and sized up columbines and caterpillars designed by Wagner Holt inside the Haggin Museum. With the exception of a Filipina woman who screamed, Let me out! Let me out! at the top of her lungs on the corner of Airport and Main, we saw no bedlam and the only violence we witnessed was an underage white boy who, angry at the barista for refusing to sell him a beer, got angry and threw a chair at the plate glass window of the Blackwater Café.

Walking from street corner to street corner, getting my direction from the trees, I wondered if Junah were still alive would this be the part of Los Angeles that he'd like best? If when visiting Ricky and me he'd insist, laughing at my chrome rims and kid-leather seats, that we take his car downtown and if Ricky, alternately, would make Junah park his 1982 Subaru tri-toned wagon inside the garage instead of on the street, less worried about oil stains on the epoxy garage floor than about what the neighbors might think.

Fuck! I missed him so much it was maddening and most likely obscene: I wanted to cut off my arm, to roll around naked on crushed glass. If I were brave enough I'd probably throw my body off a high rock because that's just about how it felt. I missed him in a way that's hard to explain, especially to the Shrink or, worse yet, my husband. And regardless of what either one might say it had nothing to do with some fucked up Freudian incestuous V. C. Andrews kind of plot. I never loved Junah like that and I don't miss him like that either. I miss him more than that. As though he were mine. As though I had birthed him. As though he were all the best of me.

KABUKI

WHEN I reached the empty lot across from the Geffen I realized it was almost dark, so I picked up my phone and called Puck.

You're where? Puck asked.

Sitting on the steps of, I turned around to look at the plaque on the building behind me, the Japanese American National Museum.

Where? Puck said again, while simultaneously thanking someone for coming, I could hear his fake kisses through the receiver. A giant Yoda? Honey you're breaking up.

Pagoda, I shouted.

J-Town? Sugar, what on earth are you doing there of all places?

I took a walk.

Kiss. Kiss. He was faking it with someone again. You walked? His attention was back—somewhat—on me. You're kidding, kiss kiss, right?

No. Meet me for sushi and I'll fill you in?

Be there in ten.

It took him forty-five minutes to find me, but when he did the albacore was to die for and the uni nigiri was the best I ever tasted.

AD-LIBBING

YOU SAY that every time, Puck said, reaching his chop-sticks across the dimly lit table and scooping up a roll.

Yeah, but this time I mean it.

You say that every time too, he said, wrinkling up his nose and taking a bite.

Don't waste it! I reached my own sticks across the table and pinched what remained of the sea urchin out of Puck's grasp.

Easy there Sugar, we can always order more.

Umm, you say that now, I said, with my mouth full, but who's to say the next round will be from the same cut? Prepared in the exact same way? I mean if I've learned anything about Los Angeles, I took a swig of sake to wash down my last bite, it's that everything changes. Quick, I snapped my fingers, without any notice.

Everything? Puck asked. It seems to me, that you and I, he pointed a chopstick in my direction, are pretty permanent.

That's what you think, I said, grabbing my Bambina bag and reaching into the side pocket for a worn photograph that had been torn in two and reattached with tape. But I thought, I slid the photo face down across the table to Puck, they would last forever too.

In the photo I'm sitting on the tailgate of a teal Dodge Ram, with my flannel-covered arms wrapped around my brother.

Puck scrunched his eyebrows as he looked at it.

My tits are small, my teeth are crooked and a boy's too-big Stetson sits on my head, partially concealing my left braid. In the picture, Junah and I are smiling. Hell, I pounded my drink and set the cup on the table with a thump. We're loving each other to goddamned death.

It's beautiful, Puck said carefully, rubbing his thumb gently across the crease in the photo's corner, as if he were trying to raise the brim of my hat just a tiny bit more. Or maybe trying to wipe away the tear stains? I couldn't be sure. Is that, he paused trying to find the right words, him?

No, I said, reaching for the picture, it's me.

But Puck refused to let go of the image. You didn't tell me you were twins, that you were so damn, he was searching for words again, identical.

We're not, I said, holding onto the photo with soft fingers, wanting to grab it out of his hand but too worried about its fragility to tug. In case you haven't noticed—I turned my chin up and to the left in what I imagined to be a perfect profile—we look nothing alike. And then, instead of pouring some more alcohol into my cup, I picked up the petite porcelain bottle the waiter placed between us on the table and sucked it down in three huge gulps. My mouth burned, my head rushed, and I felt hot and shivery all at the same time. I set the bottle down on the table and then said to Puck in a not-so-confidential voice, Give it to me.

He handed me the photo and once I had it back in my hands, I held it up to my face, exhibit A versus exhibit B. I mean not since Michael Jackson—I pointed to my new and old nose, my new and old lips, my new and old teeth, hair, chest and chin— has anyone looked so before-and-after different.

Oh, Sugar, Puck said. He stood up and laid several crumpled bills on the table before gently zipping the picture back in my purse and steering me carefully, in my Yves Saint Laurent platform sandals, out the restaurant door.

SYNTAGMATIC STRUCTURE

THE LAST real art I did—Luxe labeling not included—was just before I started crying. Just before I took up residency under the bed. Just before Ricky fell out of line and just after Junah fell. Morbid as it maybe was (and I don't, for the record, think it was), the last real art I did was plastered to the outside of Junah's coffin. The coffin was cardboard, or maybe pressed board—not, as you might think, because we couldn't afford anything better, but because Junah's body was so far gone, so badly mangled, that cremation seemed like the only humane thing, at least according to the man at the mortuary. And because we are from (but are not ourselves) overtly religious people, and because my father found some comfort in knowing that he could plant Junah as an Oak in the backyard, and because my mother was too distraught to speak, we went with it. And as the body was flown from the Yosemite Basin to the podunk airport in Stockton, as funeral arrangements were made and flowers and casseroles and cards arrived in an endless string, I locked myself up in the barn, not sleeping, eating only from a stale box of Wheat Thins and drinking straight from the garden hose.

I spent four days adorning Junah's casket. Dry-eyed and clear-headed, I worked until my palms blistered, until my nail beds were so thick with paint I could no longer feel my fingers. My wrists grew tingly and a stabbing pain shot back and forth between my neck and my right elbow. But I kept on, and when it was finished I carried it, all by myself, to the front porch, where I set it near a foil-covered lasagna and an amaryllis plant. I wanted to go in. I wanted to go to the funeral, but after I finished the coffin or the casket or the container or whatever the fuck it was, I just couldn't. I couldn't stand to see his body, however mangled, set inside it, and I certainly could not sit beneath the live oaks in the pasture and watch as friends and neighbors cried into their purses and Stetsons. I did the last thing I could do for him, and although it wasn't enough I just couldn't bear to share him, even in death, with anyone else. So I pounded on the front door, rang the bell twice and left.

And lest you think I'm some self-absorbed, irredeemable ingrate who couldn't even show up at her only brother's funeral, I'll have you know that the day after the funeral I did stand by myself—while my parents and Ricky waited outside—and I did watch as my brother was slid into the crematorium. In my ninth-grade World Culture Requirement I remember reading that when the skull pops, due to the intensity of the heat, the soul is set free. And more than anything I wanted to be there when Junah's soul soared. I wanted to catch it, in case it also decided to fall.

I thought it would be quick, standing there. That the flames, or whatever it was that lived behind the ascetic and antiseptic brushed nickel doors, would be so hot that his body would just disintegrate, but I was wrong. It took forever. And as I shifted back and forth from foot to foot, refusing to sit, refusing to speak for nearly three hours, I strained to hear the pop. To hear anything. But of course I couldn't. Hear anything, that is, except the sound of my own breath that, as time wore on, gradually turned into a panted hysteria.

WHEN I went back to the car I was shaking so badly that I almost dumped the cardboard box that held his remains—not a soft ash, like most people assume, since we had decided to skip the mechanical smoothing out process, preferring instead to take Junah as he was, all four and three-eighths pounds of coarse bone fragments. In the car I handed the box to Ricky, and when he took it the tears began. My mother lifted a red bottle of Seven Deadly Zins to her lips and took a long pull, and my father ground the gears as he shifted into first.

Not long after I crawled beneath my bed and refused, despite all efforts, to come back out.

BRECHTIAN ACTING

PUCK AND I got home after midnight, but when he pulled my Tank into our six-car garage, right next to The Corvette I Wasn't Allowed to Drive, the headlights illuminated Ricky's empty parking space on the left. He wasn't home.

Probably business, Puck said.

Right, I said, glad for the sake that still sloshed around with the raw fish in my stomach. And because Ricky wasn't home, and because it was late, and because ever since Junah I developed a fear of the dark, and because Puck drove my car and left his who the hell knows where, I invited him in.

Why not? he said and followed me up the stairs to the master suite, a bottle of Tanqueray Ten between us.

You know, I said to Puck, setting the bottle down on the night stand and flopping back into the pillow-filled bed, I never realized how much Ricky worked until I stopped working.

Yeah, he said, unscrewing the bottle and pouring a dash of tonic into the gin filled glasses.

No really, I said as he passed me a glass, When we were working together the dinners at midnight seemed normal, even almost fun.

And now the fun's done? Puck asked, taking a glass for himself and getting comfortable on the bed.

Now, I said, snuggling into the crook of his arm as we laid back on the ginormous bed I shared with Ricky, I'm tired all the time.

Well, art can be exhausting, Puck laughed. Especially the good kind.

Yeah, I yawned, but having a husband who is never home—

Never as in ever? Puck asked, rehearsing our well-played script. I smiled, As in ever. That's pretty damn exhausting too.

But seriously, Sugar, Puck said, twining his fingers in my hair and rubbing my scalp in small circular motions, it just feels that way, right? He's got to be home sometimes, right?

Okay fine, you caught me. I'm exaggerating. Welcome, I flung my arms wide, sloshing gin in my gesticulation, to the hyperbole of my life. If you must know, Ricky is technically home from 9:43 PM to 5:35 AM Monday through Friday, occasional Saturdays and every other Sunday afternoon. Excluding of course, I counted with my fingers, fund-raisers, extended industry luncheons, Laker Games, Hollywood premieres and other so-called appearances.

So what do you do? Puck asked. Home by your lonesome.

That's a damn good question I said. Puck moved his hand down my scalp and started rubbing the back of my tense neck. I can tell you what I don't do, I said as my voice softened with his rubbing, When he comes home at 10:02 I do not point out that he's nineteen minutes late. I do not remind him that I've waited up. I do not ask where he's been, because I know the answer. The answer is the business. "Babydoll," I said in my mock Ricky voice, "I've been up to my ears in the business." "Honey, the business is on fire and I'd sure like to take advantage of the market."

Puck laughed and in his best Ricky imitation joined in, "Sugar, without the business how would we eat?"

I turned and looked Puck straight in his cool blue eyes. Ricky doesn't call me "Sugar," I said. You call me that.

Puck shrugged and kissed me on the forehead. And then he kissed me again on the nose.

But to answer your question I said pulling back a bit, We'd eat with a fork, a knife and maybe even a spoon. But I don't say as much. Not out loud to Ricky anyhow. Because I know that's not what he means.

You sure? Puck's hand slid further down my neck to my shoulders.

Oh, I'm sure all right, I said untying the straps of my halter and rolling over so Puck could work on my back. What Ricky's really saying when he gives me the business is not *how*, but *what* would we eat and, heaven-forbid, *where*? I said, speaking into the pillows, my voice only half audible. "Ricky," I'd like to say, I said, turning my head to the side so that Puck could hear me, "without the business we'd probably eat pasta, with butter and salt, on a card table in our rented living room. But we could eat at 5:30 in the PM and we could eat *together.*"

Well isn't that pretty to think? Puck said, straddling my body between his legs, sitting on my ass and pushing down on the small of my back with his knuckles.

Wow that feels good, I said to Puck, but Ricky doesn't think so.

Well I should hope not, Puck said. If Ricky wants a full-body massage I'm going to need a raise.

No, I laughed, card table dinners together is not pretty thinking to Ricky, who maintains that when I met him, when I married him, I understood he had a certain minimum lifestyle to maintain. And don't get me wrong, ohh. Right there, I said to Puck. That's the spot. Umm. I was quiet for a while, and when Puck began to move his hands up and down the outline of my spine I continued, When I said I do, I understood about minimums, and maximums too. I mean Ricky's not the only one with an MBA. I just didn't realize that Ricky's bottom line was a clay tennis court and six-car garage. I had no idea his *sine qua non* included a household staff of twelve and twin sunken, saline-filtered, Tahoe-blue swimming pools. If I had I might have held my tongue when I came up with the goddamn business. When I said, while we were rolling about in our 150-count polyfiber Sears' sheets, Baby, I have an idea.

Puck, finished with my back, rolled over so he was curled up beside me again.

Drink? He asked, holding up the green bottle and looking at me with a soft, almost sad smile.

AND ALTHOUGH the last thing I remember is falling asleep looking at Puck's distorted image from the behind the clear green glass, when I woke up Ricky was kissing me on the forehead and prying the bottle out of my grasp.

What time is it? I asked, looking around, still half expecting to find Puck passed out beside me or on the floor, or maybe even beneath the bed.

2:30.

In the morning, I asked.

Yes, in the morning, Ricky said, unclasping the onyx circles from around my neck and helping me slip my hips out of my abstract embroidered dress.

Where were you? I asked, so tired I could barely speak.

At the fund-raiser, Ricky said, as he helped me into a paisley chemise, raising funds.

Until 2:30? I moved my head from right to left so he could undo my Buddha hoop earrings.

Until midnight, he said. Then I went to grab a drink with some of the investors at The Standard.

Oh, I said, holding my legs up Pilates-style so Ricky could remove my shoes. And did you?

Did I what? Ricky asked.

Do the deal?

We'll see, he said, turning off the light and sliding into bed beside me. I sure as hell hope so.

Me too, I said, not sure if I meant it or not. Not sure anymore what I meant. Only sure that as soon as Ricky's breathing became regulated in the bed beside me, as soon as he was fast asleep, I was suddenly very wide awake.

TREATMENT

AFTER JUNAH, my hair went dark.
They say that can happen, you know. Shock or something. But not my whole head, just a streak. Like an inverted skunk of brown tailing its way through the top left part of my yellow head. Jersi, my stylist, said on most people it usually goes white.

Well fuck me for being the exception.

He sighed, brushed a small brown strand high above my head and held it there, the ends tightly wrapped around the bristles of his brush. The rest of my hair was wet, and my shoulders and chest were covered with a silver smock. I looked at my reflection and followed the lock of brown hair upwards towards the exposed bulbs running in a straight line across the top of the mirror. There were six of them and they cast a hyper-white glaze across my face so that my skin appeared translucent. You could actually see the veins pushing blood across my forehead. It was rich. It was much too much. I looked at my lap and said, Do what you can.

Jersi looked at me, or at least the mirror image of me, and said, I'm not going to pretend that it will be easy Cupcake, but I think, although the texture's changed, that I can bleach it out, maybe add a few psychological highlights.

That's when I started screaming. When I couldn't stop.

Losing Junah isn't something I like to talk about.

So I'm not going to.

What I will say is that sometimes I wonder, if Ricky wasn't on liquid time, if he didn't sleep only four and a half hours a night, if I would be able to stay awake and pretend not to go crazy, pretend not to know that it's impossible to only sleep four and a half hours a day, pretend not to care that if he isn't sleeping here he must be sleeping somewhere, right?

But where?

And with whom?

And if he slept, say, six or seven hours like most people, would I make it? Would I be able to lie beside him night after night and hate him? Night after night in some sleek and silly nightie with my arm almost touching his thigh, with my head almost touching his chest. (If I actually touch him, he says, Mags go on your own side. Like we're six and seven in the backseat of the station wagon and have drawn imaginary lines to mark territory. Pretend there is a chain saw running down this line, Junah would say, tracing the vinyl ribbing that ran the length of the upholstery, and if you cross it you will loose your arm. That's how it is with Ricky, only now it's a bed and we're twenty-nine and thirty-four.) For eighteen months I've lain here, almost insane, almost ready to leave, almost ready to scream: I'm not touching you! I'm not touching you! I'm not touching… But before I can finish, Ricky's alarm (set to New York time) sounds. If we were in New York it would be 7:30 AM. But we're not in New York. We're in Los Angeles, or some Hollywood extension thereof. And in Los Angeles Ricky will shower and shave and dress himself up in gray slacks, a lavender shirt and paisley tie because it's the outfit I have laid out for him. On the back of his belt I have written I LOVE YOU in Mauve-a-licious nail polish. He won't notice. It's been there for three months.

Should I say it again?

That he doesn't notice anything?

When he actually does notice he's liable to shout. Then I will have to go to Bloomies and buy him a replacement. It will be something to do. Something besides trying to peel the label off a bottle of gin in one fluid, untorn piece. Something besides imagining my hangover is morning sickness. Something besides seeing Junah die, over and over and over again in the backspaces of my mind.

TAKE THREE

STORY AND LIFE

THERE ARE three things in my life that I wish I could undo. The first is so obviously Junah that I won't even risk the cracking of my voice in saying it out loud. The other two—so pale in comparison that they might as well be transparent—are moving to Los Angeles and taking Adair's advice.

Every morning for a week after our little incident at the MoCA I pretended to sleep until Ricky left for work and then I got to work myself. Not, mind you, on the rhinestones or anything remotely connected to art. No, I set to work spying, prying and otherwise meddling into all of Ricky's affairs. I searched his accounts for excessive or unusual purchases, I recorded and redialed numbers appearing more than once on his iPhone, I retrieved the trash from his hard drive and read through his e-mail. I phoned restaurant managers from Sunset to Wilshire and requested facsimiles of business lunch bills. I watched hour upon hour of outtakes. And on Friday, I conferred my findings with the Shrink.

CHARACTER REVELATION

THE SHRINK didn't want to talk about undercover infidelity operatives, instead she wanted to talk about sex. Which was easy, because there was nothing to talk about.

Nothing? she asked, her pen scraping against her legal pad as she spoke.

Nope, I said, There's absolutely nothing to say. And then I decided: Not. To. Say. One. More. Thing. For the entire rest of the session.

The Shrink, for her part, said a lot. That the French referred to orgasm as *le petit mort*. The little death, she translated. And she said she thought that was a very accurate description, especially for someone in my current situation. That sometimes emergency sex was the best way to feel again. That if anything, orgasms were a great stress reliever. That without physical intimacy, mental intimacy would be harder to obtain. That if I pretended to be interested in sex I might actually find I actually am.

I sat closed-lipped and played with my scarf. I tried, unsuccessfully I might add, to tie it about my head as Dior, Ricky's new intern had. I wondered if he'd fuck me, give me just a smidge of polite attention if I could get the scarf just right? I wondered if the Shrink knew I was interested in sex? That I'd love to have it, and often, and soon, but that my husband just wasn't interested? Or if he was interested, he wasn't interested in having it with me? Or if he was interested in having it with me, he was never home long enough to accomplish anything short of sleep?

And when the Shrink said, near the end of our session, in frustrated desperation, You know Magdalena, if you're going to refuse to say anything I don't know why it is you come, she almost won. She almost got me to open my mouth and shout: I come because Ricky and I have a deal: if I go to the Shrink he'll drive me. And although I can't count on much, I know that at least once a week, for forty minutes there and forty-eight minutes back, I'll be alone. With my husband. In the daylight. In a car. And although that may not seem like much, believe you me, it's all I have.

But even though I wanted, very much, to say as much, I just opened the door and walked out, tossing her my scarf—Isadora Duncan style—as a parting gesture.

Back in the car Ricky handed me a shot of wheatgrass juice and an orange chaser. He sucked his own smoothie through a straw and asked, So, did she say anything interesting?

No, I said, tossing back the wheatgrass and sucking on the orange rind, wishing it was gin and a lime, respectively. She told me a fat pack of lies.

STEP OUTLINE

YOU KNOW, Ricky said, pulling away from the curb as though he were driving a much smaller, much faster car, the secretaries at the office listen to Ryan Seacrest every morning, and they have this game where you call in and try to convince your significant other to come home in the middle of the day. He fiddled with the stereo dial, as if he expected to magically find it on demand.

You mean like just quit work and come home? I asked, hitting the OFF button.

Right, but you do it all live, on the radio. They have some sort of two-way connection where you call in and then give them your significant other's number at work and then they connect you and if you can convince them to leave work and come home—

Agree to it on the air?

Exactly. Then you win a prize. Concert tickets, dinner on Sunset, free CDs, radio stuff.

I wonder if they give away trips to Palm Springs?

Magdalena, everybody gives away trips to Palm Springs.

Well then we should play.

Like you need another trip to Palm Springs, I mean it's not as if you can't just buy one with a prepaid gift card at Bristol Farms. And besides, you know you'd never be able to get me to agree to come home in the middle of the day.

Sure I could.

Really, Ricky said, looking in the side mirror, but not over his shoulder as he switched lanes. Try it.

I stretched out my finger and thumb and curled up my middle three fingers into a pretend phone.

Hell-Oh, Ricky said in his overdone radio personality voice, This is Ryan Seacrest on air live with Mrs. Magdalena de la Cruz. Longtime-listener, first-time-caller. Magdalena you ready to play?

Sure am, I spoke into my finger phone.

All rightie sweetie, why don't you tell our listeners just who it is you'll be calling.

My husband, Ricky.

And where's Ricky today?

At work. He bottles water, I said knowing in real life Ricky would die if I said as much.

Good old H_2O. Well Val, our production assistant, is going to ring Ricky up, and when he says "hello," you're on. You ready?

Ready, I said.

Ricky made several fake phone ring noises and then put down his radio mic and, becoming himself again, picked up his hand-phone, Hello?

I summoned the tears that I'd fought back before and let them fall loudly from my eyes. Ricky, I said in my serious hysterical voice (as opposed to my frenzied hysterical voice) I…I need you to come home right away. I hiccupped and sobbed again for emphasis. I was opening up a cantaloupe for lunch and I slipped with the knife, you know the samurai-ginsu Global knives, the good ones we got for our wedding that will cut through chicken bone? Well, I cleared some snot from my nose and said, I slipped and cut off my finger. The little one. Chopped it completely off. I need you to come home right now. There's blood everywhere.

I let out one more soft whimper before turning the tears off. Well, I said, looking into Ricky's stunned face. Would you come home? Did we win the trip to Palm Springs?

Are you feeling all right? Ricky asked.

What do you mean?

What I mean is that's how you'd get me to come home? You'd scare me half to death with a made up emergency?

Well, did it work?

Of course it fucking worked. Only an asshole would stay at work after a call like that.

So I won! I said, clapping my hands together and making the mental flight to Palm Springs.

No, you didn't win. You fucking scared me half to death is what you did. I probably would have drove home at eighty miles an hour and slammed into the side of some brick wall because of your little prank. And besides you didn't play by the rules.

You never said there were rules.

You're *supposed* to try to get me to come home by flirting and talking dirty. You're *supposed* to make me hard, not scared to death.

Well you didn't say that, I said.

So you just decided to pick the sickest thing you can think of?

No. It wasn't the sickest thing. I mean it wasn't like I cut off my whole hand, or my arm. It's not like I fell on a nail and gouged out my eye. It was just a finger. My pinkie one.

Yeah, but you cut it clear off. On the drive home I'd be imagining how it was all small and bloody sitting in a Ziploc baggie with ice cubes or something. Probably turning blue or green or whatever color severed fingers turn when they get cut off.

They turn gray, I said, quietly. I've seen it.

First the body slams against the ground. Then the life oozes out. And after a while, when some kind embalmer tries to assemble everything into some sort of humanity but gives up when the family insists on cremation, it turns gray.

All of it.

The fingers, the forearm, the space behind the knees, the face, now too mutilated to recognize.

It all goes gray.

CAUSALITY

IT GOT very quiet in the car. I focused all my energy on not crying, which meant I cinched up my brows, clenched the door handle with white knuckles and took deep breaths of air through my mouth.

Ricky put his hand on my knee. I let him keep it there. The quiet continued.

Ricky slid his hand up my recently laser-treated leg—you have to keep on top of veins; one day they're little purple threads, the next day they're knotty varicose ropes—and played with the kumquat beaded hem of my Betsey Johnson German chocolate mini-dress. I slid my body to right, so that my hip touched the door, but Ricky gripped my thigh tighter. The car hummed gently through the floorboards. Deciding, for once, to actually take the advice of the Shrink, I moved away from the door just a bit and slid closer to Ricky. I put my own hand on top of his and squeezed. At the next red light he turned his face into mine and slowly kissed me with open lips. Our tongues were shy, our movements slow but not clumsy, and I suppose that is what differentiated us from the countless teenage couples who had mirrored our motions in cars—arguably less nice ones—across the greater Los Angeles metropolitan area.

We drove down San Vicente and turned left at Santa Monica Boulevard. At the next red light, North Doheny, I turned towards Ricky. I pushed Junah to that far, black backspace of my mind and I took a deep breath. The smell of Dove soap and freshly cut grass swirled around. I pressed my lips into his. Trying. Wanting.

Yet still, I didn't feel anything.

Which means I wasn't exactly fibbing, on the curb, when I told Ricky the Shrink had been feeding me a fat pack of lies.

In fact, like most things I make up, it was now pretty much true.

THE WAR ON CLICHÉ

LOOKED to the dash, 4:43 PM. In another hour Los Angeles would switch places. The freeways, already congested with the exchange, would be jammed in both directions as gardeners, housekeepers, pool boys, and handymen keeping up the homes on the Westside made their way east to Downey, Inglewood, El Monte and Echo Park while lawyers, bankers, producers, executives and industry types, working downtown, made their way west to Bel Air, Beverly Hills, Westwood and Malibu. Aspiring actors would stop circulating their headshots and start passing out menus. Musicians would climb down from billboards and arrange drum sets in someone's cramped studio apartment. It was a slow parade of poorly documented domestics making the long walk to the neighborhood limits, because public transportation is restricted from entering designer drives (see decrease in property values) and chic canyons (see smog, see noise ordinances, see intentionally narrow roads that curve and chicane).

According to my navigation system, downtown L.A. is exactly 12.62 miles from Rodeo Drive (Start out going Southeast on N RODEO DR toward ELEVADO AVE. Turn LEFT onto S SANTA MONICA BLVD/LITTLE SANTA MONICA BLVD. Turn SLIGHT RIGHT onto BURTON WAY. Turn SLIGHT RIGHT onto N SAN VICENTE BLVD. Turn RIGHT onto S LA BREA AVE. Merge onto I-10 E. Merge onto CA-110 N via the exit—on the left—toward PASADENA. Take the 4TH ST/3RD ST exit— exit number 22B. Take the 6TH ST ramp). On a good day, say on a Sunday at 3 AM, you might get there in the twenty-three minutes, Google Maps suggests. On most other days it will take you anywhere from forty-seven minutes, not including parking, to an hour and a half.

An hour and a half, without parking, to go 12.62 miles seems extraordinary in most instances, but it's one of the only things in L.A. that actually make any sense; it's one of those collegiate conundrums of place and space that can actually be solved, QED. My sociology professor would go nuts over it: income times quality of life divided by a quotient of perceived happiness, expressed or otherwise, minus assets, including but not limited to green cards, 401Ks, IRAs and dental insurance, and it takes a hell of a lot longer than twenty-three minutes to navigate from Olvera Street to Rodeo Drive. In fact, I've heard it said that, although it's walkable in less than an afternoon, it can sometimes take upwards of five generations to make the trip.

Ricky, I suppose you could say (provided you're not the type to perpetually remind me that California was actually once Mexico and so Ricky wasn't making the trek, rather he was making his return—as long as you're not one of those kind of people, you'll most likely agree) that Ricky made the trip in two generations and some change—which beats my fifth-generation white-ethnic slide down from Pollack Hill by quite a mean feat. The traffic must have been particularly light. Maybe he took the surface streets or maybe, oh the genius, he took the carpool and didn't get caught!

It was barely five when we pulled into the drive.

Ricky was about to make his way into the garage when I screamed: STOP!

THE PROBLEM OF SURPRISE

JESUS, MAGS, what the hell? Ricky asked after he slammed on the breaks, scanning the drive for an imaginary cat, a seagull with a broken wing, a crazy pile of barbed wire and shards of glass. But there was nothing but perfectly paved concrete interlaced with hand-painted tiles, imported from Mexico. We both knew that.

Seriously, he said, slamming both hands against the steering wheel.

I can't, I said quietly. I just can't do it anymore.

I wanted him to say, Can't do what? So that I could begin the list of my grievances: everything that once upon a time I could do, but that now, in Los Angeles and without Junah, I just couldn't.

But he didn't.

He didn't ask. And he didn't answer. And, in fact, he didn't say anything at all. Instead he put the car in park, unlatched his seatbelt, opened the door and walked out. He walked out and left me, keys dangling and door open, just sitting in the parked car in the dead center of our circular drive. Sitting alone with the radio and the deet deet deet of the electronic key-in-the-ignition reminder.

I watched him, as he tried first the front door, and then the side. Immelda was playing Bunco with the neighbors and would be gone until at least ten. So both doors were locked. I gave a small smile to the reflection of myself in the side mirror and leaned over to pull the driver's door shut. Maybe he heard the quick click of the locks as the door shut, or maybe he saw me out of the corner of his eye in the mirror, because he didn't return to the car to try to wrestle the keys from me so he could get inside. Instead he did something shocking. He did something so completely un-Ricky-like that it can only be called outrageous. He walked to the front of our house, pulled up his trousers and took a seat on the antique porch swing that hung from delicate brass chains off the lip of our veranda. He sat (sans gardener or landscaper or any other hired help to instruct and otherwise oversee) on the front of our porch and he swung from our swing.

CONSISTENT VERSUS INCONSISTENT REALITIES

WITHOUT RICKY, I put my feet on the dash, reclined my seat and fished about in the glove compartment for a yellow package of peanut M&Ms and a green bottle of spirits. I reclined for a while. Missing Ricky. Missing Junah. Missing the way my breasts used to be, small and comfortable, even with a seatbelt digging across my chest. But now, I wondered how it was so easy to slip from happy to hell? It was as if the line that used to be delta-thick was now the L.A. river: a dried up trickle, so easy to cross it might as well be concrete. And once you realized that you could just skip across, say one mean thing after the next and get away with it, it was hard, so hard—after the worst thing you could imagine had already happened—to go back. To be understanding and compassionate to other people, who might very well have their own shit to deal with, when it felt so god-awful on the inside.

I wanted to unroll the window, open the door and yell across the yard to Ricky. To say: I'm sorry and I'm sad. I miss my brother. I miss you. But most of all I miss us. But I wasn't brave enough. I sat for a while, trying to wonder if, when Ricky wasn't looking, I could make a mad dash for the house and manage to get inside and rebolt the lock without him trailing after me.

If it weren't for the house I could have forgotten Ricky in an afternoon. Just put the car in reverse and drive wherever the road takes me. But there's a goddamned house, which is worse than a goddamned dog. I want a dog. And not one of those stupid fluffy white yappy little things, a real dog. A Mastiff or a Great Dane or an indiscernible farm breed like Gideon. I tried to buy a cat once but Ricky made me take him back. Can you imagine that? Taking back a cat. I mean it's not like a purse or a belt or a few dozen wilted roses or even a car. But a cat? They take them back. They look at you real funny, but they do take them back. And just like the bag or the belt, they ask what the problem was.

The problem?

This is where you stretch your manicured hand out to the cat, ruffle it up near the back of its ears and, with fingers woven between the carefully brushed fur, scratch all the way down until you reach its tail. Where it immediately arches its little kitty ass straight to the sky. With a few loose hairs still in between your fingers, look at the pet shop lady and say, as though you were from Beverly Hills, It didn't match the rug. I mean I thought it would, but the color was too close and so in fact they clashed. Next time I'll be sure to bring a fabric swatch. Or pretend you're from the Valley and say, I was hoping it would go on sale. Do you know when the next cat clearance will be? Or don't pretend at all; just say you're a woman narrowly escaping the fourth stage of grief in Beverly Hills. Say, my husband is an asshole and he says he's allergic but I know for a fact he's not; he's just pretending to be allergic like he pretends to be allergic to smoke, so I can't.

The pet shop owner will try to be funny. While making goo-goo faces at the cat and glaring at you she will say, But you don't smoke do you, kitty-witty? She will reach for the cat, a blue tabby, and she will take a long time, putting on a big show of detangling the cat from the brown Bloomingdale's bag the cat's in. Then she will ask if you would like your money refunded and the cat will stretch out a paw and bat at your ring. Don't bother with an answer. Just walk out as quietly as you can in Louboutin heels on tile floor and try not to cry.

GIVE THE SLIP

IT WAS getting dark now. In the side mirror I could see that Ricky had stopped swinging and was instead obsessively pacing the front porch while texting. I still had over two-thirds of my king-sized package of Peanut M&Ms, half a bottle of Tanqueray Ten and a trunk full of Diamond Myst. If I rationed correctly I could most likely last all night. I shook a blue and a yellow chocolate-covered peanut into my hand and was surprised to see them glowing. Okay, not glowing really, but illuminated by a pair of headlights pulling up behind me in the drive.

I turned around in the front seat and saw a convertible Jag, with the top up, idling behind me. It wasn't Puck (he drove an Audi), and we had bought Immelda a Mini Cooper. For a second I thought it might be Dean, in his wife's car, but then remembered after he got made she bought a Bentley with her off-shore account. And besides, though it was dark and I was looking straight into headlights, the outline of the driver was svelte, not stocky. I checked my reflection in the vanity, combed my fingers through my hair and was reaching for my gloss when I noticed Ricky was getting in on the passenger's side. I pushed open my car door and stepped out into the drive just in time to see a personalized license plate that read: J'ADIOR backing out of my drive.

AESTHETIC EMOTION

WITH TIME, trying not to cry gets easier. Now that doesn't mean the tears don't fall, but usually there's a small bit of warning before the spill. A small enough spell wherein you can, perhaps, not embarrass yourself by running after the other woman's car, shouting and tossing cuss words at your husband. A span of maybe two or three minutes where you can, instead, grab the keys from the Tank, unlock the side door and step inside your dark house. A teeny tiny moment where you can walk up the stairs to the big white bedroom you share with your husband and throw yourself down on the oversized bed, or ravage his side of the closet, or lock yourself in the bathroom. Like I said, it's a small window, but with time it does get easier.

THE SHRINK, before I wore her out, told me whenever I felt the tears coming on I was to look whomever was nearest directly in the eyes.

When the tears begin to fall, don't fight it, she said, just focus. She put her hand on my chin and tipped my face, kindly, towards hers.

It worked for a while, her tricky little trick, but eventually, I learned how not to cry in front of others and instead how to keep the tears for myself. Because there was no one else at home and because it was, if not impossible, then very, very difficult to catch Ricky's gaze as he motored about with his mistress in a unconverted Jag, I walked the halls to my vanity and stared at myself in the starlet illuminated makeup mirror.

AFTER JUNAH, I changed everything. I mean obviously. But short of a corneal transplant—and trust me, even I'm not so far gone I'd go there—the eyes are hard to alter. Sure you can lift the crow's feet. You can pull the brow back and up so it's taught against your forehead. You can even have your lashes extended so far that they flit up against your sunglasses, leaving little black mascara specks on the tinted glass. But the eyeball itself, the cornea, the pupil, the iris and its aqueous humor, well you pretty much have to live with all that.

I reached my fingers up to my face and held my left eye open. With my right hand, I gently put my pointer finger into my eye and popped out my colored contact. My eye went from blue to gray in a moment. I stayed focused. Eyes each a different color, I wondered which would cry first. Undoubtedly it would be the gray one. The one with the small brown fleck near the bottom edge that perfectly matched the eyes of my dead Polish twin. Undoubtedly, if I could just stay focused. Keep my eyes open and not half-shut in the hypersleep place that I couldn't quite control.

RICKY HAD been gone maybe an hour when the panic started. Although the logical Magdalena that I once was whispered rationalizations like: Any minute now he'll knock on the door. He'll pick up his phone and call me. Even though he just got in a car with another woman without so much as a goodbye, he still loves me. He still loves me and he is not fucking Dior the whore in the dimly lit parking lot of Rock 'n' Roll Ralphs.

ADAPTATION

THE SHRINK has prescribed small white pills to dull my vision, my anxiety, my compulsion for panic. The pills, I tell the Shrink, those pills, I tell Ricky, make me sleepy. Asleep I cannot see straight.

That's exactly the point, Ricky says.

The point is, the Shrink says, sleep.

But if I don't stay awake all night reckoning with the memories, how can I be sure I will have recorded all the details of Junah before the fall?

Already, his smell has worn. How can I cement him before I lose the sound of his voice, the scar above his ear, the shimmer in his smile?

When I am hung over from my prescription it means that I'd begun obsessively thinking. Again. This means I gave in to the small yellow bottle with the little white pills because my fingers were going numb with reckoning: Rain falling down a chimney that no longer burns wood sounds like ping-whoosh. The Santa Anas blowing the trees that drag across the south wall—with some focus these become Central Valley oak and not SoCal palm. The far-away bark of the neighbor's dog could be Gideon. And then later, or earlier rather, in the wee parts of morning. I can most certainly sense a ghost making his way from the kitchen into the foyer. The creak that goes hee-haw is his phantom boot on the first stair. Don't breathe. Don't move. The creak that goes haw-hump is an ephemeral too-big hand on the banister.

To take one white pill means to fall asleep for fourteen hours. To take two means to be temporarily dead. I do not want to die.

I merely want a familiar body to sit next to me in the car, to lie next to me in the night while I classify moments. Ricky. Puck. A dog even. Someone to think about outside of myself and the memories of Junah's dying I can't help but let in.

SEMIOSIS

WE DIDN'T identify Junah after the fall. We—my mom, my dad, Ricky and I—were all too hysterical, or in Ricky's case helping to calm the hysterics. And so when our neighbor Mr. Stroud dropped by to see if he could help, Ricky gave him the job. I don't know what I would have done in that situation.

Wait. Actually I do. I would have done what I did, which was to climb into Junah's bed, pull the covers around my ears and scream. But had I been Ricky in this situation? Well, let's just say I like to think I would have manned up and gone myself. I would have driven out to the airport with a cop and the corner to positively ID my dead brother-in-law. I would have done that, even though I knew the image would be forever engrained on my memory. Etched into the back of my asleep eyes for the rest of my life. I would have done that for my wife and for her parents, to be sure. So that later, when they were collectively going through the denial phase, I could gently assure them that, yes, it was Junah. I saw him with my own eyes. My own 32-year-old, capable, related through marriage, unbespectacled eyes. I would not have trusted it to the ageing Mr. Stroud, a farmer three acres to the left. I would have gone myself. I would have done at least that much.

But Ricky didn't.

And so, inside the DeYoung Memorial Chapel, I asked. To look inside. Even without looking, I knew it was him. Even though in my heart I hoped that it was some other blond boy and that Junah, a bit dehydrated and a bit disorientated, was secretly making his way back to us, alive, from Wawona Meadow.

(Laney, it was such a trip! One minute I was packing in and the next I was completely lost. Good thing I took that wilderness survival class last fall. I mean, surviving for three days on raw redwood bark and half a canteen of Coconut Water, well it's not the best of conditions, but I made it work.) I knew it was him before the phone rang. I knew it was him when I heard my mom scream. I knew it was him when my heart snapped. And if I had any remaining reservations, I knew without a doubt that it was my brother Junah, and not some other poor unfortunate blond boy, when they handed me a Ziploc bag with his harness, his watch, his Petzl William screw-lock carabiner, but no shoes.

I knew it was him when they didn't hand me shoes.

But when the man in charge of the cremation asked if I would like a moment to say goodbye, I said yes. And when no one was looking, I looked inside. To be sure.

PARADIGMATIC ANALYSIS

I DON'T know when I fell asleep, but when I woke up Ricky wasn't there. The clothes he had worn the day before were in a small heap by the door to his closet. Not in the hamper, mind you, but in a pile directly adjacent to the hamper, just like every other morning. Which meant, although he hadn't slept with me, he had made it home.

I rolled over to look at my bedside table, hoping that if there were a scone and a soy latte we could forget yesterday. Just pretend, like most everything else, that it had never happened.

No such luck.

The table was empty. I stepped out of bed and walked down the hall to the guest room that had a view of the garage. When I pulled back the drapes, my car was still in the drive, door ajar, just as I had left it. Which meant that, unless Dior the Whore was chauffeuring him around again, he was somewhere inside our house.

I'll skip giving you the room-by-room home-tour and tell you, instead, three of the more interesting places I've hidden, where of course Ricky was not: he was not in the garage in a parked vintage Corvette, curled up in the fetal position; he was not in the wine cellar alphabetizing bottles of Lodi red; and he had not decided to see if he could fit into the oversized armoire of guest bedroom number four.

The last place I looked, where of course he was: the bathroom attached to my studio above the garage. I knocked three times before opening the door, Please oh please don't let Ricky be dead in the tub, I pleaded as I turned the handle.

GHOST LIGHT

B EFORE JUNAH actually died, and just after I outgrew my
childish attempts on his life, I thought he actually had died
and it nearly scared me to death. We were fourteen and fifteen,
respectively, and we were home alone, which was a pretty big deal
considering it was a school night and it was after dark. Our parents were at some sort of town hall meeting concerning the long
stretch of greenbelts that separated Lodi from North Stockton.
And because the proposed legislation was about Eight Mile and
whether or not to allow the construction of a strip mall behind
what was now Chavez cherry stand, the meetings got rather heated and lasted well into the next morning: the fruit and asparagus
farmers on one side, the middle-class suburbanites—desirous of
larger stadiums for their high schools and newer tracts for their
homes—on the other and in between Ronnie Buck and J.T. Ga-
ramendi (the town developers), their pockets bulging with cash
for the sell-outs. My parents were on the green side, as opposed
to the greenback side, and my mother decorated the bumper of
her Volvo with a glossy red sticker that read: DEVELOPERS GO
BUILD IN HELL. My father, a self-proclaimed quiet farmer who
just wanted to be left alone to tend his grapes, gave impassioned
speeches about sprawl, gentrification, oak trees and egrets, and
was frequently quoted in the *News Sentinel*. In the morning, my
mother would perch at the high kitchen counter on a yellow
stool, her glasses just about to fall off her pointy nose, and read
the articles aloud while the family ate Johnny cakes and peaches
around the kitchen table. When she finished a column, she'd take
a sip of heavily sweetened coffee from an ancient teacup passed

down from my Polish grandmother, push her glasses back up on her face and reach for the scissors, the sound of shears slicing through newsprint mixing easily with the clicks of tines on teeth and knives on plates.

It had started as a normal night, Dad packing boxes of fly-ers and supporting documents into the Volvo, Mom icing small sugar cookies in the shape of trees and toads that read: SAVE ME. Junah and me in the barn, peeling the veneer off the rafters and tossing a masticated tennis ball to Gideon. No matter how hard or how long Junah threw the slimy green ball, Gideon would always fetch it. Bounding his shaggy mutt body in the hay, off the front porch, and even through an old, open, wood-framed window, Gideon was just happy to be.

In the valley, it was the time of year when the air changed. One day in September it would be 102 and then, with not so much as a Delta breeze to quiet the heat, the frost began to form on the vines at night, collecting in whimsical drops on whatever remained of the heavy, unpicked fruit. It was one of those nights when the air tasted so good that you couldn't stay inside, and so that night, without much else to do, we decided to walk the levee.

It had been a hot, dusty valley day. The kind of day that starts out hot and then grows exponentially hotter. The kind of day where the plows start up at seven—and not in the AM, like they do in the fall, but at night. As we walked the levee that separated our farm from the Stroud stead, Gideon sniffed out gophers and asparagus shoots with equal discretion, while Junah pointed towards the flood lights mounted to the roof racks of Warren Stroud's tractor and said, squatting down so his eyes were level with the light, It's got to be ten times harder, farming at night. At 6 AM it's hard enough, but at least you have light. Something to shield your eyes from, something to wear a brimmed hat against. But at night, he picked up a clod of sticky clay dirt and chucked it into the levee water, it's got to be ten times harder. To walk out the barn without shielding your eyes, to ride around on the Deere in the dark.

I never thought too much about it, I said pulling at one of the white danglies that hung off my cut-off shorts. But it's interesting. To beat the heat, I'd figure, though how do you suppose they keep the lines straight?

Instinct, Junah said, still squatting and squinting on the steep levee side.

And when I close my eyes that's the picture I have of him:

Tall. Bent at the middle and caught in the lights of a plow above the levee. His feet boot-clad and brown with dirt, his jeans torn at the hem and his t-shirt white and ringed with sweat. The dust his hands stirred up as he traced the dirt, unearthing clods and rocks and roots, made him indistinguishable from the waves of particle light the tractor beams spit his way. And then, just like that, with the turn of the tractor he was gone.

I thought for a moment that it was a trick. Something about my eyes adjusting from the direct light of the tractor to the muted light of a few far-off stars, but even after a moment, even after several moments, he was gone.

Junah? I called out, scanning the rows of grapevines stretched out to my left, Where are you?

He didn't answer, but Gideon did. Bounding up beside me like I was about to hand out treats, he licked my hand and barked twice. Quiet! I said. Then I turned, retracing my steps to the spot where Junah had crouched just a moment ago.

June-Bug you bastard, where the hell are you?

I could still see the lines his fingers had traced in the dirt and his boot prints walked southeast, like mine, but then stopped.

Gideon barked again and then started to whimper. There was something inside that told me something wasn't right. Something inside that pushed up the panic instead of just assuming, like I usually did in these instances, that Junah was playing hide-and-seek in the vineyard. That he was off chasing a peacock or simply faking me out. Even still I willed him to pop up and shout: Gotcha! Maybe throw a crawdad at my chest and then sprint towards the house where he'd dig into the whole carton of ice cream with a spoon, leaving the freezer door flapping in his haste.

Junah Francis! I shouted again, This isn't funny, where are you?

And then, when there was no reply, a final, Junah I'm calling Mom and Dad.

Laney Bamberger, that you carrying on over there? Mr. Stroud hollered, reaching the end of another line and turning the tractor back around.

Yeah, it's me, I said, holding up one hand to shield my eyes from the manufactured light, while with the other holding on to Gideon's collar—he had something against Stroud, or rather, Stroud had something against him.

You okay, honey? He asked, giving the squint eye to the dog. What's all that shoutin' 'bout?

Yeah, I'm fine Mr. Stroud, I waved him on. Knowing full well that to tell my parents would be one thing, but to involve the neighbors (the hardworking neighbors as my father so fondly referred to them as), well that would be quite another. But then, bathed in light, I looked down the incline and saw Junah's boot, bobbing about on the scummy levee surface.

I don't know what the words were that I screamed, or even if there were words at all. I just remember a strange sound coming from somewhere inside as I slid down the levee's bank and splashed, mouth open, still screaming, into the reclaimed water.

JUMP CUT

EVERYBODY IN the valley has their own version of the story: the story about the kid who gets drunk and drowns in the levee. It happens every three years or so, just after prom but before graduation or sometimes even on the first warm night after winter. The kid, most always a boy, most always a jock, was drunk and stupid, drunk and brave, drunk and young, drunk and showing off, drunk and—take your pick. Whichever you choose, he was above all drunk and forgetful that levee walls are slanted V-like and the algae sediment too slick to counter. So the drunk kid slips in, or jumps in, or falls in or whatever and then splashes about while the other kids laugh and drink and toss him a beer, sure he'll soon be able to get himself out, not realizing when the splashes turn from amusement into struggle. Not realizing until it's too late. Occasionally—and these are the stories with the happily-ever-after—someone will be sober. Occasionally disaster is narrowly avoided by someone who thinks enough to tie a thick rope to whomever's truck has the biggest bumper, lasso the swimmer and pull him up hog-style. But Junah wasn't drunk and unless he lost his balance, hit his head...how the hell?

JUNAH, I screamed, splashing through the water, holding up his boot and waving it at Stroud.

Junnnaaahhhh!

MID-ACT ANTICLIMAX

JUNAH WAS down the street at Jennifer Anne's. The story, when it came out, had something to do with her county fair lamb; and Junah, having spotted it escaped from its pen out of the corner of his eye, took off after the wooly critter with wordless stealth. To sneak up on it, he said. To catch it by surprise. And quietly too so that Gideon didn't catch on and give the lamb a scare. The boot, well he didn't know who's it was, but yeah, funny thing, it did look an awful lot like his. Maybe I should have slapped him. Maybe Mr. Stroud should have given both of us a firm scolding and perhaps even a licking, but when I saw Junah sitting on the porch holding out an asparagus spear to Jennifer Anne's lamb, I could only run to him. And Mr. Stroud, wore out from shouting and lifting me—hysterical—out of the levee hog-style, could only do the same.

And I wish I could say it ended there, an alarming misunderstanding. But it didn't. After I thought Junah was dead, after I had to live, again, with the empty thought of life without him, I knew I could never lose him. Just as sure as I knew I someday would.

SUPPORTING CAST

T WAS weird, but—as I stood in my studio bathroom holding my breath before flinging open the door that led to the oversized tub—I felt it all over again: the warm creep of the levee water, the dim beam of the tractor light, searching for Junah's bloated body, my own body flooded with fear, my eyes barely held open. Only this time the terror was unnamed. Clearly I didn't adore Ricky, at least not like Junah, but I had loved him beyond reason and up came sick feeling all over again. The twitch in my left eye. The deep breath before looking into the tub for a body. But, thank the Mexican God of Catholicism and Cigarettes, Ricky wasn't floating in the basin, his neck snapped from a slip. He was lying in the tub, fully-dressed in clothes of his own choosing, leafing through a bound business document and sucking on a cherry cough drop.

I shut the door and pretend not to hear him through the door as he yelled after me, Figured someone should get some real work done in this studio. Just like, when I saw him in the kitchen thirty minutes later, I pretended to be civil.

Pretending to be civil was infinitely easier than pretending that my heart was not about to fall out of my mouth. Pretending that anything higher than my knees didn't hurt was so much more manageable than pretending Ricky didn't fuck Dior. Pretending that the way Ricky used to look at me was void of sadness and disgust was just better than acknowledging the reality of his vacant gaze.

STAGE LEFT

N AN attempt to make up for the awkward standoff, drive-off, cut-your-finger-off insanity of the past night I made my way to the kitchen to make omelets.

Now I'm not going to pretend that I'm one of those women who's so far removed from the kitchen that she doesn't know where the eggs are, much less how to crack one. I may not be able to light the pilot or clean the crisper in the Sub-Zero, but I can make a mean Hungarian goulash or a chili verde with bite, and without question I can beat an egg.

Which is exactly what I was doing, beating, when Ricky breezed in and made his way towards the blender. As I whisked and stirred, making progressively more noise with each flick of my wrist, I watched him add two scoops of protein powder, a cup of soy, six strawberries and a whole banana to the glass pitcher. It was only when he reached for the egg carton and found it missing that he noticed me.

Denver or Spanish? I asked pouring the eggs into the sizzling pan.

He hesitated. I saw it in the movement of his pointer finger as it reached to press the liquefy button on the blender.

I watched the eggs bubble around the edges of the pan and pointed with a knife towards the chopping block where I had neat piles of diced ham, green peppers and cheddar and alternately potatoes, onion and green olive.

Wow, Mags, I wish I could have gotten some advance notice on all this. He looked to his watch and then back to me. It's just that I have the Pettersen proposal in T-minus thirty. He pressed the liquefy button. Sorry, babe.

No worries, I dropped a handful of cheese into the pan and flipped the eggs, smacking the pan down hard against the stovetop.

Stop it, Mags. I don't have time for all this right now. I'm a little stressed, in case you can't tell. And the numbers aren't coming through like they used to.

What? I asked, ignoring the eggs and turning to face Ricky. Since when don't our numbers add up? Do you want me to go to the office and take a look? I began mentally scanning the business section of my closet. Definitely the vintage Chanel suit with the lambskin skinners.

No, Ricky said, almost immediately, putting a wrinkle in my imaginary wardrobe. He very deliberately stepped around me and made his way to the shelf that kept the stainless-steel travel mugs. Stay home, he said to me. Take Puck to the spa or something.

No, really, I said, turning the heat down and handing Ricky the matching lid for his mug. It's no problem.

I have it under control, Ricky said, but if you really want to do something you can help me find my driving goggles.

Third drawer of the buffet, I said, like a reflex.

Not my regular ones, my driving glasses. I'm taking the 'Vette. Top down, you know?

I paused for a second, tapped my spatula against the side of the pan and then, calling his bluff said, Upstairs in your closet, second shelf on the left, the summer accessory section.

Great, he said, heading up, taking the stairs two at a time.

I pushed stop on the blender, poured the contents into his mug and placed it next to his briefcase.

Once I was sure he was upstairs, I opened his briefcase and looked inside. In addition to the Pettersen proposal, a pack of spearmint-flavored Orbit gum, three proofs of the new ad campaign and a Forbes article on the IBWA Bottled Water Hall of Fame, there was a handwritten note from Dior:

Congrats on the Aqua Award. Enjoyed working with you on our little project last night. If you need anything…

I picked up the note and hid it under the toaster. Then I picked up the skillet held it over Ricky's briefcase and slipped the omelet inside.

When Immelda, followed by Ricky wearing his hopelessly goofy driving goggles, came down the stairs I was standing by the front door, Ricky's briefcase in one hand and his protein shake in the other.

Careful, I smiled to Ricky, the 'Vette doesn't have cup holders and you wouldn't want to make a spill.

Right he said, setting the Corvette keys on the valet and picking up the keys to the Mercedes instead.

Have a nice day, he said, kissing me on the forehead and making his preoccupied way out the door.

You too, I said.

The door shut.

AFTER HE left I stood looking at the doorframe, listening for the throaty purr of the CL 63 as it slid out the drive. But I couldn't hear it. What I heard instead was Immelda smacking a rug against the banister inside the house and the invisible sound of a gazillion microparticles of dust smacking against walls and couches, hardwood floors and Tiffany lamps.

While Immelda worked her magic against the upholstery, I decided to go for a drive. Taking a cue from Ricky, I knotted a cherry scarf around my head, pushed my Didion frames against my cheeks and slipped my fingers into the soft white leather of my driving gloves. If it was a top down day, I was gonna take the 'Vette.

ACT RHYTHM

I LIKE to drive. Not to anywhere in particular because I have no place in particular to go, but I'm addicted to freeways. The 405 to the 10 to the 110 to the 101. It's so L.A. I used to like driving more when I had a piece-of-shit Escort. It was a stick shift and unreliable and I never knew where I'd end up stranded. Since the move to L.A., nothing's been unreliable, at least in terms of cars and appliances. Whenever something breaks and I attempt to fix it, Ricky goes all red in the face.

Magdalena, there are people for that, he says.

I used to be afraid of *those* people. When I first moved to L.A. my mother would download stories off the internet about everything that happened to L.A. women. Then she would e-mail them to me. Her favorites were car jackings and wives raped in their own homes by plumbers and pool men. For a good year and a half, whenever the people would come over to carpet, clean, deliver or fix, I would sit on the porch with my cell phone and a container of carefully concealed Mace. One day the guy who was delivering our Hepplewhite sideboard was early. Can you imagine that? Early in L.A. So I didn't have time to prepare. I actually had to talk to him. We had a very nice conversation about yachting. He had just bought a Tartan 37-footer named *Molly Putz* and we talked about tacking, marina fees, tall teak toe rails and shellac. Fuck me, but who knew? I suppose it figures, though, the amount of money Ricky pays him—correct that, the amount of money we pay him—to deliver, times seven or eight deliveries a day, damned if I wouldn't buy a boat too.

Now I consider breaking things just for conversation. Like

the Tank. It's silver and colossal and has a gazillion cylinders, so I run over things for adventure. It started with those little concrete blocks that separate parking spaces; initially I had to escape an irate gas man, but once I realized I could do it, I started to run things over on a regular basis. My favorites are orange tubes. Not the cones, those get caught in between your tires and can't clear the muffler so you end up dragging them for a block or two and people look at you funny. But the orange tubes, they're taller and usually stuck to the asphalt by a black hexagon. They're also a harder plastic so when you run over them you get a nice *click-thump* rather than just a *chub*. The trouble is the tubes are usually located on on-ramps to alert your attention to cement dividers, so it's quite a trick running over the tubes and still clearing the concrete. A trick I'll most likely be avoiding today, considering the 'Vette and all. I mean I'll be the first to admit that I'm not the pinnacle of caution, but I'm not exactly malicious either. Although I should add—not many people know this—when you're in a Polo White '53 'Vette with a personalized license plate that reads ARTGRL, you can't see the front from the back, parking's a bitch and you can forget cutting anyone off.

The best part about freeways is the lane change. I like to cross from middle to fast without hitting the reflective bumps that divide the road. It takes a lot of practice, especially at speeds above sixty, but if you tune into the blinker, if you play the clicks of the flashing green light like a metronome, you can usually succeed provided some asshole—the type who refuses the courtesy wave—doesn't speed up when he sees you attempting the merge. I always give the courtesy wave; it's like waiting the requisite three seconds before making a left on yellow: survival. If I were a cop, I'd ticket anyone who didn't wave. It's inexcusable. Almost as bad as strutting down Rodeo with a Prada knock-off bought from a vendor on Venice Beach or fucking another woman's husband.

I said *almost* all right?

CROSSROADS

I LIKE to drive.

This is different from driving well.

Which will make it totally easy to believe that I crashed the car. On purpose.

I mean who would question it, right?

Not the purpose part, but the crash.

Think James Dean meets Isadora Duncan, but without the scarf-decapitation part. Camus with Grace Kelly beside him, snugging up in a convertible to catch a thief until they accidently hit a tree, but without the fatal injuries part. Or Jayne Mansfield, on the tail end of a tractor trailer in a particularly dark game of chicken, without, of course, the death part. And if it were big enough and loud enough in front of our office, or better yet snarling up traffic on Sunset, it might actually be believable, right? Or at least visible on the sixteenth floor where Ricky, taking a break from his canoodling with Dior to see what all the fuss is about—the sirens and honking and general fracas—might be forced to peek out his window. Look down and see me, standing on the hood of the crumpled Corvette, a survivor!

STRUCTURE

W/HEN WE first moved to L.A. my favorite thing to say was, That's so L.A. I used it to describe just about everything from fake boobs to traffic. Then I got implants and started to drive. Drive not to go someplace, but as sport. On the 10 you can pick out the regulars from the tourists. Those who merge left just before the lane ends and then have to merge back right again versus those who know the La Brea shortcut: exit but don't ever get off. During a crunch you can save five minutes plus if there's a pile-up. My favorite time to drive is early morning and right before dark. I like the added thrill of the sun in your eyes. It throws mirage into the game and the DJs are at their prime.

Sig alert on the Santa Monica Freeway West, the Shady Lady hums through my speakers. Since nobody's going anywhere anyhow I'll take caller number nine for some naked rush hour bingo.

I kid you not. Bingo. Naked. In rush hour.

Shady Lady here. Name, make and license plate, please.

Oh hi-yee! I'm Alyson, with a y, and I'm in a silver 325i on the 10 West, wearing pink and black—

Which, as you may realize, is the physical description of a gazillion people on the 10, but everyone plays along.

Okay listeners we're on the prowl for a silver Beemer license 1MY325I. If you see her, honk. And Alyson, you know the rules: you lose a piece of clothing for every honk you hear.

As if there isn't enough honking on the 10. As if taking your clothes off while stuck in traffic weren't so L.A.

After a while Ricky banned me from saying it ever again. First off, he huffed, nothing is *so* L.A., and secondly, we are *not* in

L.A., we're in Beverly Hills. It's a totally different thing.

I said okay, but I really wanted to point out that differentiating himself from Los Angeles proper was, itself, *so* L.A. Of course, Ricky doesn't understand this. Ricky doesn't understand a lot of things. For example, Ricky is really happy about my career in art. I am bored out of my fucking—

My fucking phone is ringing. Vibrating around in the ashtray while it sings Ricky's *Take Me Out To The Ballgame* ring.

Hello?

What the hell, Mags?

I know. Traffic's a bitch, isn't it?

That's not what I'm talking about.

What? Honey, you're breaking up. I'm on the 10, near the Robertson exit. You know how it gets spotty, I lied. He was coming through clear as water.

That was the Pettersen proposal you breakfasted on. Pettersen, as in how I plan to pay for that gas-guzzling G500 you're motoring about in.

He wasn't fooling anyone. I knew he paid cash for the Mercedes. In full. And besides he never planned on anything. We were above that now.

I'm not motoring about in the G500. I'm in the 'Vette.

You're in what? Ricky said.

What? I repeated. Babe, I really can't hear you.

Get off the freeway, Ricky said. Go straight home. No. Wait. Just park. I'll send someone 'round to get you.

I set the phone in my lap and fiddled with the radio dial.

Love you too, I said. Call you back when I get better recep—I tapped the end call button.

I WAS in the fast lane, cruising along at ten, maybe fifteen miles an hour. I sighed and flipped on my blinker, not because Ricky told me to, but because it felt like time to make a graceful exit, to head for the hills, to cruise the canyons. I took Robertson north through SoRo past Pico and Olympic and Wilshire as the used car dealerships of Crestwood melted into the kosher delis of Beverlywood turned to the lavish boutiques of Beverly Hills.

The phone rang; I let it go through to voicemail.

The phone rang again; I clicked the reject button.

The phone rang a third time; I answered, didn't say anything and then hung up.

Before it could ring a fourth, Ricky's smiling face dancing across the ID panel of the receiver, I clicked messages and clicked again on voice mail. Phone to my ear, the mechanical voice asked for my password.

Blonde, I said into the voice recognition system.

Error, It spoke back. Please speak or press your password again now.

Blonde, I repeated.

Error, it said again. Please speak or press...

I took the phone away from my ear: 2-5-check-the-road-6-check-the-road-6-check-the-road, I typed when, 3-check-the-road, the light at the intersection of Beverly turned yellow and instead of speeding up the car ahead of me, a fucking blue Mini, slowed to a fuck! stop. I slammed on my brakes and checked the rearview simultaneously. My hands sweat through the soft white leather of my gloves. I wasn't going to stop in time. I cranked the wheel hard, too hard, right and—though I almost made it into a boutique parking lot—I rolled instead into a giant pole.

When I opened my eyes there wasn't any smoke or a geyser of water from some broken gasket like I expected. There was no airbag so the steering column remained intact, and I hugged the wheel desperately. I looked around expecting a crowd, but with the exception of a couple of gawkers from the outdoor café across the street no one stared. In fact, no one had even stopped. I unbuckled my seatbelt. This was so exactly not how I had planned it. No on purpose. No fanfare or paparazzi. Not even so much as a traffic detour. Just a lopsided solitary accident.

You okay? An espresso-drinking kid shouted from across

the street. I waved my gloved hand affirmatively in the air, I'm fine. I opened the driver's door and then shut it again, afraid to step outside and assess the damage. Instead I looked to the giant pole and followed it up, twenty feet, maybe more, to where a billboard advertising exotic car rentals and private planes was perched high above. The phone rang a fourth time. I opened the door again, this time without looking; and, still without looking, I stepped out onto the sidewalk and walked down the street in search of a bathroom, a bar and a straw in exactly that order.

TYPECAST

A T THE Ivy I tossed the valet my keys and, when he looked bewildered towards the curb where my car did not sit idling, I shrugged and pointed toward the billboard a half block down. The long-haired girl who passed out menus politely pretended not to notice my tears as she led me to my table of one and sat me outside near the faux-fence beneath a white umbrella. I sat facing south, my back to the wreck, and because it wasn't yet noon I ordered three chocolate chip cookies, which were soft and gooey, and a bottle of cabernet that I insisted upon pouring myself. Between my first and second glass I sent a 911 text to Puck. Instead of typing anything I just held my phone above my head and snapped a picture in the direction of the billboard, a picture of the menu and my cookies and my bottle of wine. Between my second and third glass I counted the number of nights in the last year Ricky was supposedly away on business: ninety-three. Between my third and fourth glass I ordered three more cookies.

Mag-da-lane-a! Is that you? Adair, smelling of lilac and followed by Cheri, sashayed over to the table and bent down as if to kiss me on the cheek. I shoved an entire cookie into my mouth and said a mumbled, No.

No, honey, I've never met you before in my life, and if you'll excuse me, I brushed some crumbs from my lap as I reached for my Berkin bag, I've got to be going. I stood up, slapped a credit card on the table and left, Cheri looking incredulous and Adair no doubt smirking in my absence.

I flew past the long-haired girl who said something like have

222

a nice day or maybe valet and when I reached the curb I walked fast in the opposite direction. I knew that speed—as opposed to, say, direct eye contact—was the only way to keep back the tears that were dangerously close to welling over. I knew that if I walked fast enough in my heels, that if I could breeze past the boutiques and flower shops and designer hardware stores, the Juicy and the amaryllis and the clawfoot tubs, the tears would stay in. But if I slowed, if I faltered, if the glue or nails or whatever it was keeping my heel to my sole should separate and crack and cause me to fall in a sort of half heap on the corner, the tears would slip out, the tears slide out, the tears are starting, slow at first and now frenzied. A frenzied sobbing ridiculous girl, tied-up in a cherry-red scarf, sitting on the curb in a Jackie O. dress with her taffeta petticoats riding up in a pout around her knees, crying about a broken shoe, a broken car, a broken heart and so much more.

DEUS EX MACHINA

WITH ONE bare foot in the gutter and my butt still seated on the curb, the tears were still turning, pouring out tumultuous when I met Quentin.

That bad huh? he said, sitting down beside me but not too close. Just kind of there, at a safe distance, but there all the same.

I pushed my glasses hard against my face, Yes.

He didn't ask more. Wasn't one of those people who pretend to be concerned about blubbering women on the sidewalk. He just sat down beside me and lit a cigarette.

For me it was a better version of those walk-up psychics who, walking down Melrose, sense your aura could use a little cleansing and feel the need, for a small fee, to schedule you a reading. Quentin was in the right place at the right time, or maybe I was.

He said, Crying get you much?

I stopped then. Maybe even I laughed. Ricky doesn't like it when I cry. The first time I cried I thought he was going to start crying, too. He got all cute and crazy and for that moment I could have gotten away with anything. But later, Ricky didn't care anymore if I cried or not. He thought that two years was enough to get over anything, including Junah. He started calling me melodramatic. Then he said, You cry so much your tears have lost their meaning. That really made me cry.

What Ricky didn't know, couldn't possibly understand, was that the tears were a good thing. That my heart still had enough of him in it to cry over. When the tears stopped it would be worse. Much, much worse. But I didn't say as much to Quentin. What I said instead was, Cigarette?

He flipped out a package of Lucky Strikes.

I took one and held it lit in my hand a long time: inhaled, coughed, exhaled, before I said, When I was sixteen I convinced my daddy to let me borrow his 1936 Chevy Pro Street pickup.

I'll bet you did, Quentin said, smoke escaping as he spoke.

Cotton-candy blue and newly restored, he threw me the keys, much to my mother's horror, and said, Drive safe. Clearly I wasn't listening or maybe I was more concerned with securing my scarf to my hair. I turned the wrong way down a one-way street and collided with an officer of the peace. I cried.

Huh, Quentin coughed, looking down my legs to my lavender toenails.

But a quiet, one tear dripping from beneath my large gold sunglasses kind of cry, and said I was sorry. I got off.

Quentin shook his head and put out his cigarette on the chipped gray curb before crushing the butt with his shoe, Goddamn girls.

I ignored him and, cigarette still in hand, pushed back a cuticle. With daddy I cried huge, hiccuppy, my life is going to end here and now kind of sobs. I got off again.

Yup, Quentin said, and shrugged as he pulled in his legs. He had a lot of leg, legs that nearly reached his chin, and he hadn't the faintest idea of what to do with them hunched along the curb. Probably when he went out for a smoke he would perch on the fire hydrant or lean up against the wall watching people pass, but next to me his awkwardness was thin and comfortable, his tallness familiar. He had long hair that wasn't stringy or greasy but voluminous, and it sort of waved in unkempt curls around his shoulders. He would have made a beautiful girl had his Adam's apple not jutted out considerably. He made an all right guy too.

But, I said, you can't just keep on doing it. The crying. And getting away with it. The crashing. It's like after a while when they run your plates their little computer thingy spits out Crier.

That's funny, Quentin said. Like at the dentist. After my name it reads Biter. They've got us figured out.

Anyhow, I continued, letting the cigarette grow slowly into ash, I just did it again, only different, in my '53 Corvette.

Had there been water in Quentin's mouth, had he been sucking on candy or chewing tobacco, surely he would have choked it up his nose, but because his mouth was dry and his eyes locked with mine, he simply let down his shoulders and said, You have a '53 'Vette?

Well I did, I said, motioning towards the street. But now it's kind of wrecked.

And you're sure it's a '53?

That's what they tell me.

As in first model run and you crashed—

Yes, I said before he could finish.

He didn't say anything then. He pulled out his cigarettes and banged them against a strip of silver duct tape on his palm. Maybe he didn't believe me. Regardless, he reached into his wallet and held out a card. I took it but I don't think he intended to give it to me. I could tell by the way he paused when pulling out his wallet, the way his finger twitched a little when it went beneath the photo of him and a pretty red-haired girl to retrieve it, the way he held it in his hand a little too long, so that the corner was wet with thumb perspiration before he handed it over. He said the guys at La Cienega Collision specialized in classics and could work something out. He said he had a cousin or something. He said, Tell 'em Quentin sent you. And then he said, What color?

ARCHPLOT

ASSHOLE.

The '53 'Vette only comes in one color: Polo White with red interior. I would have said as much to Quentin and his little trick of a question but it didn't really seem relevant.

Help me up? I said instead, holding out my hands.

He hesitated again, for just a moment too long, and then, tossing his cigarette into the gutter, he grabbed my hands in his and pulled me up off the curb.

His hands were dry and calloused, something I didn't expect from such a pretty face, and the tape across his left palm was sticky.

Standing up on the curb, one red d'Orsay pump on my foot and the other heelless and broken on the sidewalk, I was still shorter than Quentin who stood in the street, in a vintage pair of Pumas, holding my hands.

Unusual.

Not only because I'm taller than most girls, but with three-inch heels and a step up from the curb, I'm usually taller than most boys, too. But as I stood looking at Quentin, I had to kind of tilt my head to look him in the eye. When our eyes met he dropped my hands, but kept looking at me intently.

What? I asked, smoothing out the flounce of my dress.

Nothing, he said, stuffing a long-fingered hand into his front pocket, you're just tall. Or taller, rather.

Not taller than you I said, breaking the gaze—which had, in fact, dried up my tears completely—and moving my eyes up his face to the sky.

But I'm a guy and you, he said, with a squint, are not.

No, I said, shaking my head, I very much am not.

Hey, he said, pulling his hand from his pocket and reaching out in an apologetic gesture, tall is sexy. I like tall, especially on teary, shoeless girls. My delivery's usually cooler—it's just that I can't shake the feeling that I know you from somewhere.

Now it was my turn to smirk. Yeah, that's real original. But no, sorry to say, I don't think we've met. But if you want, to meet me I mean, I'll buy you a tall drink of something.

He paused and looked to an invisible watch on his naked wrist, Isn't it kind of early?

I pulled my phone from my crocodile Birkin bag, It's 12:42, I said and waited, tottering on my one good shoe, my other barefoot on tiptoe.

He picked at the tape on his left palm, looked me over and then said, Okay, but not here.

STAGE RIGHT

QUENTIN MADE it a point not to drink on the Westside. He claimed all the bars were conspicuously pretty and the glasses they poured their sugary spirits in too tall. He liked a short glass and a dirty bar. Especially, he said, as he held open the door of a utility truck so I could slide inside, if I'm going to drink—in the daylight—with a girl like you.

He drove us all the way downtown to a pretty dirty place called the Redwood Bar.

The Redwood was cozy and dimly lit, or at least it appeared to be from the outside. And although I wasn't exactly dressed for the salty pirate panache that appeared the chosen décor, I would have gladly saddled up at the bar next to Quentin while the bald and tattooed tender poured us something strong, preferably with ice. The trouble was, the bar was closed. Well not closed to everyone, just closed to us.

If you have to get technical, the sign read RESERVED. Reserved for an all-girl Japanese garage-rock baby shower, and I don't know about Quentin but I sure as hell hadn't brought a gift.

Shit, Quentin said, as a thin girl wearing fishnet tights and fluffy Mini Mouse ears pushed past us and into the bar. This is exactly why I don't drink in the daylight.

Good thing I do, I said. Quentin laughed and shook his head, Good thing, he said as he followed me a half block over and three blocks down to the teal and mustard splendor of Foodcourt. Piñatas of all sizes hung from the ceiling, and as we walked down the crowded aisles—*menudo* or *sopa de albondigas?*—their crepe-paper tails brushed against the height of Quentin's head.

Near the back was a liquor store. Not a bar exactly, but there were bar stools, and if you could manage to get the cap off your Negro Modelo or Dos Equis, well then you could sit on a worn Formica stool and drink. I mean it's not exactly gin, I said, looking Quentin straight in the eye, but at least it's something.

Cheers to that, Quentin said, as he used the counter top to remove first my cap and then his, making sure to rub both bottle lips on the underside of his t-shirt before handing one over to me.

Thank you, I said, as I tipped my bottle in his direction.

I do what I can, Quentin said, and he took an unusually long sip.

And then it got quiet. To fill the space between speech, I took successive sips of my beer while Quentin busied himself by picking at the duct tape stuck to his left palm. The floor was filthy and although I didn't care much about the bottom of my bare feet— though probably I should have, Ricky would have—I made sure to hang my purse off the bend of my knee. Which meant that every so often the stiff strap would slide down towards the floor and I would have to quickly hitch it back up before the crocodile touched the gum-soiled cement. It was something to do while figuring out what the hell to say to the tall stranger seated on my right. And yet, here's the thing: sitting silently next to Quentin felt all right. It was comfortable even. I had all sorts of things I could say, like: Where are you from? or What do you do when the sadness gets so heavy you think it will crush you? or Ever killed anybody? but for the first time in a long time I didn't feel the need to say anything. And it felt good. To sit. And drink. And be quiet, together. Especially when, as my purse strap slid down for the gazillionth time, it was Quentin who rescued it and, sliding his finger across my knee and up my leg, set the strap right.

Between the two of us we finished off seven bottles of Bohemia, and then Quentin slid off his barstool and held out his hand to help me off mine. I grabbed the hand, still sticky with duct tape, and I rubbed my thumb down the back of his wrist, to say thanks.

He looked at my thumb. At my hand holding his, and he squeezed.

Just what exactly are you hiding under there? I asked, touching the tape gently, sure that beneath it was a machete wound or, at the very least, a saber-toothed shark bite. Quentin shrugged and looked at his invisible watch.

Gotta get to work, he said, kicking a half-eaten churro on the sidewalk between us. I'm twelve minutes late already.

I looked him over then, his tattered blue jeans and tight white t-shirt. Definitely not business, but not a waiter either. Most likely blue collar, but maybe, I crossed my fingers in my mind, maybe an actor, maybe a poet, maybe just maybe Quentin did art.

Where's work?

On the Westside, he nodded towards his yellow utility truck. Some blonde supposedly drove her car into a billboard. I'm the guy who has to fix it.

I smiled and stepped out of my one good shoe. Barefoot on South Broadway between Third and Fourth, I waved and walked in the opposite direction of Quentin who walked down and then across the street.

CLIMAX AND CHARACTER

STANDING IN front of the Guadalupe Wedding Chapel I waited for a cab, and when it arrived it wasn't yellow. It was green with a billboard for Viagra on the roof.

Why isn't anything like the movies?

I got in, cringed as my bare feet touched the gritty floorboards and told the driver to head west, towards Diamond Myst.

I could have called Ricky. I could have called his secretary and had her send over a driver and the company car. Hell, I could have called our Mercedes dealer and had them drop off a loaner Tank, but I called Puck and left a message: Keys at the Ivy, car at the pole. And I sat on the grubby vinyl bench seat in my frilly-fru-fru dress as we drove to the office because I wanted to see Ricky's face when I told him about the 'Vette.

I gave the driver a fifty and asked him to wait. Said that I'd only be a minute. And as I rode the elevator up to the sixteenth floor I rehearsed what I would say to Ricky. I anticipated the dramatic pause I would leave for him to explode, for me to burst into tears, for him to come to his senses and embrace me in an it's-okay-it's-only-a-car-I'm-glad-you're-all-right-hug. Or, alternatively, not come to his senses in which case I'd start screaming and create such a high-profile and thoroughly public ruckus that he'd have no choice but to lower his voice and apologize, embracing me in a slightly less sincere, yet still forgiving hug.

A hug, that's why I needed to go to the office in person. If only Ricky would hug me again, like he used to, like he meant it.

I TOOK a deep breath and walked out of the elevator. His secretary was on the phone and as she saw me approach she covered the mouthpiece with her hand and whisper-said to me, Ricky's in a meeting right now.

Right, I said gliding past her in my bare feet.

No really! she said, as my hand reached for the doorknob to Ricky's office, It's best if you don't—

I opened the door.

Inside, instead of finding a half-dozen important looking executives scratching their heads and shouting over one another about cost analysis and market figures, there was just Dior sitting in Ricky's silver Herman Miller chair, her feet on his desk and her hair falling long across her back. Just Dior and Ricky (!) who was leaning over her shoulder, close enough to smell the rosemary mint of her shampoo, close enough to brush his lips against her naked neck as they talked in low whispers.

Wow, I said, with no hint of exclamation.

Mags, Ricky said, he stood up and took a few steps away from Dior, what are you doing here?

Walking in on a very important meeting, apparently.

Dior stood up. She smoothed her charcoal gray pencil skirt over her thighs and looked, embarrassed, to her stocking-clad feet as she stuttered to explain, We were just going over the Luxe figures...

No really, I said walking across the plush pile rug, make yourself comfortable. In fact, since you aren't using these, I picked up her shoes, Chloe peeptoe pumps, I'm sure you won't mind if I borrow them. I broke mine when I crashed the 'Vette. I paused then, as I dramatically put first one foot, and then the other, on Ricky's desk and slid on Dior's shoes.

You know, Ricky, the 1953, only three hundred ever made, John fucking Wayne sold it because he was—like me—too tall to fit in it, Polo White 'Vette you bought from the *Neiman Marcus Christmas Book* Fantasy Section and gifted to me last Christmas? Well I ran it into a billboard. On purpose.

I didn't wait for him to respond. In fact I didn't even look at his face. Throughout my entire monologue, a monologue completely contrary to the ones I'd composed on the elevator ride up, I looked only at Dior. Then, turning on borrowed heels, I left.

IDEALIST, PESSIMIST, IRONIST

DIOR HAD sharp green eyes and big feet. I had to take precise, planted steps and hold on to the front of her pumps with curled toes to keep from stepping out of them. Thankfully, I could take it slow. After walking out of the office and not slamming the door I realized that no one was following me. That Ricky wasn't running after me. That I was in the elevator, and then the lobby, and finally back in the green cab, quiet and alone.

No really, completely alone.

The cabby, keys still in the ignition and cab still running, was nowhere to be found. I opened the back passenger-side door, grateful it was unlocked, and sat silently inside. I pushed my oversized sunglasses tight against my cheeks and waited for the tears but they didn't come. So I reached my arm through the small opening in the Plexiglas partition that divided the cab into front and back and honked the horn. Nothing. I picked at the layers of pink and red netting that stuck out from the bottom of my maraschino dress. Still nothing. I reached my arm through the divide and gave two more honks, longer this time and if at all possible with attitude. When he still failed to arrive I picked up my phone and sent another text to Puck.

411, I typed and then snapped a self-portrait of me inside the cab. It wasn't an emergency anymore, it was just a fact. Fact: I was sitting in the backseat of a green cab in front of the building that Fact: housed a cooperation that I created, but Fact: no longer worked for while my husband Fact: quite possibly screwed an intern with excellent, but Fact: expensive taste, which made me wonder just how much were we paying her that she could afford Chloe anyhow? JesusMaryandJoseph, was I blind? Of course we were paying her a fucking fortune. She was fucking the CEO.

Solidarity my—Pilates-toned, laser-treated, sunless-tanned—ass.

I reached my arm to the front, about to honk a fourth time when the cabby appeared, carrying two double ice-blended caramel macchiatos with whip. He handed me the one with part of the paper still attached to the top of the straw.

I took it, felt the cold of the ice as it perspired through the plastic cup and said, Thank you.

No problem. He placed his drink in the cup holder and looked at me through the rearview, Where to?

Home, I said. I want to go home.

CONTROLLING IDEA

MAYBE MY mother was right. Maybe it was time to go home to the brown ranch I grew up in, because suddenly I wanted nothing more than to crawl under the green-gingham bedspread of my childhood and sleep. I wanted to love Ricky as I loved Junah: completely. I wanted to love him to death. And not in the I'm so furious I could kill you kind of way, but in the I love you so intensely, so madly and insanely that I sometimes dream of pushing you off tall places, of suffocating you in your sleep, of beating you senseless with a shoe, my love for you is so fierce.

THE GAP IN PROGRESSION

LICKED the whipped cream from the top of my drink and debated telling the cabby to head north on the 5, but figured a seven-hour metered ride through the central valley might be pressing my luck, so I gave him my address in Beverly Hills.

He let me out, by request, at the end of the circular drive, near the side door. I handed him another fifty and offered to throw away his coffee cup. He declined, gave me a funny half smile and headed back down the drive.

Just after he turned left onto Bedford and the lime green of his cab disappeared into the lush foliage that lined our street, I realized I didn't have my keys. That they were probably still neatly hung on a hook, sans car, in the valet box at the Ivy—which was really fucking fabulous, especially since Immelda was most likely at her yoga class. So, without even trying to knock on the door that led to the big house, I went through the garage to my studio.

INSIDE I headed towards the bar, which was artfully disguised behind a Cindy Sherman (original) print, when something decidedly male coughed. I grabbed a Costco-sized bottle of gin by the neck and spun around, holding the green glass in front of me like a weapon. Puck, sprawled across the chaise and flipping through fashion magazines said, No thanks, I'm not thirsty.

Damn it, Puck, you know how I am...how I get... I unscrewed the cap of the bottle and poured.

Long day?

You don't know the half of it, I took a sip.

Try me, he said sitting up and smoothing out a spot next to him for me to sit.

So I sat and I tried.

The car and the cookies were easy to explain. Quentin—a little more difficult—so I decided to leave him out—but Ricky and Dior and Dior and Ricky, how do I even?

So I tried.

RHETORIC

WHEN RICKY started saying mean things—and by mean I mean those really mean things you can't come back from—when he started saying those really mean things they sounded like: Maybe if you made something of yourself instead of making yourself another drink like your mother, maybe then you'd stop blaming everyone else for fucking up your own life.

They sounded like: I never knew there could be so much space between two bodies on a California king bed, so much space it may as well be the loneliest place in the world.

They sounded like: Who are you (his finger pressing pointedly into the saline filler of my tits, his eyes looking cross at my Jeuvedermed lips) and where is the girl I fell in love with? Just where exactly is that girl right now?

THE NATURE OF CHOICE

WAIT, LET me get this straight, Puck said, when we were eating Thai takeout from white cardboard boxes and I had finally managed to get out most of the story of Ricky, and Dior, and that damn Corvette.

When you walked in on them, they were—wait for it—whispering?

I pushed a piece of bamboo shoot around the bottom of my takeout container with my chopsticks and said, Technically, yes, but—

No buts, Puck held his hand out—STOP—in front of me, I just want the facts.

Yes, I nodded, while putting a piece of green curry chicken in my mouth.

And they were fully clothed?

Except for those, I pointed towards Dior's shoes.

Okay, so no one was untucked, their lips were not locked and everybody's hands were above the breasts?

Yes, but—

But what?

But I could tell.

Mags, Puck said, sliding closer to me on the couch and putting his head on my shoulder, are you sure you're not confusing what you want to happen with what is actually happening?

Why on earth would I, would anyone, actually *want* their husband to cheat on them?

I don't know, said Puck. You tell me.

Tell you what? I said, pushing away from Puck. That if I had a baby, a boy around five or six, that maybe I could just look the other way while my husband fucks half of L.A. Maybe, for the sake of the family I could just suck it up and make out with the pool boy? Well I won't. Because I don't need to be reminded that I don't have a kid or even a kid brother because Junah, as you know, is dead.

Magdalena, don't.

Don't what? I stood up spilling glass noodles across my lap.

Don't go there, Puck said, trying to redirect my anger with the calm of his voice.

Why not? Maybe there is exactly where I should go. Maybe I should just go out and fuck senseless the first married man I find. Fuck him to even the score. Fuck him to find out how it's done. Nail him and then take notes. I mean why wait? Why lounge around my house in Beverly Hills becoming the best bimbo I can be all the while waiting to walk in on my replacement? Why not just load up the Tank with Saks' summer line and leave?

Well maybe you should. Leave, Puck said. Go back to your ranch or whatever it is. But I can tell you one thing, fucking a married man isn't going to make Ricky love you more.

Fuck you.

No really, maybe you're right, he said, dangling my key ring in front of me. Maybe you don't belong in L.A. You can take the girl out of the valley but—

Seriously, I snatched my keys from his outstretched hand. I am just barely holding on here and you think a weekend with Mom and her bottle, watching Dad barbecue his dinner in the shed, is going to snap me back to reality?

Well I sure as hell hope something does, because it's about time you realize Junah isn't coming back.

I slapped him then, straight across the face, with my keys still in my open palm.

He didn't say anything. Not even ouch. Instead he pursed his lips into a thin, tight line and left. The lingering smack of hands and keys against soft face flesh echoed in the studio air.

TAKE FOUR

THE INCITING INCIDENT

I WANT to be the *other* woman. You know, the one who fucks your husband while you're PTAing with the kids, the one who spends alternate Tuesday, Thursday and Sunday mornings with your fiancée while you're Yoga-wrapped in a salutation to the sun. I want to wear ninety-dollar panties and do it doggy-style. I want to hang half-off the tailgate of your boyfriend's burgundy F150 while he fucks me like a racehorse. I want to swallow. I want to suck.

But I want to do other things too. I plan to listen well and I won't nag. Not about the laundry or the bills or the baby. I won't be the one who pressured him to marry me when we were twenty-three and I sure as hell won't make him make nice to my parents.

Home-wrecker.

Harlot.

If you had asked me two days ago I would have told you I preferred things the old fashioned way: Highway 99 over the 5, tangerines with seeds, marriage. But not today.

Today I say, Fuck it. Or rather, Fuck me. Because today I want to be unfaithful. I want to know, firsthand, how it's done.

THE POLITICS
OF STORY DESIGN

LEAVING DIDN'T take long really. I mean not as long as you
might think. For some reason, the leavers—divorcées and
otherwise—always try to make you believe they've been meditat-
ing on their departure for years: *Do I go? Do I not go? If I leave will
I maintain my eligibility on his dental plan? If I stay will I maintain my sanity?* Turns out all it takes is one really long day and—
poof—the car you didn't crash is packed and you're wearing the
other woman's shoes and angling for cones on the interstate.

Driving the Tank with one hand, I grabbed my purse with
the other and dug for my wallet. There, after some major shifting, searching and serious break squealing, stuck between my
Bloomingdales charge and my black AmEx was a card for La
Cienega Collision with Quentin penciled on the back.

THE QUEST

SUPPOSE I was expecting to find Quentin greasy and under the belly of a '67 Barracuda Formula S or maybe a Lime Lite Green '69 GTO, something classic with a loud engine and some muscle. He'd be on his back on one of those roller thingies and I'd walk up, straddle his long legs and fish him out. In my mind, it would take him a moment to realize I was there. Maybe a guy named Sal or Tony would give a low whistle or a Yo Quentin, to clue him in, but probably it would be just us. And he would look down or across or however it is you look out from under a car and see my ostrich-feathered pumps, the dimple above my left ankle, and ever so slowly he'd come. Sliding on his back until he was firmly between my legs. He'd be polite. Shielding his eyes from the noon sun and leaving a greasy smudge across his forehead, he'd say, Hey, while trying to sit up and I'd say Hi, putting my foot on his chest and pushing him down, and out like a cigarette butt. He'd pretend to be surprised, maybe even a little shocked, but while his eyes were widening his hand would be climbing the backside of my calf, pulling me down onto him. He would taste dirty—that I could be sure of—like smoke and unwashed grapes and wherever he touched me it would leave a mark. Slippery brown fingerprints that I would wear like Tiffany's: showy and proud.

I'd unzip his denim jumper slowly, lingering on the whiteness of his chest, his uneven tan lines and his rippled abs. Or better yet, I'd get on all fours and unzip him with my teeth, tugging at the little steel pull, leaving small traces of MAC as I went. My hands on his shoulders, knees on the oil-spotted concrete, I'd wink and work my way down. When I reached his cock I'd slow, just slightly, push my lips into an o-shaped kiss and blow. Not him, but on it until it pressed against the zipper, rose beneath the denim and pushed against my throat, wanting to be released, and then I'd tug, on the pull, until I had passed it, until I was halfway to his left knee and then, slower than before, I'd lick my way back up. I'd linger on the waistband of his baby blue boxers, following the elastic bit with my tongue from his hipbone to his navel; I'd bite onto the center and again rip down. And his mouth, no longer able to stand the strain of surprise, would relax and he would aaahhh while he maneuvered his way under my dress to unfasten my vintage carnelian bra. He would be clumsy, looking for a clasp instead of a tie, but by the time he found the bow and gave the strings a tug, my dress would be up around my hips and I'd push down onto his dick. And we'd fuck. Right there on the garage floor, rolling back and forth on the dolly with each thrust. And when we were through we'd toast ourselves with Kentucky straight bourbon.

But when I got there, Quentin wasn't in and instead of Tony and Sal there was a boxy receptionist with extra-long turquoise nails, named Wendy, who informed me that Brick, the guy on the front of the card, was out to lunch and, Ain't no one working here named Quentin, hon. But I left the bottle of Booker's, with a note and a fifty just to be sure, and checked into the Beverly Hills Hotel.

LEAVE ROOM FOR THE ACTOR

RICKY'S SISTER Cheri was the first to introduce me to the Beverly Hills Hotel. After our little outing on Rodeo we went to the Cabana Club to get our wits back about ourselves over icy-cold mango margaritas, blended, no salt. Salt bloats. I'm actually allergic to mango, but when I tried to say as much, Cheri started in on the Polo Lounge and how she really couldn't believe Ricky hadn't taken me there yet. Although I had convinced Ricky on more than one occasion to put on a jacket and take me out, we had never actually stayed at the Beverly Hills Hotel.

And so today when the concierge asked if I had a reservation I said, Of course. Bungalow Five for Mrs. Ricky de la Cruz.

He typed on his keyboard, scanned his screen and looked back at me. I removed my sunglasses from my face and gave him an icy stare.

I apologize, ma'am, but the first name is?

Magdalena, I continued to give him my best do-you-know-who-I-am glare while clicking the arm of my sunglasses against my teeth, but it's under my husband's name, de la Cruz. As in de la Cruz owner and founder of Diamond Myst water.

This was a first. Not that I hadn't namedropped before, but I had never namedropped in the "do you know who I am" style. In fact, I vowed never to be so blatantly appalling after I overheard Tori Spelling throwing a fit of her own at Wrap Scissors Paper on La Cienega when the counter girl wouldn't let her use the ribbon-cutting scissors to cut through a cardboard box. These scissors have a special blade, the girl explained. Do you know who I am? Tori exploded in a bad bit of Hollywood entitlement.

I could buy this entire store if I wanted so give me the damn scissors. Undoubtedly she probably could buy the store, or at least she could have if she made up with her mother. Hell, if she made nice with Candy and got back in the will she probably could buy the whole block, Beverly Center included, but that didn't give her special scissors rights.

Of course, Mrs. de la Cruz. He was reddening a bit in his cheeks.

Is there a problem? I asked.

No, no problem, he said, clicking on his mouse repeatedly, maybe it's under your address.

My address?

Yes, you do have an address?

Of course I have an address. 730 N. Bedford, I blurted out before I could think better of it.

Bedford, in Beverly Hills?

Yes, about three blocks that way, I pointed.

Right, he said.

It's the foyer, I lied. A total nightmare so we're doing a complete remodel and the pounding, I held my black American Express card to my temple in a dramatic gesture, is more than I can stand. I'll probably be here for an extended stay. I smiled and the boy behind the counter smiled back at me, but this time his grin was different, less quizzical and more compassionate. As if I wasn't the first Beverly Hills housewife to walk out on her husband and take up in the Hotel, blaming the carpet or the plumbing or the goddamned paint that's taking forever to dry.

YOU'RE IN luck! He exclaimed, as he swiped my card, It appears that Bungalow Five is already occupied, but we do have the Sunset Suite.

Impossible, I said, near tears. I always stay in Bungalow Five. Your staff assured me that Bungalow Five would be reserved for me beginning this afternoon.

Do you remember whom it was exactly that you spoke to, ma'am?

I looked at his name badge and said, Ian, does it look like I have time to take names?

Not at all, Mrs. de la Cruz.

You know, he said, as the tears pooled behind my glasses and I struggled to look him directly in the eye, not many people are aware of this, but Lana Turner stayed in the Sunset Suite with four of her seven husbands.

Really? I asked, refusing to make eye contact by staring off at the banana leafed wallpaper.

Really, he said, as he reached across the marble counter and patted my hand. I thought that might be of interest to you, since you're redesigning her foyer and all.

Well, technically, I smiled, it's my foyer now, but I appreciate what you're saying. The Sunset Suite'll be fine.

Fabulous, he said, tapping my hand once more before typing something into his computer. I'm sure you'll have a lovely time during your stay with us, and if you need anything, he gave me his card, give me a call.

Thank you, I said, palming his card and handing him my keys. My things are in the car, I'll be in the Cabana Club. Let me know when it's ready.

HOW THEY managed to get my things upstairs without suit-cases I'll never know. Maybe they used large green lawn bags, or maybe they just backed the Tank up to the service eleva-tor and tossed everything inside. Maybe misplaced L.A. wives were commonplace and they had a system. Whatever it was it worked—by the time the bellhop came round to the pool, where I was sitting on an umbrella-covered lounge chair and sipping on a piña colada, my clothes were all perfectly hung on glossy wooden hangers in the walk-in closet of my new temporary $2,000-a-night residence.

I had considered, briefly, the Four Seasons, renting one of those penthouse thingies and drinking my liver larger, but the Beverly Hills Hotel wasn't in walking distance of anything and they had the most adorable little pool-side palms. So if Quentin didn't get the bourbon maybe he'd get an inkling for a swim. Maybe I should call and inquire. Maybe I should call 411. Maybe I should call my mother. Maybe I should dial 209-555-2855 and let it ring until I'm home. Just crawl right up the line and fall out onto the hardwood floor of my mother's yellow kitchen and cry.

No, fuck that. If I wanted tears I'd drive back to Ricky and I'd cry him a whole new line. Saline Spritzer, he could call it and bottle it up in a Diamond wrapper for $2.95 a liter.

Remove the phone from the cradle. Look at the handset until the Beverly Hills Hotel desk clerk says, Ma'am? And then wonder how you slipped? How you slipped from Miss to Ma'am without a lift or a tuck or a stomach full of embryonic fluid and stretch marks the size of Japan.

Hang up.

Pick up and dial Mom.

And in between the repeating deet deet deet of the busy tone slip still further into a past life, a life with meandering country roads and apricot trees and not a whole lot more.

THE WORLD OF A CHARACTER

WHEN THE busy beeps stopped and my mother said hello, I said, Hi.

Under my breath I said, I'm sorry.

To myself I said, about Junah. It was my fault that he died.

Laney, my mom asked, is that you sweetheart?

Yes.

Where are you? You sound far away or hollow. Maybe both. I hope you're not talking to me on that cell phone while driving. You know that's dangerous, especially in L.A. I have an article somewhere around here that I've been meaning to send to you, I could hear her open the heavy door of her file cabinet and sift through her alphabetical magazine index, that says people who drive while on the phone, even if they wear a headset, are thirty times more likely to get in a wreck, and in Los Angeles, she was still sifting, it more than quadruples.

I'm not driving, so you can stay on the line.

Well where are you? The connection sounds hollow.

I'm in Santa Fe, I lied.

New Mexico, or is that some kind of trendy new L.A. hot spot? New Mexico.

And you're there because… her voice was on the verge of panic, but I could tell she was exhibiting some restraint just in case I happened to be there on business instead of say, her worst fear, escaping the wreckage of my burnt-to-the-ground-in-a-riot home.

Because I need some time to think.

You can't just think at home? What, California isn't big enough? You need to fly to another state?

I didn't fly, I lied. I drove so I could think.

About what?

I don't know. Stuff. Me and Ricky. You and Dad. Great big breaths. Junah—long pause—stuff.

She was quiet. Too quiet.

Mom?

Yeah.

I'm sorry.

For what?

But I couldn't say it. So instead I just said, For all of it, you know?

Yeah, she said, uncorking another bottle, I know. But I'm over it. You should get over it too. And while you're at it, stand up straight, and get some comfortable shoes. Those heels you wear will give back problems by the time you're thirty-five. Get a haircut that doesn't take two hours to blow dry. Laugh at yourself and, for Christ's sake, stop thinking so damned much about your relationship. You honestly think anyone gives a damn?

I tried to answer but the beeping of call waiting cut off my words.

Answer it, Mom said, maybe it'll be someone who can help you stop thinking so much.

Okay I said, but when I clicked over it was a voice I didn't recognize. A musical male voice that said, Hey.

THE FIRST STEP

EY.
Hello?

Hey, the voice said again. So I was thinkin' that since I was in the neighborhood I might be able to borrow some ice?

Quentin?

Yeah?

Are you hurt? Do you need me to bring you some ice?

No, said Quentin, laughing, inhaling. I was wondering since I was in the neighborhood if I might borrow some ice and perhaps a glass to put it in because I have a bottle of bourbon.

I surveyed the room, which, in the two days I had been there had magically transformed—not unlike myself—into a hot fucking mess. No, um, yes, I said.

No ice?

Yes. I mean, no.

Before Quentin called I had been sorting my wardrobe by season, as opposed to say, designer or texture. Although I had tried to shove errant parts of Fall 2006 under the California king-sized bed bits of brightly colored Dolce and Gabbana and Gianfranco Ferre stuck out from beneath the ruffled bed skirt. I grabbed a pile of panties—the green, aqua and lace pile—and pushed them into the drawer with the Beverly Hills phone directory and shopping guide.

I have ice, I said, shutting the drawer.

Enough to spare?

I could hear his fingers drum against the stained teak of the concierge's desk, Mind if I come up?

No, I mean yes. Just. Come up.

Hang up. Grab the cheesecake box. Where to put the cheese-cake box? In the tub. Everything that doesn't fit under the bed goes into the tub. And then he knocked. A loud knock followed by two short raps all with knuckles, and I peeped out the peep-hole and saw him sway with the bottle, half outside the frame, waiting for an invitation.

I took a deep breath, unlocked the door and said, Come in. Sit down. Ice.

Before he arrived I thought I would fuck him. Fuck him to fuck over Ricky, to even the score of my lopsided marriage, but there Quentin was: tall, with thick tan shoulders, leaning in the jam. He had a very long chest, big arms and dark brown hair that grew long and away from his temples in boyish waves. The bour-bon he held in his left hand, and with his right he kept smooth-ing away a piece of imaginary hair that had fallen into his eyes. I watched him survey the room, but what's more I could feel him. The way he sized up the mahogany breakfast table, littered with Kleenex, the green leafy butts of bitten strawberries and an over-turned magnum of Laurent Perrier Grand Siecle. I could feel he had misjudged the situation too.

I wanted to explain that I had brought the booze with me, that I hadn't paid $210 for alcohol as the room-service menu claimed, that Ricky and I bought it by the case for $165 a bottle from a wholesale guy in Napa—but it wasn't true and, besides, I didn't want to point out the extravagance. In case Quentin didn't know. In case Quentin didn't fucking care. He looked to the table and then to the chairs—all seven and the desk and loveseat cov-ered by clothes: bras wrapped around the armrests, blouses and coats over the backs and pants piled in unfolded heaps on the seats. When Quentin stopped surveying the room and began to assess me, I shrugged and looked sideways to the bed, which was made, but by no effort of my own.

In my memory it seems that he made the trip from the door to the bed in two steps, but maybe that's just how it seemed. What

I know for a fact is that when he decided to come all the way into the room, he never took his eyes off me. I tried to look back at him, but I could feel my eyes grow red and puffy. I hadn't had time to put on any lip-gloss, not to mention fix my hair, which was tied up in a tousled ponytail. So when he did sit down, on the far right corner of the bed, the corner closest to the balcony and opposite any pillows, I left the room.

Glass, I said, pointing to the bourbon he still choked by the neck, but rather than heading towards the bar, I slipped into the bathroom and locked the door.

What was I doing? I had seen the picture in his wallet. The one of him and some redheaded girl sitting knee-to-knee on a merry-go-round. I mean who the hell rides a merry-go-round anyhow? And who's to say she wasn't his sister or an old roommate from college? That they were even still together? Though the trembling of his fingers, okay, not trembling, but the slight tic...the slight tic in his fingers as he reached beneath the picture for his card...I mean, who's to say?

But I knew. Staring at my gray eyes in the mirror, massaging my temples with my index finger, I knew and yet I pulled out the rubber band, brushed my fingers through my long hair, smoothed on some gloss and walked back out to Quentin with a glass in hand—all the while knowing full damned well: Quentin had a wife.

I sat in the middle of the bed and I brought the ice with me. It sloshed around in the carafe and gave me something to look at, something to do besides move my leg half an inch closer to Quentin when I thought he wouldn't notice. It was a strange game we played, holding the bottle a little too long so our fingers touched when we passed it between us. Adjusting and repositioning, slowly. Fighting for possession of the awkward space between us.

RICKY AND I were about the same height: six-foot, though Ricky always said he was six-two even when in my three-inch heels I towered over him. Quentin, however, had to be six-six, though he seemed still taller, his legs stretching every which way, uncomfortable.

I reached over and rubbed my thumb over the back of his wrist, like I had near the Foodcourt. Maybe he wasn't thinking, or maybe he wanted me to see it, but he turned his hand over and there, in his palm, un-duct-taped, was Sarah.

Sarah, he said, just to get it out there. Something other than floral fabric to keep us apart.

Sarah, I repeated and then coughed on some ice. In my head I had already peeled back the layers of his duct tape. I had read her tattooed letters aloud.

He shrugged. I flinched. He grabbed my hand tightly in his, positing my palm so it covered the green-black lines of her name, and, sitting up just a bit, he reached into his back pocket and pulled out a stretch of silver tape. One-handed, using his teeth, he managed to pull a strip of tape off its coil, and letting go of my hand, just briefly, he stuck the sticky silver over Sarah's name.

Better? he said, leaning back on the bed, rubbing the underside of his thumb against the bare skin of my shin.

Better than what? I wondered. Tape or no tape Dior knew Ricky was married, and I knew Quentin held Sarah when he wasn't hiding out in hotels holding me. I slid back, letting my head rest against the large down pillows—Was this how you had an affair?—and pushed my legs out so that suddenly Quentin was in the space that would be my lap if I were seated. He leaned back so that my legs tucked neatly beneath his arms, one on each side of his waist, and I waited.

What was I supposed to do? Ask, Wanna fuck? Want me to suck your dick with my finger up your ass until your head explodes and then you can go home and hug your wife? Want to hug me instead? I said nothing.

Quentin continued to run his fingers down my legs, tracing some invisible pattern.

I got other tattoos, he finally said, running his nails from my knees to the arches of my feet.

I wiggled my toes, I figured as much.

One right here, he said tracing the line of my calf, and another, he said, turning on his side and then on his stomach, so that his face was now near my navel, right here. His hand was moving along my waistline, creeping up ever so slowly under my shirt, but it stopped. He stopped.

And one more, he continued, turning us both around so that I was on my side also and his fingers moved across my back, that stretches from right here, he traced my shoulder blades, to right here, he ended at the small of my back.

I suspect he wanted me to ask what they were, to ask if I could see them. But I was silent, imagining a Julia near his back, a Carlotta running up his inner thigh and an amazing Grace stretched out strong on his right pectoral. Instead of speaking, instead of moving, I stared out the window and look at the palms as they swayed in the wind.

This is what happens when you let things talk themselves out. Suddenly, just like a Double Mint commercial—double your pleasure, double your fun—we were hugging and not fucking. Not doing anything you're supposed to do when you're on the run from your own life and wrecking another woman's home. But because I couldn't say her name, because I was never really able after the first time to say Sarah out loud, what I said instead was, Maybe you should go.

THE GIFT OF ENDURANCE

BUT HE didn't. He sat up and took off his shoes, then his shirt and finally his pants. See, he said, spinning around before falling back onto the bed. On his back Quentin was covered in gears and teeth. A pendulum stretched down his torso and was anchored by a weight near his waist. Tick. Tock. Exposed and unclothed he looked like the insides of my grandfather's pocket watch. What the hell was I supposed to do? Wind him up?

But the tattoos made it easier. Like him, I began by tracing. He had two symmetrical gears circling his thigh and one enormous cog, with what he called an escape wheel, on his chest. Its locking teeth stretched up his breastbone and a ruby disc circled his nipple in a neat ring. I started in on the pendulum, tracing its path down toward Quentin's pelvis until I reached the anchor of his navel. It wasn't inked on the inside and looked kind of funny, a bit too small for the weight of a clock. I moved my index finder around inside it and then back down the other leg, moving dangerously close to his hard dick.

Tattooed flesh feels different. Unreal and slippery almost, like the soft leather of overpriced shoes. When I turned him over, his back was all levers and pulleys. I tasted them, sucking with tiny kisses, and they tasted different. But maybe it had nothing to do with the shape or the color; Quentin tasted different than Ricky. I bit down. Right in the middle of a left-shoulder spur, I bit into Quentin's flesh and he flinched.

No, he shook his head with his tongue pressed against his lips. No marks, he said aloud and I knew why. I thought Sarah, I thought Ricky, and I turned away from Quentin and bit into my own flesh. Just below the shoulder I sank my teeth into my skin and sucked until it bruised.

I have tattoos too, I told him. They just haven't been inked yet.

My clothes came off easily, like in college when my roommate Stephanie and I used to snip the seams of our panties halfway so that later, when they came off, the boys thought they'd ripped them. When we were both completely naked, I couldn't see much of Quentin at all, we were lying too close, but I could feel him; the entire fucking clock of Quentin and his hands were moving their way over me. Every curve of his body, every ink-drawn line was taking possession and suddenly I couldn't get Sarah out of my mind. How did she manage Quentin's watch? Or worse yet, did she have her own? Somewhere on the small of her back, was there a cuckoo and a squawking beak attached to a bird that just wouldn't shut up:

That's not how Quentin likes it. That's not how Quentin likes it, like the goddamned Tiki Room.

I don't know exactly what I thought infidelity was supposed to feel like, but it sure as hell wasn't this. When you ask around they always make it sound fantastic. Like fucking your brains out, sex times seven. But this was awkward, uncomfortable even. Maybe it was different because we knew we wouldn't get caught. Even if Ricky did track me down, he wasn't the type to bust down a door. And Sarah, who really knows? Maybe, like me, she was wrecked. Maybe, just knowing Quentin and I were inside wouldn't be enough. She'd need to see it. She'd need to know how and why. She wouldn't bust down the door but she'd slip in quietly. Climb the palms up to the balcony and slip in through the French doors. Perched on the end of the bed, she'd smooth out the covers and whisper, Lean back. He likes it when you arch. Push in, not down. Get on top. And before I could tell what had happened, Like this, let me show you, she'd shove me off and we'd switch places. Sarah on Quentin and me in the corner, where I finally could scream, I feel something, Ricky! because I'd know how it was done. How someone could cheat on their bereaved wife and get away with it. How someone could fuck a man they knew full well was married and not even mind. Maybe being the other woman would teach me something too. Teach me how I could make my husband love me. Teach me how to be more than just a wife.

But here was the kicker: flat and still on my back, I was the other woman making love like the wife. No, this wouldn't do at all. So I arched my back and he slipped right out.

Surprise, I said and climbed on top, and that is how it was done.

THE POINT OF NO RETURN

I WASN'T afraid until he'd finished. He wove his fingers between mine, thrust up and said, Dangerous.

Dangerous could have meant a hundred things. For starters
we weren't protected and if dangerous didn't mean hepatitis C
it most certainly meant thousands of tiny sperm spinning and
swimming their way up the birth canal and smack into fertil-
ized eggs. I could have told him I was on the pill, but I wasn't,
and lying beside him in our Beverly Hills bed I wanted danger. I
wished for imaginary feet pushing out from the inside. I wished
for illegitimacy and scandal and betrayal. What I got instead was
a now-quiet Quentin, rolling over onto his side and blowing soft
circles of air on my chest. My nipples contracted and shriveled.
He stuck out his finger and pushed one down.

They real? he asked, peering up from the nook in his arm.

No. I said, putting my own index finger on my left boob and
pressing down.

Thought they were supposed to be cold then, he said letting
a few more fingers touch down before he cupped it.

The cheap ones I guess. These are saline. Twenty grand.

Like the ocean.

Tears. I filled them all myself.

Hurt?

Unreal. I mean I hear it's worse than childbirth, but how
would I know? What I can tell you is that I couldn't brush my
teeth for two weeks. I couldn't reach my arm high enough, Immelda had to…. I stopped.

Quentin pretended not to notice, How'd they do it?

They went in through the armpit, I said, lifting up my arm so he could see the staple-like scar. On strippers and the girls who pay $3,500 off some ValPak coupon, they go in on the underside. Just cut a smile and stuff in some silicone. I suppose it works, but not as well. The way I had it done was with a balloon. They put it in and injected the saline through a tube. It happens gradually, over a few weeks. You can adjust the size. B today, D tomorrow.

Like so that people won't notice?

To cut down on stretch marks. I had a few, in the beginning, but with the vitamin E you can hardly notice. And this way your nipples come out in the middle. With some girls they're lopsided, or pointy, like to the sky.

Yours look good. He bent down, took the left one in his mouth and blew a raspberry, and then he moved over to the right and tugged at a nipple with his teeth.

They repositioned them. Even better than before.

How big were they before?

Little.

Like lemon little? Lime little? Cherry little?

They were Chicken Little, okay. Grade A, organic, sunny-side-up egg yoke little.

He laughed, Are you happy?

With the tits? Yeah, they're all right. I have a big ass so they give me balance. You know, I'm proportional now. And it's not like I take them seriously or anything. I mean as soon as I could do my own hair I threw a busting-out party. Invited all kinds of people and put them on display. I mean that's what they're for, aren't they?

Guess so.

Like tattoos.

Tattoos are an art.

He was squeezing now, first the right, then the left.

Really.

Yeah, they mean something.

So what do they mean?

Depends on the person.

You.

He had each nipple pinched between his thumb and index finger and was twirling the skin back and forth.

Me? The twirling stopped. He only held.

What do yours mean?

Mine mean I like gears—and pendulums and old-fashioned clocks.

That's deep, I said, reaching under the bed for something to cover my breasts with.

Well, it's kind of like a club, you know? You can't just go running off at the mouth with just anyone. Then you might as well join a frat and get matching Greek letters or some of that Old English gang shit.

So we fucked, I said, my voice muffled by the sequined tank I was pulling over my head, and then I told you about my boobs, but you can't tell me what your tats mean?

Tattoos. You're not some biker-chick in some Bakersfield bar. He looked around for his own clothes and started to pull them on. And until you get one of your own my lips are sealed. Besides—he was fishing for shoes in a pile of Prada—gotta go.

Home?

I just gotta leave is all.

Want a shower? There's soap and stuff around here some-where. I never use the hotel stuff—it makes your skin dry.

Nah, I'm all right.

But won't she. I mean the smell?

I like your smell. I like you, too. He was dressed, up and making a move for the door.

Hey, Quentin?

Yeah?

He was in the frame again, half in, half out. The spinning mauve floral of the rug was reaching out for his left shoe.

I could feel you, you know. Your fingers. The pinching. It's not like I didn't.

He winked, long eyelashes briefly closing over the green of his left eye, and held up the bottle of bourbon.

THE PRINCIPLE OF TRANSITION

E VEN AFTER Quentin left, the room felt full. I lay on the
bed bare-assed, my sequined lace camisole stretched over
my designer tits, and followed him home in my head:

Tuesday.

Two-thirty in the afternoon.

A hotel full of daylight adulterers: doctors, lawyers and in-
dustry-types who kept their other women high in the recesses
of the Beverly Hills Hotel, their offices in Westwood or Mid-
Wilshire, their kids in Harvard Westlake and their wives in kicky
heels, sashaying down Rodeo or Robertson. The afternoon ty-
coons had their inter-marital relations for lunch. Maybe they
made jokes about it in the elevator: talked shop, switched hits
and anted up. Maybe, like Quentin, none of them showered;
and, wearing the scent of another woman, they waited for their
Jags and Benzes, over-tipped the valet and drove back to work
with the windows rolled down. How many would Quentin run
into as he made his way from my room to the street? Hallway to
elevator to lobby to valet, I'd guess five at the absolute most, but
what of it? Was Quentin the type to even give a damn? Chances
are he'd walk straight out the front door, nod to the bellhop, by-
pass the valet and the endless stream of newly waxed town cars
and walk three blocks to Rexford, where his car (something old
but well maintained, something with muscle) was waiting where
he parked it: under the spotted shade of a palm.

He smoked, I'm sure, three maybe four cigarettes on the
drive home, and no doubt he stopped for gas. Maybe that's what
they did with the smell. Mixed with smog, smoke and Exxon,

the Chanel floral, amber blend of orange blossom, Sambac jasmine, iris, floating vanilla and lilac express lost their hold as they slipped around exhumes and exhaust. Maybe I rubbed off as Quentin wore on, a mint in his mouth and one of those princess red gas station roses stuck in the cupholder, waiting, with an exaggerated flourish, for Sarah. Maybe he'd make her dinner, runny spaghetti with white toast; and because he was guilty, and because even the smell of burnt bread and fresh basil wouldn't be enough to cover his afternoon absence, they'd fuck ferociously on the tan linoleum floor, Quentin rubbing his head beneath Sarah's small chin and tugging at her breasts with his teeth. Sarah, no doubt, had big ones. Jugs, Quentin probably called them, and to tell you the goddamned truth, I'd like to believe that she was stupid, fat and clumsy.

But, and here's where I roll onto my stomach, push my head into the down of my pillow and say it smothered, so maybe no one will hear: I know it's not true. I fully admit that. Sarah fell in love with Quentin and he with her and so she's obviously something—although what she is, I don't really know. Who she is to me is no problem. She is not tall, she is not blonde and she has not recently left her husband to take up with a grandfather clock in the Beverly Hills Hotel. To me that is enough. But to Quentin, who she is to Quentin, that I cannot even think. Because thinking that would, by some screwed-up twist of logic, require the inverse: Who am I to Quentin? And who, pray tell, is Ricky to me?

SYNOPSIS

IN THE most basic of terms Ricky is my husband. And once upon a time we were lovers, too. This is the guilt talking, right? The post-coital running of the mouth that starts the mind wandering while the funk of some man other than your husband is beginning to drip from between your legs? Why is it that sex is so messy and why doesn't this get taught in high school? No, seriously. If more girls knew about the slimy white spunk they will inevitably spend the rest of their lives sopping up, they might hold out longer. It's kind of like your period. You spend all of age eleven, and half of twelve, chanting tiny mantras for its arrival, and then when it hits—usually in a white bikini at the community pool in Lodi—you wonder why the fuck no one warned you. I mean really, speaking of a solidarity among women, shouldn't it start there? A stalwart sisterhood of truth and vindication with in-house biologists specially trained in the advancement of the elimination of dripping funk, where the first rule of membership would be honesty and the second allegiance to your fellow female. With a system like that I could be home with Ricky right now, tanning by the pool and drinking a Piña Colada; but as is, some intern bitch had to go sleep with Ricky, and I had to go hunt out Quentin so that I could learn how it was done. And Sarah, poor, oblivious Sarah, is a good two hours away from her first clue—and when she finds out (if she finds out), will it even matter?

COMPLICATION
VERSUS COMPLEXITY

WHY WAS I with Quentin? Well, there's the whole Ricky thing, and not the fact that I just walked out of his life. I mean the other thing. The small bundle of rhymes-with-maybe thing. Maybe Mags when we sell the water; maybe Mags when we buy a house; maybe Mags when I work less and you go a month without crashing the car. Maybe without you Ricky, maybe how about that? And before you get all judgmental and tell me how terribly fucked up I am to leave my husband and go search out a sire like some frickin' Cher song, let me tell you that you have not earned the right to say shit until you have peed over a plastic stick. You can't speak a word until you have sat, the second Monday of every month for a year and a half without exception, with your pants around your ankles, watching a thin stream of golden-yellow piss bounce against an indicator strip and then spill into the toilet. You cannot tell me one thing until you have attempted to button yourself up while simultaneously holding the stick between your first and third fingers, and you have absolutely no voice until you have taken your mother's car without asking and driven halfway to Rio Linda to buy a home pregnancy test from a drug store where you're hoping like hell there'll be no one you know.

FLASHBACK

MAGDALENA BAMBERGER was seventeen, unmarried and a senior at Tokay High School; anonymity was therefore important, almost as important as her desire not to be pregnant. Unfortunately, for her, she had woken up nauseous for the past two weeks. She hadn't missed her period, but then again it wasn't due for another eight days. So she was probably jumping the gun driving Eight Mile Road in search of a Thrifty Drug where she was sure no one from Lodi would recognize her. As a volunteer at the local day care (Monday and Wednesday) and convalescent home (Tuesday and Thursday), she was exposed to everything: mono, strep, meningitis, cooties, and so it was highly likely that her nausea was merely a strange vein of stomach flu the kids or the old folks had been passing around. For the first week this seemed the case; however, near the end of the second week, right around the time she started vomiting like clockwork, Magdalena stopped calling her affliction the flu and started calling it Ariel.

She had sworn to name her first child Ariel in the eighth grade when she got a hold of Sylvia Plath and spent nights under the covers in a flashlit tent. When the baby actually did come out she would undoubtedly name it Madison or Madeline or Marianne, but right now, in the three-minute wait on the indicator strip, Ariel would do.

What Mags will do when the strip turns pink is uncertain. The father, a sweet but over-determined kid, won't be of much help, which Mags doesn't mind because she doesn't plan on mentioning it. However her own father, sweet Jesus, her own daddy will do what every good valley daddy does and convene a search party to hunt out the bastard and cut off his balls. The thought of her brother Junah, Uncle Jerry, cousin Wade, the neighbors and half the Lodi wine-growers association hunting down the unfortunate soon-to-be-father and then tying him to the bed of an F-150 while pelting him with cork brings a giggle to Mags' lips as she impatiently stares herself down in the bathroom mirror waiting for the strip. Nothing has changed yet, and as she again sizes herself up in the glass, reflecting on her posture, she is reminded of her mother.

Her mother, oh Christ, her mother will positively come unglued.

MAGS BOOSTS herself up on the counter and sits beside the sink. She swings her heels against the linen cupboard for five or six beats and then jumps off the counter and onto cold linoleum where she takes another step up on the scale. It reads 107, which is somewhat of a relief, but then again the stomach flu named Ariel is probably about the size of her pinkie nail and so she again jumps up on to the counter and leans her cheek against the medicine cabinet. When she'd imagined situations such as this, Magdalena always figured she'd be surrounded with loud but well-intentioned girlfriends: the feminist who'd have already scheduled the abortion; the sentimentalist who would go on and on about onesies and layette sets and buggies with yellow wheels and attached umbrellas; and the dreamer who wouldn't say much of anything, all the while secretly wishing it was her with her pants around her ankles pissing on a stick. The four of them would cram into the bathroom with some chocolate mint ice cream and wait it out together. Kinda like in summer camp when all the girls would get it in their heads to go blonde, taking turns tinting each other's roots and massaging the dye in with rubber gloves. But, a natural blonde, Magdalena was alone and the strip went from one line to two and thus begins the second saddest story I know.

VOICE-OVER NARRATION

W ITH THE rather large exception of Junah, the saddest story I know is about a girl who got knocked up the first time she put out. You know the story: young, yada, just about out of high school, dada, with an acceptance letter to UC Berkeley tucked beneath the padded bras of her underwear drawer. She's tall, a little too tall, so that she's not really conventionally pretty but she's smart. I suppose there's a story variation about the dumb, short, pretty girl who goes and gets preggers too. But I have no experience with that version, so I'll stick with the one I know best. This girl, let's just call her Magdalena, she's like the valedictorian or artistic editor of the school yearbook or some such what-she-thought-then-was-meaningful-but-turned-out-years-later-to-be-trivial type shit and because she has a pact, a very sacred and valued pact with Jenny and Jennifer Anne, her two best friends in the world, she loses her virginity a month before prom so that when prom night rolls around it won't hurt. See, I told you she was a bright one. But now for the irony: It wasn't even about the boys. It was about the girls. You see, these three, they loved each other with sister-blood, and the only way any one of them could imagine doing it was with the others in close proximity. And so it was that these three little virgins all ended up holding hands on a California king, while three faceless boys—maybe they were brothers, maybe they were triplets—hammered away from above, so elated to be getting ass they overlooked thirty identically manicured fingernails attached to three sets of tightly held hands. Hell, if any one of the girls had read *Fear of Flying,* or had been born after the internet, probably they would've bought a big purple vibrating dick and undone each other amidst a group hug, but they were from a small town and so they used boys. But sex, with boys, is messy. And even with condoms—fluorescent orange, glow in the dark, school colors—and all six hands all gripping tightly onto something or other, it juiced out. Sploshed over the latex and, somehow, made its way up the pipes past the DO NOT ENTER sign and into Magdalena's baby box where it bit hold of an egg and held on.

Three weeks later she was ten days late.

So Magdalena took some Midol—like a lot of it—because it's the one thing she could find with promise: *Do Not Take if Pregnant. This Drug has been known to Induce Miscarriage.* Betting on some little pink pills, Mags came out—in red and violet gushes and all over the porcelain tub—the big winner. Like I said, it was a small town. And if she had read *Fear of Flying* or if she'd had the internet, or even a frickin' Planned Parenthood, she might have done something different, but instead she held tight to the soap dish and her younger brother's hand while she downed pill after pill until her stomach seized up, her ovaries cramped, her face went white and it worked. Out came the blood and she was bloody unstuck.

It worked so well, in fact, that nothing stuck ever after. Not even much, much later, years in fact, when she actually wanted it to. And for a while she thought it was Ricky. But now, with her panties still tangled in the sheets of the other room, Quentin's just a single line of blue too.

IRONIC ASCENSION

HAVEN'T seen Jenny or Jennifer Anne since high school, and last I read—courtesy of Mom's newspaper clippings—they were Teaching for America and engaged, respectively, but I think of them both, a lot. Especially, when I'm tanning, bleaching, waxing or tweezing. Sometimes, it's almost as if they're still with me, you know? Or maybe it's just that I wish they were. Because maybe then I'd have someone to call, someone who would rush over to the Beverly Hills Hotel and reassure me that what I did was right, absolutely acceptable, considering the circumstances and all.

Instead I call Ricky. But not work, or his cell, because well then he might actually answer. I call home, because if I've learned anything from being wedded to the water baron of the western states, it's that he's never home.

So I dial and then listen to my own voice tell myself that I'm not home. I have no idea what I want to say to the beep, but I'm pretty sure it sounds like Save Me. Which is really silly, considering. But still it's there like a badly drawn dream: my need for a happily ever after. Instead I hang up before the beep and then call back. When my voice sounds I pull the phone away from my ear so I don't have to hear myself jabber again: Hi, this is Ricky and Mags, we're so sorry we missed your call... And when I hear a faint beep I pull the phone back in and whisper into the line:

Ricky it's me. I'm in Santa Fe. As in New Mexico and not that trendy new grill on the corner of Santa Monica and Kings Road. I needed some time to think, but tell anyone who asks that it's art or something. Make up a convention if you have to. I don't much care and I'm sure neither do you. If you need to reach me try my cell.

And then I hang up again. I tell myself this is because I don't want him to worry. I don't want to see myself on flyers posted all over WeHo, or on the six o'clock news: Ricky solemn, rational, demanding my captors to return me safely. My mother hysterical, her swollen eyes covered with sunglasses too big for her face, unable to speak.

Or not.

This is just what I tell myself.

Deep down I know the message is for me. So that I can stop telling myself Ricky hasn't called because he hasn't noticed that I'm gone.

PROGRESSIVE COMPLICATIONS

IT'S AMAZING how quickly I came to need Quentin. Without discussing the details we fell into a pattern. He'd arrive, half-in-half-outside the door, signaling his entrance with a low knuckle rap. I'd await that rap Tuesdays after one, Thursdays after six and precious, perfect Sunday afternoons. He'd arrive at various other times too, unannounced, unafraid and sometimes I'd answer and sometimes not. And even in the Nots I'd see his need, usually in the form of a note or small trinket, written mostly on bar napkins but sometimes also on actual paper enclosed in envelopes. He'd push these small missives under the door and whenever I'd return from anywhere, weighed down by designer bags of obscene dimensions, I'd insert my hotel key and catch my breath as the door pushed open and I looked to the floor. Mostly I saw the expensive Berber carpet, but sometimes—and the joy at these moments is too hard to explain except to say it was a joy not unlike the days when Junah still lived—sometimes there'd be his letter.

I'd bend over, sometimes a Adho Mukha Svanasana pose, sometimes a complete crocodile twist or even a little boat. I'd pose and breathe, the letter inches from my cheek, chin and eyelashes, and I'd let the moment linger, breathing in deep through my nose, feeling the air fill the bottom of my lungs, feeling my lungs press back into my spine. The smell was of shag, to be sure, and industrial hotel carpet cleanser, but sometimes there'd also be a whiff of something new: a linger of Lucky Strike, the scent of a guitar string just before it snaps and, once, though this brought decidedly less joy, the smell of a girl's nail polish remover, the non-acetone type. His handwriting was stretched and slinky. It curled around the "M" and "l" of my name with abandoned precision, never fully centered, always almost about to run off the envelope before it reached the final a curve.

Barefoot, in child's pose, in downward-facing dog, I'd meditate above the letter. If it were enclosed I'd imagine what the sweet words were that were written on the insides. If exposed I'd linger on each word before I forced it into a sentence, into a recognizable phrase:

Mag-da-lane-a (accompanied by half and whole musical notes as though it were a score, my name a song) Mag-da-lane-a last night. Mag-da-lane-a last night I. Mag-da-lane-a last night I was at a party. In Silver. Silver Lake. And. And although you were not. You were not. Not. But. Not but you. Not but your voice. Your voice was. Was. But your voice. Your voice. Voice. A deathless song. Song full. Full of money. I was at a party. Money. Party. Mag-da-lane-a. Your. Yours. Yrs. Quentin. Quent-in. Quen-tin. tin.

He stole, to be sure. Lines from songs, from books and poems. He claimed it was his right as a musician. That music required sampling. That it was born on repetition of a few good chords strung over and over again in endless repetition. He had a band to back up his theory. A band and a day job because he still, let's not forget, lived in L.A. But unlike most Angelinos in the industry he didn't supplement his craft working wait staff at some trendy bar *du jour*. He worked manual labor putting up and taking down billboards across our urban skyscape.

Wait a minute! I asked when he told me, You don't work at the auto shop?

We were facing each other in the tub, our legs intertwined, his body slightly angled to the left so as not to have the faucet uncomfortable in his back.

Naw, he said, scooping up a handful of soapy water and splashing it against his face. The shop's in the family, but I'm not. In the shop. My uncle Al runs it with a few of my brothers and my cousin, Salvatore. It's a good business, they rake in a shitload, but not for me, you know? Spending my days under the belly of some automobile looking for oil drips and unclutched parts, naw. I need to live above ground.

So what you're saying, I said, untwisting the sheath of my hair from the rubber band that secured it and letting it fall wet-ends into the tub, is that you chose billboards to be closer to nature?

Kind of. But they chose me too. All stretched out, so high in the sky. And the view. Have you ever been fifty or sixty feet above ground?

I took a deep breath. What kind of question was that? I mean innocent enough for most people, but for me? Considering...? I considered how far I wanted to go, with Quentin, and then because I didn't exactly want to go there, at least not yet, because I wanted my relationship with Quentin to be free and unattached from the strings that tied me to Junah, I chose my words carefully and said, Not without ropes.

Fuck ropes, Quentin said, apparently not noticing the pre-panic in my voice. You don't need ropes to look over a city so filled with people and possibility that anything could happen. And you. Above it all, looking down. Once I tried it there was no coming down. It's like that with most things. The rest is up to...

He paused.

I waited.

The rest is up to... He took a mighty big breath of air.

Would he say God? Chance? Luck? Fate? I was naked, chin-deep in a tub with a man who I only recently learned was not a mechanic, as I had initially supposed, but was instead a billboard technician. Is that what they're called? I knew he was married. I knew he smoked and was tall. I knew the precise location of all his tattoos and he knew my tits were fake and filled with salt. But what else really did I know? Not the names of his brothers. Not the school he attended for junior high. Not his favorite color or song, none of the things that typically make up the courting ritual. And yet I knew enough.

The rest is up to the rest, I said, pulling up on the soap dish and rising out of the tub. As I stood up bath water fell from my body in soft splashes and a sparkle of bubbles piled on my breasts and hips. Quentin stuck out his long finger and gently popped a few of the full bubbles clinging to my backside. I lifted my left foot and watched the sudsy water slide from my shin, across the top of my pointed toes and back into the tub, before placing my foot down onto the fuzzy bath mat. Lifting my right foot behind me, I shook it gently before placing it next to my left on the mat. And then I stood there, naked before Quentin, feeling his eyes move across my back, which was still slightly slouched from the lingering remnants of junior high when I was the tallest girl in the school. From my shoulders his gaze moved down my spine, resting on the soap-bubble freckles just above my ass, and from there he moved down further still to the curve of my butt as it met the tops of my thighs. Standing with knees and ankles touching, ballerinas and super models—unless they're the bulimic kind—have three perfectly spaced boat-shaped openings between their legs: one between ankles and calves, one between calves and knees and one between knees and thighs. I had spent the last seven months in Pilates and spin classes widening the width of my boat-spaces, and I wondered as I stepped from the mat onto the cold marble tile if Quentin appreciated my work? But the touch of the marble started the march of goose bumps working their way up from my feet and so I grabbed a plush pink BHH–monogrammed robe and slipped into it, tying the sash in a loose knot around my waist and effectively ending the show.

The rest, he replied, scooping up more water and splashing it across his face, across his long hair, making no move to get up or get out, content to spread out in the space my absence made and plunge his head beneath the water's surface.

When he went under my first thought went to Junah, the only other boy with whom I'd shared a bath. My second thought was don't go there. Push Junah to the back. Push Junah under.

At least for a little while. At least until you're alone. Now is the time to sit down on the short leather vanity stool and pretend nothing's wrong.

I sat down on the short leather vanity stool and put my feet up against the adjacent wall where an assortment of hand towels hung. I counted: one alligator, two, and he surfaced, a pile of suds artfully arranged on the top of his head.

Nice look, I said, motioning to his head with my chin.

He rolled his eyes upwards as though he could see his skull from the inside out and then, using a prunish hand, patted the bubbles down into a flat cap. With the other hand he scooped up a new batch and smoothed them over his chin and cheeks.

Ever play bathtub barber? he asked.

I pulled one of the wash towels off the rack with my toes and none-too-gracefully flicked it into the water.

No, I said, even though I had.

You missed out, he said, bending his index finder into a crooked razor and shaving off the suds on the left side of his chin. If I had a Tupperware cup I would have dipped it into the bath and ladled out a glassful over his soapy head. Lean back, I would have told him, using my hand as an eyebrow shield, careful not to let the soap drip into his eyes. But the Beverly Hills Hotel is for predictable reasons without Tupperware, and they don't have those little plastic cups wrapped in cellophane like the Holiday Inn either. Instead they supply goblets and flutes and other beverage containers bearing stems that hum when clinked with the flick of a finger. So I fished the washcloth out and hung it, drippy and wet, over Quentin's head where I squeezed, letting the collated water hit his head in rivulets, unconcerned about his eyes.

Hey, he said, shaking his head back and forth like a wet dog. Hey, he sucked in a drip of water off his upper lip like a baby bird. Hey.

HEADSHOTS

THE MOOD, if there ever was one, was gone. I settled back
on top the short leather vanity stool and said while combing
my hair, Our housekeeper, Immelda, has a sister, Immaculate,
who now works for Priscilla Presley but who used to work for
Bruce and Demi back when they were together, before Ashton
started the urban cougar thing. Anyhow. She told Immelda, who
told me that Demi and Bruce only bathed in Evian water.

Can you imagine? I asked Quentin, a long, wet strand of
blond held in the bristles of a flat brush held out before me,
Bathing in water imported from France?

But Quentin didn't reply. Instead he raised his left eyebrow
ever so slightly higher than his right, framed his hands like a
camera and put them in the air as though taking an invisible
photo of me.

I ignored him and kept brushing. Evian? It's so presumptu-
ous not to mention impractical. Immaculate said it used to take
hours, heating the water so that it would be warm enough to
bathe in, and what, with all three kids—

Hey, do me a favor, Quentin interrupted. Comb your hair
forward will you?

Like this? I said, as I bent over and shook my head so that
my layered locks covered my eyes.

Yeah, Quentin said, adjusting his phony camera again and
angling it to the left. Now tuck half behind your ear.

I did as I was told.

No the other ear, Quentin said, still positioning his hands,
fiddling with an invisible zoom.

I switched ears, wondering what he was up to.

No, like this, he reached up and adjusted my chin so that it was raised to the right and well above my chest. And put your shoulders back.

Why?

Shussh! Quentin said, leaning forward and resting his elbows on the ledge of the tub, now close your eyes.

You're not going to splash me or something silly, are you?

No. Just trust me, will you?

Trust me. Fuck. And there it was again. Those two words that I just couldn't let go.

I took a deep breath. Promise? I asked.

Promise, Quentin said, holding up both hands to show me his uncrossed fingers.

Okay, I said and shut my eyes.

The water in the tub rippled slightly. Maybe, like I always feared, Quentin was about to make his final exit. Just slip out while I sat eyes closed, and when I opened up he'd be gone. In the other room the TV was on, and I struggled to hear past the cheesy laugh lines of some syndicated sitcom for more clues. I tried to elevate my senses, to be perfectly motionless so that I might sense the heat of his body and his tiptoes out across the tile. But all I heard was a soft Click. And when I peeked out—just a quick blink with one eye—to see if it was the click of the door or the click of Quentin's imaginary camera, Quentin shouted, I knew it!

Shit, it was a test then? I opened my eyes just a crack and he caught me, untrusting.

Did I lose? I asked him, pushing back my hair and opening both eyes wide.

Lose what? Quentin asked.

The game, or whatever it was we were playing.

Huh?

I held my own invisible camera up to my face and said, Click-click.

I wasn't testing you, Quentin said, as he lifted the drain to let the water out, I was framing. I knew I knew you, he said. I just had to get the position right.

Position?

I put you up, Quentin said, standing in the tub, bubbles stuck to his thighs and chest and knees, partially obscuring the tattoos.

Excuse me?

On a billboard, he said, reaching for a towel, off Sunset and Doheny. The wet hair gave you away. You were clinging to some blond boy and a bottle of Crystal Geyser, right?

Diamond Myst, I said. Biting the inside of my cheek and looking to the floor.

Whatever, he said, wrapping the towel around his shoulders like that boxer I used to date, and strutted off naked into the next room.

ZED CARD

SO WHAT are you anyhow? Quentin asked later while we were wrapped in the sheets. Model? Actress? Some sort of bottled-water heiress?

None of the above, I said as I turned my back to Quentin and looked out the window towards the skyline. I'm just a ditzy blonde who happened to be in the wrong place at the right time.

Bullshit, Quentin said, turning towards me like a spoon and running his index finger across the small of my back.

I always wanted to be one of those girls who had dimples right there, I said. You know, so when you're backside up in a bikini at the beach or when you bend over and aren't wearing panties under your cut-off jeans, guys will stare.

I'm pretty damn sure guys stare at your ass regardless.

Thanks, I said blushing, scooting an inch or two closer to Quentin's naked body with my own.

But, he slid away from me an inch or two, so he could keep his finger on the spot, it would be a cool spot for a well-placed tattoo.

I almost said, Ricky abhors body art, but I caught myself and said instead, Don't you think that's a little trendy? A little too 1992?

If you got a rose, yeah. Or a butterfly. Or the Chinese fucking ideogram for Zen. But I'm talking about something different. Like text.

Text? I rolled over to face him and found that as I did so my boobs pressed up against his forearm. How is text any different than the kanji symbol for hummingbird?

Because, one, it's in English, and don't you dare go and get Latin or French or some other shit unless you plan on moving there. And two, I'm thinking not just one word, or even a phrase, but a full fucking sentence.

Isn't that a little bit dangerous? I asked. I mean a gear, I looked straight to the circle around his nipple, can mean lots of things, like movement or friction or—

Or the futility of time, Quentin interjected, staring at me through a squinted eye.

Exactly, I said and smiled. It's ambiguous. But a word, not to mention a full sentence, well that's pretty damn clear, isn't it?

That's why it would work, especially on you.

What do you mean especially on me?

Oh please, he said, as if you don't know.

No, I said, I don't. Enlighten me.

The space between us on the bed seemed to be widening with each word we said.

I mean, look at you.

I winced, and pulled back so that there was only an inch between me and falling off the bed.

No, he said, closing the gap between us a bit and reaching his hand out to stroke my cheek, I didn't mean it like that. Or rather, yes I did. But not the way you're taking it. Fuck. I mean look at you outside yourself. Look at you like someone on the street sees you.

I had nothing to say, so I just lay there, blinking, pushing my tongue against the tip of my palate. I saw myself like that every time I looked in the mirror. Because when I closed my eyes, when I imagined myself as me, without the aid of digital cameras or reflective surfaces, I saw the girl version of Junah. But when I opened my eyes, when I stared into the glass, I saw a stranger. The only thing that remained the same, the only thing it was impossible to augment and the only thing that still linked me to Junah was my eyes. Height aside, I saw a perfect blonde body pretending to be me—the new me, now, as opposed to the me who used to be—blinking. Blinking, I said nothing and waited for Quentin to dig himself out, or perhaps further in.

You're fucking flawless, Quentin said, and you're funny.

Ha, ha. I said, laughing while tucking the sheet around my body.

No really, he said, you are. And not in a ha-ha Laugh Factory way or in that asinine, flirty, I-can-get-what-I-want way—

I raised an eyebrow.

Well, I'm sure you could if you wanted to—but you don't.

I don't?

No, you, he said, standing up naked on the bed and pointing a finger at where I still lay, you have wit, which is what makes you so damn stunning.

Really? I was starting to smile despite myself. My cheeks were pulling back and my laugh lines were beginning to show.

I mean a fine ass, well that's a dime a dozen, you know that. But a witty ass, now that's something!

Thanks, I said, loosening my grip on the sheets, I think.

You're welcome, Quentin said, reaching down to grab the sheet and pulling it off me in a flourish, leaving me naked and exposed. Now about that tattoo. He scanned my body, How would you feel about *Caution: contents not what they appear.* Right about, he lifted my left leg and traced a line from my inner thigh to my ankle, here?

Maybe, I said, looking up at him, but I think I prefer here, I traced my hipbone from side to thigh, and I think if we're going with a caution, I'd prefer *Caution: contents may shift under pressure.*

Brilliant! Quentin said. That's exactly what I'm talking about. Why I like you, I mean.

You do? I asked.

Well, sure, he said. You think I show up here for the view?

I laughed. Well you never know, it is rather spectacular.

Naw, he said stretching a long leg on either side of me and bouncing gently up and down on the mattress. I like you. And I like the view from right here. He pulled out his imaginary camera and took another pretend picture. Click-click, he said before asking, Don't you like me, too?

Yeah, I said, I like you all right. But I'd like you even more if you stopped prancing about and fucked me.

No problem, Quentin said, as he bounced down to his knees and then threw himself on top of the bed. That I can do.

CHARACTERS AREN'T PEOPLE

DIDN'T exactly tell Quentin that I was married to Ricky, not in so many words. Nor that I was married at all, but I knew he knew. Even still, I didn't want him to feel as though he had gotten one over on me. As though we were even or something. And besides, two unhappily married people sneaking around hotels to have affairs at three in the afternoon seems so hopelessly forty. If L.A.'s taught me anything it's that you can only be forty at sixty-five.

I'm twenty-nine—take it or leave it—but no matter how you put it, twenty-nine is way too fucking young to be playing at middle age. Twenty-nine is I-can-still-pass-for-twenty-two prime. It is not scrambled egg-whites with spinach—steamed— and a cup of fruit on the side. I mean sure it's like that at home, but in public? Honey, on the Sunset Plaza it's give me a table near the sidewalk with eggs Benedict, extra bacon and some of those sour-cream battered French toast halves. It's yes I can eat anything I want and still fit into these size twenty-five extra-long Sevens, for all mankind. Let's not be silly, I never was one of those girls who said non-fat before latte. I mean for me it just happens and if it doesn't, well, then so-the-fuck-what?

So what if I'm lying here, artfully draped in Egyptian cotton, next to Quentin, making assumptions about his happiness at home. I know there's a possibility that he's actually in love with Sarah. That maybe it's not like the made-for-TV movies and Harlequin books:

Magdalena flips back her hair with a perfectly manicured hand and says breathily, "I honestly hope they're happy together."

A sincere, single tear drops down her petal-soft cheek. She cinches the lavender sheets around her ample breasts and looks out the window towards the palm trees swaying softly in the breeze, "Nothing would make me happier than if they were happy."

Right.

But I'm not delusional. I'll admit there's a slight possibility that Quentin isn't escaping a frigid marriage, that Sarah isn't a prude. Maybe even, although this is where it gets hard, there's something about being with me, something about lying on top of my tall body that makes Sarah's small body exciting. Maybe the truth isn't that Quentin came by because he wasn't getting enough; maybe he came because he already had. Enough, that is.

It was getting late. Later, in fact, than Quentin had ever stayed on a Sunday before, and as he lay naked on the bed blowing smoke rings towards the ceiling I got up and walked to the window. His visits were getting longer, which meant his leaving was getting harder, which most likely meant that my experiment had gone on a little too long. In the beginning my intentions were educational: I would fuck Quentin to figure out how Ricky got away with fucking around on me. But somehow the more we did it, the fucking, the more talking we did too. And talking as we were it was suddenly becoming very apparent, at least to me, that Quentin was more than sex. What he was exactly, especially to me, well, of that I wasn't quite sure.

I mean, isn't it entirely possible that—maybe I should call Adair and she can run it past the girls?—when Quentin took up with me his relationship with Sarah grew stronger?

And isn't it also possible that Ricky never cheated on me? That maybe I just made it all up?

Or is that one maybe too close to maybe-not?

Maybe not what? Quentin asks, his arms bent at the elbows and tucked neatly behind his head.

Not anything, I said, wandering back into bed, beside Quentin and wondering when I had stopped thinking to myself and started thinking out loud.

It was quiet for a long time. The sun set fast and when it was completely gone Quentin sat up and looked for his shoes.

So about that tattoo, I said, leaning back into his lap as he sat on the edge of the bed and tried to put on his shoes. If a girl were serious, serious about a tattoo in the shape of some text that did not resemble a Chinese fucking ideogram or fraternity brand, where might that girl go to get it done?

Quentin let out a laugh that was more like a snicker and said, while tugging a tight bow in his shoelaces, Well, if that girl were indeed serious, and if she were to get a tattoo, the one she's describing, she'd have to go to Long Beach and make an appointment with a man named Tuttle.

Tuttle? I said, as I hung an arm over the bedside and playfully untied Quentin's left lace.

Tuttle, he said again, tying again. He's the only one who will know how.

Nothing closer? I asked, reaching this time for the right lace, before Quentin playfully swatted my hand away. Like something on Sunset?

Nope, Quentin replied in a voice that echoed with the suspicion I'd never go through with it. But good luck, he said, kissing me on the forehead and slipping off the bed and towards the door. Lyle Tuttle only inks Hell's Angels and rock stars anymore.

THE SILENT SCREENPLAY

I KNOW he didn't mean it, but the anymore stung. Almost as much as the click shut of the hotel door. Almost as much as the noise I imagine Junah's body made when it ran out of air and hit dirt. Almost as much as the slap of my open fist with a handful of keys against Puck's baby-soft cheek. Almost as much as Ricky driving away in the dark with Dior. As though—in the anymore—there was a hint that there had ever been a time when Lyle Tuttle inked regular people like husbands and infidels and desperately lonely bottled-water girls; a time when Junah clung, breathing, suspend from ropes; a time when Puck was my best friend and not my whipping boy. If I hadn't slapped Puck, if I hadn't—literally—knocked the best friendship I've had out of my life, I would have called him up and invited him out on a field trip to Long Beach. We could have bought bikes and gotten inked and revved our engines, together. But instead I was left. In a hotel room. Alone.

REINVENTING GENRES

LEFT ALONE in a hotel room, in the dark early evening of a Sunday afternoon, has just got to be the opening line of a blues song somewhere. If I knew a little less about art and a little more about music, I'm sure I could sing it to you, but I've been known to be a bit off key and so I'll refrain. There's a voice in the back of my head that says maybe I should paint it. Maybe I should splash up some color and stick on a few rhinestones, use the blues to make a masterpiece, call it "Magdalena In and Out of Love, or at Least Bed" but just what color is infidelity exactly? And how big is the rhinestone that would catch Ricky's eye?

Bigger than a Sweet Tart, that's to be sure. Bigger than a bread box, a hope chest and even my car, big as it is. Bigger than big is the flash, the glitter and the gleam. Bigger than me and then maybe he'd know that, even with Quentin, I miss Ricky.

Maybe, in fact, especially.

COLD CALLING

AFTER QUENTIN'S exit I didn't quite know what to do with myself. Tuesday was still a day and a half away and so, lacking anything better to do, I picked up the phone, got Ian at front desk and asked for Tuttle.

When I was patched through to the shop I put on my best Barbie voice and said, I need to talk to Lyle.

The guy on the other end said, Yeah honey, what about?

And so I said, because why the hell not, Who the fuck do you think this is?

Guy said, Just a sec. And in a sec Lyle was on the line. And in another sec I had an appointment on Monday at four. And it was just. That. Easy.

Making up with Puck, however, I knew would not be. So I called his agent.

BZ and I went way back. Or rather BZ and Ricky did and so, according to the Hollywood rules of acquaintance, so did we. He was the ex-husband of one of Ricky's sisters, I can never remember which, and because of this Cheri or Sherry got 5 percent of whatever Puck made.

No, really.

It's another one of those L.A. things that took me a small while to wrap my mind around but, now that I understand, goes something like this: In L.A. it's always about who you know. And if the people you know know someone who's in the know well then you know them too. Or better yet, if the people you know know someone who's known well then you're known by association, which can, in fact, mean very big things for you and, by the rule of reciprocal association, big things for the people you know. Which is why it makes sense to know people, especially in L.A. And because I knew BZ through Ricky, who knew him through Sherry or Cheri, which practically made him family— my ex-brother-in-law if you don't mind the fact that he was married to and then divorced from Cheri or Sherry, or maybe even both, years before Ricky and I met—I subsequently knew that Puck was recovering from Moroccan jet lag (he and Keanu were on location working on the so-top-secret-I-can't-tell-you-the-title *Matrix* prequel) and that he had said—this is a direct quote from BZ who heard it from the makeup girl, who no doubt told Cheri or Sherry or both, who then obviously told Ricky, or at the very least Ricky's mother, which was much, much worse—that my situation "was so far gone it was sad."

And when BZ said as much to me on the phone, all I could say was, Ouch.

And then I hung up.

Cold phone in my hand I desperately wanted to call someone else, but there weren't many people left to call. My mother thought I was in New Mexico and was probably preoccupied in her Lodi kitchen drinking a bottle of merlot and affixing brightly colored stickers that said *Bueno!* and *Muy Bien!* to the tops of passing Spanish exams. Adair and the girls were probably out with their boyfriends or husbands or maybe even their husband's boyfriends at Chin Chins or Cha Cha Cha, and although there was always room for one more I didn't think I could handle another round of them. Not on a Sunday anyhow.

Which left only Ricky. And Immelda, who were probably at home watching reruns of *The Sopranos*—in Spanish subtitles— on my couch. I paced the suite naked walking in and out of the bedroom, bathroom and living room divides. I opened the door just a pinch and flipped the DO NOT DISTURB sign over to reveal the PLEASE MAKE UP ROOM sign. I turned up the stereo and turned down the A/C. I threw myself on the unmade bed and buried my face in the pillows. As I breathed in I realized, if only for a moment, that I expected them to smell like Ricky. They didn't. And don't be so judgmental, they didn't smell like Quentin either. They smelled of grapes and chlorine and very dry cork. They smelled of Bamberger merlot just before the press. They smelled of home.

I reached for my purse, shook a couple of pink and blue pills into my hand, swallowed them dry and sent a text message to Puck.

CRISIS

9 11. LONG BEACH. tattoos. please? yrs, mags.
He responded: Go 911 yrself.

It wasn't exactly what I was hoping for, but at least it was something. And it was a quick turnaround, which meant, undoubtedly, he was stomach down, sprawled on his faux-rabbit sofa thumbing through *Variety* and waiting for his iPhone to ring.

So I tried again: pretty please?

But he didn't reply. So I went into the bathroom, sat at the vanity, reapplied some mascara and nothing. I checked my phone, it had all the bars. I turned it off and then on, just in case, but no.

I called down to ask Ian to saddle up the Tank and made my way to Long Beach, alone.

SPECIAL EFFECTS

CONTRARY TO what Quentin may have said, Lyle Tuttle's tattoo parlor is not in Long Beach. It's in the back of a bike shop in Bellflower. The bikes were all Harleys and shiny with chrome, and tacked up to a grease-stained wall were a grip of hand-drawn girls in bikinis and one-piece suits stretched up against palm trees or lounging in inner tubes. Some had super-short cut-offs with small danglies of denim touching their thighs, and others had coconuts or half-shirts tied in knots above their navels. I walked along considering each one. Considering myself done up as one, with high heels and coifed hair, looking as though I were waiting to be slapped against the freshly scrubbed bicep of a seaman from the 1950's.

Yum.

Lyle Tuttle was in the back and when someone hollered, Four o'clock, he didn't keep me waiting. So Sugar, what's it gonna be? he asked, eyeing first my hips and then my breasts. Text, I said, pulling from my purse the Basquiat postcard from the MOMA gift shop Ricky bought me when he wouldn't buy me the painting itself. I held it out to Lyle but he didn't take it. Instead he readjusted the bandana that was holding back his ponytail and he made what sounded like a grunt. He had a ridiculous amount of armpit hair, the most I had ever seen on anyone, and he smelled sticky or like bologna and I realized I kind of liked the smell.

Sit down, he said, pointing to a barstool with a swivel seat and no back.

I sat, hanging my Fendi bag over my bare knee, and soon learned Lyle Tuttle didn't do custom orders, especially not custom orders taken from reproduced pieces of art printed on a museum postcard. Lyle Tuttle gives you the tattoo he thinks you need and he doesn't care particularly if you want it on the small of your back or circling your wrist. Lyle Tuttle gives you the tattoo he thinks you need in the place he thinks you need it, and when he told me to take off my shirt I did. And when he told me my bra strap was getting in the way, I took off my bra as well.

Naked from the waist up in the back room of a Harley shop, I sat on a stool with a swivel top and watched Lyle carefully add black ink to a steel vile attached to a gun. He turned it on and off twice and he said to me, Ready?

Hell no, I wasn't ready, but I knew if I said as much, if I hesitated for even an instant Lyle would turn off his gun and walk away forever, leaving me to sit shivering, half-undressed on a barstool in Bellflower. So I took a small breath and said, Ready.

Lyle Tuttle grunted and picked up another stool, identical to mine, and set it down in such a way that when he sat down he was straddling my small body like a hug.

And suddenly, right there, like that, I was all right. No, I was better than all right. I can honestly say that, at that moment, I had never felt more safe in my life.

Ready, I said again to Lyle, who switched the gun to his left hand before he switched it on.

Lyle decided I needed a moth adorned sentence running vertical down the lower part of my spine. *Le papillon de nuit*, he said. The gun was on in Lyle's left hand, and it hummed. With his right hand Lyle grabbed my right shoulder and began to squeeze while massaging the muscle in a circular motion. With each small circle he inched his index and pointer fingers closer to the line where the sharp curve of my breastbone was lost behind the fatty skin of my boob. With his left hand he inked the moth and then the text while with his mouth he made quiet words into my ear.

Can you feel it pushing against your skin? Ripping into your flesh?
Do you want it deeper? Longer? Harder?
Sugar?

THE CASTING COUCH

DIDN'T fuck Lyle though maybe I almost wanted to. I did not fuck Lyle although I knew it was probably part of the gig, the way around not being a Hell's Angel or a rock star. Because I did not fuck him he used brown institutional paper towels to blot at the blood that formed in the crevices of the delicately drawn wings on my back. I deserved this.

I said, Ouch.

Lyle said, don't use Neosporin. Don't sun. That'll be $175.

I wished I could pull three perfectly rolled hundred dollar bills from someplace magical, like my cunt, but unfortunately I hadn't the foresight to think of such a thing, so like a dumb-ass I wrote Lyle a check.

Don't worry, I said as he looked it over with a squint—I had made it for four times the amount he told me. It'll clear.

I'm sure it will, Sugar, he said as he tucked it into the pocket of his worn and greasy jeans. Of that I have no doubt.

OUTSIDE, THE sun was a little too bright, but instead of getting back into the Tank, which I left with the last of my cash—a fifty—near some kids on the curb, I sat on the steps of the bike shop, smoked an imaginary cigarette and tried to figure out what the fuck I was doing. In the Central Valley I'd be quite a sensation, sitting skirt around my thighs on the dirty-ass steps of a bike shop, taking drags of a cigarette that didn't exist. But in Los Angeles, or some Long Beach/Bellflower extension thereof, I'm just another girl with a back that burns like a motherfucker and a purse full of pharmaceuticals.

I dug out my phone and dialed.

Okay, so I didn't exactly dial numbers, rather I said "Puck" into the handset and after a brief pause the phone rang. It rang three times before someone, a girl, picked it up.

Hi-ye, she said, Puck's place, and then she giggled. And he giggled. I heard him in the background. A distinctly Puck-like giggle of the we're-talking-shit-about-those-girls variety.

I didn't say anything. I just crossed my fingers and held my breath.

Umm, like hell-oh? she said again.

Hi, I said. Is Puck there?

In the background I heard him say, Ask who it is.

He said to ask who is it, the girl said.

She sounded young, but she couldn't be that young. Not four-years-old, I-repeat-everything-as-I'm-told young. I was being played. She was playing with me. And I had to take it. At least if I wanted to talk to Puck. So instead of saying, Listen here Sweetie, on the front of the phone is a little screen and when I call my picture pops up. I know it does, because I was wearing my I-can't-believe-I-spent-so-much-on-a-white-linen-that–you–just–spilled–cabernet-on—before—I—could—even—wear—it—in—L.—A. dress when Puck snapped the shot in the rolling green hills of Cotes de Bordeaux. And underneath that picture, in case we haven't met, is my name: Magdalena. But instead of saying all that, I just said, Magdalena.

She said Madge-da-lane-ah, the girl repeated and I heard a muffled cough, or what might have been a cough but what most likely was a pantomime because when she returned to the phone she said, He said to tell you he's not home.

I hung up and sat down.

I closed my eyes and pushed my fingers into the sides of my eyelids until the red haze I was seeing turned into a dark black spot. I breathed. I took air in and then, as gently as I could, I let it out.

I was going to need a bath. A hot one.

And a real cigarette.

And one hell of a bottle of gin.

EXTERNAL CONFLICTS

BACK AT the hotel I was admittedly half-drunk, in a half-full tub. My body art burned and itched in a god-awful way, even when pressed up against the cool porcelain back. Unbelievable, I thought as I tied my hair in a knot on top of my head and reached over the side of the tub for another drink. I was blasting a recently burned copy of *The Barbie Coffin's* latest single, "Baton de Colle." It was Quentin's band and I was trying to love it, hence the volume, the alcohol and the perpetual repeat, but in all honesty it just wasn't my thing.

When the phone rang I was sure it was Ian asking me to turn the racket down, so I ignored it and let it go to voice mail. But when it rang again, I picked it up.

Ian hesitated before saying, Mag-da-lena?

Yes?

I know you've placed a hold on all your calls, but since you're on the line would you care to receive messages at this time?

That depends who's calling.

Well there's a gentleman in the bar. He's been waiting about forty-five minutes. I told him you were taking a siesta and that I'd notify him when you were receiving visitors.

Send him up. I'm receiving visitors now.

I'll get right to it.

Thanks Ian, you're a peach.

SURVEY BEATS AND
LOCATE TURNING POINTS

IT WASN'T Tuesday or Thursday and it was far from a Sunday afternoon so for a brief moment I breathed a strange excited air thinking the gentleman in the bar who was currently making his way up to my suite might be Puck, or better yet Ricky, but when I heard Quentin's knuckles rap I knew it wasn't so.

It's open, I hollered above the drumming of the dead Barbie band.

The door opened slowly as Quentin shuffled in and took a survey of the room. My hair was piled in an artful, but wet sloping mess on top of my head, secured with two take-out chopsticks, and I wasn't wearing lip-gloss. I had, however, managed to get out of the tub and slip into a camo tank and hip-huggers, covered by a tangerine kimono with red and magenta dragonflies buzzing round the armholes—I didn't want Quentin to see the tattoo. It was still raw and red. Maybe when it had healed over. Maybe when the scab fell off.

Hi, I said to Quentin.

Hi, he responded, walking over to the stereo and turning down the noise, shaking his head and kind of quietly laughing as he did so.

Glad you decided to accept visitors, he said, I was going broke down there at the bar. Do you know they charge $24.50 for something called a Tahiti Martini?

Well they use real lychees, I said.

Fuck, for that much they'd better use real crystal and let you keep the glass.

I giggled and slid my feet over a smidge so he could join me on the lounge.

I didn't know you were the Tahiti Martini type, I said, stretching my feet back out over his lap.

I'm not, but we're doing a tall wall on Sunset and there was a conflict with the squeegee jockeys so we got off early.

A tall wall?

You know when they paint the entire side of the building with an ad for Spiderman or something.

You mean like where his eyes become the windows and he looks like he's climbing up nineteen stories strung from a web?

Kind of, but we're more sophisticated than that now. We do the windows too and from a distance you can't even tell.

What about from close up?

Close up it's pretty good, though I don't know what it's like from the inside. I've always wondered what they see.

I'm pretty sure they can't tell the difference, I said thinking of the giant bottle of Diamond Myst we had painted on the west wall. Most companies use dual panes and they're tinted in such a way that you can't really tell what's going on outside.

Right, he said. You would know.

There was some silence while I adjusted the chopstick in my hair.

So, Spiderman, that's what you did today?

No, we're starting a Target wall, Quentin said, pushing my feet off his lap and walking out to the balcony, where he lit up a smoke.

Shut the sliding glass door, I shouted out to him, I don't need smoke in here today.

Without saying a word Quentin did as he was told.

While he was out on the balcony I repositioned myself on the lounge where I busied myself with makeup, trying to discretely paint and line my lips with my right hand while I held my left over my mouth as though I were about to cough. I didn't have a mirror, but I could see an outline of my mouth in the polished base of the table lamp, and although I was grossly disproportioned by the convex surface I managed the lips just fine.

When he came back inside I had a freshly done-up mouth, which he failed to kiss. Instead he said, Maybe this was a mistake.

You mean us? I said, suddenly still on the settee.

No. Not quite, he tried a small laugh. Maybe we should just keep to our appointments next time. I don't know about this dropping in stuff.

I didn't ask you to come—

That's what I mean, he said, pushing his heel down into his shoe and reaching for the laces.

But, I finished, I'm glad you did.

He paused, I can't say I feel the same.

What do you mean? I was standing up now, making my way to the door to block his departure.

I mean I guess I thought you were different when I wasn't here.

Different how?

Like you did something.

For your information, I told him, I do do things. I do all sorts of things.

Like what? he said, suddenly sounding a lot more like Ricky than I ever thought him capable.

You know what, I said reaching for the doorknob and opening it myself, I don't need this.

No really, what do you do all day? Is this it? he said.

Is what it?

This, he untucked an arm and motioned to the room, the growing mound of glossy shopping bags, the take-out box from Chin Chins, the view.

Yes, I said. I hotel all day. I spa and I sun and more often than not I call down to the valet and he brings the car round unless I don't feel like driving whereupon I hire a limo and then I spend the afternoon nursing a latte through the boutiques of Rodeo and Robertson.

Sounds like a tough life, Quentin said.

It is, I said, defiant. You don't know the half of it. But something in the way he was looking at me, past me, said he did know. He knew all too well.

Fuck, I said, holding on to the doorframe to keep from shaking. Do you think that it's nothing? That I spend my days doing nothing? I do exactly the opposite. I spend my days trying to do something, anything, so that I have something to pour the nothing into. Doing nothing is easy. It's doing something that's hard. Doing something meaningful or monetary all day…I mean, how on earth do you begin?

Quentin laughed, finally, and not in a sad or sarcastic way. He laughed out loud and for real. Come on, he said. I'll show you.

THE NOT SO A-LIST

SERIOUSLY, HE said. Get dressed. I wanna show you something.

What, I asked, my faced buried in down.

It's an outing, he said.

I don't know, I said.

Well I say you should, he tossed me a pair of Juicy peach capris.

Rolling over slowly and leaning back on the bed I slipped my feet into the leg holes and slid the sweats up onto my bare ass, cinching the drawstring tight around my waist. I reached for my bra and quickly put on my shirt so Quentin wouldn't see my back, while he dug through the closet looking for shoes.

Don't you have any shoes with laces? he asked.

Sure, I said, pointing to a pair of cranberry corset-inspired Manolo pumps with ankle ties.

That's not exactly what I had in mind, Quentin said, picking up the shoe and examining it briefly before placing it back in the closet. Don't you have any tennis shoes? he asked, poking around in the closet again.

I don't play tennis, I said. It's almost more excruciating than golf.

I wasn't being literal, he said. Sneakers? Converse? Adidas? Gym shoes? You go to the gym don't you?

Yes. In those, I said, and pointed to a pair of rhinestone en-crusted flip-flops.

You wear these to work out in? Quentin picked one up and ran his finger along the sparkly sole.

No, I wear them *to* the gym. *At* the gym I wear my running shoes.

Okay, he turned around a bit exasperated and I could tell I had almost gotten to him. Wear your running shoes then.

I can't, I said, enjoying myself. A-of-all they don't match with what I'm wearing and B-of-all they're at the gym. I keep them in my locker.

Of course, Quentin said, and turned back towards the closet. I laughed.

Having fun? he asked, still sizing up the closet's contents.

A blast, I said. Where are we going that I need sneakers?

It's a surprise, he said, reaching back into the closet and grabbing a small brown paper bag.

Put that back, I said, jumping up from the bed and walking towards the closet in two long steps.

Why? he asked, opening the bag and removing one tiny peachy-pink slipper.

I froze, half wanting to tear the shoe away from him, half struck by the sight of the dusty ribbons I had hand-sewn into the seams with teeny tiny stitches.

Hey, he said. No heels, laces…do these still fit?

I don't know I said, gently taking the slipper from his hand and rubbing its soft leather across my cheek. I sat back down on the bed and held the sole of the shoe up to the bottom of my foot. I think they're too small.

Just try, he said, you never know.

I took a deep breath expecting, like some backwards Cinderella story, to be immediately turned into ash. But when my foot touched the slipper, first the left and then the right, nothing happened. They were a little stretched out—my pinkie toes bobbed about and did not stay snugged up against my middle toes—but I took hold of the ribbons and wrapped them in a tight X-pattern up my ankles and ended with a double-knotted bow just above the neck of my foot.

Okay, I said, desperate to *pas de bourrée*, to *arabesque*, to *échappé* and *jeté* out of the hotel. I grabbed Quentin's hand and tugged him out of the bedroom. Let's go already.

STUNT DOUBLE

EACH SOFT-SOLED step I took down the hall, in the elevator, through the lobby and out the door of the hotel resonated with danger. My hand in Quentin's, step by step, we were breaking the rules. Maybe if there had been a third, Puck for example, or one of Quentin's cousins from the auto shop, Treena or Adair, someone other than just the two of us, standing in the lobby surrounded by banana-leaf wall paper and waiting for the valet to pull Quentin's car around. Someone to make excuses in case we were seen by someone from the water set, by Quentin's uncle, by Venus, Donna or, oh the horror, Cheri. Three can be explained as a meeting, a business dinner, a group outing. Two can't be so easily explained. Especially when one of the two is wearing pink ballet slippers, two Blonde Lizard chandelier earrings and no panties, while the other of the two is wearing paint-splattered Diesel jeans, a vintage Syd Barrett concert tee and green pumas. We deserved to be caught, I was thinking, and then a beige minivan with a ladder tied to the top pulled up and the valet held open the passenger's door.

That's us, Quentin said, dropping my hand so he could pull a twenty from his wallet. You coming?

You drive a minivan?

Don't worry, he said, the rear windows are tinted. You can sit in back if you're worried about what the world might think. He tugged open the sliding side door and walked around to the driver's side leaving me to make up my own mind.

I climbed in next to him and the valet closed both doors before we drove off.

That's not what I meant, I said, clicking my seat belt across my lap. I just thought you'd drive something older.

What, you don't think the Aerostar's a classic? This baby here, he patted the dash, is timeless.

I can see that, I said, noting the sloping bow of the ceiling and the duct-taped vinyl upholstery.

And besides, it fits three amps, the drums, a dozen cans of paint and a 22-foot extension ladder.

Good to know.

Quentin made a left on Beverly and another left on Crescent Heights. We passed Santa Monica Boulevard and Melrose.

Where are we going? I asked again, terrified he'd gotten it in his head to take me to Sunset and there was no way I was pulling up in front of Katana, North or even the Whiskey-A-Go-Go in a minivan, however timeless.

You'll see, he said.

Right, I said and continued to keep track of the street signs: Norton, Fountain, Sunset. On Sunset we didn't turn right or left and I let out my breath. Instead we continued straight, passing Selma Avenue and Mt. Olympus, and—just before Crescent Heights turned into the windy roads of Laurel Canyon—we took a right and headed east on Hollywood Boulevard.

Can I have a clue?

We're not going out, we're going up, he said.

Up how? I asked, feeling a new kind of terror creep into my stomach.

Up there, he said, pulling into an alley on the corner of North Stanley and pointing to a billboard that advertised Diamond Myst.

Maybe I'll stay in the car, I said, eyeing Puck holding a water-logged me, larger-than-life as we bobbed about in the Pacific, and the words A DIAMOND IN THE ROUGH, printed in bold, below.

Well I'm going up, Quentin said. Could you at least give me a hand with the ladder?

Fine, I said, unclicking my belt and opening the side door.

While Quentin worked the knots on the driver's side, I struggled to undo the double figure-eights on my side without injuring a nail. When the ladder was unhitched, Quentin lifted it off the roof and over his head, setting it down against the Myst ad.

We'll need this, he said, expanding the ladder and locking it in place, to get past the barbed graffiti wire. After that we can climb up the utility pole using the attached rungs.

You can, I said, if that's what you want. Even looking that high makes me dizzy.

Look, he said, I don't know what's up with you and heights, but you're not going to fall, I can promise you that.

Really, I asked. You can promise I won't fall? You can promise I won't come crashing thirty gazillion feet to the ground? You can promise you'll save me and all that.

He kicked at some loose gravel with his sneaker and stuck his fingers in his pockets, slouching. No, he said, you're right. I can't promise anything. Maybe you could fall. Maybe an earthquake will hit and knock us both over. Maybe you'll sneeze and I'll slip and we'll both, as you say, come crashing to the ground, but it's doubtful, and if it does happen we'll fall together, that I can promise.

Why would you want to...how could you promise a thing like that?

STICKING WITH THE SCRIPT

SEVERAL THINGS happened after Junah's body came tumbling off the rock. I wasn't there to see it, you know that, so
like me you have to trust what the EMT said, what the ranger said,
what six out of seven of the wilderness youth brigade on spring
break from the outdoor recreation program at Oregon State said.
We have to sort of piece it together so that it makes sense. Had I
been there, had I not driven back to the ranch to work on water,
you could have trusted me when I told you Junah didn't fall from
anything, but as you know I left him and down he went.

The EMT said he was lucky. I mean, he said, trying to be
sympathetic, trying to empathize, who of us wouldn't want a
sudden death? Most Americans, if polled, attest that they want
to go quickly, and your son, Sir, Ma'am, he nodded in the direction of my parents, did just that. It was instant, he said as if that
was any kind of consolation. He didn't suffer.

Instant? I thought, as I held on to Ricky, trying to form
words but only able to choke on my sentences. Instant? What the
fuck about falling is instant? Sure it's only seven or eight seconds
of falling, but can you imagine (like I imagine daily) what those
seconds were like? Of trying to stop the falling? Of watching the
rock as it slips past your grasp? Of knowing you're alive and just
waiting for your body to smack against the ground, to take the
life right out of you? What's so fucking instant about that?

The ranger concurred, The young man was dead on impact.
Those poor kids from that Oregon school did an amazing job,
really. They came to his aid in a matter of moments, attempted
CPR, assessed his vitals, but he was already gone.

And six of the seven "poor kids from that Oregon school" who had to bear witness to the death and the horror of my brother's broken and bloody body all said the same. They said he was a badass. Soloing with no rope thirty or forty feet above ground. They had been climbing with him all morning and collectively agreed that he was the safest, most levelheaded, badass climber they had ever met. Which of course begs the word, "until..."

He was the most level headed, until...

He was the safest climber they had ever met, until...

He was a badass soloer until...

...he fell to his death.

Until he fell to his death.

Until.

PROPS

MY PARENTS didn't stick around for the ceremony, for the certificates of valor handed out by the Mariposa County Chamber of Commerce to the brave rescuers of their dead son. And I didn't blame them. My mother was still reeling from "dead on impact," and my dad, who had never shed a tear a day in his life that I can remember, was holding his hat in front of his face, yet still you could hear him sobbing.

I would have left too, were I able to stand. Had I a voice I would have asked Ricky to pick me up and carry me out of the fucking Greeley Hill Library conference room, but I couldn't say anything. And so we sat, Ricky and I. And somewhere after the certificates were handed out, but before the informational session on rock climbing safety began, the seventh of "the seven poor kids from that Oregon school" approached me and held out a brown paper bag.

I thought, he said awkwardly, I just didn't...know.

I let go of Ricky then and wrapped myself around that poor boy. Sobbing into his shoulder he held me, awkward, as he tried to whisper into my ear that he was the first one on the scene. That he was sure Junah had been climbing barefoot—what a badass!—but that when his body hit the ground he was wearing... He pushed me away a little and tried to take something out of the brown paper bag.

I shook my head and held his arms in my hug.

I know I wasn't supposed to touch the body, he said quietly to my neck so no one else could hear. But after I knew he was...and before the Ranger got there...well, I took these. I didn't want anyone to think…I'm just saying, I'd want someone to do it for me.

Thank you, I said, taking the brown paper bag and letting the poor kid go.

Gently, Ricky tried to take the bag away from me. Either to help me in my grief or to look inside. But I held tight, and then, when he tried again, I stuffed the small paper package into the chest of my black dress. It's mine, I said fiercely. Don't fucking try to touch it.

GRIP

YOU GO first, Quentin said, holding his arm out chivalric towards the ladder. Climb to the fifth rung and I'll be right behind you. We'll go step by step together, and if you slip, if you fall and crash to the ground, so will I. I'll fall beneath you, maybe I'll even break your fall. What do you say? he held out his hand.

I say no, I said as I walked to the ladder and tested its stability by shaking it a bit.

I say absolutely not, I said, stepping with my soft slippers onto the first rung and then the second and then the third.

I'm right behind you, Quentin said as I stepped onto the fourth and then the fifth rung, making sure both feet were parallel before leading the right foot up another notch: right foot, left foot, feet together; right hand, left hand, hands together.

It was very slow going, but Quentin didn't seem to care. I'm right behind you, I'm right behind you, he kept whispering.

About five feet below the barbed wire my iPhone, attached to my waist by a plastic clip—hopelessly uncool, I know, but I forgot my purse and had nothing to put it in—rang. But not just any ring, Ricky's *Take Me Out to the Ballgame*, ring. Deet de de de de deet deet, it sang as I climbed. I wanted to push the reject button. I wanted to turn it off. I wanted to answer, but to answer, to reject, to power off would mean removing one of my white-knuckled hands from the cool metal of the ladder and there was no way in hell that was going to happen. So we climbed to musical accompaniment.

When we reached the massive loops and swirls of barbed wire, intended to keep taggers and people such as ourselves from reaching the billboard's shelf, the ringing stopped and Quentin said, Now this is going to be the tricky part.

You didn't say there was going to be a tricky part, I said.

Well there is, and this here is it. What you have to do is swing around to the back of the board, where the rungs are, but don't push off or the ladder will wobble, and lift your leg extra high or else you'll be snagged by the barbed wire.

I looked at the board, the wire and the rungs as Quentin gave instructions. I want to go down, I said.

But you're over halfway there, Quentin said. It's quicker to go up than it is to go down.

I want to go down.

I'll make you a deal, Quentin said as my phone began to play Ricky's ring yet again. Just try it once. Stretch up as tall as you can and see if you can reach the rung with your leg. If you can't we'll go down, no questions asked.

Buy me some peanuts and cracker jacks, my phone sang, I don't care if I ever—No really, I said, I can't. And if you'll excuse me, I started to take slow, small steps back down the rungs, I really have to take this call.

Quentin nodded, but he didn't back down. Instead, he swung his body around the backside of the ladder and made me face him, our knuckles inches apart, our chests brushing through the cold steel as he went up and I went down.

WRITING FROM THE OUTSIDE IN

O N THE ground I leaned up against the hood of Quentin's van and stared at the picture of Ricky that flashed across my caller ID. Putting a hand over my mouth and the receiver to help muffle the noise in both directions I said, Hi.

Hi, Ricky said.

And then there was along silence where neither of us said anything.

How are you holding up? he finally said.

Fine, I said. You know, considering.

Considering what? he asked.

Considering, I wanted to say, I'm in a mild tiff with my lover who is currently without ropes fifty feet above ground, and if he doesn't die I just might, from the sheer terror of the memories and all. But instead I said, Considering, you know, us.

What about us? Ricky asked.

I don't know, I said. I thought maybe that's why you called.

It is, he said, kind of. I've been thinking about us and I think we need to talk.

Yeah, I said. We probably do.

So how about if I fly out to Santa Fe and then help you drive back.

How do you know I didn't fly out here myself? I asked.

Because you're too scared to fly, at least without a purse full of sedatives and a licensed psychiatrist. Your car's gone. And your mother called.

Oh, I said, wondering how even in a simple lie I managed to get so caught up.

So how about it?

How about what, I asked.

How about I fly to Santa Fe and we drive back together?

Sure, I said, knowing he never would, knowing that something would come up—Fiji, an important merger meeting, a date with Dior, a melted iceberg—something always came up.

Where are you staying? he asked.

I'm moving around, I lied, not wanting him to do something crazy like call the hotel to confirm. How about you call me when you land in Albuquerque and I'll pick you up.

Sounds good, he said.

Good, I said.

And then there was more silence. I took a deep breath and looked up to where Quentin stood, hands in his pockets on the ledge of death. Because I couldn't think of anything else to say I said, Do you love me?

Of course.

Not because you have to, but like you used to, I said. Do you love me like you used to?

Magdalena, Ricky sighed, I need to be efficient today so that I can catch the next flight out of here. I love you. Bye.

But not like you used to, I said to the dial tone.

UNRAVELING THE
NARRATIVE THREAD

THE CAR ride on the way home was awkward. I stared out the window and would have fiddled with the door locks, except in Quentin's car nothing was automatic and it might have seemed silly to push and then pull the button thingy by the door. So instead I picked at a loose piece of rubber that was sticking out of the dash and tried to count my intake of breaths.

Hey, Quentin said, reaching his hand over the stick shift and rubbing my knee, heights aren't for everyone. It takes practice to know you won't fall.

That's when the tears came. The impossible body-shaking, snotty, hiccup mess of soul-melting sorrow.

Fuck, Quentin said, taking his hand off my knee so he could downshift and pull over with minimal commotion. You okay?

No, I shook my head as the story of Junah began to slip out. I'm not okay at all.

DREAM SEQUENCES

AFTER JUNAH died I was sure he would come for me. In a dream, in a cloud, as a door-to-door soap salesman. I prayed to God a lot then. My God, not the Catholic one. Apparently this is the bargaining/denial/rage stage, but I didn't see it that way. Maybe it's because I'm still not to the acceptance stage, but to get to the acceptance stage I would have to know just how exactly it feels to fall to the ground and when your body hits the earth in some sort of deafening smack what it feels like and does it feel alone?

I know that accepting Junah's death has everything to do with the feeling of body to ground. But short of leaping off the same cliff, I only have moments like the ones just before sleep when I feel as though I'm falling and I don't fight it. I don't jolt awake and reach out for the bed, instead I try to stay there, in the perpetually plunging moment, and I pray—not to God—that this is Junah. That if I fall with him, I'll have my sign.

DRAMATURGE

KILLED him, I said to Quentin, on the side of the road.

Woah, easy now, Quentin said, as he put the van in park and moved out of the driver's seat, over the stick shift, and squished himself into the bucket seat on the passenger's side with me. He put both his arms around me and let me cry.

It was supposed to be a joke, I was getting eye make up all over the silkscreen of Syd Barrett. It...I...I stole his shoes, I said. It was supposed to be a joke. It wasn't supposed to kill him.

Quentin, God bless him, didn't ask questions. He didn't say, "Who?" or "Where?" or even "You killed someone! What the fuck?" Instead he scooped me up so that I sat in his lap, and he stroked my hair as I talked into his chest:

They were teriyaki orange with spumoni-colored laces. And I thought it would be funny. I thought it would be hilarious if I just swapped out his shoes and replaced them with—the tears came, pushing past my lids again—these. I held up my foot and flexed my soft-soled ballet slipper. I thought...I didn't mean for him to...and I planned to tell him. When he opened his bag, I planned to be there, after the joke, to trade back my shoes for his. But I wasn't. There. And his shoes were with me, one hundred thirty-one point six miles away.

Quentin swayed and held me tighter as I continued, telling him things that I don't think I had even dared to admit to myself:

And what makes it worse, what makes it so much worse, was that he clearly found it funny. Junah and I were good like that. We were...twinned like that. I knew he knew it was funny because he wore them. He wore my fucking pink ballet slippers soloing onto a 43-foot rock just so he could tell me about it. Just so he could take my joke and make it even funnier. But he fell. Because unlike rock-climbing shoes that stick, ballet slippers are supposed to slide. They're supposed to glide across the slick bamboo floor. They're not—

Shussh, Quentin said, kissing first my mouth and then each and every tear that still clung to my face. Shussh, he said again as I hiccupped, wiped snot on his shirt and struggled to breathe. Shussh, he said again, as he bent down towards my foot and kissed first one pink-toed slipper and then the other. He loved you, he said, looking directly into my puffy red eyes. Your brother loved you, and he'll never, ever, love you any less.

SUBSTANCE

THE NEXT day I woke up alone, tattoo still snugly hidden beneath my tank, without so much as an indent on the pillow next to me to prove that Quentin had—not ten hours ago—lain beside me. I showered, got dressed, called down to Ian to request a town car and then waited in my I ♥ L.A. tank for Puck to pick me up for our standing nail/wax/Rodeo appointment at half past ten.

When I bought the tank, for $168.50 shortly after the water boom, Ricky said carefully, so that I would understand, that my shirt was for tourists.

People in L.A. do not wear t-shirts that say I heart L.A., he said, unless they are in L.A. on vacation from Minnesota—which you are not—and even then most of them have the good sense to wait until they're back in Duluth before they wear them in public.

But why not? I asked, holding the shirt out and attempting to determine which size I needed by pressing it up against my body while it was still on the hanger.

Because it looks stupid, Ricky said. I mean that would be like going to Hawaii and dressing your kid up in one of those t-shirts that say, "Grandma and Grandpa went to Hawaii and all they got me was this dumb t-shirt." It wouldn't make sense because you're already in Hawaii and the kid is wearing the shirt there. You see?

No I don't see, I said, putting the small back and reaching for the extra-small. I don't have a kid and we never took him to Hawaii. So you're not really making sense.

It's just dumb, Ricky said, wearing a shirt that says I love L.A. when you live in L.A.

But that's just it, I said, taking the small and handing it to the sales clerk standing nearby. I'm being glib.

I think I wore it once to the beach while Ricky was at work, and then I forgot about it in my closet. Just as, apparently, Puck had now—intentionally—forgotten about me. So I stepped into a town car and went alone.

At Nail Bar I sucked down Cosmopolitans and stuffed my cheeks full of marshmallow chocolates while Vietnamese women buffed my calluses smooth. Although most of the wives in the water set preferred to get their nails done at the Four Seasons Spa where they give "European-style" manicures—which are no different than any other type of manicure with the large exception that the floor is Spanish tile, the price is three times as much and girls doing the nails are white—I still preferred the low-overhead Asian joints.

Or at least I did when they were seemingly owned and run by the girls themselves. Lately, in every shop, or at least the ones I frequent, in addition to the polite, skinny nail girls, there is also a boss man. At Nail Bar his name is Norman and although he doesn't do nails he sits at the front desk and takes all the money, tips included. In hushed whispers I tried to express my distaste for Norman to the older woman seated next to me but she was, in her own words, Entering a euphoric state, honey, and not in the mood to discuss gender politics.

Sorry, I said and leaned back into the vibrating faux-leather of the massage chair.

Sensing I wanted to talk, Lily, the girl who was massaging my left calf, said, You married?

She knew I was married. I came in weekly and every week we had the same chat, but it was part of the ritual, part of the short list of English words she most likely knew.

Yes, I answered, smiling.

How is your husband?

I looked at Lily, she was kneading her thumbs into pressure points just above my ankle. Her hands were powerful, despite the tired look in her eyes.

I don't know how he is, I answered, honestly. I moved out.

Lily pressed deeper, pinching my Achilles.

That's why I ask, Lily said in perfect English, if you're married. In L.A. you have to ask every week.

I smiled, for real this time, and a noise, half laugh, half sob, escaped from somewhere deep in my throat.

You okay? Lily asked.

Yeah, I said, sinking back into the pleather massage chair. How are you? I asked Lily as she moved on to my right leg.

Still married, she said. Norman, she nodded her chin to the front desk, he's my husband.

Oh, I said, not really knowing what else to say. I was quiet until the phone rang.

When Norman answered Lily whispered, Nail Bar was my idea. To sell drinks and do nails at the same time. Used to be fun working here. Then Norman got fired from his job with Cal-Trans. Now it's not so fun here.

I know exactly what you mean, I told her, taking out a twenty and discreetly tucking it in between the acetone and cotton balls on her nail cart.

WHEN I was back in the car, speeding to Pink Cheeks to get waxed, I started feeling stupid. You know, like when you're at a party and you think of the perfect comeback only after you've left? It was like that. Only reverse. Had I really just complained to my underpaid manicurist? Had I really just pretended to empathize, no, to compare my life to her life? My own voice mimicked me in my head, "My life isn't so fun either." What a bunch of bullshit. *Poor me. I live in the Beverly Hills Hotel. Poor me. I'm fucking the next Eddie Vedder while my oblivious husband is footing the bill. Poor me. I'm just like you.* Oh my God. As if I really believe that. As if I actually think I have anything in common with Lily, who actually has to work touching other people's feet as though she likes it for a living? Fuck me.

And then I was scared.

Soon I was actually going to have to think about what the hell I was doing. Already the pieces didn't match up. The longer my affair with Quentin lasted, the more it became apparent that Ricky wasn't in fact cheating. He was most likely working. Hard. I was the one who had issues. I was the one who couldn't keep the faith and was literally fucking up after murdering my own brother.

At Pink Cheeks, a place supposedly frequented by all of Hef's girls, I went into my cubicle and, thankfully, didn't have to talk. Although some of the other girls shouted their personal lives into cell phones or through the curtain divides, I silently unrobed and spread open my legs. As promised, in six sheets of sharp pulling I was hair free and on my way to Escada.

320 North Beverly Drive, I told the driver and he made the next left.

North Beverly Drive is one block east of Rodeo and developed largely for tourists. It has stores like Victoria's Secret, Banana Republic and the Gap, affordable so that the masses visiting from Duluth can say they bought something on Rodeo even if they didn't buy it *on* Rodeo exactly. I told the driver Beverly and not Rodeo because Puck and I had agreed there was something too *nouveau riche* about getting dropped off on Rodeo. I much preferred to get dropped off one street over and walk around the block.

As the car rounded the corner to Escada I fished in my clutch for some gloss, applied a small amount to my bottom lip and then blotted, checking my work in the tinted window of a Hummer as we passed.

MAGDA! ARMUNDO shouted, sashaying through the store and into my outstretched arms as I walked through the door.

Mundo! I shouted back as we kiss-kissed first one cheek then kiss-kissed the other.

Well aren't you just the package, he said, looking at me, my clutch, my double Ds, my derriere. To think, it was days ago—

Ages, I correct him.

Eons ago, he smiled and swatted me on the ass, that you were just some ill-fitting farm girl from, where was it again, Kentucky?

Lodi.

Might as well be Kentucky, and now look at you, he paused for dramatic effect. You are positively sooooo L.A.!

I looked at myself in the full-length mirror and I didn't see me. Not the me that I carried around in my mind. Not the me that in any way at all resembled my brother Junah. My Polish nose had been replaced with a smaller, less pointy version. My eyebrows had been waxed and arched and lined into perfect floating commas above gray eyes that had been Lasiked into perfection. My skin had been peeled and buffed and bleached and bronzed into a tight mask free of sunspots or laugh lines or anything remotely real. My tits had transformed like a really lucky thirteen-year-old who goes away to summer camp and comes back the most popular girl in class. Anything that might have once said "I grew up outdoors on a grape ranch in the sun" had vanished and was replaced by a Los Angeles vixen varnish. And my hair, try your luck, pick a strand, one in a hundred says you won't—hell, even I won't—be able to spot which shade, which lock is my natural blond.

I looked fake and felt a little sick. The burning sensation that was largely due to the waxing of my parts was creeping up into my stomach, into my chest, into my cheeks. I took a deep breath trying to still the panic, and threw up.

INSTANT REPLAY

I F MY life were a movie and had instant replay, my puking all over Mundo, all over Rodeo and Escada's designer dresses would have been worthy of an Academy Award in special effects. Touted as overly showy and unbelievable by some, the projectile-range of my vomit was astronomical. It would have been awesome too, if the store was not one of Beverly Hills' elite and was instead a tree house filled with thirteen-year-old boys. If I had been back on the ranch, Junah would have appreciated it. He would have glowingly told of my aim to his friends. And then, he would exclaim with wild gesticulations, Laney barfed chunks all over everything. How about that for cool?

But at twenty-nine and some change, with clumps of breakfast stuck to the sash of my knitted angora bolero, it wasn't cool at all. It was the opposite of cool. It was the third worst day of my life.

THE GAP

THE FIRST worst day of my life involved a phone call from a sympathetic ranger who manned a first-aid station at the foot of an impossibly large rock. It was summer and the business was off to a rough start. Ricky had just left the accountants in Berkeley and then driven over to my parents' place to work out the kinks in our reverse osmosis project. And because the accountants had given him the runaround and because no one would invest until the osmosis project was kink-free and he couldn't quite unkink it himself, I left Junah in the mountains to join Ricky and my dad in the field. We were waist high in Tokay seedless and I was attempting to explain to both of them the best way to achieve efficient hyperfiltration without energy recovery or pressure exchange, only this crazy bird, a magpie maybe, I don't remember, kept splashing down into the center of my project as though it were a bath and flipped the water that I was vainly studying all over his little birdie back. Ricky and Dad were stitches over the thing. I tried to be serious, shooing the bird with my left hand while I explained the process, but Ricky and Dad were laughing so hard they could hardly breathe, let alone listen, and that's when it happened. When we heard Mom scream.

Dad sprinted for the house so fast he nearly broke his leg on the length of PVC pipe I had recently rigged to the aqueduct. Ricky looked around, bewildered. Choking on his laughter he was suddenly solemn and followed slowly behind Dad.

I, on the other hand, didn't move. I had heard that scream before, when I was seven, and I knew. Maybe Junah and I really were twins and the umbilical chord that we had shared at birth was finally cut, the tail knotted and left to rot like a black-eyed pea on a newborn's navel. I knew it was Junah and not, say, Grandpa who was getting on in his years. I knew it was Junah and not cousin Wade who drank too much and then challenged the Larsen boys to chicken fights along the levee. I knew it was Junah and not an intruder or a fire or a mouse because I felt it. I felt it like my own back was breaking, my own face crashing as it hit the stone ground.

THE THIRD worst day of my life pales in comparison to first by leaps and bounds, pales so ghostly and sickly green that it tarnishes his memory by even mentioning it in the same breath. But the second worst day, which came after the third, was closer to the same kind of Junah pain. It was the day I realized infidelity wasn't fun.

KEEPING THINGS MOVING

AFTER BLOWING chunks in Beverly Hills I did the only thing I knew how. I ran out the door and around the block to where the driver was waiting on North Beverly and I said, I want to go home. But this time I did not mean the house on Bedford or the Beverly Hills Hotel. I meant home, home. The place where I was from.

The driver looked bewildered. Said something about how he was only contractually able to drive as far as the airport without first getting permission from his supervisor and so I said fine. Take me to my car. I'll drive the rest of the way myself.

THE DRIVE up I-5 is one long agrarian slog. It's slow and mindless and, with the exception three hours in of Kettleman City (which is comprised entirely of fast food restaurants and gas stations built beneath a freeway underpass) and the Danish décor of Pea Soup Andersen's two hours after that, there's not much but an endless expanse of land and livestock, orchards and sky. In my rush to leave L.A. I forgot to restock the CDs, and so it was just me on the road with static, an occasional mariachi march and some feel-good love songs for lovers after dark. First it was Foreigner wanting *To Know What Love Is*, followed by Michael Bolton's *How Am I Supposed To Live Without You?* By the time REO Speedwagon couldn't *Fight This Feeling Anymore*, I killed the radio. The last thing I needed was Rod Stewart *Telling Me Lately* or, worse yet, Celine Dion and her *Power of Love*. So there was silence. And in the silence I drove straight and followed the beam of my headlights as they illuminated hubcaps and tumble-weeds on the shoulder.

At Harris Ranch I stopped to gas up. Stepping out of the car the first thing I noticed was the smell of cow. It was a warm night in the great Central Valley and the air was moist with dung and the fresh scent of alfalfa. I walked from my silver Tank into the convenience store, where the light was harsh and unnaturally yellow. I pushed my sunglasses back against my face and paced the aisles. I grabbed a pack of peanut M&Ms, then I went for water.

A long time ago, when we were happy and first beginning, Ricky and I were frequent convenience store stoppers. We could spend an entire weekend exiting and entering off and on ramps going from 7-Eleven to Shell, Circle-K to Arco and Exxon, scanning the refrigerator sections for liquid. And not, mind you, just any liquid, but water, our water. In the beginning it was usually stored on the bottom next to the gallon jugs—large opaque containers with little labeling and no frills—used for filling radiators or cross-the-border trips to Mexico. We'd work quickly and quietly, one of us (usually me) distracting the counter boy with inane questions about the quickest way to get to, say, Salida, while the other rearranged Cokes and Sprites and Mountain Dews, moving Diamond Myst from the bottom shelf to eye-catching, eye-level locations. We'd snack on corn dogs and powdered doughnuts and drive for miles, moving our empire up, one plastic bottle at a time.

In front of the refrigerated coolers I scanned the shelves for water, which nearly seven years later wasn't hard to find. In fact, there were now so many brands and bottles that collectively they took up nearly two cooler cases. Diamond Myst was sandwiched between Fiji and Aquafina, third row from the top, while our Luxe line sat nearly four rows below, beneath the Evian and Perrier! I looked quickly at the station attendant and then, holding the door open with my hip, I pushed the Evian to the back and stocked nine or ten cool bottles of Luxe in front of it. It wasn't a full run, but single-handed and short on time it was the best I could do. Then I grabbed a 64-ounce, sports-top bottle of Diamond Myst and made my way to the checkout.

I DROVE the remaining 187 miles to Lodi with the window down, so I could taste the air; and when, after the urban cityscape of Stockton and the cloudy black waters of the San Joaquin Delta melted back into the pastoral of Lodi, I pushed down on my blinker and exited onto Eight Mile Road.

When I was a kid Eight Mile Road used to be just that: eight miles. Junah and I would test it on the odometer of the Chevy. It was eight miles down a two-lane country road west from the docks at Herman & Helen's Marina that led through the channels of Rio Linda to Pixley Slough by the Union Pacific Tracks ending up at Highway 99 where it continued another eight miles—well, eight point six, if you want to get technical—east past the Central California Traction lines to Jack Tone Road. Now it stretched a proposed eight lanes and twenty-two miles. There were two golf courses, a Target and hundreds of felled oaks to make room for the tract homes. When I exited I had to pay special attention to stoplights, which seemed to multiply each visit; but even still, as I turned left onto Thornton and right onto Devries, as the country reclaimed itself under the protection of a precious greenbelt, as the manufactured ranches and man-made lakes of Beck Homes turned into the real ranches of my neighbors, there was the wood strawberry shack with its hand-painted sign and dirt drive on the shoulder. And even if the Cardinales did tear down their yellow barn and erect a boutique and state-of-the-art tasting room where they sold sips for $10 a glass, at least they still kept their land.

When I pulled in to the long dirt drive bordered on both sides by grape vines and rose bushes, I half expected my dad to be out in the barn, fiddling with some stray part, coaxing it to come unstuck or bending the renegade tine of a pitchfork back into alignment, a single bulb hanging from the ceiling. But he'd leveled the barn months ago and in its place now stood what looked like an upscale wine bar and marketplace.

I got out of the car and made my way to the front door where I rang the bell and waited. Inside I could hear mixed voices and laughter. When my mother opened the front door she was holding onto the stem of a Riedel glass (a gift from Ricky and me three Christmases ago) and she looked flushed and happy.

Laney, baby, hi. What are you doing here? I mean, I thought you were in New Mexico. She said, stepping back and holding open the door.

I lied, I said. I never went to New Mexico and I, I really don't know what I'm doing here. I just needed to get out of L.A. is all.

My mom looked over to where my father and their guests, a dozen or more couples dressed in various vineyard-logo polos, swilled wine and mingled. Well come on in, she said, kissing me on the cheek, we were just having our monthly Wine Brats tasting. Can I get you something to drink?

No, I said, smiling and giving a small wave to the crowd before heading towards the kitchen. I think I'll just go upstairs and take a bath. It was kind of a long drive.

Mom followed me into the kitchen where she gave me a quick, Sorry honey, is this a Ricky situation? whisper.

Yes. No. The tears were building behind my eyes.

Go take a bath, she said, kissing me again on the head. They should all clear out in an hour or so. Then we'll talk.

THE LAW OF CONFLICT

IN THE tub of my childhood, my long legs cramped up against my chest. I hadn't known I'd miss the valley heat, the air thick with corn, the calm before the temperature hit the century mark. I hadn't seen the beauty in a place that smelled like cow shit; I hadn't seen the strength in the sweaty valley men who bent in back-breaking swoops to load eighty-pound bushels of asparagus bedding onto lowered tail gates before the frost. Maybe my mother was right. Maybe I needed to move back in so we could be alone together. I grabbed an ice cube from my water glass and rubbed it across my forehead when my cell—on silent mode—started vibrating and bouncing all over the soap dish.

I reached blindly for it, wondering if I knocked it into the bath would I electrocute myself, and didn't check the caller ID before flipping it open. I hoped it would be Puck. Puck calling to say he accepted one of the many apologies I kept leaving on his voice mail, with his agent, written in lip-gloss on the window of his car. Puck calling to say that it wasn't really that bad, that he still loved me and was coming over with some sushi and Dove bars. But it wasn't Puck, it was Ricky.

Hi, he said, I'm here.

You're where? I asked, pressing the phone closer to my ear and tossing the towel in the direction of the sink.

At the airport, he said. In Albuquerque.

In Albuquerque, I repeated, feeling the vomit rise up all over again.

Yep, pick me up?

I…I can't.

You busy?

No, I mean, Ricky, I'm sorry. I'm so sorry.

No big deal, there are tons of cabs around.

No, that's not it. I'm not in Santa Fe.

I'm confused, he said, an announcement for the arrival of Flight 817 from Tucson echoing in the background. Where are you?

I'm in a bathtub. In Lodi. It's just…I never thought you'd actually fly to New Mexico.

I could hear his frustration rise through the phone. I told you I was going to come, didn't I? I texted you my flight information and everything.

I haven't been checking my phone. I didn't think…sorry.

So am I, he said and hung up.

Taking the iPhone with me I plunged under the water and waited. Although the phone made some bubbles and a weak beeping noise, nothing happened and so, when I ran out of breath to hold, I came back up.

FALLING IN LOVE WITH ALL OF YOUR CHARACTERS

THREE THINGS you need to know about Ricky that I haven't told you yet:

1) EVERY MORNING, no matter what, he drives to The Coffee Bean and Tea Leaf to buy me a soy latte and a currant scone. He gets up, showers and picks up the clothes I have laid out for him. When he puts his socks on he sits on the corner of the bed and kisses my face all over. He notices how the red stripe in his socks matches the red alligators on his boxers and how the red alligators match exactly with the vertical stripes on his Hugo Boss tie. Not only does he notice, but he says, Babe! Babe, he says, you always do me right. When he pulls on his pants he makes sure to leave the band of his boxers showing, he rolls up his left leg and bends over, with one foot on the bed, so that tie and boxer band and sock all touch. Then he smiles, re-adjusts himself and kisses my face again. He leaves and shouts up the stairs, I love you, before going out the door. When he's gone I roll over to his side of the bed and breathe in the scent of him on his pillow. Twenty minutes later he's back with my scone and latte. He leaves it on the bedside table, kisses me on my face for the third time and says, Are you going to have a productive paint day?

I look up at him and say, Yes.

2) EVERY MORNING before he goes on the coffee run I ask Ricky if he really has to go to work today. If he couldn't just stay home, just this once. Usually he says no, kisses my face and makes a remark about somebody supporting this family.

What family? I ask. There's only you and me.

But one day, a Tuesday in May, the only day in the whole of my recollected memory, Ricky actually said yes. Of course I didn't really hear him, so used to him saying no, and I waited for my pre-coffee kiss pretending to be half asleep. Why not, I heard him say, taking off his key-lime tie, navy striped shirt and matching lime and blue argyle socks, I'd like to see just what it is that you do all day.

I peeled one eye open slowly, to be sure I wasn't dreaming, but there he was standing in front of his closet looking for sweats.

3) CONTRARY TO what a lot of people—myself included— say about Ricky behind his back, he didn't sell out. Not his Berkeley social consciousness or his Mexican-ness. In fact, like most of the critical mass at Cal, he made the connection between money and power rather early, but instead of rallying against it, instead of picketing the Bay Bridge because they wouldn't let the working class commute across on bicycle or unfurling bloodied banners from the top of the Campanile to demonstrate the horrors of factory farms, Ricky buckled down and bought stock in the corporate monopoly.

I mean, he'd say late at night, a pot of organic free-trade coffee brewing between us, staging a protest isn't going to make the machine stop. In order to stop the machine, you have to be the man who runs the machine. The man who owns the machine. The man who fucking made the machine in the first place.

So your plan is to buy social consciousness?

No, even better, he said. I plan to sell it.

And although it didn't seem possible, that's just exactly what he, no wait, we went and did.

I KNOW, I said there were three things you should know about Ricky, but that's only because three rolls off the tongue better than four. This is the last one, I promise. And stay with me because it's good:

4) IT ISN'T entirely true that the reason Ricky is never home is because he works all day. He works a hell of a lot, don't get me wrong, but—and I think with the exception of the kids at the center and their probation officer I'm the only one who knows, so don't go blabbing it around for philanthropic publicity reasons—every Thursday night Ricky volunteers as a crisis mentor at the Los Angeles Juvenile Detention facility. He listens as boys, sometimes a young as seven or eight, tell him about their gang bangs, their sexual conquests, their rap sheets and how in the third grade they would drink their own urine out of a Wolverine thermos because their Uncle/Cousin/Neighbor/Father was sexually molesting them and they thought, if only they could make themselves disgusting enough, then maybe the Cousin/Uncle/Neighbor/Father would stop.

Sometimes the kids cry. Sometimes they lunge at Ricky with sharpened pencils or Plexiglas shanks. He doesn't pretend to understand. He doesn't pretend that he didn't go to Berkeley. He doesn't try to relate by telling a similar story about his own life or attempt to paint the bleak image with hopeful pastels. He just listens. He listens for as long as the boys need to talk.

THE STORY IMPERATIVE

W HEN MY mom came upstairs she sat on the worn mint bathmat and handed me a cup of jasmine tea.

Laney, she said after I had poured my heart out, there are surprisingly many things that a husband does better than a lover. Maybe the sex isn't always as exciting, and maybe he doesn't remember to open the door every time you approach the car, but there are things you realize that only a husband can do right. You know like when you're trying to put on a necklace with a tricky clasp? Your husband will know how to fasten the clip without snagging your hair. He will know the curve of your neck like his own. He will kiss you behind the ear when he's finished and he will know that the smell he's inhaling is, what's that expensive perfume you're always wearing?

I swallowed the tea that was in my mouth and said, *Joy* by Jean Patou.

Well, Ricky will know that it is *Joy* not because he's refined enough to tell the difference between orange blossom and lily of the valley—

It's orris, I interrupted.

Orris, orange, whatever. The point is he will know the difference because, at one point, he bought you a bottle of *Joy* and you wore it and whenever he smells it he thinks of you.

But it's so much more than that, I said, setting my teacup and saucer on the side of the bath and dipping my washcloth back into the lukewarm water. It's so black and so bad and—

My mother held her hand up to my mouth. No, she said, it's not. It could be if you want it that way, but if you stop right there, right now, it can really be just as simple as that.

CHARACTER IS
SELF-KNOWLEDGE

COULD IT? Could it really be as simple as the smell of perfume and the fastening of tricky clasps? Initially I seriously doubted it could, but after a week in the valley, after a week of driving dirt roads, bits of gravel stuck to the undercarriage of the Tank. After a week without room service, or valets, or makeup. After a week of using Noxzema and Crest and wearing underwear from Walmart beneath my mother's too-short Lee jeans (I hadn't thought to pack any of my things. I just got in the car and left). After a week I began to think that maybe it could.

I mean, undoubtedly Ricky was still mad as hell about the whole Albuquerque thing, and Puck was still pissed and not returning my calls, and Quentin, as well as half my wardrobe, was all but abandoned in the Beverly Hills Hotel; but just maybe, with the right props and an ample bit of humility, it could happen.

WHEN I decided I wanted to go back home—and by home I mean the house on Bedford and not say Lodi or the Beverly Hills Hotel, when I decided to go back there—I knew it wouldn't be as easy as driving back down the 5 to the 405. Exit on Wilshire, a left on Santa Monica, another left on Maple. A right on Carmelita, one last right onto Bedford and walking in through the front door. If I came home like nothing was wrong, like I really was in Santa Fe adorning the canvas with dusty rose and turquoise paint, would anything change? Has Lindsay Lohen been to rehab? Is water wet?

I needed something, some sort of irrefutable way to get Ricky's full and undivided attention so that I could tell him, so that I could scream: I'm in on the Joke and I don't find it funny.

The revelation, when it happened, wasn't nearly as shocking or as sudden as say my maternal urgings in the paper goods aisle of Bristol Farms. In fact, the solution was scattered up and down the sides of I-5.

Between Pea Soup Andersen's and Harris Ranch, the monotony of flat brown land undulates into the greenish hills and valleys of Crow's Landing. And spotted about Crow's Landing, spaced in increments of exactly 4.3 miles apart were the shamrocked signs of Shane P. Donlon, Ranch Broker. The first one, on the right, partially secluded by an almond tree, was:

1,900 ACRES OF GROUND.

EAST AND WEST IT'S ALL AROUND.

The second, a little further down the road and nailed to the trunk of a peach tree, read:

IN THE MIDDLE CROW CREEK

CAN BE FOUND.

The third, continuing the rhyme, was bigger and ran the length of a wooden fence:

IT CAN BE YOURS.

HOW DOES THAT SOUND?

And the fourth, biggest of all and phone number inclusive, stood on its own pole, billboard-like in the middle of a high green hill:

ALL YOU SEE HERE CAN BE YOURS!

S. P. DONLON PRIVATE TOURS.

And no, I wasn't going to buy up four hundred acres of land in the middle of nowhere. I didn't plan to force Ricky into a move or stake my claim on a field of summer fruit trees. What hit me were the signs. Pretty little rhyming couplets spread out, not along a desolate stretch of the Golden State Freeway, but rather scattered, intentionally, on Sunset, Melrose and Mid-Wilshire. Signs that Ricky couldn't help but notice planted perfectly along his path to work. Art.

UNSCRIPTED

BUT FIRST I had a stop to make, and I don't mean Kettle-man City or Castaic. First, I had to make a visit to a champagne-colored Craftsman bungalow in WeHo. First, I had to pull up, without hitting a car wash, without even changing out of the pair of elastic-waisted track shorts I borrowed from my mother (and I don't mean the sexy terry-cloth Hard Tail variety, I'm talking your average navy blue nylon, mid-thigh, made for jog-walking track shorts courtesy of Big Five Sporting Goods). First, I had to pull up and apologize, in person, to Puck.

I got out of the Tank without checking myself in the vanity. I had no idea what I looked liked, but I was pretty sure it was real. As I stepped on the stones that led to Puck's front door I took a deep breath, and when I reached his porch I made my hand into a fist and I knocked. I waited, breathing and squeezing my calves tight then lax, tight then lax. I brought my hand up to knock again, but just as I did the door opened and darling Nikki, in a bandeau bikini no less, stood on the other side.

Hi-ye, she said.

Hi, Nikki, is Puck here?

Ummm, do I know you? she asked, twirling a long strand of hair on her finger and looking at me, puzzled.

Yeah, I'm the girl from the shipwreck ad, I said pushing past her and making my way inside.

Right! she said, looking me over. I totally recognize you now.

Right, I said and made my way through the living room and into the kitchen, where through the large picture windows I could see Puck floating in the pool on his purple raft while six or seven beautiful people lounged under lavender umbrellas or splashed on the Baja bench of the black-bottomed pool. As I opened the sliding glass door that separated the kitchen from the deck I caught a glimpse of my reflection. My hair was pulled into a messy knot and stray strands escaped at almost every angle. My eyes were unlined, my lips bare and my eyebrows, even though they were blond, could use a good waxing. But that was nothing in comparison to the white trucker tank with orange and yellow stains down the front that I pulled from a ragbag in my father's shed or the puff of the nylon as it pulled against the elastic waistband of my midsection. I stepped through the door and out onto the deck.

Puck, I said, shielding my eyes from the bright Hollywood sun as I walked towards the pool, I'm sorry. I'm so sorry I don't even know how else to say it.

Everyone got quiet then and stopped applying cocoa butter and sucking down strawberry-peach daiquiris; it was finally like the movies where the action stops and all eyes were focused on me. But then, not half a beat later, when they turned, looked, surveyed and decided I was unworthy of their gaze, they all went back to whatever it was they were doing before, as if I were invisible. As if I were the help. Everyone that is, except for Puck, who rolled off his raft and, getting his hair soaked in the process, swam out of the pool and over to where I stood.

I held out my arms and he held me. Dripping with tears and chlorine, respectively, he said into my hair, So this is what the real Magdalena looks like.

Yes, I said into the tanned smooth skin of his neck, this is me.

And, pulling away ever so slightly so he could look at my face, he said, Well I think you're beautiful. Much better in real life.

Then he scooped me up like a baby and holding me in the cradle of his arms, he jumped into the deep end of the pool.

THE QUESTION OF
SELF-EXPRESSION

ALTHOUGH THE Pink Palace had been relatively ac-
commodating to all of my, shall we say, whims, I have a
feeling even Ian will put his foot down when it comes to art.
Especially art-in-the-large. Especially art-in-the-large involving
spray paint and rhinestones and gallons of hot glue and acrylics. But that isn't a problem, really. I mean it might pose a threat
to those less imaginative than I, but as you know I have more
than enough time to make things up and so Puck and I devised
a plan: I would maintain the Beverly Hills Hotel as my primary
residence, but every morning instead of getting up at ten and
sunning by the pool, or shopping, or lunching or waiting for
Quentin, I would instead get up at seven (yes, in the AM) and
sneak into my studio. My studio above the garage. My studio attached to my sprawling American Federal Revival estate.

Just how exactly I was going to do this without garnering
suspicion from the gardeners or confrontation from Immelda
had yet to be determined, but Ricky, well, there's very little risk
of running into him.

Gearing up for a proper stakeout I called Ian at the front desk
and requested a rental car. While he worked out the details on a
long-term rental with Enterprise—apparently (oh the horror!) no
one at the Beverly Hills Hotel had ever asked to rent a Ford Escort
before—I put on a black mini-dress, wide-brimmed hat, oversized
Chanel glasses and set to work. If I wanted to outwit Immelda
I'd have to show up precisely between 7:30 and 8:45 each morning. She has a daily routine and the 75-minute slot between 7:30
and 8:45 was dedicated to morning mass at the Good Shepherd

Catholic Church. Because the Good Shepherd is located on one prime piece-o-property (who says the Catholics are having financial troubles?), Immelda walks the seven blocks to North Bedford. So as long as I park down the street and walk in from the opposite direction (say Lomitas to Rexford instead of Roxbury to Santa Monica), I should be fine. As for my entry, well lucky for me: since it was built in 1930 it had, in addition to the garage and front entrance, a service entrance out back. As far as I knew Immelda never remembered to set the alarm, and besides I could disarm it by entering the code if she did. What? Did you think I'd have to shimmy up the rain gutter? Hitch a rope and swing from the palms?

The real challenge would be getting out.

The real challenge would be art.

It had been so long since I had done any real (as my mother would say) art that I didn't know how to begin. For two days I avoided work by stocking up on supplies. Puck and I drove to World Supply and then, because they only had six-dozen bags of magenta rhinestones left in stock, we drove to Sterling Art in Irvine to get a few dozen more. The next three days' work was avoided through research. Puck, in serving as my unofficial personal assistant, was familiar with our accounts and was put in charge of the financial aspect. His job was to figure out just how much four prime-location billboards would cost and how, without Ricky catching on, we could get the money wired from our reserve bank in Panama. I mean running up a charge at the Beverly Hills Hotel was one thing. Dropping a couple of million on rhinestones and billboards was quite another. While Puck busied himself with the financial and logistical matters I drove to the library in Beverly Hills and instead of checking out predictable museum books, I pulled out the less glossy, obscure titles. With Florine Stettheimer, Gwen John and Tamara de Lempicka, I poured over portraits, studying brush strokes, chin lines and the proportion of parts. With the Jennys—Saville and Holzer— I poured over attitude, extremity and exhibition. With Cindy Sherman, I fell back in love with the still.

I envisioned my finished product to resemble an Alberto Vargas calendar had the pin-ups painted themselves. A vintage *Esquire* Vargas, but with a little more skin and—obviously—a hell of a lot more sparkle. I checked out a book called *Painting Faces and Figures* and embarrassed myself each time I referenced its pages. Appalled by lines like "Experiment with major gestures of a composition using a pencil sketch and thumbnail grid. Then, transfer your sketch to a canvas by means of a grid," I nonetheless found them instructive. Though how in the hell I was going to find a canvas as big as a billboard I had no idea. That, coupled with the proportional mathematics of transferring an eight-by-eleven-inch pencil sketch to a thirty-by-fifty-foot wall was enough to induce panic. But I refused to curl up on the couch and sleep until the task was more manageable. I had been sleeping on the couch for almost two years. It was time to wake the hell up.

To get the gesture straight I needed a model, but because I had snuck into my own home and was working in secret, Immelda was off limits. So, standing with my back to a full-length mirror, wearing nothing but my panties, I looked over my shoulder and snapped a digital photo of myself with my iPhone. It wasn't perfect by any means, but it held its shape, and although the resolution was low I was able to e-mail it to my laptop and begin a digital recreation.

Using Photoshop I broke my body into thirty-two self-contained one-by-one-inch squares. It would have been as easy as a click of a mouse, but I resisted the urge to streamline my thighs, to exfoliate my underarms, to smooth out the dimples in my exposed derrière. If I was going to make my debut as Magdalena-Larger-Than-Life I was going to do so uncensored. I was going to do it right. Truth be told, the only changes I made weren't with me at all, they were with the fabric. I changed the sea foam lace of my panties to a subtle black Lycra and then—doctoring, enlarging, enlivening the text of my tattooed flesh—I typed in Arial Narrow: IF YOU LIVED HERE, YOU'D BE HOME RIGHT NOW and promptly stuck the words down the spine of my back. On the screen the text was black and fairly generic, nothing as beautiful as Tuttle's tiny real-life design, but on the board I envisioned it glowing. I envisioned the world's largest rhinestone collection all meticulously glued together reaching up from my bum and sparkling in the Sunset Boulevard sun.

Using five-by-five-foot particleboards it took me three days to transfer the thirty-two original squares of my body into enlarged forms. Considering the letters that would adorn my panties were approximately three feet each, and considering there were thirty-two of them, not to mention one two-foot apostrophe, I knew it was going to take at least three more days to set the rhinestones straight. For nearly a week I lived on coffee, peanut M&Ms and whatever Puck phoned in from Pink Dot. Although I returned to the Beverly Hills Hotel to shower and occasionally sleep, I spent most of my time sneaking in and out of my studio.

On Tuesday at 1 PM I was applying small samples of paint to my thighs and arms trying to match the exact shade of my flesh. On Thursday at six I was engaged in an oil study of hair, trying to capture the depth of blond curls as they cascaded down my bare back, and on Sunday, precious Sunday afternoon, I was burning my fingers on hot glue and rhinestones and taking small breaks to soak them in ice.

I know by the notes he left behind, piled on the rug inside of the door, that Quentin came by, but when I returned to the hotel in the late hours of night, in the wee hours of the morning, I was too exhausted to read, but not too tired to care.

And then, when I was least expecting it, there was a knock on the door. Removing the satin mask from my eyes I rolled over to look at the clock. It was 12:30 in the morning on a...Friday? I pulled an overstuffed pillow over my head and tried to ignore it, but there it was again, a muffled but still present long-knuckled rap rap rap. I got up and walked to the door. I didn't need to check the peep hole, only one person in the world knocked like that, and when I opened the door there was Quentin, standing half in, half out of, the jam.

Hi, he said, as he stood leaning, picking on the duct tape that covered his left palm.

Hi, I said and let him in.

THE TRUTH

CAN'T, I said...I just.

I know, he said in a shy way, reminiscent of the first time he came knocking, standing half in, half outside the door. I'm not here to... He blushed and looked down, and then stepped all the way inside and grabbed my hand. I missed you. Talking to you, ya know?

Yeah, I said, sitting down on the sofa, I know. I missed you too. We sat there then, awkward, like some stupid after-school special.

So, he said, finally, breaking the silence, What have you been doing, you know, lately?

Art.

So that's it? Art is what you do?

Well, I said, deciding to just go for it, not so long ago I was executive vice president for Diamond Myst Water Distributors. And before that I was their chief financial officer. And before that I was an investment banker.

Woaah, Quentin let out a slow whistle. What'd ya do before that? Mine opals in Australia? Create a zero-balanced spending plan for the state of California? Drive ambulances for the Red Cross?

No, I said, allowing my lips to form a small grin. No, before all that I was a grape farmer and before that, my voice caught just a little, an artist.

Now there's something I know a little bit about, he said, getting more comfortable on the couch and slipping out of his shoes.

Really? I asked with a smile.

Yes, really, he threw a throw pillow from the chair beneath

him in my direction. You think I worked seven years in the advertising industry as an understudy and two in the billboard union without picking up a thing or two about visual techniques? What's your medium?

You'll laugh.

I won't laugh.

Promise?

What, do you work with your own urine or something? Are you one of those feminists who think a file cabinet full of used tampons is art?

No, it's worse than that.

Worse than tampons and urine?

Rhinestones, I said. I use rhinestones.

He laughed.

I threw the pillow back at him, but I had more force and better aim than he did and so it knocked him square in the chin.

Ouch, he said rubbing his face.

That didn't hurt.

How would you know, he picked up the pillow and fingered the fringe. These little beaded things, these rhinestoney things are kind of hard, not to mention sharp.

Quentin, I'm serious.

Rhinestones, huh?

And paint and a hell of a lot of glue.

He held out his hand.

I crawled over to where he sat and took it. We shook and then he pulled me close. He tried to slip me out of my kimono, out of my clothes, but I shook my head a soft, No.

So he curled his body around me and held on, and I held him too. We had nothing more to say, my lips on his hand and my head on his chest. Our legs were intertwined, bent and pushed up against the coffee table. He worked his fingers through my hair. He brushed it out with his short nails, fanning it across my kimono-covered back, and then he gathered it neatly, wove his fingers between the blond strands and held tight before falling asleep.

CHARACTER VERSUS CHARACTERIZATION

I WOKE, still stretched out on the floor at 2 AM, to the sound of Quentin searching for his shoes.

Don't go, I whispered.

He sighed and reached a hand over to my cheek, brushing away a strand of hair.

I have to, you know—

I know, I said, but this is...I mean. We can't see each other anymore.

Yeah, he said, slipping on his left shoe and making a bow with the laces, I know.

He bent over and kissed me on the forehead and then, with only one shoe on, he made his way towards the door.

It was funny, but I finally felt guilty. Like all the cheating before was just warm up and this night, after I had sworn it was over but fell asleep with Quentin anyhow, was the real deal: not sex, but infidelity, in the raw. And I felt it. Just as I felt, for sure, in my heart, that there was absolutely no way Ricky would ever or did cheat on me.

Quentin! I said, jumping up and chasing after him, grabbing his arm and pressing into his wrist flesh with my nails. Don't go.

He smiled a small, sad grin as he pried my polished nails from his arm.

I need your help with something, I said, moving my body between him and the door.

All right, he said taking two steps back, but then it's done?

Then it's done. But I want to go up the billboard first. I want you to take me, all the way to the top.

He paused, and then exhaled as though it were smoke.

I looked at him hard, and then held up my hands in an imaginary camera. Click.

Go get your slippers on, he said.

ON RISK

GOING UP the second time was like the first only harder. I took the rungs slowly. One at a time. Methodical.

Don't look down, Quentin said. Reach up. Be tall.

I am tall, I said, with my feet squeezed into my peachy ballet slippers.

Good, Quentin said as we made our way to the landing, because here comes the hard part.

The hard part?

Bend your knee, Quentin said, his hands on my lower back, and plant your foot down solid.

Solid, I said, my arms and thighs shaking. Okay now, swing around, Quentin said, lifting my torso. I reached out an arm, grabbed hold of the rung and swung around.

Breathing deeply for four counts I clung to the backside of the billboard.

Good work, Quentin said, now one more thing and you're done.

I thought you said you'd climb with me, I said, looking down and across to the ladder where he stood. Not enough room, he said, I'll be there in a sec. But first you have to reach up and open the trap door.

You're joking right?

No. See that cord? He pointed to a rusty chain above my head, Pull down.

I knew about trap doors and tree houses too, but reaching above my head to pull a yellow rope in the garage and reaching above my head to pull a rusty chain forty feet above ground were two completely different things. You mean I have to let go?

Just for a second, he said. Pull on the cord and the door will open up, then you can climb through it and onto the platform.

I breathed a count of four again and then reached up. I pulled the chain took another deep breath and I let Junah go.

I climbed, the seven remaining rungs and emerged just under the oversized "X" of Luxe. Leaning my back against the ad, I slid down into a sitting position and was still.

Isn't it amazing, Quentin asked, popping up through the trap door and walking on the outer perimeter of the platform, pointing out at the lights of the city.

Even though I somehow felt perfectly safe, just as Quentin promised, I still couldn't walk to the edge. Instead I sat holding onto the side beams of the board and said, Ever wish there were things you could do differently?

All the time, Quentin said, lighting up a cigarette, taking a drag and ashing over the side.

No, not life, I said, but in art.

Art? Quentin asked.

Yeah. You know, if you had a blank canvas, say the size of this billboard, what would you do?

A love song, Quentin said. Maybe something by Billie Holliday.

Well, isn't that precious, I said, holding out my hand for a drag.

Quentin passed over his cigarette and said, Well how about you? What would you do?

I took two very, very small scoots away from the back of the platform and looked up to the billboard where my blond hair hung in wet clumps over my bluish lips. Close as I was, the image was distorted and slightly out of focus, but I stared intently anyhow and tried to honestly figure out what it is I would do, if, as I had been wanting for so long now, I was given a do-over.

Well first, I said, I'd simplify. I held up my hands in a frame and like Quentin would I took an imaginary picture: click-click. I'd do away with the hunky blond boy, the boat, hell, the whole ocean would just dry up and instead I have...me.

You? Quentin asked, smirking. The distressed damsel without her prince?

No, I'd do away with the damsel stuff too. It'd just be me, naked, except for some rhinestones. And panties.

Of course, Quentin said. Nothing says water like a half-naked chick and some rhinestones.

It may not say water but, correct me if I'm wrong, it certainly says "drink me," does it not?

Well, that depends, Quentin said, grinning.

Depends on what? I asked, unbuttoning my shirt and feeling the sense of something old and forbidden creep into my chest.

On the rhinestones, Quentin said, looping his finger through his belt buckle and looking at me, curious.

Well, I was thinking, I said, shrugging out of my shirt and unhooking my bra, that it'd look something like this:

I stood, tits pressed tight against the filthy billboard. Turning so my profile was visible over my bare shoulder I looked to Quentin and said, What do you think?

I think, he said, walking slowly, surely, over to where I stood, that is exactly what I was talking about. Only better.

Better?

More, I don't know, intimate.

Intimate?

Discrete. I don't know. Smaller than I expected, but just better. When did you get it done?

A week or two ago, I said, still pressed against the board as Quentin traced the tattooed lines of Tuttle's text with his finger.

Hurt much?

Like crazy. But in a good way.

Like you wanted it to?

Exactly.

Yeah, I know that feeling. Most people usually want it to hurt.

There was a long silence as Quentin continued to trace down to the last little letter at the tip of my tailbone.

Anyhow, I said when he was finished, I figured I could replace the ink with rhinestones, on the board, I mean. And make them bigger, of course.

Course, Quentin said, his thumb slung in the belt-loop of his jeans. I reckon that might be pretty damn hot.

Hot enough to make you sweat? I asked, pushing away from the dusty billboard and reaching for my discarded shirt.

I'd say so.

Thirsty?

I'm buying what you're selling, Quentin said. It may not have a hell of a lot to do with water but with you like that, he pulled out his imaginary camera again and pretended to review a shot, I'd buy a whole jug.

THE DECLINE OF STORY

DESCENDING FROM the billboard wasn't difficult. I mean it wasn't a piece of cake or anything as sweet as that; but with Quentin going first and me following after, left foot, right foot, both feet, we hit solid ground in about half the time it took us to go up. In the van on the ride home, I took my shoes off and examined their soles. They were dirty, and running through the pad beneath the forefoot was the faint imprint of the rungs. I massaged the leather with my thumbs and, by the time we reached the Pink Palace and Quentin let me out, the indentation was almost invisible.

NOTE CLOSING VALUE AND COMPARE WITH OPENING VALUE

BECAUSE IT was, as promised, officially done, we didn't have sex and we didn't sleep together, either. Instead we stayed up half the night and talked.

So, not that you're an expert in these things, but now what? I said, my lips loose after a few too many sips of gin.

We live with it, Quentin said, walking across the room to get a pack of cigarettes off the top of the TV.

What?

I live with it. You live with it. And we never, ever, ever tell, he said slowly as he navigated a cigarette out of the pack. And if it slips off some asshole's tongue, he paused to light and inhale, always, always, he exhaled, always deny.

Funny, but isn't that a rap song? I shook my hips and started swaying while humming "Wasn't Me."

No, Quentin grabbed my shoulders to stop my dancing, the lit end of his cigarette barely grazing my left arm. Looking at me, suddenly serious, like he might slap me until I understood his point, he said, Don't tell him. His cigarette had turned mostly to ash and he took one long drag before squashing it out on the disposable plastic lid of an old Starbucks cup. Telling him is selfish. You'll feel worlds better to cry and confess and get it all out. But he won't. Not even after or if he forgives you. Telling him is unfair. If you love him, you won't.

And there it was, smacking out in hard words against the air: how to cheat and get away with it.

But what wasn't there in words, what Quentin didn't say out loud but said, instead, through the force of his fingers as he pinched the cigarette butt was that how to cheat and how to live unfaithfully were not mutually exclusive. What his mouth held back but his body told was that, to the canon that included Junah falling, his feet bound up in soft pink slippers, I could now add my betrayal of Ricky to the secret backspaces of my mind. And in the wee dark moments of early sleep and in the foggy daylight of morning, I'd have to live with it, alone.

Feeling cold and slushy drunk, I stopped talking and walked Quentin into the bedroom. He slipped into bed and pulled up the covers, and I pulled the drapes tightly closed before I went to sleep on the couch.

STICKING WITH THE SCRIPT

A T 7:30 in the morning I woke to another knock on the door. I looked around the dark room, confused. And then pulling back the curtains to let in a little light I peeked into the bedroom where, sure enough, Quentin lay sleeping, his feet poking out from beneath the down comforter. Another knock, this time louder and more persistent.

Fuck, I thought, as I grabbed a robe and tied it tightly around my waist, who on earth could it be? The knocking continued, still louder and any hopes I had for the possibility of room service or housekeeping vanished as the knocking sounded less and less polite. I pulled the bedroom door shut and peeked through the peephole.

On the other side, dressed in jeans and a black leather jacket, was Puck. I opened the door.

Oh thank God! he exclaimed as he burst through the door, Magdalena, we have a little problem. He paced back and forth from the balcony to the bar.

What? I asked. Gazing nervously to the door Quentin slept behind.

Well, he stopped his frantic pacing and sat down. Well, I don't exactly know how to tell you this, he reached into his jacket and pulled out an envelope covered in foreign postage and a red air mail stamp.

Just say it, I said, my heart thumping. I was suddenly certain that Ricky found out about Quentin. That he was so upset he moved to our hacienda in Los Cabos and inside the envelope were papers for divorce.

Well, I think I may have found out what Ricky's been hiding. He looked down, as if he were almost embarrassed himself, and then he looked back at me.

Tell me, I said, the fear escalating, because I was now entirely certain of what wasn't inside. Inside there were not explicit photos of Ricky and Dior naked and buck wild. Even though I hoped for it—to help ease my own Quentin guilt—my heart told me that there wouldn't be a magazine clipping of Ricky caught by the paparazzi smooching some starlet at a charity benefit. And I was positively certain that, unless Quentin had written it to me, there would be no sappy and overly sentimental love letter.

Here, Puck said, as he pushed the envelope across the coffee table to me, I think you should see for yourself.

I looked at the envelope, took a breath and pulled it open. Inside was a bank statement from the Banco Confederado de América Latina, and even though I didn't speak Spanish the numbers were clear; Diamond Myst was dry.

Although it sounds odd, I was relieved. I'd been broke before, hell, hadn't I been wishing my entire stay in L.A. that things could go back to how they used to be?

It's not quite as bad as it looks, Puck said, reaching across the table and taking my hands in his.

It's okay, I said, somehow sounding more reassured than Puck as I looked at the negative numbers before me.

That's just the Panama account. You still have money in the bank here in the states; you own the corporate office, the plant in Fiji.

Yeah, but the mortgage on the office? And the overhead, the exportation fees, we just lost $473 million, didn't we?

Mags, Puck tried again, it's not that bad, you still have the house.

You mean the one I'm not living in?

Magdalena, Puck asked, when is that last time you looked at the books?

I opened the balcony door. I needed some air. The books? How come I couldn't remember?

I don't know, I finally admitted, one, maybe two months ago.

Try nineteen.

Nineteen? And suddenly it all made sense. The long hours. The emotional detachment. The meanness. He wasn't cheating on me. He was treading water. Our water. My water. While I slept, Ricky was trying his hardest to keep the business afloat.

I sat down on the floor and leaned my head against the wall. So now what?

From what I could gather it was the Nestle and Pepsi people that did it. Aquafina, Vittel. They have vending machines, Sweetie. And exclusive contracts with Disney and McDonalds.

Stop, I said. I get it.

Do you even know what's happened to the advertising department since you left?

I shook my head.

I'm just saying, Puck said. I don't think it's over.

I didn't know what to think. Not only was my installation—my first real artistic attempt in years—evaporating, but my life, or rather my lifestyle, was slowly dissolving too.

Honey, Puck said sitting next to me on the floor and rubbing my head. You can get it back. Maybe not all of it, but if you try really hard I think you can reclaim the important stuff.

Just then the toilet flushed. Puck and I both looked towards the closed bedroom door.

Plumbing acting up? he asked.

Yeah, I said, pretending not to hear Quentin coughing into the sink as he ran the tap water.

You didn't, did you?

No, I said. I slept on the couch.

So…? Puck looked at me, curious.

So, I said standing up and pulling Puck up with me. Now we go out and reclaim the important stuff. I grabbed my car keys and my sunglasses and, still wearing my pink robe, I pulled Puck out the door.

THE LOSS OF CRAFT

THE FIRST thing that had to be scaled back were the bill-boards. It was doubtful I could afford one, much less four. And the one I hoped I could still have would need a bigger purpose. Not that it still couldn't be a message to Ricky, but—and this partially killed me—in order to justify spending half a million dollars that apparently we didn't really have, I had to make it utilitarian. I had to splash on some Myst.

I went back to my studio and stared at my oversized self-portrait. My left arm was on my hip and my right arm was half-hidden behind my torso, but if I did a little digital editing and a bit of revision to the upper nine panels, with work I could extend the right arm up and over my head and place in my outstretched hand a sparkling glass bottle of Luxe, cap off and pointing down-wards, one single, precious drop of liquid headed for my head.

Wow, said Puck, when he saw the revised rendition on my Macintosh screen. Love it, but how in the hell are you going to manage to get the bottle cut out suspended above the billboard like that? I mean I know you're good at what you do, but don't you need a crane or something?

Don't worry, I told him. I have a friend.

THE STORY TRIANGLE

TROUBLE WAS, Quentin had always come to me and now that I needed him I hadn't the first clue how to find him, so I got in the Tank and made my way back to La Cienega Collision with a fifty and a bottle of Oban.

You again? Wendy asked, her long tangerine nails tapping the Formica counter.

Yeah, I said, setting the fifty and the bottle in front of her greasy computer screen.

She looked at the bottle and then she looked at me. I wasn't wearing much makeup and my tiny-tee had paint splatters across the chest.

I'm a little untucked today, I apologized. I've been busy at work.

Hey, no skin off my nose, honey. But as for your little gift here, she pushed the bottle and the bill back towards me, we're not interested.

I looked her in the eye and asked, How much?

How much what? she tried to play dumb.

How much is it going to cost for this note to get to Quentin?

What's it worth to you? she asked, drumming her nails incessantly.

Honestly, I pushed the bottle and bill back towards her, it's worth my sanity, my marriage and my artistic integrity. I opened my purse and pulled out my checkbook, How much?

Wendy picked up the bottle and turned it around. She fingered the fine malt label. Do you know, she said, that in Scotland they give tasting tours? Kinda like Temecula, but with Scotch.

Never been there, I said. But it makes sense.

I was there last summer, she said. It stayed light for twenty-one hours a day, and even when it got "dark," she used her orange talons to make quote marks in the air, it was more like twilight than night.

Must have been fabulous, I said.

No, she said, taking the fifty and putting it into the pocket of her jeans, there's something really fucked up about living in a place that doesn't have night.

Oh, I said. I didn't really—

Get out of here, she said. I'm keeping the bottle, but he'll get the note.

Thank you, I said as I walked out the door.

Whatever, she said as the screen slammed shut.

THE NOTE Wendy gave Quentin wasn't nearly as poetic as the ones he wrote me, but considering the situation it was the best I could do. In it I told him I was grateful. I told him it was over and I asked again, even though he didn't owe me a thing, for his help.

P.S. I penned, *I considered enlisting the Guerilla Girls, but I don't know if they work in rhinestones.*

HE SHOWED up, his beige minivan parked in the circular drive of the Federal Revival, at exactly 11 AM. Immelda had Sundays off and, as expected, she was getting her hair set and styled at Spa 415 and wouldn't return until at least two. In addition to the van, Quentin had brought a crew and a crane, and I led them all through the yard and up to the studio the back way.

THE END OF THE LINE

IN MY mind I had always imagined my billboard would go up in the secret of the night. That I'd hitch the painted panels to the top of my rented red Escort with bungees and nail-gun the five-by-five squares to their expansive platform by the light of a full Hollywood moon, but in real life a five-foot-by-five-foot piece of board, even the particled kind, is pretty freaking heavy—especially when it's been doused in rhinestones and layers upon layers of now-cooled glue. So instead of attaching a tool belt to the hip of my custom 36-inch-inseam Hudson Supermodel jeans, I deferred to Quentin and the billboard professionals, preferring instead to dictate through a megaphone with Puck on the ground.

The spot I had chosen for the erection was on the Sunset Strip just above the House of Blues. Originally, I had wanted a tall wall, but when I had called Chuck at Viacom, the best he could do was a twenty-by-forty-foot traditional, even after I reminded him of the little favor he owed us after Ricky threw some weight around during the Outdoor Advertising merger meeting. A tall wall, he said, would be opening up (at a half price discount for the wife of Ricky de la Cruz) in twenty-two days and if I could wait that long—

I'll take it, I told him referring to both the board and the half-price discount, but I'll need something facing east and ready by Sunday, too.

Facing east and ready by Sunday, I had my space. As I stood below watching my ass grow ever larger while Quentin and his boys secured my half-naked body nearly fifty feet above ground, I felt—for the first time since Junah—something akin to butterflies. Something akin to joy.

THE PROBLEM WITH POV

A LTHOUGH I paid nearly five hundred (thousand) for my
billboard on Sunset, I would have sold the house if I could
have been with Ricky as he drove to work on Monday. I would
have given my breasts, my nose and my diamond engagement
ring to see his face as he glanced casually up at the sign, to be a
bug on the windshield after he slammed on the breaks and threw
the car into reverse to look once more. I wonder if he recognized
me by my ass? If he knew each dimple and precise contour of my
thighs? Or, if he had to look further up, to the profile of my face,
half hidden behind a blanket of blond.

If I had been in the car I would have said, That's me trying to
say "I'm sorry, I want to come home, I want back in the business"
in the only way I know how.

TAKE FIVE

THE END

A WEEK and a half later I was, without ropes and without a net, forty feet above West Hollywood where Doheny meets Sunset doing some routine maintenance to my billboard—you know Windexing rhinestone and squeegeeing the thin layer of smog off my ass and thighs—when my phone rang. I glanced at the caller ID panel: KISF Audio Marketing. Thinking it was someone returning my call from the Outdoor Advertising place, I slid my finger across the screen, careful not to coat it in acrylics, and pressed the phone up against my ear.

Hello, I said.

There was a soft sigh, like a whisper, and then a cough.

Hello, I said again about to hang up. Who's this?

Magdalena? the quiet voice said just as I was about to tap END call. It's Ricky.

Ricky? You sound terrible. Are you okay?

No, he said. I'm not all right.

What is it? I asked, sitting down on the high work platform and dangling my feet over the edge. Did you get in an accident? I scanned the road below, imagining his Spyder trapped beneath a Hummer. Glass everywhere, and Ricky sitting on the concrete curb, a bloody towel pressed to his forehead. Where are you?

I'm home, he said.

Home? I looked to the clock on my phone, it was 11:30 in the morning.

I was chopping a cantaloupe, he said, and I slipped and cut my finger off.

With one of those Samurai-ginsu knives we got for our

wedding? I asked my voice now just about as shaky as his. The really sharp-cut-through-chicken-bones knives?

Yes, he said. Will you come home? There's blood all over the place.

I'm on my way, I said, beginning my descent, rhinestones still stuck to the front of my t-shirt, a tack hammer and industrial-strength glue wrapped around my utility-belted waist.

WHEN I started up the Tank, I heard Ryan Seacrest confess to his listeners something about how one of the unfortunate dangers of dealing with a live audience were sickos like us. As an apology from the station he would be awarding our forfeited trip to Palm Springs to caller number sixteen, but I didn't care. I put on my blinker and snuck out into traffic.

Ricky, like most Angelinos, doesn't believe in the blinker. He maintains that by initiating the blink you actually hinder any small chance you have of actually getting over. The guy on your right, when he sees the click-click of the yellow light, will speed up and close in on the gap. But I disagree. One of the remarkable things about Los Angeles, one of those things that no one seems to talk about, is how we all do manage to get where we're going. We slide from the fast lane (wave) to the middle lane (wave) to the slow lane (wave) to the exit ramp (blinker off), and we merge. It may not be singularly graceful or without incident, but 99.9 percent of the time we do manage to make our exits, our left turns, our way home.

FADE OUT

IF HOLLYWOOD had her way things would have worked out with the water. We would have rebounded from the fall with an unquenchable vengeance and restarted our liquid upstart in recyclable aluminum cans. It was something I had been thinking about since before the boat—ease of packaging and transport, not to mention the ecological aspect and a profit margin (when compared to plastic bottles) in excess of 218 percent. It would be the low-end version of Luxe, sold to third-world countries and those who couldn't afford to pay more. It was genius if you could get past the aesthetics, if you could see past not being able to see through the can. With water in cans and not bottles Ricky and I could have lived, together, in our big house in Beverly Hills. We could have restored the Corvette and lived happily ever after. But if you look at the outtakes or perhaps maybe the director's cut you can piece together the real story, and it doesn't take a genius to figure out the backside of water looks remarkably similar to its front. Off screen we didn't climb aboard *Chelsea Girl* in matching topsiders and nautical caps and sail off into the Malibu sunset. No, after the credits stopped rolling, we saw the Shrink together and Anheuser Busch beat us to the canned-water craze. Rather than being bought out for $4.1 billion, Diamond Myst went bankrupt and we didn't try to save it. Instead, we spent our energy trying to save what was left of us.

Ricky, Immelda and I moved to a three-bedroom, two-bath with a carport on a tree-lined street in Silverlake. With my parents, we invested what remained of our savings in a wine-bottling technique that used plastic corks. Ricky got a job teaching high school economics; and, after selling two-thirds of my closet on eBay, I was able to afford a small studio space in Echo Park where I work, without rhinestones, on art.

As for the nine people I know in the San Joaquin Valley— and by know I don't mean the people I swill wine with, I mean the nine people who I've bent over with picking grapes in a hot and dusty field—those nine people might never believe it; but Los Angeles, beneath the pixie dust and beyond the Sunset strip, is really nothing more than a desert where the water is scarce and we're all thirsty.

LETTEREDPRESS
IN ASSOCIATION WITH
THE O.O.C. AND THE J.D. MULHOLLAND FOUNDATION

PRESENTS A BRIDGET HOIDA NOVEL

So L.A.

EXECUTIVE PRODUCERS JACK & LYNN HOIDA
LEADING MAN JESSE MULHOLLAND

BASED ON THE PERPETUAL ENCOURAGEMENT OF KATHI DUFFEL

DIRECTOR OF [ALTERED] GEOGRAPHY & ETERNAL MOMPAIR
CARA CARDINALE FIDLER
LINE PRODUCER, PENCIL EDITOR & FOREVER FRIEND
JENN STROUD ROSSMANN
BEST BOYS WILL & JEFF HOIDA

PRODUCTION COORDINATOR & SPECIAL EFFECTS NAMI MUN
SCRIPT SUPERVISOR JENNIFER DEITZ   VOICEOVER ARTIST NICK PETRULAKIS
SEGMENT EDITOR AUGUSTUS ROSE   GAFFER, GRIP & BOOM PAUL HEIL

PROSE ADVOCATE SALLY VAN HAITSMA

DIRECTED BY
STELLA D. & WEST H. MULHOLLAND

ON LOCATION IN LOS ANGELES:

PERCIVAL EVERETT   AIMEE BENDER   CHRIS ABANI   DAVID ST. JOHN
CAROL MUSKE DUKES   WILLIAM HANDLEY   VIET NGUYEN
THE LITERATURE & CREATIVE WRITING PROGRAM AT USC
RICK REID   SAMUEL PARK   SALVADOR PLASCENCIA   TUPELO HASSMAN
PAMELA MACINTOSH   GRACE TODD   &   KAREN MULHOLLAND ANGELUS

ON LOCATION IN BERKELEY AND THE EAST BAY:

MAXINE HONG KINGSTON   TOM FARBER   SHAWNA YANG RYAN
CHRISTIAN DIVINE   BENJAMIN BAC SIERRA   MARIKA BRUSSEL
UC BERKELEY ENGLISH DEPARTMENT   HOYT HALL STUDENT CO-OP
SUMMER 2011 TIN HOUSE PALS   INVISIBLE CITY AUDIO TOURS
& MOST ESPECIALLY   THE GROOP ON ASHBY AVE.

PRODUCTION TECHNICIAN, VISUAL EFFECTS & GAL OF GREAT GUMPTION
SARAH CISTON

DIRECTOR'S CUT

IF HOLLYWOOD had her way things would have worked out with Ricky. He would have taken me back and I him and we would have lived, together, in our big house in Beverly Hills, happily ever after. But if you look at the outtakes or perhaps maybe the alternate cut you can piece together the real story, and it doesn't take a genius to figure out things with Ricky could only work out in the movies. Off screen there are trust issues, body art, a pile of staggering debt and joint custody of a crumpled Corvette. So you may as well know, after the credits stopped rolling we didn't exactly kiss and make up. We didn't have hot burning sex and I didn't find myself ecstatically pregnant. No, instead of all that, Ricky and I split right down the middle. He downsized to a smaller house on the Westside and I moved to a studio in Silverlake. I see him around every now and then, and we smile and wave and sometimes we even do lunch.

As for the nine people I know in the San Joaquin Valley— and by know I don't mean the people I swill wine with, I mean the nine people who I've bent over with picking grapes in a hot and dusty field—those nine people might never believe it; but Los Angeles, underneath all the rhinestones and the pixie dust, is really nothing more than a desert where the water is scarce and we're all thirsty.

ABOUT THE AUTHOR

BRIDGET HOIDA is a graduate of UC Berkeley and has a Ph.D. in Literature and Creative Writing from the University of Southern California. She is the recipient of an Anna Bing Arnold Fellowship and the Edward Moses Prize for fiction. She was a finalist in the Joseph Henry Jackson/San Francisco Intersection for the Arts Award for a first novel and the William Faulkner Pirate's Alley first novel contest. Her short stories have appeared in the *Berkeley Fiction Review*, *Mary*, and *Faultline Journal*, among others, and she was a finalist in the Iowa Review Fiction Prize and the Glimmer Train New Writer's Short Story Contest. Her poetry has been recognized as an Academy of American Poets Prize finalist and she was a Future Professoriate Scholar at USC. This is her first novel. Visit BridgetHoida.com.